OTHER BOOKS BY JONATHAN FAST

THE SECRETS OF SYNCHRONICITY
MORTAL GODS
THE INNER CIRCLE
THE BEAST
THE GOLDEN FIRE

THE JADE STALK

JONATHAN FAST

E. P. DUTTON NEW YORK

Copyright © 1988 by Jonathan Fast
All rights reserved. Printed in the U.S.A.

No part of this publication may be reproduced or transmitted
in any form or by any means, electronic or mechanical, including
photocopy, recording, or any information storage and retrieval
system now known or to be invented, without permission in writing
from the publisher, except by a reviewer who wishes to quote
brief passages in connection with a review written for inclusion
in a magazine, newspaper, or broadcast.

Published in the United States by E. P. Dutton,
a division of NAL Penguin Inc.,
2 Park Avenue, New York, N.Y. 10016.

Published simultaneously in Canada
by Fitzhenry and Whiteside, Limited, Toronto.

Library of Congress Cataloging-in-Publication Data
Fast, Jonathan.
The jade stalk.
I. Title.
PS3556.A779J3 1988   813'.54   87-30123
ISBN 0-525-24650-9

Designed by REM Studio

1 3 5 7 9 10 8 6 4 2

First Edition

This book is dedicated to Sterling Lord,
cherished friend,
gentleman,
and agent extraordinary.

Contents

ACKNOWLEDGMENTS ix
1. THE MAGIC PILLS 1
2. AN HONORABLE DEATH 10
3. THE PRINCESS HAS A PLAN 22
4. LESSONS IN THE JADE CHAMBER 36
5. A PRESENT FOR THE EMPRESS 42
6. THE ENCHANTED PILLOW 48
7. THE FORTUNE-TELLER 57
8. THE NEW ABBOT 76
9. THE VINAYA MASTER 87
10. AN AUDIENCE WITH THE EMPRESS 101
11. THE EMPRESS HOLDS A DEBATE 113
12. A VICTORY AND A DEFEAT 124
13. RENOVATING THE TEMPLE 133
14. THE TAOIST'S REVENGE 144
15. THE BUDDHIST'S REVENGE 152

16. THE BOXER IN MORE TROUBLE   *162*
17. THE BOXER LEARNS TO PAINT   *169*
18. BUILDING THE MING-T'ANG   *187*
19. THE GIANT BUDDHA   *196*
20. A TRIP TO THE SOUTH   *201*
21. THE GREAT POET-PAINTER   *211*
22. THE BOXER IS BETRAYED   *227*
23. THE BOXER BECOMES A GENERAL   *246*
24. THE BOXER RETURNS   *264*

ACKNOWLEDGMENTS

The author gratefully acknowledges the following authors and publishers for the use of the excerpts quoted in the novel. Excerpts on pages 44 and 46 are from *Buddhism in China, a Historical Survey* by Kenneth Ch'en, Princeton University Press, 1964. Excerpts on pages 110 and 111 are from *The Platform Sutra of the Sixth Patriarch* by Philip B. Yampolsky, Columbia University Press, 1967. Excerpts from pages 118 to 120 are from *Sources of the Chinese Tradition* by William Theodore De Bary, Columbia University Press, 1960. Excerpts on pages 193 and 194 are from *Political Propaganda and Ideology in China at the end of the 7th Century* by Antonio Forte, Naples, 1977. Excerpts on pages 212 to 214 are from *Translations from the Chinsese* translated by Arthur Waley, Alfred A. Knopf, 1919.

A greedy man dies of moneymaking,
A hero dies for fame,
A politician dies from striving after power,
The common people avoid death.

   —Chia Yi (201–196 B.C.)

1 THE MAGIC PILLS

The boxer Huai-i was handsome and taller by a head than any member of the crowd that had gathered in the marketplace to observe his demonstration. His shoulders were broad, his hips narrow, his long-lashed eyes as black as ink sticks, his lips as thick and shapely as the calligrapher's brush. Except for the kerchief tied about his head, and a gray loincloth knotted around his groin, he was naked so all could see his well-formed muscles and smooth skin.

While waiting for the crowd to gain in size, he broke stacked tiles with the side of his hand, caused a rope tied around his chest to snap by the mere act of inhaling, and suffered the thrust of a wooden post into his gut with barely a wince.

He had to put on a good show, for the South Market was itself a spectacle to contend with: one hundred twenty streets, each of them a bazaar teeming with shops and warehouses. The poorer merchants were sheltered from the sun by rush canopies on frames of lashed bamboo, the wealthier ones by elegant tile roofs that rose gently at the eaves, like the waves of a tranquil sea. At any time of day one might see camels from Samarkand wobbling under the weight of the treasures piled upon their backs; a mandarin who had fallen on bad times, pleading with an arrogant Uighur moneylender; a political dissident being led through the streets to his execution; or a troop of Persian acrobats standing on each other's shoulders. And if such sights weren't distraction enough, the irresistible odors of roasting pork, duck, and dumplings streamed from the open screens of the teahouses and restaurants. In the wine shops and taverns, courtesans strummed bent-necked lutes and sang songs that inflamed men's blood.

Since the Empress Wu's decision to move the capital here from Ch'ang-an, commerce was thriving. And commerce was everything. If people could pay their taxes, fill their bellies, and shop all afternoon for pleasing trinkets, then it was a good age indeed. As for those who starved and suffered, as long as they were not seen, or their voices heard, they were of no matter. The Buddhist temples might care for them. In that regard, the age of her reign was no different from any other age.

The boxer was one of those who had starved and suffered. His father had eked out a living in the honorable profession of farmer until the ever-escalating triple tax of grain, linen, and labor had driven him from his land. Not only was he ordered to send the court a portion of all his rice and millet, and the bolts of linen his wife stayed up nights weaving, but also to give his eldest son for twenty days of forced labor, dredging the Great Canal. That same year his middle son, accused of stealing a bowl of rice, was sent to fight the fierce Tibetans as punishment (thus were the armies of the Middle Kingdom recruited). The two older sons had died during their service, the former beneath a hundred feet of sliding mud, the latter with a barbarian arrow in his lungs.

Without them the farmer could no longer grow his rice and millet. He and his wife and their third son, who was then only a child, fled their home, seeking to escape the tax collector. If they could just reach the south. People said life was easier there. But they had only traveled a short distance when the mother caught the fever and perished. A few months later they found themselves in a province where locusts had picked clean every growing thing. They ate grass roots and tree bark and white stones—anything to fill their bellies.

The father starved to death but the third son, being only twelve years old, the age when a human being is most resilient, survived.

He went from town to town, begging food in return for a day's work. Because of his size and strength, he was always employed. Finally he reached the city of Lo-yang, and the wonderful marketplace where the mandarins had so much cash that they seemed to throw it at the merchants in handfuls, as his father had once thrown handfuls of seed on the upturned earth. This was a place, he decided, where a man could live without working himself to an early death.

Because of his good looks, widows, spinsters, and even the occasional married woman whose husband was away, took him in and cared for him. He learned to be very good at pleasing them. He had a talent for it, as other men did for carving wood or playing a musical instrument, and nature had further suited him for the work by making the part of his body that pleases a woman exceptionally long and thick.

He also had a talent for boxing, as he discovered in the street fights that constituted an education for boys who grew up in the poor part of a city. What he knew of technique, of kicks and holds and punches, he learned from other boys who knew only a little more than he did. Lacking tenacity and a good teacher, he could never be a real boxer. Instead he learned to be a show-boxer. He learned how to perforate a tile to make it break more easily, to fray a rope so that it would pop under the slightest pressure, to find old logs that had been bored out by ants until they were soft and light as pastry. And he learned how bouts that appeared spontaneous could actually be staged as carefully as any piece of theater, to sway the crowd and open their hearts as well as their purses.

No doubt some of the observers gathered there knew he was second-rate. But to most of them the huge boxer, with his grunting and swaggering and flexing of biceps, was a delight. The men saw in him a symbol of the power and freedom and courage that was lacking in their own lives; the women, a dream of physical pleasures such as their work-weary husbands could never provide.

Now that the crowd was sufficient in size, the boxer called for challengers. A short, grizzled, savage-eyed Korean stepped forward. Though he was at least a decade older than the boxer, his step was light, his motions quick. He wore, in addition to his robe, a leopard skin around his shoulders, the sign of a warrior. He was one of the thousands captured during the war against Koguryu years before, then freed by the benevolence of the old emperor. The purple ridge of a scar crossed his right cheek, from the edge of his mouth to his ear, and a portion of the shell of his left ear was gone, the evenly scalloped border suggesting the bite of human teeth. The crowd stepped back to make room. The Korean threw his fur piece on the paving stones, untied his rope belt, and slipped off his robe. He faced the boxer barefoot, wearing only a loincloth, and a black band around his forehead to hold back his hair.

The two men circled each other, silent in concentration, their open hands raised in front of them, fingers loosely spread. The boxer could not resist stealing a look at the crowd, just to see if any really pretty young women had come along. The instant of inattention was all the Korean needed. He attacked with lightning speed, feinting toward the groin, then stabbing at the eyes with rigid fingers. The boxer saved his eyesight with a parry and countered with an open-handed blow to the kidneys. The Korean punched the boxer in the stomach. The boxer kicked him in the groin.

It went on like this for some time, the boxer enjoying superior strength and reach, the Korean benefiting from his small size and speed.

Finally the Korean, seeing an opportunity, raised his leg and snapped it straight, slamming his heel into the boxer's jaw. The boxer's head snapped backwards. The crowd rushed to get out of his way as he teetered and fell, his head striking the paving stones with a sound like the note of the wooden fish that the monks used to accompany their prayers. That he was dazed only momentarily bore testimony to the thickness of his skull.

When he did open his eyes, he found himself gazing up at the face of a servant girl, no more than seventeen years of age, youth like an early dew on her skin. She had been sent shopping for the Spring Begins celebration that was only a week away, and her donkey was laden with all sorts of provisions, including bags of freshly baked hempseed cakes and jars of oil for the many lamps that would be burned.

"A fox fairy, come to bewitch me," he murmured, struggling to focus his eyes to determine whether she was really as lovely as he supposed. After all, it was spring, and he felt particularly light-hearted despite his awkward situation.

Embarrassed, she covered her face with her hand. She was wearing a modest gray upper robe with a white blossom pattern, a long turquoise skirt, and a pink brocade vest fastened by a ribbon beneath the bosom. Her hair was piled high and held in place with ivory combs. Her feet, in silk slippers, were tiny enough to set his heart racing. Judging by the quality of her clothing and coiffeur, she held a high rank in the staff of an excellent home.

"I'll make quick work of this Korean turtle spawn," he assured her, "and take you for tea and a walk by the river."

He grinned at her and, with an effort, reached a standing position, albeit a wavering, weaving one, as though he were poised on the deck of a junk navigating the roughest sea. The street dust clung in piebald patterns to his damp skin.

The Korean charged, howling, fists a blur. A blow to the temple, a blow to the head, and the big boxer was down again, blood trickling from the corner of his mouth, a bruise over his eye swelling like a pigeon egg and turning green. Such brutality toward an already enfeebled opponent made the crowd shake their heads and murmur disapproval. The Korean couldn't have cared less. He took a running start for a leap that would land him, knees first, on the boxer's throat, but at the last instant the servant girl, to the astonishment of the onlookers, intervened.

"Have you no sense of propriety?" she demanded in a voice that quivered with indignation.

The Korean stared at her dumbfounded.

"When the lion lays low his rival," she continued, "does he not cease his clawing and leave the other to lick his wounds and recover? So it is in nature, and so it must be with man. Though you are a barbarian, while you live in the Middle Kingdom you should observe its ways, that you may improve yourself."

This not-quite-accurate observation of the animal world pleased both the Taoists in the crowd, with its reference to the rightness of Nature, and the Confucianists, with its patriotism and moral tone.

She knelt beside the boxer, seeming to tend to the bruise over his eye, but in fact drawing a small cloisonné pillbox from her sleeve. She pressed a pill, as large and brown as an acorn, between his lips and said under her breath, "Chew this. It will make you strong."

Despite her efforts to conceal what she had done, nearly everyone in the crowd witnessed the administering of the pill, and speculated as to what its effects might be.

They learned soon enough.

The boxer's eyes, half-closed with pain and fatigue, snapped open. His nostrils flared, his lips curled in a snarl. He sprang to his feet with vigor astonishing for one who had taken such a beating.

Though the Korean tried to smile, his confidence was shaken by the display. His face paled until the scar on his cheek stood out like a brushstroke on white silk. He acted courageous, circling from a distance, then closing in, hailing kicks and blows upon his opponent. The big boxer blocked his every thrust. Then, seizing the Korean by shoulder and groin as though he were a sack of millet, the boxer lifted him over his head and hurled him at a nearby fish stall. The fish vendor and his customers ran for cover, and just in time. The Korean hit the lashed bamboo canopy, knocking it down, and landed in the wooden trays where the salted fish were displayed, striking with such impact that the slippery fish flew out from under him and rained down on those unfortunates standing close by.

The boxer took a deep breath, straightened the kerchief tied on his head, and saluted the crowd.

He did not have long to enjoy their adulation, for a moment later the fish vendor was after him, shaking his fists and screaming that his customers had been scared away, his goods destroyed, his stand ruined. The boxer and the Korean, slipping and sliding on the fish underfoot, fled in opposite directions. The fish vendor ran first this way, then that, uncertain about which man to pursue. By the time he decided to chase the boxer, his chance of catching him seemed slim.

The people surrounding the servant girl took little notice. They were more interested in the strange pill she had given the boxer. At first she denied that there had been any pill at all; then, realizing that everyone had seen the act of mercy, and that denial was useless, she admitted the truth. A Taoist herbalist who lived in the mountains had molded them for her father, whose vitality had been drained by a terrible illness. Concocted from cinnabar, rhinoceros horn, eagle's claw, and a dozen other ingredients, these pills, which had cost all her family's wealth, would endow even a frail old man with the vigor they had witnessed in the boxer. Though she had sworn to bring them straight to her father, she was so moved by the boxer's plight (as well as his good looks, though she did not admit that) that she had decided to spare one. After all, she had twelve pills altogether.

"I will give you one hundred cash for one of them," the old woman beside her whispered. "You'll still have ten pills left. They are so powerful that they will certainly be enough for your father."

"I'm sorry," the servant girl said. "I cannot."

"I will give you five hundred cash," said the man standing beside her, a wealthy merchant.

"There is no point in discussing it," she said. "I must go now. If I don't return home soon, my father will surely die. I have tarried too long already." She took hold of the donkey's rope and began to lead him away.

"A string of cash," the man said, "a whole string of cash! Look, I have it right here." He reached inside his robe and brought out a thousand small, round copper coins strung together like a necklace by a string passed through the square hole in the center of each. "Think what you can buy! Enough rice to feed your family for a month, or silk to make a dozen robes."

She stopped and turned, overwhelmed by the temptation. "A whole string?" she whispered. Her lower lip trembled.

"I will give you a string too," the old woman said. "You'll still have nine pills for your father. That will last him until you visit the herbalist again and have him make more."

"I cannot," she whispered, but at the same time her hand strayed to her sleeve and brought forth the cloisonné box. She watched her own actions with horrified fascination, as though control of her fingers had been wrested from her by some demonic spirit. She handed one to the old lady, who slipped it greedily into her sleeve, and another to the merchant, who did the same. More people came forward with strings of cash or little sacks of gold dust, while others offered her carvings of jade and ivory combs. As soon as the pill had changed hands, the buyer hurried away lest the girl return to her senses and demand that the wondrous medication be returned. In the end, she found herself standing in front of the broken fish stall with one single pill in her hand.

The few members of the crowd who remained watched her in pity, the foolish girl who could not resist the lure of cash.

"What have I done?" she whispered to herself, and began to weep. Head bent to hide her misery, she led her donkey from the marketplace.

The servant girl stood on a bluff by the River Lo, where the willows trailed a thousand fragile branches, like beaded curtains, across the water. The moss gave underfoot, the mist swirled about like a dancer's veil. Usually she loved this place of nightingale songs and rushing river sounds, loved to come here to contemplate nature.

But today the rich perfume of spring was more than she could bear. She walked to the very edge of the bluff and stood watching the water swirl and eddy and throw up white foam as it crashed against the rocks. How simple to take the step and be washed away, leaving nothing behind but a few lines of verse, as the cultured mandarins sometimes did.

It came to her all at once, as though whispered by the breeze sweeping through the branches.

The willow arches like the gate of my birthplace,
The nightingale sings like my mother.
Ah, River Lo, rock me to sleep.

Her own death ode. It made her shiver.

She turned away from the water and saw the boxer and the Korean hurrying toward her through the mist.

"What kept you?" she demanded, grinning at them, despite her irritation. The sight of these two good-for-nothings always made her smile. "It is nearly the Hour of the Monkey."

"The fish vendor chased us twice about the town before we lost him," the boxer said. "Then we were so exhausted that we had to stop at a tavern for a few cups of rice wine and some oysters. We ran into a couple of old friends and began trading stories."

"Old friends?" she said suspiciously.

"Singing girls," the Korean said, his grin revealing a mouth full of black and crooked teeth.

"Singing girls!" She raised her fist as if to strike the boxer, and he backed away, shaking his head.

"No, no, don't believe that treacherous turtle spawn. They were nuns and they were lost and hungry. We gave them a few coppers. It's the truth, I swear it on my father's ancestral tablet." He watched her expectantly.

Her expression softened. "You're terrible," she said. "I never know when to believe you."

"Believe him when he says nothing," the Korean said.

The boxer glared at his friend. Then he smiled at the servant girl. "Forgiven?"

She nodded. "Forgiven."

"Well, good!" He rubbed his palms together. "Now, how did we make out this afternoon?"

8

She opened her purse and shook the contents into his cupped hands. "Five strings of cash, three ounces of gold, and some very nice bits of jade and ivory."

The boxer howled with delight, and the Korean began to dance a jig right there beneath the willow.

"Do not carry on so," she cautioned them. "Someone will discover our charade and it will be prison for all of us."

"Don't worry," the boxer said. "A few more hauls like this, and we can retire these sick fathers and mystical herbalists. Then we'll buy our inn, and a carriage with tarpans to draw it, fine robes and lacquer ware, and a dozen concubines."

"Concubines?" she said, raising an eyebrow. "You talk of concubines before we are even married?"

"All rich men have concubines," the boxer said, wounded that she would deny him this simple pleasure.

"We'll see about that," she said, touching his chin teasingly with her forefinger. "I'll keep you so busy on the pillow that you will have no time for concubines. But let us hurry and divide up our earnings, for my mistress said she would be home at nightfall, and I still have many chores to do."

AN HONORABLE DEATH

The servant girl's mistress, Princess Ch'ien-chin, eighteenth daughter of Kao Tsu, the emperor who had founded the glorious dynasty of T'ang a generation before, lived in a splendid home of many courtyards to the east of the palace.

The boxer and the servant girl reached its high outer wall by sunset. She led the donkey around to the stables while the boxer hid in a place where the poplars grew particularly thick. When she saw that the stables were unattended (the Turkish groom frequently stole away to the kitchen courtyard to drink plum wine), she called to the boxer, who hurried to join her. The air was rich with the scent of hay and manure. The horses, mistaking his heavy step for that of the groom coming with feed, whinnied and stamped and extended their necks through the bays for a glimpse of him.

The boxer searched stall after stall for her, his heart beating faster as he realized this was a game of hide-and-seek. There she was, leaning against an upright post in an empty stall at the very back of the building, her eyes half-closed, her head tilted back, her lips awaiting his kiss.

Finding their heights too disparate, he swept her up, hands

beneath her armpits, and trapped her between the upright post and his body, so she could feel his hard member beneath his loincloth.

"Put me down," she said, laughing.

"On one condition," he replied, setting her on her feet. Without a trace of shame, he tugged the ribbon that closed her brocade vest. The front fell open.

"Not here," she pleaded. "Not now. I'm late as it is. If the princess finds out . . ."

"Don't deny me," he said, his long-lashed eyes melting her resolve.

She looked around again, and ascertaining that they were still alone, that the shadows were sufficient to conceal them, and would only improve in their capacity to obscure as the evening wore on, she whispered, "All right." And added, "But quickly now. And we must be quiet."

She slipped off her vest and her upper and lower robes, folding each item neatly and stacking them across the top of the bay, where they wouldn't be sullied in the dirt. Then she took off her white silk under-robe and laid it across the floor of the stall, to serve as a mat for their lovemaking. After an instant's hesitation, she also drew the ivory combs out of her hair and pulled at her tresses a few times with her fingers so that they came free and tumbled to her waist.

"You're very beautiful," he said.

She said nothing, but smiled and lay down on the outspread robe to watch him undress.

Although she had seen only a few men naked, some of the other women who worked for the princess had been mistresses to many, and loved to pass the hours comparing their experiences. When, during one of these discussions, the servant girl had used her forearm to demonstrate the length and breath of the boxer's member, they accused her of exaggeration; when she refused to reduce the dimensions, they giggled and pleaded with her to share him with them. At such times she felt special, as though she were the possessor of some rare treasure.

As they prepared to lie together, an element of fear heightened her perceptions. She was always afraid, at first, that she would be split up the center as if by a wedge. But then his patient ministrations relaxed her, made her lips swell with blood and her fluids run, so that when he finally entered her, there was no pain but only a wonderful sense of being filled up. Such was his skill that, even though she was mounted on this weapon, she could surrender herself to him entirely without fear of being injured. The possibility of abandon was what made it exceptional.

Though they intended to be quick, they lingered a long time over their lovemaking. She could not hurry him on a warm spring night such as this, after he had boxed so well that afternoon, and they had collected so much cash and so many trinkets. What was an extra hour or two? The princess had other servant girls. Perhaps she would not be missed.

Afterwards he fell asleep, as he always did, and she lay awake in his arms, listening to his heart beat, and to the soft, snorting sounds of the horses as they rustled in their sleep. She thought about the wonderful life they would have when they bought their inn. If he wanted concubines, she decided with postcoital generosity, he could have concubines, though such second-class wives were often dangerous. Hadn't the Empress Wu once been a mere concubine of the third rank? And look at her now, Empress Dowager, ruler of the Middle Kingdom.

The servant girl must have dozed too, for she was awakened by torchlight and voices. She opened her eyes, and among the circle of heads staring down at her, she recognized the Turkish groom, the fish vendor, several of the princess's menservants, and Princess Ch'ien-chin herself, wearing a most displeased expression.

"That's him," the fish vendor was saying, "the one who wrecked my stall. And she is the girl who wept while she filled her purse with ill-gotten cash."

For a moment the servant girl believed herself to be having one of those dreams in which, contrary to logic, one appears naked before the important people in one's life. But the moment was too detailed and enduring to be a dream. She grabbed her lower robe and drew it across herself and the boxer to hide their nakedness. Waking him at times like this, after he had enjoyed her love, was no easy task. She shoved him and shook him and pinched him before he finally opened his eyes. Quickly appraising the situation, he sprung to his feet, snarled, and assumed a boxing pose, his open hands anticipating the attack to come. It was all a bluff, of course. The others stepped back, except for the princess, a woman who was not easily intimidated by size or strength.

"Come quietly," she said, as a mother warns a naughty child.

She was a plump woman of fifty-four, but old beyond her years, with thick ankles and a face like a fallen dumpling. "If you cause a commotion, I'll see to it that you witness your own skin being stripped from your body."

Even the horses had ceased to stir.

The boxer brought his hands behind his back so that his wrists could be bound with rope.

One of the servants lowered his lantern to provide his companion who was tying the knot with better illumination. A ray of light fell upon the boxer's member. The princess gasped in surprise. Using a stick that was lying near her feet, she raised the limp thing, as a traveler might lift the head of some enormous cobra he found dead on the road.

"Extraordinary," she whispered. "It is like the great sword of General Kan. How sad that it will see no more battle."

The boxer was left in the kitchen courtyard, guarded by five menservants with bamboo canes, until the magistrate could arrive. Others led the servant girl to the princess's apartments. Though for years they had been her closest friends, tonight they avoided her eye. Dishonor was like the scar of the pox that could never be ignored or forgotten.

The sitting room where they brought her was simply and elegantly furnished. A large, black-lacquered armchair, a low table on which rested a vase of indigo glaze with a few peonies arranged within it, a rosewood desk inlaid with small rectangles of ivory and mother-of-pearl. A hanging scroll depicted, in palest tones, a fisherman tossing his net, and above him mountains, strange dark forms hunkering toward heaven. A wick floating in a dish of oil gave off an amber light, a musty smell. Sheets of oiled paper, stretched across the latticework screens of the east wall, let in the moonlight. The bamboo blind at the entranceway was rolled up and tied at the top of the doorframe, allowing the warm night air to circulate through the chamber. From where the servant girl stood, she could see a part of the courtyard: a stone bench, a smooth white stone, iridescent in the moonlight, and a small, twisted tree of extraordinary beauty.

Some time later the princess appeared, wearing scarlet robes and gold brocade slippers; a long gauze shawl, narrow as a ribbon, was draped over her shoulders. She lowered her plump form into the armchair, moved about until she was comfortable, then motioned languidly for one of the menservants to stir the air with a fan. On its broad paper paddle were two delicately painted phoenixes engaged in circular pursuit.

The servant girl knelt before her and kowtowed, banging her forehead violently against the floorboards, but the princess was unimpressed by the gesture of humility and remorse.

"You've been very stupid," she began. "You have enjoyed a good life serving me, security, a roof over your head, enough to eat, and the occasional glimpse of Heaven's Daughter Herself." (She was speaking of the empress, who was often referred to by this honorific.) "Yet now you go and break your rice bowl for a man who, in all likelihood, does not know the character for his own name."

"With all respect to my lady," she whispered, "I love him."

"You love the part of him that is like a horse."

The servant girl merely bowed her head, it being inappropriate to respond to such a remark.

"He is not even a clever thief," the princess continued, "who commits his crime so close to home. The fish seller had only to go about the marketplace describing the two of you to learn that you were my servant. He proceeded directly to my home, demanding compensation for the damage that had been done. He said you sold pills that you claimed to be elixirs. I myself had begun to wonder about your activities because of your tardiness on market days. How long have you and the boxer practiced this deception on the good people of Lo-yang?"

"A few moons. No more. We only wanted enough money to marry and buy an inn, that we might support ourselves."

"An inn?" Her high eyebrows rose even higher. "*You* would buy an inn?" She couldn't help herself, the idea was so preposterous. She began to laugh, and kept on laughing until her face grew red and hot, and she had to wave at the servant to fan more quickly.

"I plead for your mercy in his behalf," the servant girl said. "You've seen yourself that he lacks the cleverness to create such a scheme. It was all my work. Do what you wish to me, but let him go free. He is a simple, good soul who has never harmed anyone."

The princess shook her head in astonishment. "How love deludes us! Obviously this lowborn swindler is the tortoise that drags the snow-white crane into the mud. I have already sent for the magistrate and shall give you both into his hands."

She heard the servant girl choke back a sob.

The princess gazed at the young woman kneeling motionless before her, and recalled her years of service. Such memories produced a certain nostalgia. In time her expression softened. "You have served me well. You have been honest, industrious, and loyal, and have refrained from spreading gossip at the marketplace. I suppose I owe you something in return."

The princess whispered to one of the men, and he left the room and returned a few minutes later with a small, flat, black lacquer box, which he passed to the servant girl without looking at her. She opened it and regarded its contents with terror; but then she grew calm and removed a dagger from the velvet cushion within the box.

"This is the solution of the mandarin," the princess said gently. "In general it is not for servants. But you are a girl of unusual virtue."

"Thank you so much," she said, bowing once more. "Might I ask one more favor?"

The princess nodded, faintly irritated. Why were servants always thus, responding to gestures of generosity with demands for more?

"I am lonely and frightened of what is to come. Could my precious one tread the Dark Pathway beside me?"

"I suppose," the princess sighed after some deliberation. And she said to the manservant, "Bring the other prisoner here. Then go stand in the courtyard, in order that they may have a few minutes to themselves."

"Thank you so much, my lady," the servant girl said. "Your compassion challenges Heaven's own. The historians will memorialize your sense of propriety for ages to come."

"My charity will be my ruin," the princess remarked to no one in particular, "and the historians will find me inconsequential." With this, she rose and left.

The servant girl remained kneeling, gazing at the dagger she held in her lap and thinking, for some reason, of her father, long dead, and a wooden doll he had once made for her. The boxer entered, standing so tall that his forehead struck the doorjamb.

"They have set me free," he said, grinning, and rubbing the

bruise above his eye with the back of his hand. "I don't mind telling you, I was worried. I suppose they have decided that it was nothing but some innocent mischief."

She gazed at him sadly and held up the dagger. "They've set us both free."

He looked at her closely. "I don't understand." Then it dawned on him. "Wait, you don't mean . . ."

"We've very little time. I know this is the coward's request, but let me go first. I am neither very strong nor very brave. I am sure that I will not sink the dagger deep in my breast before fear and pain overwhelm me. Then you must kill me quickly so that I do not suffer overlong. As a boxer, you must know how to kill with a blow. Do me this service, then hurry and join me in the Pure Land, where we will enjoy each other for all eternity to come."

The boxer gazed at her. He opened his mouth but could find no words to speak.

"You will be all alone," she went on. "There will be no one to help you take your own life, as you have helped me take mine. But Heaven will help you."

"I do not want to die," he whispered, fear in his eyes.

He looked down at the bamboo fan that had been left on the floor, the phoenixes chasing each other in a circle.

"The willow," she murmured, "arches like the gate of my birthplace. The nightingale sings like my mother. Ah, River Lo, rock me to sleep."

"What's that?"

"A poem that came to me today, when I was standing beneath the willow tree."

"I did not know you could make up poems!" he said, trying to distract her, hoping to gain time. "Tell me some more, for I love the sound of it even when I do not grasp the sense."

"We have no more time," she said. "We must act quickly, for common people are not afforded such opportunities twice. Goodbye, my beloved." She was rushing now, as though worried that if her momentum slowed for even a moment she would lose her courage. She gazed up at him, her eyes swimming in tears, then stood on her toes and kissed him. She knelt on the floor and pulled open her upper robe so that the valley between her small breasts was exposed. Then she seized the dagger with both hands and, setting her teeth in anticipation of the pain to come, plunged the blade into the pale skin below her breastbone.

She gasped and jerked forward, striking the low table with her shoulder, overturning the vase of peonies, which rolled off the edge and shattered against the floor. The flowers fell here and there, while a few petals that had been shaken loose drifted in the shallow pool of spilled water. The puddle spread, the water racing along the cracks of the floorboards. Laboriously she raised herself with her hands so that she could see her lover. Her face was mottled and covered with sweat, her features contorted. The irregular dark blot of blood spread across her upper robe with astonishing speed.

"Please," she whispered. "Kill me."

The boxer could neither speak nor move. He felt an icy numbness in his arms and legs, and also the sensation that he was observing her death from some distant place.

She crawled across the floor and, reaching him, pulled at the hem of his robe. "Kill me," she pleaded.

He couldn't bear to look at her. All he felt was a strange compulsion to clean up the spilled water. He imagined that if he could only hide the flowers and pieces of broken vase, it might all be better.

"Please," she whispered, tugging at his hem. A bubble of blood formed at her lips.

He ran from the room, into the courtyard where the menservants, thinking he was trying to escape, beat him senseless with their bamboo canes.

They took the boxer to one of a row of dark, windowless stone wards set behind the Board of Punishments at the Tribunal, to await his trial. Owing to the backlog of cases, his wait might last many years. When they pulled open a heavy door reinforced with iron bands, he caught a glimpse of men sleeping upon a wooden bench that ran along the rear of the ward. They snored, mumbled, tossed, and turned. They were skeletons dressed in rags. The smell from the open toilet hole in the corner made him gag.

The guards departed without a word. The door shut behind him with the finality of a coffin lid. He heard the key turn in the lock, the tumblers fall into place. It was pitch black. He walked with hands outstretched before him, like a blind man. Vermin scuttled out of the way of his footsteps. Finding the bench, he felt along it, seeking an empty space. He touched strange flesh and greasy shreds of clothing. Finally he pushed aside some bodies, unnaturally light and yielding, and curled up on the bench. Sleep came quickly, despite his smarting wounds—the troubled, tossing sleep of the prisoner, the sleep that brings no peace.

Sometime during the night he half woke, pleased by the feeling of a warm body beside him. In his dream, it was the servant girl, sharing the hull of a dragon boat that sailed across a smooth purple sea. The sail was scarlet silk, and a golden banner fluttered from the masthead. In the morning, the body beside him, a prisoner freshly dead from contagion, was cold and stiff and rank smelling. Revolted, he pushed it onto the floor, where it lay until the guards came to dispose of it that afternoon.

Following a breakfast of a small bowl of rice that still had stones and grit in it, he was permitted to walk in the courtyard. After the gloom, the sunlight seemed impossibly brilliant, as though the surface of every wall and step and stone had been fitted with mirrors. He had to cover his eyes, as if blocking a blow. The air was as sweet as a flower garden, although only gravel crunched underfoot. The prisoners walked in a circle. Some wore heavy iron collars that bent their spines, others leg and wrist manacles. Some spoke of murders or robberies they had been accused of, while others admitted that they were merely witnesses to crimes, or plaintiffs who had brought lawsuits against one another, for in Middle Kingdom justice, everyone involved in the judicial process, with the exception of the magistrate himself, was detained, and shared at least a shred of the guilt.

Although the ward had no windows, slots beneath the eaves allowed enough light for him to scratch a simple calendar in the brick. While occupied with this task one day soon after his incarceration, he felt a gentle touch on his back. A man with a ferret face, shifting eyes, and long, nimble fingers was squatting behind him, wiping his welts with a damp rag. His hair, shiny and black, was drawn back behind his ears, and his sleek beard reached halfway down his chest.

"You took quite a beating, old friend," the prisoner said. "The wounds are open still. If they ain't kept clean, the lice will crawl in and breed in your blood. It's a bad way to die."

"Lice?" the boxer said.

The other prisoner scraped at the floor with his fingernail. An inch below the surface, the earth was teeming with insects no bigger than poppy seeds.

The boxer, moved by this small act of kindness, introduced himself and told of the circumstances that had led to his imprisonment.

"They call me Pinch Purse," said the prisoner who was administering to him, "and this here's my friend, False Brush. Oh, he don't look like much now, but he used to be quite the imposing figure. Nothing less than personal manservant to Li-hung, the crown prince."

False Brush started at the mention of the prince's name. "Is Beloved Master coming? But we cannot greet him like this." He looked around at the prison with dismay. "The palace is in shambles! The guards are ungroomed and out of uniform. We must put things in order at once." False Brush came closer, until his wild, bloodshot eyes were inches away from those of the boxer. "That's why Beloved Master went away, you know. He couldn't bear the disorder. He is a very refined soul—very refined! He could spend an entire day gazing at one particular mountain vista or writing a single line of verse. If only we can straighten up, he'll be back, I know he will."

Pinch Purse whispered to the boxer, "Lost his mind when the Empress Wu poisoned his master, her stepson. That was ten years ago."

"I've heard she's a ruthless one," the boxer said.

"Ruthless ain't the word. She killed her own baby to help her career. That's the advantage of being cheap millet like you and me. We don't have to have nothing to do with the mandarins if we don't want. Sure, their lives seem fine—silk robes, grape wine, writing poetry all day. But show me one who don't wind up with a dagger in his heart or exiled to the edge of the world."

His mind was not all that had been lost, the boxer decided, as he watched False Brush on his knees, scrubbing the floor with an imaginary brush. Judging from his smooth cheeks, sweet voice, and baggy skin, he was also a eunuch. He had probably been quite a plump capon once, but a prison diet reduced him to this. (Castration was performed when any man took employment in the palace, to ensure that he would sire no heirs who might be mistaken for princes.) Wispy hair, tangled, matted, uncut for years, covered his face like spiderwebs. At times only his eyes could be seen peering through it; at other times he parted it with his hands, as gently as a woman separating skeins of silk, and then his face would appear, his dead white skin hanging in sacks beneath his eyes, and bagging at his cheeks and chin.

The boxer wondered how long it would be before his own good health crumbled beneath the onslaught of disease and parasites, the poor food, the lack of light and sleep. His hair would grow thin, his teeth rot, his bones turn soft, his spine curve like that of an old man. Without his strength and his good looks, how would he support himself? Womanizing was his only talent, show-boxing his only art. He would be lost! Hopeless! If only he and the servant girl hadn't been discovered, she would have shown him how to make an honest living as an innkeeper. Innkeeping was a trade a man could practice even when he was too old and feeble to carry wood. She was so clever. Thinking about her, he wanted to weep.

"He may be mad," Pinch Purse said of his friend, who was still scrubbing the floor, "but he ain't dimwitted. He can read and write as well as any mandarin."

The boxer was impressed. For him the process of drawing and understanding the complex characters of his own language had always seemed almost magical. "Could he write something for me?"

"Provided it's short. He's only got a bit of paper and can't concentrate on anything for too long."

"It's only a few lines."

"False Brush?" Pinch Purse said, tapping his friend on the shoulder. "I hate to interrupt your work, but my friend here, he's got an important message for the prince. Could you write it down for us?"

Seized by the urgency of the request, False Brush rushed to retrieve his writing kit from a hole behind a loose brick in the wall. The old wooden box was so chipped and worn that the boxer could barely make out the lacquer design on the cover. All he had was a pathetic scrap of paper covered with characters except for a corner of it, a bit of ink stick, a brush with a dozen hairs, and the nail of his thumb for a palette.

When the boxer expressed skepticism, Pinch Purse pointed out that men had written great poems with less.

False Brush moistened the ink stick with some spittle and made a pool of ink on his thumbnail. Then he pulled the brush through his lips to give it a fine point. You could see he was eager to demonstrate his skill.

"The willow tree," the boxer began in a tentative voice, "the willow tree curves like the door of my house—no, that's not it. Curves like the gate of my house? The willow tree—just give me a moment. I'll remember it."

But he could not recall the servant girl's poem, and by the end of the week even her face and the sound of her voice, whispering lovingly to him in the straw, were as distant as the memories of his childhood.

3 THE PRINCESS HAS A PLAN

Princess Ch'ien-chin invited her great-niece, Princess T'ai-p'ing, to tea, in order to share the delicious gossip about the servant girl's ill-fated love affair. The younger princess was the fifth and favorite child of the Empress and therefore a useful ally—if not a safe harbor, then at least a buoy in the treacherous, shifting sea of court politics.

The younger princess shared her mother's classical beauty, eyes that curled up at the corners like the egret's wing, a fine nose with flaring nostrils, and the smallest bud of a mouth. Her face was a long oval, and her chin came almost to a point. Her form was plump (for in times of poverty and famine, men desired the plump woman as they disdained her in times of plenty), her feet sufficiently small to excite even a jaded suitor.

Alas, her excellent features were wasted, in the opinion of the elder princess at least, for the younger princess affected the barbaric manners and dress of the Turks. Like many of her peers, she was infatuated with things Turkish, believing them to be more filled with passion and vitality than those staid customs and manners of her own society, as well as more capable of shocking her elders, in which act she took the greatest pleasure, as do children of all times.

Not only had she, with brazen disregard for propriety, ridden to her aunt's house on horseback rather than by carriage, but now she appeared in the outlandish outfit of a horseman of the steppes: a tall felt cap, a jacket with open lapels and tight sleeves tied with a sash at the waist, as well as men's trousers and high leather boots.

Her great-aunt, receiving her in the sitting room, did her best to appear unshaken by the display. She exchanged pleasantries and offered the younger princess a seat where she could gaze out at the courtyard, at the smooth white rock and the twisted tree just coming into blossom.

A servant brought them a rare tea known as "Forest of a Thousand Fragrances," and curds and fagara with which to flavor it. The cups, small and round and fashioned of green porcelain, were as fine as the shell of an insect when the soft insides have rotted away. Another servant girl brought a red lacquer tray with plates of peaches from Samarkand and pistachios from Persia. The former, it was said, bestowed immortality, the latter, sexual vigor. The cost of this small repast would have fed a peasant family for a year.

"What, revered Aunt, has become of the blue vase I gave you?" the younger princess said, when she was seated and sipping her tea. "I cannot help but notice that it is no longer on the table where you usually display it."

"A servant girl broke it," the elder princess replied, delighted to be provided with such a graceful opportunity to turn the conversation to the subject she had prepared.

"I hope you punished her well."

"There was no need. She took her own life. With a dagger."

"All over a broken vase? My compliments to you. Propriety must certainly flourish in your home. You should be pleased with yourself."

"I might go on to speak of something else, and leave you with the impression that things were as you said—that it would reflect well on myself and my household—if there were not details that I believe you will find amusing."

And she proceeded to tell of the boxer and his false bouts in the marketplace, the intervention of the servant girl and her fabricated tale of her sick father, the useless pills sold to the onlookers at exorbitant prices. She told how she had apprehended the two lovers while they lay naked in the stables and offered them the opportunity to end their lives honorably rather than suffer beneath the slow, cruel wheel of Middle Kingdom justice.

Then, like a bit of sweet peach after bitter tea, she supplied the part of the story she reckoned most piquant; how his cowardice was such that he had failed to uphold his end of the suicide pact, or even provide a death-blow to his lover after she had stabbed herself!

When the younger princess did not react with the anticipated gaiety, but instead grew thoughtful and quiet, the elder princess began to worry that she had made a grave miscalculation. As the silence lengthened, she grew more and more anxious. After all, she had spent many years cultivating the young woman's friendship. The room grew insufferably hot, the sweat trickled down her armpits. Such mistakes had been known to result in a fall from favor.

After what seemed an interminable time, the younger princess said, "Tell me again of his Jade Stalk. Show me its dimensions with your hands."

The elder princess held her hands some distance apart, then made a ring using the thumb and index finger of both hands to indicate its circumference.

"You would not exaggerate?"

"It is perhaps larger, for I have only seen it limp."

"And his face—was it comely?"

"He was quite handsome, with splendid teeth and clear eyes. His lashes, when they fluttered, were like the wings of the butterfly."

"And the rest of him?"

"Tall, as I have said, with excellent muscles, a broad chest, and narrow hips." She could stand the suspense no longer and spoke up, determined to learn whether she had erred in judgment.

"But are you not at all amused by my story? Do you not find it the least bit interesting?"

"I find it interesting indeed," the younger princess replied.

"Then why do you look so solemn and question me in this odd manner?"

Now the younger princess saw how upset her aunt was and hastened to reassure her.

"Old aunt of mine, you need not worry. Your story was delightful. But like any good story, it has inspired in me other thoughts. Let me share them with you now, that I may benefit from your wise counsel."

Here she paused to instruct the servant to pour her another

cup of tea, and peel and slice one of the peaches. The fruit, velvety and pliant, oozed juice as the knife slipped into it.

"What would you think of this boxer," the younger princess said, weighing out each word as though it were polished jade, "as a lover for Mother?"

"For the Empress?" The elder princess gasped, and held her hand over her chest, as though her agitated heart might tear through ribs and skin.

"I know it seems outrageous, but stop a moment and consider the sense of it. Though but a year has passed since Father's death, how long do you suppose it has been since they shared the pillow?"

"I could not guess." The elder princess seemed embarrassed by the question.

"Not since the day I was conceived, twenty-one years ago. So mother tells me."

"I have been that long without a man's love," the elder princess said solemnly. "It is not an uncommon experience for widows, or wives who have fallen from favor."

"Dearest Aunt, what rules apply to the sparrow do not govern the behavior of the phoenix."

The elder princess frowned. While she was not as flamboyant as the Empress, she was certainly no sparrow.

"We would not dream," the princess continued, "of asking a man to live for twenty-one years without the warmth of a woman's embrace. The instant he is through mourning, we encourage him to take another wife and a dozen concubines. Yet if the widow does not live out her remaining years in solitude, we are shocked."

"It is propriety."

"It is a way of keeping women subjugated. After all, what do we call a widow? One who waits only for death. Believe me, it is not so among the Turks. Among the Turks the widows may marry or take lovers as they please. They are treated with the same respect accorded to men. More or less."

"You children with your talk! Turkish this, Turkish that." The elder princess shook her head.

"Mother bears all the responsibilities of a man—why should she not enjoy the same solaces? Answer me that!"

"I—" the elder princess hesitated, taken aback by her great-niece's anger. "There is no reason, of course."

"Poor Mother! Though her face remains as tranquil as the

reflecting pool on a summer eve, and her voice as gentle as the wind chimes, we who are close to her know how she suffers. She sleeps poorly, worries constantly, is troubled by headaches and stomach cramps. She must control the government almost singlehandedly, for our child Emperor is incapable of making even the simplest decision for himself. And what a host of problems the old Emperor has left her! Bad harvests, peasants fleeing their homes to avoid tax and forced labor, corrupt administration in the provinces, and careless promotions in the army."

"And that dreadful rebellion."

"That was worst of all," the younger woman agreed. "Let me tell you something, old aunt of mine. She pretended to be untouched by the rebels' polemic, but only I know how deeply it hurt her. Particularly that part which said she had 'a heart like a serpent's and a nature like that of a wolf.' Time and again she comes to me in private and asks, 'Am I really thus? Part serpent, part wolf?' And of course I reassure her that she is nothing of the sort."

"You are the only one she can confide in. Thank heavens she has you."

The young princess bit into a slice of peach, and laughed as the juice of it ran down her chin. The servant rushed to supply her with a towel, but she had already wiped her mouth on her own long sleeve.

"But these are excellent fruit!"

"I will send a dozen to your home—if there are that many to be had."

The younger princess leaned close and, her mouth still moist with peach juice, confided, "Only yesterday, Mother told me about a dream. She was walking through the palace gardens when a great stallion appeared. It knelt down so she could mount it, then galloped away with her on its back. A terrifying ride they had, she told me, but also a thrilling one, leaping chasms, fording streams, riding through rings of fire. In the end she had to kill the horse by crushing its skull with an iron mace, lest it destroy her first. Then she threw herself on its corpse and wept."

"Perhaps we should give her a horse," her great-aunt suggested earnestly.

"Oh, aunt of mine, you are too simple! A man is what she needs. Particularly now that it's spring."

"But certainly not a swindler."

"All men are swindlers. It is a question of degree. There are more important factors. While his physical endowments sound wonderful indeed, it is his cowardice that attracts me. As with all positions of privilege, being Mother's concubine carries certain risks. It will no doubt swell a man's head and fill him with all sorts of illusions about himself, since men are prone to that sort of vanity and self-deception anyway. This man's cowardice will prevent him from stepping too far out of line."

"But what of his low birth and crude manners?"

"I will teach him to behave. If the Empress fancies him, she will change the situation of his birth. All is within her power."

"What if he proves to be a poor lover? After all, the size of the Jade Stalk is not everything."

The younger princess considered the question for a few moments. "I suppose someone should put him to the test, just as the Empress's food is tasted before she puts her chopsticks to it."

She took a bite of peach and, licking the juice from her lips with a quick, pointed tongue, winked.

The elder princess gasped.

In prison, time moved like a tortoise crossing a muddy river bottom. By the third day, the boxer was certain that he had been there for a week, and that someone was tampering with his calendar.

The day differed from the first and second in one event. At the Hour of the Monkey, which time the boxer knew because it was then that the second bowl of rice came, two guards opened the heavy wooden door and led False Brush away.

"Where are they taking him?" the boxer asked.

Pinch Purse only shook his head.

The screams came later, while they were eating, spitting the stones and grit from their mouths as they chewed the uncleaned rice. The boxer had never heard so harrowing a howl as that of False Brush's high, screeching voice. He felt a chill, and the short hairs on his neck bristled. Able to eat no more, he put down his bowl. The others, having grown accustomed to all the sounds of human suffering, fought over it like dogs.

Later that day, False Brush was returned to the ward. When the guards let go of him, he took a few steps and fell to the ground. One of his arms, pried from the socket, seemed attached to his torso at a crazy angle. The dislodged end of it stretched his shoulder into a strange shape, as though a sphere had been slipped beneath the skin.

The boxer, having often witnessed this type of injury during sparring sessions, knew what to do. While some of the other prisoners held False Brush facedown on the bench, the boxer straddled him and, with one hand on the displaced ball at the end of the bone, the other in the middle of the arm so that he might use it as a lever, snapped the errant limb back into place.

False Brush screamed from the pain of it. Later he sat up and, cradling his bad arm, moved it slightly. He smiled with gratitude.

"Who did this to you?" the boxer asked.

"Those who lick the Empress's hands and then steal the scraps from her table."

"He's talking about Chou Hsing and Lai Chün-ch'en," Pinch Purse said, "the Empress's watchdogs. They think the madness is an act, and that he's really an agent of the Li princes, waiting for a chance to help overthrow the Empress."

"Who are they?"

"Nobody. Just the rightful heirs to the T'ang throne. Where have you been?"

"I don't pay much attention to politics," the boxer admitted.

"The name of their clan is Li. When the Empress ain't babbling about how she loves them, she's having their throats sliced, one by one. She wants to get rid of them so she don't have to worry about them being restored to the throne."

Pinch Purse turned to his friend. "What did they ask you this time?"

"The same as always—the names of my accomplices. I told them the Sun, who helps me rise in the morning. And the august Earth—for without him to stand on, I would go flying off into the sky."

At night the boxer spoke silently to his ancestors, his father and mother, his grandmothers and grandfathers, offering them deals in return for his freedom (as if they had any control over the matter). He would never steal again if he could walk once more through the South Market; he would never deceive anyone if he could just once more take a pretty young thing to the pillow; and if they could somehow give him back his old life, he would uphold every Confucian virtue (though he had only a hazy idea as to what those virtues were) and never again desire wealth, or a fine house, or handsome clothes. He would travel to the south, where life was easier, and become a farmer like his father, for farming was a virtuous profession. He would lead a simple existence, venerating his ancestors and his Empress. In the spring he would plant, in the fall he would harvest. On festival days he would kick up his heels, but the rest of the year he would be a model of propriety. All these things he swore he would do if he could only taste freedom again.

On the fourth morning of his prison stay, the guards came for him.
"What's going on?" he asked, as his wrists were lashed cruelly behind him. "Where are you taking me?"
No reply.
He tried to behave with dignity, as he had seen False Brush do. But when they slipped a leather bag over his head, pulling it tight around his neck with a drawstring, he panicked and lashed out. A lucky kick knocked the first guard off his feet, a ramlike butt of his head caught the second in the stomach. He struggled and flailed for all he was worth, but trussed and blindfolded as he was, he was no match for them. He felt himself grabbed from behind, and after that he remembered no more, for he was knocked unconscious.
When he woke, the bag was still over his head, obscuring his vision, muffling his hearing. The air within it was rank and hot from being breathed over and over again. Burning sweat dripped down his forehead into his eyes. The throbbing in the back of his head made him want to cry out loud. If he could have remained perfectly still, it might not have hurt so, but he was riding in some sort of oxcart that bumped and jogged incessantly. Since the magistrate and the torture rooms were both on the prison grounds, a long trip could mean only one thing: that he was being taken to the marketplace to be executed.
The thought that his death was imminent made his senses reel. No more women, no more drinking with friends, no more visiting taverns. No more eating roast pig or swimming in cold streams during the summer heat, or boxing before an appreciative crowd. Death was a leather sack stuck on his head for eternity.
Though he had been in prison only a short time, he had heard much talk of executions. Among the prisoners who had been sentenced to death, the subject was an obsession. A hundred cash, it

was said, could buy you a quick, painless death from the executioner. If you were to be sliced, he would sneak a dagger into your heart so that you did not have to witness the removal of your hands and feet; if you were to be strangled, he would give your head a jerk, breaking your neck before the slow tightening of the braided rope took away the air; and if you were to be decapitated, he would see to it that the ax was swift and sure.

"*Pssst!*" the boxer hissed. "Anyone there?"

Somebody sitting beside him grunted.

"Are you the executioner?" the boxer asked.

"Executioner?" Coarse laughter.

"I've heard," the boxer went on in a whisper, "that you'll hasten a man's death for a hundred cash."

"He offers me a bribe, this piece of putrid camel's meat!"

"Shhh! Quiet! It's not a bribe I offer. I simply ask regarding a rumor I heard in the prison."

"Just a rumor, eh?" Then, after a silence: "How much cash have you got?"

"Fifty with me. And my friend the Korean will get you another fifty later."

"You think I would trust a Korean?"

"He's true to his word," the boxer said.

"Give me the fifty. It's not much, but I'll see what I can do."

The boxer, because of the uncertainty of his daily existence, always kept fifty cash in the hemmed sleeve of his robe. He told the other man where to find it. He felt him tugging on his sleeve, heard the hem being ripped open, the jingle of coins falling into his palm.

"Have you got it?" the boxer whispered.

The other voice grunted affirmation.

"Tell me, then," the boxer whispered, "what's it to be? Please say decapitation!"

"You'll be sliced like fresh pork," the other voice said.

At which point the boxer's bowels gave way.

The other voice spent the rest of the journey complaining about the stink of it.

In time, the cart stopped. Curiously, there were none of the sounds of the market that he had anticipated, but only the trilling of songbirds, the distant notes of a bent-necked lute like jewels suspended in air. The stairs he climbed were smooth and solid rather than the crudely built ones that led to the executioner's scaffold, and only three in number. The sounds grew faint, as they do when one enters a dwelling.

They loosened the drawstring and pulled off the bag. The air on his hot, moist face felt like a mountain wind. He was in the bathroom of a fine home. The afternoon sun coming through the wooden lattices was blinding. The floor was of ceramic tile, cerulean blue, and the moldings and floral medallions on the walls were carved and lacquered in a manner that would have pleased the most demanding mandarin. A wall scroll featured a poem in bold calligraphy, and a drawing of three plump and lovely women bathing beneath a waterfall. An enormous bronze basin, decorated with a hammered relief of lotus blossoms, had been set out and filled three-quarters with water. As he watched, a servant boy ran in, emptied a bucket of water into it, paused to gawk at the boxer, and ran out again. Round stools with red lacquer seats were arranged around the tub, along with pitchers, brushes, and stacks of silk scarves.

Two menservants in black caps, the ties of which trailed like drooping rabbits' ears, and bright red robes belted low on the hip, stood before him, their bamboo canes raised and ready to strike. Three women servants were also in attendance, their hands folded and heads bent in respect.

"Where am I?" the boxer demanded. "Whose home is this? Am I to be executed?" He advanced toward one of the menservants.

"Watch your step!" the manservant said, flourishing his cane.

One of the women servants came forward and untied the boxer's hands. When she tried to unhook his belt, he pushed her away. The manservant swung his cane; the boxer groaned and staggered backwards as a red welt rose across the side of his head. The servant girl approached a second time and the boxer made no protest.

When she took off his under-robe, the other girls giggled at the sight of his penis. The menservants smirked and whispered.

At their direction, he climbed into the basin, into the cold, invigorating water. The servant girls sat on the stools around the tub, scrubbed him with a lotion of peas and herbs, and poured pitchers of water over his head to rinse him. They were gentle with his welts. They washed his hair, ears, armpits, and groin. Afterwards they dried him with silk scarves, and dressed his wounds with balm. Then they brought him a fresh white under-robe and a black outer robe, all clean and crisp, and a red belt to tie it at the hip. They gave him socks and woven slippers, as well as a black cap like those the servants wore, with ties that hung like the ears of a rabbit.

"I'd like to know what's going on," he said.

Nobody replied.

Flanked by the two menservants, the boxer followed a loggia around the courtyard. They passed through a moon gate in a stone wall into a second courtyard. Here were reflecting ponds, twisted trees, gravel walks, and arching bridges, all the elements of the classic garden, but rendered in miniature, so that while the courtyard was of limited size, the garden seemed a sweeping expanse of countryside. Knowing that for cultivated people, sights such as this brought them nearly to a swoon, he sought a state of elation, but all he attained was awe at the cash it must have cost.

The tiled roofs of the house, he noticed, were glazed a gorgeous yellow. The eaves turned up gently and the joists were ornamented with terra-cotta dragons, their jaws spread, their forked tongues licking at the air. Such architectural niceties were reserved for mandarins of the highest rank.

In time they arrived at the loggia at the far end of the courtyard. The servants opened a sliding screen and stood aside that he might enter. It was a bedchamber, a woman's. A mirror of polished steel hung from a stand above a makeup tray. The clothes box, lid askew, held robes of shimmering silk. A canopied bed, raised on a platform and enclosed on four sides by painted screens, was an elegant little room within the larger room, where solitude was sure to be complete. A servant girl, as perfect as an orchid, stirred the air with her fan. The odor of musk was vaguely discernible.

"We will be waiting in the courtyard," the first manservant whispered. "If we hear that anything has gone amiss, we will rush in and beat you to death. Don't think you can escape us."

The boxer said nothing.

The two menservants left the room.

The boxer looked at the servant girl who was moving the fan. She averted her eyes. He turned and looked out the entrance, at the courtyard where the guards stood with their backs to him, their canes resting on their shoulders. What should he do next? He certainly didn't want another beating.

He was startled by a woman's voice, low-pitched and commanding, coming from within the bed he had presumed empty. After all, it was midday.

"Take off your clothes," she said.

"Who's that?" he said, squinting to see through the screens that were the walls of the bed. But it was too bright outside, too dim within to discern anything more than her silhouette.

"You'll learn in good time," the voice replied.

"Am I to be executed?"

"If you do precisely as you are told, and satisfy me by properly performing the Clouds and Rain, your life will be spared for today."

"Clouds and Rain?" His brow furrowed. "Forgive me, but I am not a learned man. If you could explain—"

She sighed, an impatient woman forcing herself to be patient. "You know of the yin and the yang, the essence of that which is female and that which is male?"

"I am not a dog. Even we who live by our hands learn some things."

"The yin are the clouds that rise from the valley; the yang is the rain that falls from heaven. When they meet, the rain penetrates the clouds, they become one. Now do you understand?"

The boxer gazed at the floor, baffled. Then a great grin spread across his face. "You mean—?" he began.

His heartbeat quickening with anticipation, he took off everything but his under-robe and climbed into the confines of the bed. At first he saw only the whiteness of her body on the rush matting, and the dark triangle between her thighs, like a bit of onyx inlaid in jade. Her hair fell loose across the glazed ceramic square of the pillow. The covers had been pulled down so that they concealed only her ankles and feet.

As his eyes grew accustomed to the light, he saw that she was young, and beautiful in the way of the aristocratic women he had seen in the company of mandarins. The long oval shape of her face came nearly to a point at the chin, and her individual features were equally fine and well proportioned.

"Well?" she asked, amused by the way he stared at her. "Does what you see please you?"

He tried to talk, but his throat was so dry and constricted that he could make only a croaking sound.

"Yes," he managed, finally.

"It is better than an execution, is it not?"

"Yes," he croaked. "Much better."

"Now," she continued, raising herself up on one elbow, "let

us see this Swelling Mushroom of yours that they liken to the limb of an oak."

Leaning forward, she pulled open his under-robe and, reaching between his thighs with her graceful fingers, raised his member to the light.

She drew in her breath with surprise. "Old Aunt did not exaggerate."

"Old Aunt?"

"Never mind. Have you yang enough to make the Vigorous Peak?"

"I'm sorry, but I do not know these expressions of the poets."

"It is what we say when what has been soft grows firm."

He was embarrassed. "I slept little and ate poorly at prison, and several times was beaten. Now on the way to my execution I find myself in a strange house with a strange woman, who makes unusual requests of me. It is not the best situation for creating this Vigorous Peak, as you call it."

Although she was only twenty-one years old, she was already an authority on the subject of arousing the male. She raised her knees so that the covers slid slowly down her legs. At the sight of her slim ankles, her tiny, graceful feet, his face grew flushed. His breath quickened and his Jade Stalk, suffused with yang, swelled to such a size that she laughed in disbelief.

Yet when he rose to mount her, she held him off with her index finger.

"We will start your instruction right now. Be attentive, boxer! Later, when we act the Clouds and Rain, that will be your examination. If you fail, you will resume your journey to the execution place."

"And if I do well?" he asked boldly.

She ignored him. "The first thing you must learn is to wait. While the rains come fast, the clouds gather slowly. You must cultivate a woman's yin by kissing her, by gazing at her Golden Cleft, by caressing her breasts, stomach, and buttocks." As she spoke, she took his hand and moved it all about her body, revealing those favorite places and the touches that brought the most joy. She showed him the hard press of the palm on the Golden Cleft, and the delicate stroke of the fingertip that was appropriate for the Jeweled Terrace. Her body was soft and warm, and smelled of musk. He did whatever she asked.

When she was ready for him, she made him kneel above her, resting his weight on his knees and elbows, and touch her Vermilion Gate with the tip of his Jade Stalk, again and again. When in time her Golden Cleft grew flooded with yin, she warily allowed his entrance. Ignorant of the size and flexibility of her opening, and knowing that his life hung in the balance, he began cautiously, first the head, then a bit of the stalk, then a bit more. To his surprise, she grew impatient and, grabbing his buttocks, steered the rest of him in until the entire length was buried inside her.

It was here that even the most constrained women lost their self-control, and would gasp, weep, and babble endearments. Imagine, then, the boxer's surprise when she kept instructing him in the same cool, dispassionate voice.

"At first push on slowly, as a snake does when squeezing into its hole to hibernate. Then flail out to the left and right as a brave general breaks the enemy's ranks, and rise and plunge low, like a junk on a turbulent sea."

In time, however, she began to have difficulty keeping her voice level, and her words in logical sequence.

"A slow thrust should resemble the carping of a roll as it—"

"What?"

"The rolling of a carp, I mean to say, as it fights the fisherman's hook. Try it now. Yes, good! Now thrust quickly, like birds"—a gasp escaped her—"like birds darting against the wind. Though one style comes easily to you, and brings pleasure, do not cling stubbornly to it lest you—"

And then her words gave way to a moan and she had to struggle to recall the point where her lecture had broken off. Yet she would not abandon it. Only at that moment when yin and yang became one was she so overwhelmed that she stopped talking altogether. She bit her lower lip and closed her eyes, and made a rough sound like the growl of a tiger in the back of her throat. Afterwards, she lay beneath him, silent, eyes closed, breath quick and shallow.

"Did I score well?" he asked innocently.

She opened her eyes and looked up at him without a trace of affection or amusement.

"Go and dress yourself. The servants will show you to your quarters."

4
LESSONS IN THE JADE CHAMBER

His quarters were the little granary near the kitchen. Every day after his "schooling," he was led there directly. The wooden door would shut behind him, and he would hear the sound of a crossbar being wedged in place. He didn't complain. It was cool and quiet within. A mat and a pillow of plaited rushes had been provided for him to sleep upon. When he banged on the door, they would bring him water, or escort him to the outhouse. Twice a day he enjoyed meals of rice and raw fish, and on one occasion when he had done particularly well in his "studies," pigs' feet in a hot and sweet sauce. He even had a companion, a cat, whose job was to keep the granary free of rodents. At night the cat would climb on his chest to sleep, and purr and push its head under his chin.

It was far better, as the mysterious young woman had pointed out, than an execution.

On the second day, while being led to her bedchamber, he saw a man kneeling in the garden, pruning a miniature pine. Obviously the man was no gardener; the purple silk robes and the gold belt with jade plaques that he wore indicated that he had reached, by birth or by cunning, the headiest heights of the Middle Kingdom's elaborate civil service. The precise degree of his rank the boxer did not know; he had never considered such knowledge important to a life like his own. What he was doing here, in this garden, was even more puzzling.

Reasoning that he might gain favor with his tutor by informing her of the interloper's presence, the boxer sneaked another look in order to better describe him (one did not stare, even at men of one's own rank). The mandarin was less a man than a sparrow, thin-boned and small, with rheumy eyes, and a wispy goatee and mustache. His nose ran constantly and he had to keep interrupting his work to pull a kerchief from his sleeve and dab at it.

"By the way," the boxer said to the mysterious young woman when he reached her bedroom, "did you know there's a fellow in your garden who's wearing the purple?"

"I know," she said.

"Don't you think you should welcome him? Fix him some tea or something. He's probably a big muckamuck at the palace."

The mysterious young woman didn't reply.

"Be nice to him now," the boxer went on, "and he'll do *you* a favor next time. That's the way of the world, you know."

"There is no need to please him," the woman said. "He is my husband."

"Your . . . ?" The boxer rose to the balls of his feet in preparation for flight. On occasion he had been caught in a woman's bedroom upon her husband's return. The beatings were still vivid in his mind.

"Fear not him but me," she said.

"I don't understand. It must make him angry, you and me . . ."

"He does as I say. And so shall you."

And so he did.

That day they studied the commoner ways in which yin and yang might unite, the Close Union, the Firm Attachment, the Exposed Gills, and the Unicorn's Horn; and those couplings that required greater flexibility and acrobatic skill, such as the Winding Dragon, Bamboos by the Altar, and the Phoenix Sporting in the Cinnabar Cleft.

She taught him how to delay ejaculation by pressing the tongue against the roof of the mouth, arching the neck and back, and sucking in the breath; and how to retain the semen by pressing the index and middle finger of the right hand firmly against the perineum at the moment of ejaculation. Knowing these techniques, he could practice the Clouds and Rain with a dozen women a night, and only gain in vitality.

On the third day of his erotic captivity, he was surprised (and perhaps relieved, though he would have never admitted it) to find his tutor awaiting him fully clothed and resting in an armchair. She wore a tight-sleeved yellow jacket belted at the waist over trousers and high leather boots, like a Turkish horseman. He wanted to laugh, but he had the sense to bow instead.

"The time has come," she said, "to teach you manners."

"I am your willing student," he replied. He looked out at the courtyard. The man in purple was gone today, but the two men-servants were there, standing with their backs to him, holding their bamboo canes. He marveled at how palatable education was, when physical pain was presented as the alternative.

"A man of breeding," she began, "does not touch a woman in public. When he walks outside with his wife, he walks ten paces ahead of her. But what happens when he walks outside with a woman who is his superior?"

"Why would he want to do that?" the boxer asked.

"Answer my questions," she snapped.

The boxer thought for a moment. "She walks ten paces ahead of him?"

"A great thinker," she murmured. "Another Confucius."

"I'm doing my best," the boxer said. "By the way, there's the matter of the fifty cash your servant took from me."

"What fifty cash?"

"One of your servants told me he was the executioner. He promised to make my suffering quick in return for fifty cash."

"Yes? And what do you want me to do about it?" She was regarding him with amazement.

"Well, I'd like it back. He took it under false pretenses. He wasn't really an executioner. Merely a servant."

"Boxer, if you like, I will find the servant who took your cash, and be sure that the money is passed along to the executioner, so that he can make quick work of you. Would that be satisfactory? Or would you rather concentrate upon your lesson?"

The boxer could think of no reply, nor was one necessary.

She continued her instructing him in about manners, moving, in time, from those of daily life to those of the court. She explained how one might recognize the rank of an official by the color of his robe and the material from which the plaques of his belt were carved. She made him memorize the various honorifics to be used for different occasions. Together they acted out the three kneelings and the nine kowtows that denoted veneration, until he could perform them perfectly.

Gathering, through the course of her instruction, that the boxer lacked even the most rudimentary understanding of Middle Kingdom government, she expounded upon that too. She spoke of the three divisions: the chancellery, which saw to the transmission of imperial decrees and their execution; the secretariat, which prepared the edicts and proclamations, as well as the annals from which the dynastic history would be drawn; and the censorate, whose members guarded against corruption within the palace walls and beyond them. Within each of these divisions were legislative subdivisions, and within them further subdivisions, and so forth and so on, like an intricate set of nested boxes, fascinating to contemplate but of questionable utility in governing so vast and many-faceted a country.

The boxer couldn't understand the point of all this talk. He had never studied anything so cerebral and complex before, and it hurt his head. Leaning close, he blew into her ear and suggested that they review the Clouds and Rain instead. She was not amused. Learn it all, she advised him, or else.

Now she spoke of emperors of the past, and of how they had relied on a council of their foremost ministers for advice, men who, being deeply rooted in the Confucian bureaucracy, were too often narrow-minded and afraid of innovation. In contrast, the Empress Wu enjoyed the excellent, creative counsel of her daughter, Princess T'ai-p'ing, and a group of learned men whom she herself had assembled, the Scholars of the North Gate. She called them this because they were unofficial ministers, and the South Gate was traditionally reserved for the official ministers.

"This Empress Wu," he said, "must be something. Look at her nerve, turning tradition on its head."

"Do not speak disrespectfully of your sovereign," the mysterious young woman replied, "not even for a moment, not even in jest."

"Sorry," the boxer said, "but I was trying to imagine her and her little girl making decisions that will change the course of history." In a falsetto voice, he imitated the way the Empress must sound, accompanying himself with appropriately effeminate hand gestures: "Shall we worship the Tao this month, or the Buddha? Shall we battle the Turks or appease the Tibetans?"

His impressions of old women had always brought gales of laughter in the marketplace, and he waited for his tutor to respond in a like manner.

"Little girl?" she said, not even cracking a smile.

"Yes, the princess. Her daughter. What's her name? T'ai-?"

"P'ing," the woman said in a voice like ice.

"Have I said something wrong?"

"You have broken your rice bowl in a thousand pieces."

"I am sorry," the boxer said. "I would gladly apologize if I only knew—"

"Then apologize right now. Bow and kowtow and thank the heavens that you are so comely, for otherwise I would have you executed this instant."

"Yes, yes, of course! Apologize I will, and gladly, but to whom? And on what account?"

"To me," she said, rising to her feet before him. "Princess T'ai-p'ing."

"Oh, no," he whispered. Then he performed the bows and kowtows precisely as he had learned them, and afterwards remained with his face to the floor, trembling with fear.

She gazed down at him with a mixture of pity and contempt. "You are forgiven. But if you ever again mention Mother or myself in this casual manner, it will be the end of you. Now rise."

The boxer did as he was told.

"Tomorrow we will celebrate Spring Begins. After we visit the Buddhist monastery for the maigre feast, I will bring Mother here and present her with a very special gift."

She paused and looked at him expectantly.

"Yes?" said the boxer, not understanding.

"The gift is you, fool!"

"Now wait a moment," the boxer said, beginning to tremble and sweat all over again. "A common knave like me for the Empress? What could she want with me? Anyway, she is old enough to be my mother. My grandmother."

The princess called for her menservants. "Lock him in the granary," she instructed them, "and call for the magistrate."

"Wait," the boxer said, "perhaps it would work. Now that I

think on it, I remember hearing that these spring-autumn affairs are often the most rewarding. The older partner supplies maturity and wisdom, while the younger provides vitality and daring."

She laughed at him, his helplessness, his desperation to survive. "You are like an animal," she said, "who thinks of nothing but a full belly and a warm place to sleep. But that is my good fortune, for an animal can be trained, while a real human spirit is indomitable."

5
A PRESENT FOR THE EMPRESS

The fourteenth, fifteenth, and sixteenth days of the first moon were the time of the Spring Begins festivities. To commemorate them, the Empress had decided to sponsor a maigre feast at the great Fu-hsien temple she had founded in memory of her mother, Lady Jung, who had walked the Dark Pathway some fourteen years before. Visiting it always brightened her heart.

When the night came, she and her youngest daughter, Princess T'ai-p'ing, and their entourage climbed the path to the temple, the mossy stone steps cut into the hillside, a way forbidden to all others. The night was warm, and the lanterns that lighted the way left a smell of perfumed oil in the air.

The princess, ever concerned for her mother's welfare, asked if she would care to stop and rest.

"Were it not unseemly," the Empress replied, her eyes sparkling with pleasure, "We would run the rest of the way, so elated do We feel this evening!"

"I know how giving a maigre feast pleases you," the princess said.

"And it is a festival day, too. On festival days We always feel so young."

She continued up the steep steps without the least sign of being winded, even though she had recently passed her sixtieth birthday. With her girlish figure, people mistook her, in poor light or at a distance, for the princess. Oddly, her aging manifested itself not in lines or wrinkles, but in her face having grown less mobile, as though time and the trials of office had thickened the skin the same way irritations will callous the foot's soft sole. Her eyes, meanwhile, had sunk deeper beneath their folds, contributing to the impression that she was a mask, and that the real woman had retreated to a place more distant and better protected.

Over robes of red patterned with green floral medallions, she wore an exquisite gossamer garment as thin as the web of a spider, with sleeves that trailed nearly to the ground, and a purple shawl embroidered with vines and flowers, draped across one shoulder and around the opposite arm. Her feet were clad in tiny brocade slippers of gold and silver thread.

"But it is more than that," the Empress continued a few moments later, as though she had been carrying on their conversation in her head and only now felt the need to speak it aloud. "The sadness that has been Our burden since the death of Our husband the Emperor seems suddenly to have lifted. As the cherry blossom blooms on the Way of Heaven, so do We feel that the dark winter of mourning has passed and Our own life may begin again."

"I can't tell you how it pleases me to hear you speak this way. I have been so worried."

"Well, worry no more."

"Mother? I have a surprise for you. Something very special."

"Tell Us at once."

"Then it would be no surprise. Plead as you like, I will not say. You must wait the whole evening to find out."

"Cruel thing! How will We ever endure all these prayers and speeches if We are wondering about what lies in store?

But the princess would say no more.

Reaching the hilltop, they saw the temple before them, a complex of low buildings surrounded by a wandering stone wall, and paused, entranced by its beauty. Thousands of tiny oil lamps, a tradition at this time of year, made the courtyards and galleries twinkle like the Pure Land of legend. The various halls of the temple, arranged around a towering pagoda, caught the moonlight in their sloping, yellow-tiled roofs. Junipers, cypresses, and pines grew about the eaves, while bamboo groves and fragrant grasses covered the steps and courtyards.

From where they stood they could see the parade of poor laity, dressed in patched robes and leading their children by the hand, pass through the temple gates. Alongside them marched an assortment of monks from neighboring monasteries, wearing saffron robes, their shaven heads gleaming in the moonlight. Rich and poor alike came to share in a maigre feast.

The Empress paused in front of the Buddha Hall to admire a lamp tower specially erected for that night, a bamboo tree with a thousand branches, each bearing a tiny oil lamp with a shiny tin spoon behind it to reflect its light. The sight of it brought a beatific smile to her face.

The interior of the hall was as magnificent as the outside, the roofbeams carved in aigrettes, scrolls, and vines, every inch of the walls painted with heavenly scenes of Buddhas, Bodhisattvas, and Patriarchs. Many statues of the Buddha were displayed on the long wooden altar, including several of solid gold, one of which was eighteen feet high and inlaid with a hundred pearls.

As patrons of the feast, the Empress and her daughter sat at the far end of the hall, along with the abbot of the monastery. The other monks sat cross-legged on their benches while the lay people crowded everywhere else. Even before everyone was settled, one of the monks began to beat on a wooden fish and another chanted a scripture in Sanskrit, the language of the Buddha:

How, through this scripture, can one reach the other shore?
We pray, O Buddha, that you reveal the subtle mystery
Explain it in detail for all sentient creatures.

Meanwhile, other monks passed out copies of the Pure Land Scripture (for the monks of Fu-hsien currently devoted themselves to the study of this text before all others) printed on folded paper bound between boards, so that the literate members of the assembly could recite it together. The Pure Land Scripture told of the marvelous sphere of existence of the same name where one might go after death, and of the wondrous Buddha named A-mi-t'o-fo who ruled over it, and the forty-eight vows that had helped him reach enlightenment.

Leading a procession past the Buddhas, the Empress and her daughter paused to light slivers of sandalwood and leave them to smolder in a bowl of sand. Soon countless, delicate ribbons of smoke were rising from the bowl, and the air was filled with the most exquisite perfume. They praised the Buddha by chanting the name A-mi-t'o-fo again and again. The close of the service consisted of a memorial, thanking the Empress for the feast (she had paid for most of it), and a maigre-feast essay composed by a monk who was especially adept with words.

Waiting through all this rigmarole had piqued everybody's appetite, and, while no one actually cheered aloud when the gong rang announcing dinner, a few of the guests could be heard muttering "Finally!" beneath their breaths. The Empress, the princess, the abbot, and a few of the most venerable and pious monks retired to the abbot's quarters for their feast, while the rest of the monks and laity went to the dining hall, where the monks regularly ate.

This former group sat on stools around a table of polished rosewood, eating from small porcelain plates with ebony chopsticks and porcelain spoons. A procession of servants arrived with bowls of the "Pure Meal of the Bodhisattvas" (that being a euphemism for vegetarian food), a mildly spiced, stir-fried stew of soft ginkgo nuts, black mushrooms, tangles of hair-fine seaweed, and small wads of wheat gluten seasoned with soy, accompanied by five varieties of boiled rice.

"Would you mind," the Empress said to the abbot, when they had nearly finished eating, "answering some questions? We have been wondering what happens to a man after the last breath has left his body."

"My Empress has been entertaining the doubts of the nihilists again."

"We admit it. In the daytime We are fine, but at night, when the court has left Us alone, and We are without memorials to read, or ambassadors to entertain, or musicians to divert Us, We fear that no part of Us will survive Our death."

The abbot cleared his throat in preparation. He was a fat man with a thick neck and a mole on the side of his nose. Sitting cross-legged on his bench, he resembled a dark mountain with a snow-capped peak. His Buddhist "scarf," a symbol of the poor patched robes that monks had worn in ancient days, was sewn together from twenty-five strips of silk, at a cost of about a thousand cash. Because of royal patronage, poverty in his temple had become largely symbolic.

"My Empress, at such dark hours you must recall the words of the Pure Land Scripture. In order that Dharmakara could be the ideal Buddha presiding over the ideal land, he took forty-eight vows. Because he adhered to them, he became the Bodhisattva A-mi-t'o-fo, who rules over the Pure Land. Let us recall his eighteenth vow:

> If, O Blessed One, when I have attained enlightenment, whatever beings in other worlds, having conceived a desire for right, perfect enlightenment, and having heard my name, with favorable intent think upon me, if when the time and moment of death are upon them, I, surrounded by and at the head of my community of mendicants, do not stand before them to keep them from frustration, may I not, on that account, attain to unexcelled, right, perfect enlightenment.

"Since A-mi-t'o-fo attained his wish, he must adhere to his vow. In other words, simply by pronouncing his name at the moment of death, a man is transported to the Pure Land, which is rich, fertile, comfortable, filled with gods and men, adorned with fragrant trees and flowers, and decorated with precious jewels and gems."

The Empress's eyes glowed, and a rare peacefulness descended upon her as she listened to the abbot's description.

"In this Pure Land," he went on, waving his chopsticks in the air as though they were brushes with which he might better paint the scene, "rivers of sweetly scented waters give forth pleasant musical sounds, and are flanked on both banks by scented jewel trees. The heavenly beings sporting in the water can cause it to be hot or cold as they wish. Everywhere they go they hear the voice of the Buddha teaching patience, compassion, and tolerance. Nowhere do they hear of anything woeful, or painful."

The Empress was on her guard again. Inclining her head slightly to the left, she smiled a sly cat's smile and said, "You say that because it is written in the Scriptures, it is so. Yet there are two versions of the Pure Land Scripture, one long, one short. Though the short one says that the mention of A-mi-t'o-fo's name is sufficient, the longer version says that meritorious deeds are necessary too. This troubles

Us, for We have done many things in Our life for the sake of Our people and Our kingdom that others might consider meritless."

The abbot shook his head. "Do not let evil people convince you otherwise! The shorter version is the true version: 'Beings are not born in the Pure Land as a reward and result of good works performed in this present life. No, whatever son or daughter of a family shall hear the name of the blessed A-mi-t'o-fo and, having heard it, shall, with thoughts undisturbed, keep it in mind . . . after their deaths they will be reborn in the Buddha country of the Pure Land.' "

They finished the meal with two more traditions of the season: little hempseed cakes, and wooden orioles that the Empress had brought along as presents for the monks. The monks received them with delight and, pretending that they were real birds, stroked their painted feathers and offered them grains of rice from the remains of the feast.

The Empress ordered that whatever cash had not been spent on food should be divided up between the monks and the laity, with a triple share to the monk who had composed the stirring maigre-feast essay. Then she signaled her entourage that the time had come to depart.

THE ENCHANTED PILLOW

The hour was late by the time they reached the princess's house. Oil lamps, blazing everywhere to welcome spring, had made the carriage ride back to the city seem like a trip among the stars. The streets were crowded with revelers singing popular songs, dancing, and playing on lutes. Street vendors peddled their hempseed cakes and dumplings and little wooden birds. The lower classes crowded the taverns while the mandarins filled the wine shops.

The Empress, who had been unusually gay most of the night, grew subdued.

"What is it?" the princess asked.

"All around Us, people are rejoicing. But how can We rejoice when We are alone? Ah, my precious, there are two terrible things in life. The first is being born a woman, the second, growing old. And the one makes the other worse."

"But, Mother—need it be that way? You are nearly the supreme sovereign of the kingdom. You can remake the world."

"Tradition is like the Yangtze when it floods. Can I hold back a mighty river singlehandedly?"

"You are not alone, Mother. I am with you."

"You are very sweet. And very young."

The princess's house was quiet. The sound of the revelry was distant now, like the cries of a retreating army. She suggested to her mother that they sit in her bedchamber and sample some wine imported from the frontier town of Liang-chou. The servant girl brought a glass decanter and two goblets decorated with the Seven Gems. When she poured the wine, it looked as dark as blood.

"A most excellent surprise," the Empress said, sampling it and savoring its warming, piquant bouquet. "We are instantly conscious of harmony suffusing our limbs. *This*"—she raised her glass—"is the true Prince of Grand Tranquility." (The Taoist sage Lao-tzu was called by the same honorific.)

Despite the expansive compliments, the princess sensed that her mother was disappointed. Evidently she had expected more.

The princess involved her in witty conversation and refilled her glass. Soon the Empress was laughing. Her voice grew raucous, her jokes randy. She loved these moments with her daughter when she could let down her hair. Whom else did she trust so completely?

The chamber's entrance was open so they might admire the plantings in the courtyard and enjoy the fragrant breeze. As the hour grew late, the sounds of the revelers died away. In time the peace grew almost palpable. The grunt of a bullfrog in the pond, the chirping of a cricket in a bamboo cage, all else was silence. The prince was in the library, reading; the servants were already asleep.

Suddenly a clatter of hooves, a clamor of voices.

"Rebellion," the Empress gasped, rising to her feet. She was hardly aware that she had spoken the word.

A servant woman appeared in her sleeping robe, explaining that it was only a fire in one of the poorer neighborhoods. Fire was to be expected when the citizens of Lo-yang celebrated a festival of lamps, for the lamps were easily upset, and the tall, teetering tenements of bamboo and oiled paper flamed like the very best tinder.

When the Empress sat down again, her breathing was quick. She drank several more glasses of wine, one after the other, before the trembling left her hands.

In time she began to speak about getting home. There were memorials waiting to be read, decisions that had to be made. She stood up too quickly and had to grab the back of the armchair for support.

"Mother, you cannot work in this condition! Be kind to yourself. Spend the night here in my house. Sleep in my bed. Tomorrow you can go to work refreshed."

"If only We could, precious daughter. But there is so much to be done."

"Then lie down in my bed and rest. I will wake you in one hour, I promise."

The Empress yawned and looked longingly at the bed. "I *am* so very tired."

"Come, then." The princess rose and, putting an arm around her mother, led her to the bed. She herself undressed her and took down her hair. Then she helped her up the step and into the bed, and drew the floss-lined covers up to her neck.

"Now, Mother," she said, "there is one thing I did not tell you. The pillow on which you are about to lay your head was a tribute from the land of the Brahmans. It is a magical pillow. She who places her head in that hollow will dream of a most splendid man visiting her during the night."

The Empress smiled, charmed by the tale but in no way convinced. "And what will this splendid man do?"

"Anything," the princess whispered, "you like." And with that she withdrew, gently shutting the doors of the bed behind her.

The boxer was waiting at the entrance to the room, according to her instructions. He had been washed and powdered and perfumed until he was as white and pure as the finest jade.

Passing him, the princess growled, "Fail me, and find your head on a pike come morn."

As she was leaving, she glanced out the courtyard and noticed, beyond the outline of the sloping roof across the way, a crimson blush of burning tenements against the night sky.

The princess, asleep in the chamber reserved for guests, woke abruptly in the middle of the night as she often did after drinking, her throat parched from the wine, her head aching, a host of questions nagging at her like ill-mannered children.

Had she properly calculated her mother's response to her little surprise? Had the boxer pleased her? Certainly he had a crude kind of charm—but he was also an oaf, and a fool. Not even a real boxer, but a show-boxer, a swindler by trade. Since the rebellion, Mother was suspicious of everyone. Suppose something he did, some stupid remark or clumsy gesture, was responsible for her losing her mother's confidence? What then?

Lying there in the dark, she ticked off those siblings who had fallen from favor: her eldest brother Li Hung, the crown prince and best of the Li princes, poisoned by Mother ten years ago, or so her detractors claimed; Li Su-chieh and Li Shang-chin, her half brothers, degraded by Mother to the status of commoners the following year; Prince Li-hsien, degraded and exiled for plotting rebellion a few years later.

The list went on. Last year, Li Ying, posthumously the Emperor Chung Tsung, not two months on the dragon throne before Mother deposed and imprisoned him for his headstrong attitude and disrespect; and her brother Li Ching-yeh, executed the same year for participating in the rebellion that had left Mother so fretful.

Of course, they were princes and a threat to her reign. But she had taken out her wrath on women, too, the old Empress for one, and the Emperor's favorite concubine, both of them left to drown in wine vats, their hands and feet cut off. Their daughters, the princess's half sisters, had also met a grim fate.

So many executions of close kin left her uneasy.

Suddenly she saw her scheme as a foolish and unnecessary risk. If her mother wanted a lover, she would take one. It was not the princess's place to do the choosing, nor to take the blame if it didn't work out.

She rose quickly from her bed, pulled an outer robe over her sleeping robe, covered her ankles and feet, and rushed through the courtyard to the chamber where she had left her mother. She raised the bamboo curtain and entered. An oil lamp was burning near the bed.

"Mother?" she whispered, opening the doors to the bed.

"She left," the boxer said, yawning and rubbing his eyes. "Is it morning? I'm so hungry."

"She left?" the princess said. "Why?"

"I don't know."

"Did you act the Clouds and Rain?"

"Yes," the boxer said.

"And did she enjoy it? Speak, you putrid camel flesh, if you wish to see the dawn at all!"

"I don't know. I couldn't tell. I finished and then she got up and left."

"May my ancestors help me," the princess moaned, sinking to the floor. "I have lost her forever."

"Perhaps I am too young. I thought that might be a problem. After all, she is as old as my—"

"Who cares what you think! You are nothing but a common thief. How could I have believed for an instant that a woman of her extraordinary refinement could have found pleasure with a vile dog like you? I must have been mad!"

She ran to the entrance and screamed until she woke the menservants, and they hurried into the courtyard. She ordered them to tie the boxer's wrists and lead him out behind the kitchen for a caning. Afterwards he was to be delivered to the tribunal, to await trial for his old crime.

She passed the rest of the night sitting on the hard wooden floor as a kind of penance, and trying to imagine life as a commoner, or as an exile in some frontier town frequented by bandits and caravan guides.

She knew when the Hour of the Rabbit had come, for she heard a Buddhist monk walking by the house, banging on a strip of iron and shouting the news, as he did every morning at that time. She called for the groom, intending to have him saddle a mount for her, but then thought better of it. Why further provoke her mother with these barbaric Turkish manners? Why indulge in these childish games of defiance when her entire future was at stake? She told him to prepare a carriage instead.

She changed out of her Turkish clothes, her pants and boots and tight sashed jacket, and ordered the servants to bring her most traditional and lovely costume, a pink floral lower robe that belted across the bosom, a turquoise upper robe, and a long gauze shawl to drape across her arms and shoulders. Instead of simply balling her hair up under her Turkish cap, she had her servant girl arrange it in an elegant bubble, pierced by jeweled pins and combs.

Appraising herself in the polished steel of her makeup mirror, she decided to go one step further. She had the servant girl pluck her eyebrows completely and then draw in the high, thin arcs known as "moth's antennae," that were the style that year. That would win her mother's favor. The Empress had been badgering her about her low, thick "monkey brows" for years.

Instead of riding straight to the Inner Palace, the Empress's living quarters, as she would normally do, and risking the humiliation of being denied entrance, she ordered the coachman to drive around to the South Gate, the one reserved for high officials (she was, after all, an important adviser to her mother).

Despite the pleasant spring weather, the palace seemed a cold and forbidding place. The South Gate, a towering stone structure built into the wall that ringed the palace, made her feel very small. She watched the gatehouse officials closely, trying to determine if they were avoiding her eye with disdain, or simply behaving in accordance with virtuous behavior. Gossip traveled like lightning around the palace; it was not impossible that they had heard of her fall from grace already.

While the princess was climbing the broad marble steps at the end of the promenade, she caught sight of White Pheasant, the Empress's favorite eunuch and personal chef, rushing down the steps, his smooth, plump face rosy from the effort, his robes flapping at his feet. She stopped to greet him. He looked straight at her and continued on his way as though she did not exist!

The eunuchs knew better than anyone who enjoyed favor at court. Now White Pheasant, who had always called her "precious niece," did not even acknowledge her!

Before approaching the Phoenix Hall, the small audience hall where her mother usually held court in the morning, the princess went to an alcove near the palace entrance to retrieve her audience tablet. According to a centuries-old tradition, no one could speak in the court if he was not holding one of these tablets. They were small rectangles with rounded tops, and they displayed the speaker's name and position, making it easier for the Empress to identify those officials of low rank with whom she was less familiar. The lower officials had tablets of hardwood or bamboo that their servants carried in bags, while the higher officials had tablets made of ivory chased with gold, which were kept in a rack in a centrally located alcove. The princess, as the favorite of the Empress, had the most splendid audience tablet of all, exquisitely engraved and ornamented. But now, when she looked for it in the rack, in the space where it was usually displayed, she found nothing.

Cold fingers of despair gripped her heart. She had already fallen from honor. Her audience tablet had been revoked. All was lost.

She rushed home and retired to her bedchamber, where she sat in solitude, mourning her fate and cursing the boxer, whom she saw as the cause of it. Recalling her great-aunt's story about the brave servant girl who had taken her life rather than suffer dishonor, she had one of her servants bring a dagger. But then, finding herself lacking the courage to follow the servant girl's example, and therefore even less honorable, she grew all the more miserable.

She went on like this until the afternoon, when a manservant appeared, announcing the Empress's arrival. The princess hurried to dry her eyes, repair her makeup, and brush back the wisps of hair that had come free from her coiffure. Making amends was always a possibility, even while climbing the steps of the executioner's platform.

When the Empress entered, the princess bowed and kowtowed.

"Why are you suddenly so formal with your old mother?" the Empress said, grasping her gently by the shoulders and raising her to her feet. "Why, how lovely you are!" she went on, surprised by the princess's appearance. "We are delighted to see that you have decided to stop dressing like a barbarian horseman."

"Then you're not angry?" the princess said.

"Why ever would We be?"

"I thought perhaps I had done something wrong. You left so soon last night."

"Many memorials clamored for Our attention. Our job is a busy one."

"And then, when I passed the eunuch White Pheasant on the steps of the palace, he did not speak to me."

The Empress laughed. "The mystery is explained. He told me he had seen a woman who resembled you almost as a twin, but was certainly not you, because she was wearing robes and fine makeup. He wondered if she might be a cousin or niece of the Chou clan whom he had not met before."

"And then I looked for my audience tablet and could not find it."

"We were feeling so fond of Our daughter that We sent it off to have it inlaid with emeralds. We will order the jeweler to work quickly, so you will have it in the rack by tomorrow."

"Well, then!" The princess smiled and took a deep breath, as a prisoner might, upon learning of his sudden reprieve. "I feel so much better. Let me bring you some tea. And I have wonderful golden peaches from Great-Aunt."

"If only We could, but We must return to our work at the

palace. Having only a brief time to relax, We wondered if We might try again your magical pillow from the land of the Brahmans."

The princess was speechless. When she regathered her wits, she said, "Mother—you know it was not a magic pillow?"

The Empress smiled. "We thought the young man surprisingly firm for a dream or apparition."

"And you are not disappointed?"

"We are delighted to know that We need not kowtow to some magician lest he make Our young man vanish."

"There's more. He is a commoner."

"He will give his peasant vitality to this tired old clan of Chou."

"And a boxer by profession. A show-boxer."

"We would see him learn a gentler trade, lest he bruise his lovely chest."

"And a criminal, Mother. A petty swindler."

"The poor are often driven to crime. Now that he is in Our care, he will have no more need to swindle."

"So you know these things and you still wish to see him again?"

"More than August Earth and Heaven," the Empress replied. "Bring him here."

"I would, but . . ." She thought quickly. "But he has gone to the market to buy you a gift. I will go get him myself. I won't be a minute."

The moment she was out of her mother's sight, she tore off her robes and ordered the groom to saddle a mount. She grabbed her trousers and jacket out of her clothing box, and the boots that she kept beneath the bed. She pulled her tall cap over her hair without bothering to take it down.

The princess galloped all the way to the tribunal. She interrupted the magistrate, who was in the middle of a trial, demanding that the prisoner she had returned earlier that day be immediately released. By order of the Empress, naturally.

They opened the heavy wooden door of the ward, and the prisoners peered out like moles. The guards located the boxer and dragged him into the sun. He had been beaten so badly that his back was crosshatched with welts and he could barely stand. She called for a bucket of cold water and a pot of rice wine. She had them pour the former over his head, the latter down his throat. That gave him the energy to hang on to her while she galloped with him through the streets of the city, back to her home. Though the magistrate was shocked speechless, the princess didn't care. Assured of her mother's favor, she could do as she liked.

As for the boxer, it was clear even to his dim intellect that he had become a commodity of value. To be wanted was to have power. The thought pleased him. All his life he had been pushed about, beaten, and treated with contempt. He had starved and wandered homeless, and slept in the streets. Now that he was someone, he was going to make things different. That was, after all, the way of the world.

7

THE FORTUNE-TELLER

One hot summer day, the princess's husband, whose name was Hsüeh Shao, sat in the bamboo pavilion in the courtyard, admiring his miniature garden. He had recently received a present from a cousin who lived in the far-off city of Kuang-chou, a rock all pitted and tortuous, carved by the elements into a fantastic shape that resembled an old woman bent with age. The cousin knew of the prince's passion for gardening, and no fine garden was complete without one of these rare stones.

All week the prince had been preoccupied with his new acquisition. Even while he seemed to be concentrating on a scroll of poetry, or reprimanding the cook for adding too much soy sauce to their dinner, his mind was on the stone. Where, precisely, should it stand? Which side should face the viewing pavilion to best exhibit its peculiarities? What plants might he arrange around the base to emphasize its whiteness, its virtue? All week he had been occupied with such delightful aesthetic decisions.

Now that the rock was positioned precisely to his satisfaction, he lighted cones of incense, concealed them within the deeper holes of the stone, and retreated to the pavilion to admire his handiwork.

Lavender smoke gathered in the still summer air, a sea of mist from which the peak rose like an enchanted isle.

The prince's pleasure, as he sat there on that hot afternoon, admiring his work, was quite beyond description. Meditating on the diminutive scale of the garden, he compressed his consciousness to elfin proportions, until he could stand in a pavilion the size of a teacup, walk a tiny footpath, or cross a rainbow bridge no bigger than a brocade slipper. Roaming this little world, whose every detail he had forged to perfection, he found peace.

A most elusive item since the boxer had joined his household.
The boxer.

The very thought of him cast a dark cloud across the perfect vista.

Everything about the boxer irritated him: the way he lay about in bed until noon, ordering the servants to braid his hair or file his nails or bring him a dish of roast pork and a pot of wine; the way he dressed up like a mandarin, rode into town, and visited the wine shops with his scar-faced Korean friend, squandering cash on singing girls; the way, returning drunk to the prince's home, he would pick a fight with one of the servants and, more often than not, end it by lifting the unfortunate fellow overhead and tossing him through a wall. Servants quit, walls had to be rebuilt. Food bills tripled. And it was no use complaining to the Empress. A woman in love, she simply smiled at the description of the boxer's exploits and allocated the taxes of another hundred families to pay for the damages.

It wasn't the cash that mattered. One longed for a certain tranquility within one's own home.

The prince did everything he could to avoid the boxer, for, when they did meet, the boxer regaled him with complaints as though he were an innkeeper. The amount of cold water was insufficient, the bed creaked, a servant's voice was grating, the rice was undercooked and not to his liking. The prince could barely contain his temper. But why ruin a perfect afternoon with such thoughts? He put the boxer out of his mind and returned to his contemplation of the garden.

Now that his spirit had explored the lower parts of the garden, it ascended to that point he had been saving for last, the peak of the new rock. Poised there, his spirit gazed down, through the swirling mist of incense, at the wondrous vistas below. What bliss! So the Taoist sorcerers must feel when they escape to the Abode of the Immortals.

From far away he heard an uneven rhythm of footsteps, but chose to ignore it. Nothing would disturb this exquisite moment. The footsteps grew louder until, from his miniature vantage point, they shook the ground like an earthquake. Suddenly the mountain on which his spirit was poised toppled sideways.

The boxer, drunk and tramping straight across the garden rather than wasting the footsteps required to follow the loggia around its periphery, had caught his foot in a miniature arbor and overturned the mountain in an attempt to break his fall. In the process of pushing himself back to a standing position, he plunged his hand into a lake, drowning the miniature lotuses, caving in the mossy banks. When he was upright again, he took a step and flattened three willow trees that the prince had spent years pruning and training.

"Stop, please!" the prince cried, half rising from his seat in the pavilion.

"What's the matter?" the boxer asked.

"My garden."

"Oh." The boxer looked around as though noticing it for the first time. "Sorry. I'll fix it up for you. Beloved *son.*" This last word he pronounced with a special relish.

"What did you call me?" the prince inquired.

"Son. That's what I came to tell you. I've been made a part of the family. The Empress thought it improper that she be spending so much time with a mere commoner. So she made me a member of the Hsüeh clan."

"No," the prince whispered.

"She memorialized it this morning, in court."

"But we are one of the venerable clans of the northeast. We are a family of poets, and sages, and scholars. We trace our lineage back to the kings of antiquity."

"Be that as it may, I am now Hsüeh Huai-i, your father. You and I will worship the same ancestors and practice filial piety toward one another. Come, embrace your father."

The boxer grinned at him and held open his arms.

The prince gazed at him in horror. He rose to his feet and backed a few steps, then turned and fled from the pavilion.

The boxer shrugged and, kneeling down, began trying to stick the trunks of the broken willow trees back in the earth.

The prince requested the presence of the princess in his library. The room was lined with shelves that were divided into boxes, and every box held dozens of scrolls: classics bearing red labels, dynastic histories bearing green ones; philosophers, indigo; and collections of poems and stories, white. Recently the prince had grown so voracious in his appetite for scrolls that he had run out of shelf space and been forced to store them in the window frames, filling the windows. Thus, on this rare occasion, his quest for knowledge had led to darkness rather than illumination. The princess had to squint to see him.

They bowed to each other respectfully.

"I have tolerated many abuses in the four years since we wed," he began when she was seated. "I have been denied my conjugal rights from the very first. I have been forced to manage the household, make the shopping lists, and settle the servants' quarrels while you were out riding about the city all night, dressed like a Turkish bandit. In the dark hours of my life, you were nowhere to solace me, and in those few happy moments, you could not be found to share them. The single reason that remains for my existence, my garden, is simply another opportunity for you to ridicule me. Through all this I have remained silent. But now I must speak, for I have reached the point where my own existence is so painful that I would just as soon end my life."

He paused and, drawing a handkerchief from his sleeve, wiped his nose, which had begun to run profusely.

"I'm sorry you've accumulated so many grievances," the princess replied sincerely, having taken time to choose her words. "I never imagined that I appeared so lacking in propriety. I regret that my duty to Heaven's Chosen has left so little time for anyone else." She hesitated. "There is another thing. I am not like other women in my feeling for men. Perhaps I was born with an excess of yang, for I feel neither attraction to even the handsomest of your sex, nor desire. But do not think that I ridicule you or your garden. I bear you great respect. The moments I have spent gazing at your garden have been among the most peaceful and fulfilling of my life."

He looked at her as though seeing her for the first time. "Is it really so? Do you really take pleasure in my garden?"

"I find it exquisite. I hope that the Pure Land where I go after death is half so well ordered and beautiful."

"Thank you." The prince bowed to her.

"Now tell me, husband, what causes you such grief—though I think I know the answer already."

"The man you brought into the house. The boxer."

She gazed down at the floor. "I thought as much."

"It was bad enough before, with him eating us out of rice, destroying our home with his brawling, and battering our servants."

"He raped one of my servant girls, and drank a rare wine I was saving for Great-Aunt."

"But now your mother has gone too far."

"Oh no. What has she done? Tell me." Her brow knit with concern.

"She has passed a decree making him my father." He clenched his fists. "It is her way of humiliating me. She hates me as she hates all those of aristocratic birth. Think of it—when he dies, my children and grandchildren will have to venerate him. Even in death I will not be free of him, for they will store his ancestral plaque in the cabinet alongside my own, and all the excellent members of my family who have distinguished themselves as generals and poets and officials since ancient times. Ah, the shame of it, the shame. I would weep."

He shook his head, and tears appeared in his eyes.

The princess raised her eyes and gazed at him. The corners of her mouth twitched. She held her hand over her mouth, but she could not conceal her laughter, for her whole body shook with it. "Forgive me, husband, but the boxer . . . your father . . . it is *so* funny. . . ."

"It is as I thought. I am nothing to you but an object of ridicule!"

He rose and started for the entrance. She ran after him and, catching him by the shoulder, pulled him roughly around so that he faced her. Being the same height as she, he found himself gazing into her eyes. She was no longer smiling.

"He has made my life intolerable too," she confessed. "Though I created him, I would gladly destroy him—if only Mother would permit it. We must work together to rid ourselves of this coarse beast."

Then she embraced him. It was the first time she had ever done so. She pressed against him, and the long dormant yang rose in him and he grew ardent. She allowed him to act the Clouds and Rain with her there on the library floor. They rolled in and out of the needles of light that penetrated between the scrolls that filled the window frames. He was aware of the smell of the stables in her hair. She brought him to climax as dispassionately as she might groom a horse. Knowing her distaste for men, it moved him all the more. Afterwards, they called for tea and cakes.

The servants, finding them sitting opposite each other on the library floor, their robes crumpled, their hair messed, the smell of sex vying with the musty odor of the scrolls, cast significant glances at one another.

"Let us have him killed," the prince said in a low voice, when they were again alone. "It would seem simple enough. Have some of our menservants wait for him in an alleyway and beat him to death."

"If Mother ever learned that we were behind it, it would be our undoing. She adores him. She gives him horses from the palace stables, and clothing that belonged to my father. No, we must wait until she is disillusioned. The love affair cannot last long. Those fires that flame brightest die most quickly."

"Nonetheless, we must get him out of our house. I cannot bear it another day."

"Could we entice Mother," the princess went on, "with a scheme to make him more available to her? That would work twice in our favor, for we would be rid of him, and she might tire of him more quickly."

"Is there some way of installing him in the palace," the prince asked, "as a music master, or a teacher of fists and kicks?"

"You know what happens to men who are brought into the palace." She reached under the prince's robes and, cupping his testicles in one hand, drew her forefinger across the sack like a dagger. "They would make her fine new stud a gelding. Mother would never permit it."

They sipped at their tea, silent and pensive. All of a sudden, the prince raised a finger. "I have it. She would make him a monk at the Fu-hsien temple. Then he could visit the Inner Palace at his pleasure." His face fell and he shook his head. "But even as I speak, I see that my plan is nonsense. How long could such a braggart uphold the laws of the brotherhood? Not longer than the time it would take to insult the abbot or steal an incense burner to trade for a pot of wine."

"What if he were abbot of his own temple? Then he would have to please no one but himself. Such low creatures as the boxer adore fancy titles and costumes even when they are empty of meaning."

"Would the Empress build him his own temple?"

"There are many abandoned temples in the city. Just a few months ago she was talking about improving the old White Horse Temple. Ah, husband, it is an excellent scheme. I see that I have deprived myself of valuable counsel by not consulting with you more often."

"Now the difficult part—convincing the Empress."

"We shall have the boxer do the convincing."

"He would never agree to it."

She inclined her head a few degrees and smiled a sly cat's smile, so that the resemblance to her mother was truly uncanny. "We shall see."

Most afternoons, while the Empress was receiving envoys, meeting with advisers, reading memorials, and fulfilling the duties of the Phoenix Throne, the boxer and the Korean were visiting the wine shops on the south side of town. Unlike the poor taverns they used to frequent before the boxer's windfall, these elegant establishments were not entered from the street, but rather through courtyards with flower beds and fountains, and galleries with gilded lanterns. The boxer and his friend would sit on wooden stools, surrounded by mandarins in green robes and lavender robes and even purple robes, and drink rare wine from agate cups.

The boxer liked one wine shop in particular, because of a Sogdian singing girl who worked there. Though her appearance was exotic, her eyes emerald green, her hair flax yellow, her figure full-bosomed and as narrow-waisted as a Roman goblet, something about her low origins and high aspirations reminded him of the servant girl. Being around her brought him peace and excitement at once.

She was the perfect counterpoint to the Empress, simple where the Empress was complex, spontaneous where the Empress was studied, passionate in her lovemaking where the Empress was a model of cool perfection. If the Empress was a steep mountain road with hazards at every turn, the Sogdian girl was an oasis with date palms and cool springs bubbling from the earth.

For an extra hundred cash, she would meet him in a little room upstairs, strum the bent-necked lute for him, and sing the latest Turkish songs. Afterwards, she would sit in his lap and they would kiss and stroke one another, and whisper endearments. Finally, when his Jade Stalk had grown large and hard, they would act the Clouds and Rain.

These liaisons were discreetly arranged by the singing girl's old "stepmother." This stepmother had once been a great beauty herself, a consort of consummate skill on the zither and bent-necked lute, who had made her fortune infatuating wealthy university students, scions of the famous northeastern families, and taking all their money. Now she was a hag with sunken cheeks and a neck like a chicken's, who wore too much rouge and was always adjusting her false teeth; and the only music she made was when she rattled the beads of her abacus, calculating what her girls had earned that day.

The Sogdian girl looked forward to the day when she had wealth enough to throw off the yoke of her old stepmother, just as the servant girl had longed for the day when she might leave the servitude of the princess Ch'ien-chin. The boxer, entertaining some hazy and distant dream of a future life with her (after the Empress's death, perhaps), gave her what money he could spare to hasten her liberation.

The wine shop offered other, more trivial diversions, such as a puppet show on a little folding stage, the puppets caricaturing all the common "types" found around town: the licentious, blue-eyed woman from the west; the greedy Uighur moneylender; the evil black Malay; the Buddhist who had become a monk to avoid the forced-labor tax; the haughty mandarin; the bumpkin farmer. The shows had little plot: the puppets drank, flirted, gossiped about the customers, and passed out. The customer at whom the puppet was pointing when it fell had to drain his cup, to the amusement of the others.

Another diversion took the form of a Buddhist nun who would stop by to tell fortunes. She was sixty, short and stately, with an enormous bosom beneath her stiff scarlet robe. Her shaved head was as bumpy as a stone. She wore the cryptic smile that was often seen on statues of the Buddha, her eyes glazed with piety.

"I sense that I am in an extraordinary religious presence," she said one day, stopping by the table where the boxer and the Korean were sitting, drinking their wine and nibbling at lichee nuts.

"You, sir," she said to the boxer, "though your past was humble, I sense that an extraordinary destiny awaits you. For five hundred cash I will tell your fortune."

"What sort of fortune-telling do you practice?" the boxer asked. "Do you toss the yarrow sticks and read the Book of Changes? Or do you refer to the position of the stars at the hour of my birth?"

"Neither, sir. I practice the most ancient and venerable art of all: reading the tortoise shell."

"Bah," the Korean said. "It matters not what method they use, these fortune-tellers are all the same." He imitated her high, pious tones: " 'Wealth and fame will be yours. You will have many sons who will grow up to be scholars, pass the examinations, and venerate you in your old age.' "

"Do you question my skill?" the nun asked. "I have read the future of emperors, and the presidents of ministries. Only professional ethics stop me from revealing their names."

"Ignore this rotten piece of Korean turtle meat," the boxer said to her. "He is of low birth, and lacking in education. I, on the other hand, am of the . . ."

"Don't tell me," the nun said, closing her eyes and pressing her fingertips to her forehead, "you are of the Hsüeh clan, of the Hundred Venerable Lineages."

The boxer elbowed the Korean. "See?"

"I see nothing," the Korean grumbled. "You've told everybody in the wine shop about your fine breeding one hundred times."

"If you are not interested in my services," the nun said, "there are others . . ."

"Sit right here," the boxer insisted, pulling out a stool for her, "and get on with it."

Smiling triumphantly at the Korean, she seated herself and removed, from the purse in her sleeve, a tortoise shell the size of a serving dish, brittle and bleached from years in the sun. She brought out a steel needle with a wooden handle, and a brass incense burner. The Sogdian girl took the burner away and brought it back with two hot coals inside it. The nun left the needle in the coals until it glowed red; then she had the boxer press it against the center of the shell. With a faint hissing sound, a series of cracks crept across the dry, brittle bone. The boxer, the Korean, and the Sogdian girl all strained to see over her shoulder. The nun only glanced at the bone and her eyes widened with wonder. She stared at the boxer and shook her head.

"No, it must be some mistake."

"What?" asked the boxer. *"What?"*

"A moment, please." She took the tortoise shell over to the screen to see it better. She seemed to stand there forever, tracing the cracks with her fingertip, then shaking her head in disbelief.

The boxer looked at the Korean.

The Korean rolled his eyes to the ceiling, that they should have to suffer such theatrics.

When she returned, she sat down across the table from him, and fixed him with her most serious gaze.

"You may find what I am about to tell you incredible," she began. But then she broke off and looked around.

Suddenly it had grown very quiet. The mandarins at the adjoining tables had stopped their talking and drinking and were listing in her direction like a fleet of purple sails in the wind. Everyone knew that the boxer was the beloved of the Empress; some bit of information about his future might be the compass setting that would steer them through the gale of a sudden policy change at the palace.

All agreed that they would be wise to continue the session upstairs. When they had regrouped in a small, private chamber on the second floor, whose decoration consisted of a vase of silvery catkins, a low lacquered table, and a wall scroll depicting three drunken men taking pleasure with a woman, the nun began again.

"This is not your first life," she murmured, holding the tortoise shell in the palm of her right hand and tracing the cracks with her left. "Far from it! You have undergone countless incarnations. Long ago you lived in the land of the Brahmans. When Sakyamuni, the Buddha, was trying to reach the Bodhi tree in order that he could experience his glorious awakening, he found himself on the banks of a river that had to be crossed. He approached several ferrymen, asking that they take him to the other shore, but since he had no cash, they refused. Then finally he found a ferryman who agreed to pole him across in return for his blessing. That ferryman"—and here she paused, and gazed at the boxer with frightening intensity—"was you."

The boxer and the Sogdian girl both gasped. The Korean muttered, "Spare me."

"In later incarnations," she went on, "you were a monk, begging at doorways, memorizing scriptures, sitting in meditation, and chanting the praises of the Buddha."

"I always felt a sympathy for those Buddhist monks I passed on the street," the boxer said.

"As I recall it," the Korean said, "you made fun of their bald heads and broke their begging bowls."

"Shut up, turtle spawn."

"In time," the nun continued, "you achieved enlightenment! The Bodhisattvas opened the gates of the Pure Land, and the Buddha himself came to greet you."

"Imagine that," the boxer said, enchanted by the image of it.

"But you would not enter that Pure Land yet! You said that as long as there were souls that had not yet experienced enlightenment, you would insist on being reborn again and again in this poor material world of ours. In other words, you chose to be a Bodhisattva. You would willingly suffer grief, illness, old age, and death, rather than dwell in eternal bliss, simply so you might help others."

"So that's it!" the boxer said.

"Pardon me?" the nun said.

"Nothing. Go on with your story."

"Yes." She gazed down at the bone, trying to pick up her train of thought. "That's what you told the Buddha. And he granted you your wish. But he said that in each incarnation you would be unaware of your previous true identity until it was revealed to you by a skilled fortune-teller."

"And you are that fortune-teller!" the boxer said with excitement.

"I suppose I am," the nun agreed, with some surprise.

"Is there more?" the boxer asked.

The nun squinted at the bone. "A little. Among the other incarnations, you were Bodhidharma."

"Bodhidharma? I've heard of him. Some old monk, wasn't he?"

"No mere monk. A Patriarch, he who brought Buddhism from the land of the Brahmans to the Middle Kingdom. As Bodhidharma, you carried the scriptures to the White Horse Temple so that it could be a center of learning for all of the empire. But now the White Horse Temple has fallen into ruin, bringing you misery."

"Is that the old place west of the palace? Funny you should mention it, but I do feel sad when I ride by it."

"Of course you do."

"As though I want to fix it up. Know what I mean?"

"Naturally. It was your temple those many years ago. You want it to be beautiful, to reflect the glory of your faith."

"Is there more?" the boxer asked eagerly. He liked hearing about himself.

"That's all I can tell from this tortoise shell," she replied.

"It's quite a lot," the Korean said, "from a couple of crooked lines." He craned his neck to look at the bone. "Show me the part where it says that the Bodhisattvas opened the gates of the Pure Land for him."

"To those of pure faith," the nun said, "the tortoise shell says everything. For those who are cynical, it is silent."

"Sure," said the Korean.

"That will be five hundred cash," the nun said, holding out her hand, while turning her head in the other direction, as though the sight of the little copper coins might degrade her.

Later the boxer and the Korean walked through the South Market to the stable where they had left their horses. Everywhere they looked, tall parchment signs, hanging from the eaves or supported by wooden frames, proclaimed the names of merchants and their products or services, while other signs simply wished well to the populace. The crowd made way for the well-dressed pair. They stopped for a shave from an outdoor barber who worked beneath a bamboo canopy, and again to buy a wooden whistle from a peddler who sold dolls, cricket cages, and fans from a plank table.

"What did you mean back there," the Korean asked, "when she said you were a Bodhisattva, and you said, 'So that's it,' as though it explained everything?"

"I can't talk about it," the boxer said. But a little later he changed his mind, so badly did he want to share the burden of his conscience.

"Remember when I told you that the servant girl had died from a caning? I wasn't being completely honest. Somehow she'd gotten hold of a dagger. According to her plan, we'd both die with honor.

A suicide pact. But it didn't work out that way. To make a long story short, she started the job and I couldn't finish it. I tried with all my might and I couldn't." The boxer's voice was very soft and he avoided the Korean's eye.

The Korean squeezed the boxer's arm to comfort him. "She was a good girl. I miss her too. But what can be done? Dry grain becomes cooked rice. She may have suffered some—but she would have suffered worse in prison. Don't blame yourself."

"Well, I don't blame myself, not anymore, because now I understand that it was the Bodhisattvas who stopped me. In order to complete my compassionate mission for mankind, I had to refrain from suicide."

"Wait a minute." The Korean stopped and turned to face him. "You don't actually believe that hairless grandmother?"

"You saw her read the shell."

"I saw her look at some cracks and spout a lot of nonsense."

"You dare call it nonsense?" The boxer's misery gave way to anger, a more comfortable emotion for him.

"Of all people, you should know a swindle when you see one."

"Before you question my honor," the boxer said, "let me remind you that I am a member of the Hsüeh family, one of the Hundred Venerable Lineages, favorite of the Empress, and reincarnation of the great Bodhikarma."

"You dog. You're common dirt like me. And it's Bodhi-*dharma*."

"I won't stand for this kind of talk," the boxer said.

"You're so drunk you can barely stand at all," the Korean pointed out, grinning.

"You'll pay for that remark."

With a ferocious snarl, the boxer raised his open hands and began to close in on the Korean.

The boxer punched and punched again. He was moving so slowly that the Korean did a little dance as he dodged him, to the delight of the ever-growing crowd. Then, leaping in the air, the Korean kicked, his foot slamming the boxer in the chest. As the boxer fell backwards, the tortoise shell with his miraculous future and past inscribed upon it slipped from his sleeve and shattered against the paving stones.

"Look what you did!" the boxer shouted at the Korean.

"Put an end to your stupidity, I hope."

Rising to his hands and knees, the boxer crawled along the paving stones, gathering up the pieces of shell as though they were the remains of a rare porcelain bowl. Somebody must have recognized him, for the phrase "concubine to the Empress" was heard circulating among the bystanders.

"I should have you tortured for this," the boxer said, shaking a fist at the Korean. It was no idle threat, for he now had the power to do so if he wished.

"Go ahead."

For a long time they took each other's measure, the boxer kneeling in the middle of the street, the Korean standing over him, hands on hips.

Finally the boxer rose, put his arm around the Korean's shoulders, and said, "But instead I'll buy you a drink."

The boxer was obsessed by the nun's prophecy. When next he met with the Empress, he announced that he had a matter of the greatest urgency to discuss with her. She was so smitten that she found his self-importance endearing. How sweet that our relationship is more than Clouds and Rain—he actually has something to say to me! Such was her line of thought.

They met in an exquisitely furnished chamber that the princess had ordered built onto her house especially for their liaisons. (Middle Kingdom homes, being little more than roofs supported by wooden beams, and walls filled in with fire-baked brick and fretwork screens, were easily expanded.)

At the clap of the boxer's hands, a servant brought iced tea and melon in a jade ice urn, and sugar crabs from the Yangtze River, so frosty that they made the teeth ache.

The Empress was charmed to see how quickly he had adopted the tastes and manners of the mandarin. Given an education and a bit more refinement, he would be indistinguishable from the rest of those who wore the purple robes and golden belts. Since her own family, the Chou, was of the northwestern clans, which had always been considered a rank or two inferior to the powerful northeastern clans, she was delighted by any evidence that aristocracy was less a sign of innate ability or intelligence than an artifice to hoard and perpetuate power and wealth.

When they were settled and served, he told her about the nun's prophecy. He got as far as his welcome at the gates of the Pure Land when the Empress's face turned as red as the lacquer of her armchair and she began to laugh uncontrollably.

"What's so funny?" he demanded.

"You—a Bodhisattva . . ." She stopped to gasp for breath.

He had never been so insulted. He rose and walked to the entrance, and stood there pretending to stare at the garden, his lower lip thrust forward in a pout.

Seeing that he was far more serious about this prophecy than she had imagined, the Empress forced herself to be sober.

"Precious?" she called.

He wouldn't look at her.

"Forgive Us?" she asked.

He folded his arms across his chest and shook his head.

"We have gifts We would gladly give Our darling," she went on in a little girl's singsong, "if only We could see him smile. A eunuch who can prepare a thousand dishes without ever repeating a taste. A broad-backed, black-maned tarpan pony who is as fleet as the wind. A bronze sword of K'un-wu with a sharkskin wrapping on the hilt, and golden scrollwork on the scabbard."

"I would rather have a begging bowl, a saffron robe, and a razor to shave my head."

She crossed the room and stood behind him. The heat from the open entrance to the courtyard blew over her, carrying with it an intoxicating smell of jasmine. She ran her fingertips down his forearms, following the contours of his muscles beneath his silk robes. Moving even closer, she drew a circle on the down of his neck with the tip of her tongue.

"We cannot bear to see Our beloved so sad, and would happily grant him anything within Our power. Yet We worry that if he becomes a monk, he will shun all the pleasures of the Jade Chamber and We shall be as lonely and sad as before."

The boxer glanced over his shoulder at her. "If anything, it would be easier to enjoy the Jade Chamber, for as a monk I could visit the palace as I pleased."

"Then you would not renounce Our love when you renounced all other things that tie you to this life?"

"Certainly not! For the Jade Chamber brings you happiness,

and happiness is closer to enlightenment than misery. Since my purpose in life is to bring everyone to enlightenment, we shall act the Clouds and Rain more passionately than ever!"

"Perhaps you are a Bodhisattva after all," the Empress said gently, "for the argument you have just made reminds Us of the talk of the cleverest monks. But what of the discipline of temple life? Could you do without your wine or your rowdy friends? Could you bear the long hours of scripture chanting and meditation?"

"If I went to the White Horse Temple, as the nun suggested, I'd be the only one there, and then what difference would it make whether I followed the rules or not? Of course, I'd *try*. I couldn't give up everything completely, not all at once. I'd cut down, little by little. In a couple of years I'd be as good a monk as anybody."

"We have no doubts."

"Then I can be a monk?" he asked with excitement.

"No," she replied, a smile playing around the corners of her mouth.

"But you said . . ."

"No mere monk. You will be abbot of the White Horse Temple!"

"Really? What a fine woman you are!" He swept her up in his arms and spun her about. She laughed to see him so happy.

"Do you think," he added sheepishly as he let her down, "that I could have that K'un-wu sword anyway? The one with the bronze blade and the sharkskin hilt?"

Although she didn't know why her mother had summoned her to the palace, Princess T'ai P'ing hoped that it had to do with the prophecy of the nun and the removal of the cursed boxer from her home.

She entered the Phoenix Hall, holding her gaudy golden plaque in her hands, her boot heels echoing against the marble floor. Everybody turned at the sound: the Empress and the young puppet Emperor Jui-tsung sitting on their simple, elevated thrones; the scribes, mandarins, and guards who attended all such sessions; and the Empress's watchdogs, Chou Hsing and Lai Chün-ch'en, who were occupying the floor at that moment, holding their own simple audience plaques, and memorializing.

Following the terrifying rebellion of the previous year, these two previously undistinguished civil servants had been appointed to ferret out disloyalty and plots against the throne, using whatever means were necessary to wrest confessions from their suspects. The method they used most often was torture, and they practiced the art (it was nothing less, in their hands) in such a creative and ingenuous manner that they had grown famous for it throughout the kingdom. Their techniques varied from the subtle (repeated drops of water on a man's head for days on end) to the traditional (immersion in boiling oil) to the wildly imaginative (flaying the skin, covering the exposed muscle with red ants, then sewing the skin back in place). They were so persuasive that even where rebellion did not exist, it was exposed and admitted to.

Chou Hsing was stockily built, with a flat, smooth face on which his features were sculpted in low relief, and eyebrows that tilted up at his nose, as though raised with pity. He knew many jokes, and loved to make the Empress laugh. Lai Chün-ch'en, on the other hand, was always serious, gaunt and severe. He had sunken cheeks, burning eyes, and long whiskers.

The princess knelt, waiting for her mother to recognize her, but the Empress indicated that the watchdogs should first finish their report. She always found an excuse to keep her daughter waiting like this, for she knew how painful it was to maintain a kneeling position in tight Turkish riding pants. By forcing her to dwell on this particular shortcoming of her costume, she hoped to encourage a return to loose silk robes.

Watchdog Lai took his turn, speaking quickly to spare the princess pain. He reported on a prisoner named False Brush, who was, despite representations of himself as a madman, suspected of being an agent of the rebellious Li princes. So far, despite their efforts, they had not succeeded in piercing the veil of his deception. They now proposed freeing him and setting spies to trail him, so that he might lead them to his co-conspirators.

The Empress agreed to consider the suggestion.

Next the Empress herself brought up a matter. It appeared that a certain Buddhist nun had given a false and outrageous prophecy to a member of the court. Though the intent of the action was obscure, she thought it safe to assume that, like most deceits at this lofty level, it augured rebellion. Having ordered her watchdogs to learn the names of all those involved, and schedule their executions, she dismissed them.

Finally she nodded for her daughter to approach.

The princess rose with relief and hurried forward, looking pale and shaken, more than could be reasonably attributed to the slowed circulation in her legs. She kowtowed and requested permission to approach the throne.

"Mother," she whispered in the Empress's ear, "I must confess all. This lying nun is no one's agent but my own. I hired her to persuade the boxer—or Beloved Father, as I have come to think of him—to become a monk so that he could visit the palace at will. You shouldn't have to come all the way to my house every time you wish to see him. You are too busy for that."

The princess glanced at the puppet Emperor, who was sitting so close that he could not have helped overhearing, to see his reaction. But he appeared to have only one concern, a cunning little wooden puzzle of a Buddha that he was studying, turning over in his hands, trying to dismantle. Although he was twenty-three, he looked like a teenager, sallow-complected, with a dusting of pimples on his forehead. His eyes were dull, his posture hunched, his responses—at the rare times when they were required of him—grunts or words of one syllable.

The Empress tilted her head to the side and gave her daughter a catlike smile. "Was that the only reason?"

"What other reason could there be?" the princess asked innocently.

"We worried that he was upsetting the tranquility of your household. After all, he has his unruly side."

"No, no, Mother. Beloved Father's companionship is always a delight. We shall all miss him when he leaves." And she added quickly, "*If* he leaves."

The Emperor glanced up from his puzzle, pursed his lips, and went back to work.

"Then perhaps We should command him to remain at your home. We would not want to deprive you of him." Her cat's smile grew even more sly.

"Mother, your need is greater than mine. I have a husband, but you have none. And I am always free to visit Beloved Father, am I not?"

"Always," the Empress agreed.

"Then you will forgive me? I was only considering your welfare. Rebellion was the furthest thing from my mind."

"We have never questioned your loyalty," the Empress said. And she added, "Or your love."

The princess smiled and lowered her head.

"You may go," the Empress said.

"But what of the matter you called me here to discuss?"

"We have just discussed it."

"Then you knew all the time? And you arranged all this—"

"If We are to keep Heaven's Mandate, We must occasionally indulge in subterfuge Ourselves."

The Emperor glanced at his mother, and the slightest smile crossed his lips.

The princess smiled too, and backed out of the audience hall, for one never turned one's back on the Empress. No sooner was she out of their sight than she fell back against one of the plum trees that surrounded the hall, and breathed a long sigh. Pulling the kerchief from her collar, she wiped the sweat off her face.

THE NEW ABBOT

Owing to the unusually heavy submissions of memorials and an uprising of the eastern Turks who dwelt beyond the Long Wall of a Thousand Li, nearly a week passed before the Empress had an opportunity to view the boxer in his new situation. When she finally saw a clearing in her schedule, she ordered her grooms to make ready the ivory carriage, the one of her five carriages that was reserved for everyday use, and, surrounded by her entourage, rode toward the western suburbs of the city.

In time she reached the gate of the White Horse Temple. What a sorry sight it was! Far worse than she recalled. The lintel across the top of the gateway had fallen, leaving a narrow triangle of an opening through which a person had to wedge himself to enter. Weeds split the paving stones in the galleries, and the courtyards were overgrown with moss. A gale wind had knocked the golden finial from atop the pagoda, giving it an odd, stunted appearance.

Her footsteps sounded throughout the great, solemn, silent Buddha Hall. A dazzling blade of mote-filled light issued from above, where a fallen poplar tree had smashed a hole in the roof. The rain had rotted the floorboards and seeped beneath the wonderful murals that were everywhere along the walls, making the paint peel and buckle. Thieves had scraped most of the gold leaf off the three Buddhas who sat at the head of the hall. The central one, Maitreya, who was nearly thirty-five feet high, had sparrows nesting on his head and in his cupped hands. Bird dung streaked his skin.

Not only had her parents been devout Buddhists, but at the age of twenty-five the Empress had lived for a year as a nun at the Buddhist convent called Kan Yeh. Though she publicly patronized Taoism and Confucianism, the faith of the Compassionate One was embedded in her marrow, and the sight of the ruined hall brought tears to her eyes. How could she have approved so many other expenditures, public works projects, palace renovations, and new temples, when the venerable old White Horse lay in such dreadful disrepair?

In the meditation hall she found the eunuch, White Pheasant, whom she had given to the boxer as one of many gifts, knocking down spiderwebs with a long stick. The instant he saw her, he fell to his knees.

"Forgive the dreadful condition of the temple, Your Majesty. When I learned of your visit, I tried to make it presentable, but it was beyond my means."

"We understand. It would require an army of cleaners and craftsmen. Where is the abbot?"

"Immersed in meditation." The eunuch pointed to the far corner of the hall. There, in the shadows, sat the boxer, his legs crossed in the lotus position, his cupped hands resting one within the other upon his thighs, his body rigid, his eyes squeezed shut, his face contorted with concentration. He had shaved his head and donned the garb of the monk: the scarlet robe, the white under-robe, the flowing silk scarf.

The Empress smiled. "How impressive! Does he meditate like this all day and all night, as I have seen certain extraordinary monks do?"

"Not exactly."

"Or does he assume this position," she lowered her voice, "when he learns that Heaven's Chosen is coming to visit?"

"More," the eunuch replied, also dropping his voice to a whisper, "when he hears the Empress climbing the steps to the meditation hall."

They had been friends for many years.

The Empress approached the boxer and stood before him for several moments, waiting to be acknowledged.

"Precious?" she whispered.

He did not move.

"Beloved?" she said.

No response.

She knelt beside him and licked his ear with her long, pointed tongue.

Still nothing.

She came back in front of him and slapped him with full force across the face.

"Hey!" he said, opening his eyes, hurrying to unfold his legs so he could move if she tried to hit him again.

"I'm sorry, but you were so deeply immersed in your meditation that I could not arouse you."

She tilted her head slightly to the left and gave him her sly cat's smile.

"Yes," he said, rubbing his cheek, which was fast turning red, "I suppose I was. Well." He stood up and bowed. "Welcome to my temple. What do you think? I was hoping White Pheasant could get it fixed up before you arrived, but . . ." He shrugged.

"It's appalling," she said. "Had We known of its disrepair, We should never have sent you here."

"Oh, it's not so bad." He looked around. "Send over a few more eunuchs and we'll have it cleaned up in no time."

He took her arm and they strolled outside, into the courtyard. While they had been inside the meditation hall, five wandering monks had arrived and were circumambulating the pagoda, chanting the Lotus Scripture.

The boxer scowled. "Who do they think they are, the turtle spawn!" He ran toward them, shaking his fists, shouting, "Get out of here! This is *my* temple! You can't just come wandering around here at any hour of the day. Get away! Get away!"

The monks, terrified by the sheer size of him, turned and ran, holding their robes at their knees in order not to trip over them.

"You mustn't do that," the Empress said. "They may have traveled many miles to venerate the begging bowl. Offer them food and lodgings, and blessings for their journey."

"What begging bowl?" the boxer asked.

"Bodhidharma's begging bowl. It is inside the pagoda, in a

special chamber. The pagoda was built to contain it and protect it, so that people like those monks could come and venerate it. It is a very rare and wonderful relic, with magical powers. You mean you didn't know?"

"How would I know that?" the boxer asked.

The Empress walked to the base of the pagoda and poked the fallen finial with her foot. It rolled back and forth on the ground like an enormous golden top. She looked at the decrepit ruins that encircled them, the Buddha hall, the meditation hall, the administration hall, the residence hall, the kitchen, and the granary. Beyond their great, sloping roofs of yellow tile, a water wheel could be seen, part of a rolling mill, so long unturned that ivy covered it like a decoration.

The Empress shook her head. "It will require at least a million cash to renovate the temple, a hundred of our finest artisans, and someone with experience to supervise the work."

"A million cash?" the boxer said. "I'll supervise the work myself."

"Have you experience with temple reconstruction?"

"Well, no. But how hard could it be? To those craftsmen who work with gold I'll say, 'Go gild the Buddhas. Be quick and do a good job or I'll cut off your hands.' "

The Empress laughed. "You have the right idea, but you must be more subtle about it."

"I will be. I promise."

"Forgive Us, but We cannot put you in charge of such an endeavor quite yet. Our ministers would accuse Us of favoritism—quite rightly—and of squandering funds. Extravagant and poorly managed building programs have been the ruin of other dynasties. They shall not be the fall of Ours."

The boxer dropped her arm, and his lips curled in a pout.

"I must return to my meditation," he said.

"Oh, please do not act this way! We have worked so hard all week just so We might have this brief time with you. Let it be a happy time. What else can We do to make Our precious smile?"

"I don't know," he grumbled. "It's so boring here. There's no excitement. I don't think I like being abbot."

"It's boring because you do nothing! Do the things a monk does, and bit by bit your life will become suffused with joy."

"Oh? Like what?"

"Good works! Give to the poor. Hold assemblies and preach the law. Convert the Taoists to your cause."

"I can't do all that by myself."

"Recruit monks to help you."

"Recruit them? From where?"

"From anywhere, silly duck. Take some initiative."

"How exactly do I make them monks?"

"Usually they must pass an examination. They must memorize a hundred leaves of a scripture, interpret it, show that they can meditate, and answer questions about the Dharma and the history of the Buddha."

"I don't know anybody who could do that."

"We will waive these requirements in your case. Ordain whomever you like. Then We will find somebody to teach them what they must know to be monks."

The boxer brightened considerably at this final suggestion. He took her arm and asked if she would like to see the residence hall. He warned her, with a lascivious look, that since he was the only resident, they would be quite alone there.

She laughed with delight and ran ahead like a young girl, slowing only to turn back to make sure that he was following her.

One day the people of Lo-yang were amazed to see a train of oxcarts, their contents concealed by tarpaulins, winding through the streets in the south side of the city, led by the strangest band of monks, all scarred, grizzled, and coarse-spoken. They leered at the pretty girls and made fun of the old hags. When they saw a long-haired Taoist priest, one of them would leap from the back of the cart with a knife clenched between his teeth and chase him halfway across town, threatening to shave his head, and occasionally even performing the sacrilegious deed.

The monks parked their carts side by side in the South Market, and pulled away the tarpaulins. Each cart was piled high with cash. The monks climbed up onto the carts so that they stood knee-deep in the glittering copper coins, like farmers in the paddies, and, scooping up handfuls, tossed them at the crowd.

At first the people in the marketplace hung back. The tableau of monks tossing money was so bizarre that they questioned their wits. But the monks kept shouting, "Help yourselves! Take what you need! Stuff your sleeves!" And after a few moments the bravest and the greediest rushed forward, fell to their knees, and began frantically picking the coins up off the street. Seeing this, others hurried to join them. In a few moments everyone was scrambling for a bit of the wealth. One man shoved his old friend out of the way to get at a pile of coins that had collected in a depression. A daughter helping her aging father-in-law hobble down the street ran from his side, letting him fall and break his brittle bones. A young man even kicked an old lady who he thought was grabbing more than her share. Each slight provoked a more violent repercussion. In a matter of minutes, people were beating each other with bamboo sticks they had pried from storefronts, and hurling paving stones pulled out of the street. By the time the soldiers arrived, three people had been killed. The monks had fled, but the street still glittered as it did after a heavy rain, with coins that had rolled into the cracks, out of reach.

The venerable censor Hsü Yu-kung picked his audience tablet out of the rack in the basilica of the Great Audience Hall and approached the throne. Though it was the height of the summer's heat, he did not sweat, nor did the hands that held the ivory plaque tremble, even though he was approaching seventy years of age. Censor Hsü was fearless. The people said of him that his character was as pure as the ice in a jade urn.

He was a tall, distinguished, gray-haired mandarin, whose skin was so fine that the veins could be seen pulsing in his neck and his temples. He wore the humped black cap with ties that hung down his neck like the drooping ears of a rabbit, the purple robes, the golden belt with jade plaques around his hips, as befitted an official of the second rank. The other officials bowed their heads when he passed, such was their respect.

"In recent times," he began, having reached the thrones and made his obeisances to the Empress and the puppet Emperor, "we have seen many improprieties centering around the Buddhist temples. We have seen householders become monks merely to avoid the forced-labor tax. We have seen wealthy families make Merit Cloisters of their estates, building little temples on their grounds in order to avoid taxation. We have seen the temples accumulate land and wealth beyond the dreams of princes, and become usurers and pawnbrokers...." A confirmed Confucianist, Censor Hsü frequently took these opportunities to rail against the "foreign" faith called Buddhism.

"Yes, yes," the Empress said impatiently, "we are well aware of improprieties and excesses within the temple walls. Get to the point, please."

The young Emperor nodded agreement. He was patting his forehead with a piece of silk that had been soaked in cold water.

Censor Hsü apologized. "I regret my circularity. I came here today to speak of a gang of men recruited from the taverns and brothels, and even from the prisons, whom Your Majesty has recently ordained as monks of the White Horse Temple. They rush about town in their scarlet robes, terrifying the populace. They rape and rob like brigands. Everywhere they go, they leave chaos in their wake. Yesterday they drove ten wagons into the South Market and threw cash at the crowds. Naturally a riot resulted. Three men were killed, shops were destroyed, and the marketplace was left in ruins."

"One moment," the Empress said. "You say they are robbers. Yet they threw money to the populace. This seems to Us charity of the finest sort."

"That depends on what was in their hearts," Censor Hsü responded. "If they did it in the spirit of generosity, then it was an act of charity. If they did it to create a riot, it was as evil an act as robbery or any other crime."

"How do you know what was in their hearts? Do you practice sorcery?"

"I have only those skills possessed by ordinary men. They are enough for me to recognize a fox when I see one."

"Well, then, what do you propose we do to bring these 'foxes' to justice?" The Empress's voice was icy.

The court was silent in anticipation. Although no names had been mentioned, everybody knew that the boxer was the leader of the band in question. Would Censor Hsü court death or degradation by suggesting that the boxer be punished?

"Since the ordination of these monks was, as I understand it, Your Majesty's work, then it is only appropriate that their discipline be prescribed by Your Majesty also."

"Well done," someone whispered.

The young Emperor glanced at his mother.

The Empress considered the censor with grudging admiration. It was no accident that he had reached such a venerable age in a profession where few men survived more than a year or two. She promised to look into the matter. Censor Hsü bowed deeply in appreciation.

The Empress decided to judge for herself the degree of truth in Censor Hsü's allegations. Late that evening she ordered a carriage to take her to the White Horse Temple. No sooner had she squeezed beneath the gate's fallen lintel than she heard a terrible commotion coming from the Buddha Hall. At first she feared that the monks had turned on her precious one, but as she came closer, she realized that what she had taken for the clanking of swords was actually the clanking of wine pots and goblets, and that the battle cries were really the voices of singing girls interpreting the latest Turkish tunes.

The moonlight, filtering through the hole in the roof, shone down like a spotlight on the boxer, who was doing a dance to the accompaniment of a singing girl and her lute, while the Korean banged time on a wooden fish. The other monks were clapping their hands or singing along, waving goblets of rice wine in time to the music. They had stripped off their outer robes in deference to the heat, and their soaked under-robes clung to their bodies. Occasionally they tossed wine on each other to cool their skin. One monk, straddling the back of a singing girl who had gotten down on her hands and knees like a horse, called out "Giddyup," and beat her buttocks with a sapling to the amusement of the others. White Pheasant rushed among them, refilling their goblets from a pot of wine that he balanced on his shoulder.

One by one the monks, noticing the Empress standing in the shadows of the entrance, grew silent. The Korean stopped pounding the wooden fish, the singing girl let her lute fall silent. Finally only the boxer was left, dancing round and round. In time he grew aware of the silence and stopped.

"Why's everyone so quiet?" he demanded.

Then he saw her too.

"What is the meaning of this?" the Empress asked. Her eyes seemed to blaze in the darkness, like smoldering incense.

"I thought we should have a 'no-barriers assembly,'" he said, referring to a kind of meeting often held at the Buddhist temples, where men and women, regardless of class, gathered for prayer and instruction.

"With singing girls?"

"Why not? They're Buddhists. At least that one is." He pointed at a girl with a lute. "At least she claims she is."

"That's hardly the point."

"Look, you said, 'Hold assemblies and preach the law.' So that's what I'm trying to do."

As they spoke, the other monks crept quickly away until, as if by magic, the boxer and the Empress found themselves alone in the great empty hall. Aside from them, only White Pheasant remained, kneeling with his wine pot, trembling in expectation of what was to come.

"You're just angry," he went on, "because you couldn't join us. You're always so busy with those memorials. Why don't you take some time off for play?"

His words echoed from the roofbeams. Standing in the moonlight, he was as white as jade. Behind him the Buddhas, stripped of their gold leaf, were vague black shapes.

"We are angry," she said slowly and distinctly, "because Censor Hsü memorialized about you in court today."

"The dried-out lizard. I'll make him take back every word." The boxer took a fighting pose and stabbed at an imaginary opponent with his right hand.

"You'll do nothing of the kind!" the Empress said quickly. "We have few enough officials who will risk their lives to speak the truth."

"So you think the old lizard spoke the truth about me? Why don't you get *my* side of the story?"

"All right," she said. "What *is* your side of the story?"

"I don't know." He hesitated. "Which incident are we talking about?"

She glared at him. "How many incidents have there been?"

"I can't speak for my monks. They get into a little mischief sometimes. As for me, I spend most of my time in meditation."

"Then you know nothing of men with knives threatening to shave the heads of Taoist priests?"

"I can explain that. I ran into him on the street corner. We were arguing about whose faith was better. You know, one of those arguments that learned monks get into all the time. A crowd gathered. He said that those who followed the Tao had great power. Then he muttered something and stared into my eyes, and the next thing I knew, I was lying on my back in the street. Well, I couldn't let him get away with that, could I? Not with all those people watching. So I drew my sword and set out after him, screaming that I'd cut every hair off his head. Well, if he had such power, why'd he run like a frightened rabbit? That's what I'd like to know." He paused and thought for a moment. "Or do you mean that other time, when I ran into that old Taoist hermit by the Bridge of Heaven and he—"

"Say no more!" the Empress cried. "The less We know, the better. Oh, help me, my ancestors." She gazed heavenward. The firmament painted on the ceiling paled alongside the real stars that shone through the hole in the roof. "What am I to do about him?"

"How about a little hug?" he said.

"You don't seem to understand the gravity of the situation. You've made a public menace of yourselves. Censor Hsü has demanded a remedy. If We defrocked you and your band of ruffians, it would set a precedent." She continued, clarifying the situation for her own benefit. "The enemies of Buddhism would take advantage of it. Every time they found a temple where some impropriety was going on—which is to say nearly every temple in the land—they would insist that the monks be defrocked. We would seem the softhearted old fool who first memorializes one thing and then its opposite. Our ministers would begin to wonder if We were still a capable ruler. Even Our own Scholars of the North Gate would question Our fitness."

"There, there, sweetness, you are too hard on yourself. Everyone's entitled to a mistake." He strolled over to her and began to stroke her neck. His breath stank of rice wine.

"Don't touch me," she whispered.

He drew back quickly.

"There must be a way," she said.

"Your Majesty, if I may?" It was White Pheasant, the eunuch, still kneeling with his wine pot. His voice was as high and sweet as a child's.

"Speak," she said.

"It seems to me that a child must follow the good example of his mother and father if he is to learn propriety, just as a scholar must study the classics if he is to pass the examinations. Yet you expect this man"—he indicated the boxer, who was listening carefully—"and his friends to become monks without either instruction or example. No wonder they fail."

"He's right, you know," the boxer said. "How could we possibly succeed without insample or exstruction?"

"How much have you drunk tonight?" the Empress asked.

"A cup or two. Hardly at all."

"But if you found a monk," White Pheasant went on, "one of incorruptible character and steadfast practice, he might set these gentleman on the path to the holy life."

"If you think I'm going to take orders from some monk . . ." the boxer said, taking the deepest offense.

The Empress ignored him. "But could these"—she hesitated, searching for the right word—"*brigands* ever adhere to monastic rules?"

"My uncle," White Pheasant continued, "once visited a monastery on P'ing-jung Mountain where they practiced a kind of Buddhism called Ch'an. The monks abhor the scriptures. Instead, they tell little stories that make no sense. They love nothing better than to scream 'Kwatz!' at the top of their voices, and hit each other on the head with sticks, and on occasion chop off each other's fingers and arms and the like."

"We have heard tell of this strange sect," the Empress said. "Their master is Hui-neng, the Sixth Patriarch. Though they behave like madmen, they are supposedly of great spiritual depth." She creased her brow and nodded. "If any spiritual practice is congenial to the temperament of Our Precious One, it is this. Thank you, White Pheasant, for the excellent suggestion. Your resourcefulness will not be forgotten. We will send a messenger to P'ing-jung Mountain the first thing in the morning. We will ask for the loan of a monk who specializes in monastic discipline. Vinaya masters, We believe they are called."

"I'm not taking orders from anybody," the boxer exclaimed.

"Be quiet."

"Sorry," the boxer said.

THE VINAYA MASTER

One day in the winter, the boxer and a few of his favorite monks returned from a hunting trip to find a monk they did not know sitting in meditation just outside the gate. He was a little man, youthful in appearance (though age was difficult to judge in monks; deprived of worry, sorrow, and fear, their faces were free of lines; having no hair, they never showed gray). His head was round and smooth, somewhere in shape between a ball and an egg, and his ears protruded like the handles of a vase. His eyes were half-closed. He had a pug nose and a little round chin. Laid out on the ground before him were an iron begging bowl and a staff with a bundle tied at the end containing his razor and a few other personal effects.

"What have we here?" the boxer said, swinging down from his horse, a gorgeous, black-maned, broad-backed tarpan, a present from the Empress. His words left a plume of smoke in the air. A quiver of arrows was slung over one shoulder, and he carried a bow beneath his other arm. A number of dead rabbits and a fox and a pheasant hung limp and sorry from a saddle thong across the horse's muscular flank. The muted browns and reds of their pelts echoed the colors of the leaves on the ground.

The other monks dismounted too, and they all approached the spot where the little monk sat.

"He must be dead to sit so still," one of the monks said. Despite this monk's shaved skull, he was easily recognized as the Korean, the boxer's dear old friend. He had sacrificed his hair to his new calling, and donned the saffron robe, but he still wore the leopard's pelt over it, lest anyone forget he was a warrior. There were other familiar faces among the monks of the hunting party, including those of False Brush, Pinch Purse, and a dozen other prisoners whose freedom the boxer had arranged by cajoling the Empress and threatening the magistrate.

"It seems to me," False Brush said, "that he is trying to fool the birds into thinking he is a rock, so that they will come and sit on his head."

Since being freed from prison, he had put on weight so that his skin fit better. He was rotund now, in the pink of health, as light on his feet as a dancer. But as for the state of his mind, he seemed madder than ever.

White Pheasant pointed to the sorry state of his buffalo-hide sandals, as well as the begging bowl and the bundle of possessions, as evidence that he had come a long distance. No doubt he was the Vinaya master the Empress had sent for. By tradition, he would sit at the gate of the monastery until the abbot—in this case the boxer—agreed to accept him.

The boxer shrugged. "I accept him. You! I accept you. Get up and tell us about yourself."

"Wait," the Korean said. "Not so fast. Let's put him to the test. Let him sit there. It's hard work, I hear. The body always wants to move. I'll bet he won't last an hour."

"It's so cold," said the boxer, watching the steam trail from his own mouth.

"What if we tickle him?" Pinch Purse wondered. He pulled a feather from the pheasant they had killed that morning, and caressed the little monk's nose with the tip of it. Though sweat beaded on his brow, he did not move.

They left him sitting there and went to the cooking shed, where they skinned and boned the game they had caught, while White

Pheasant concocted a marinade of grape wine, ginger, fagara, and soy sauce.

When they returned to the gate an hour later, the little monk was still sitting precisely where they had left him.

"He's tricking us," the boxer said. "When we go away, he moves. He eats and stretches and farts and drinks. Then, when he hears us coming, he jumps back into this position."

Like most simple men, the boxer imagined others to be practicing the same deceits he would practice himself. With this in mind, he appointed another monk to remain behind while the others went into town, to make sure the little monk wasn't tricking them.

The gardens behind the royal palace, constructed during the Sui dynasty (that which preceded the T'ang) by Sui Yang-ti, numbered among man's most wondrous achievements. Beyond the usual furnishings, the odd rocks, twisted pines, plum trees, gazebos, and viewing pavilions, there was a man-made lake six miles in length, from whose misty waters rose three islands patterned after the mystical, unattainable Isles of the Immortals in the Eastern Sea. Modeling them was a popular conceit among emperors which dated back to ancient days. It began with an emperor of antiquity named Han Wu-ti, who believed that if his royal gardeners could reproduce these three islands and make them sufficiently enticing with their craft, then the Immortals, or *Hsien,* would come flying on storkback (their favorite mode of travel), adopt them as their new home, and give up their secrets of longevity in gratitude. But since Han Wu-ti died within the normally allotted threescore and ten, it must be assumed that his gardeners were not skillful enough.

Nor had any gardeners been since.

Dozens of waterways connected the central lake with streams, lotus-clotted pools, and rushing waterfalls. Strung like exquisite beads across these were sixteen palaces built on piles above the water. Their sloping, golden-tiled roofs shone bright against the gray winter sky.

In the lavish days of the Sui dynasty, gardeners had strung fabric leaves upon the trees so they would seem to bloom year round, and floated artificial lotus blossoms when the real ones had finished their bloom. Twenty of the loveliest and most talented singing girls complemented each of the water palaces. Little mechanical figures drifted by in boats, performing seventy-two different scenes from Chinese myth and history. The Confucian moralists who wrote the dynastic histories were fond of including these budgetary extravagances in the list of events that had led to Sui Yang-ti's fall. Since those of the Sui had paid the price, those of the T'ang could now enjoy it, albeit more modestly. History is filled with injustice.

A barge was waiting on the shore, its upturned prow carved and painted like the head of a dragon. The boxer left his horse with the first eunuch and allowed a second to pole him across the water, to one of the smallest and most intimate of the palaces, that which was known as the Lotus Palace because of the thousands of pink and white flowers that clotted the waters in the spring. There he found the Empress waiting for him with a pot of hot tea. She enjoyed playing the domestic with him. Fires built in brick ovens under the floor provided some degree of warmth, but they hurried to reach the screened chamber and its bed, where they could lie close together beneath comforters of silk floss.

After acting the Clouds and Rain with the Empress, he lay beside her in bed and told her of the little monk.

"The Vinaya master," she said with surprise. "So many months have passed that We had nearly forgotten. He must have traveled all the way from P'ing-jung mountain on foot. Heed his teachings. He must be a great monk if he is a disciple of the Sixth Patriarch. You must bring him to the palace on the next possible occasion. We have many questions to ask him regarding the Pure Land. After all, We have lived our threescore. Despite Our Taoist sorcerer and his longevity potions, We shall not live forever."

"Why do you call him 'Patriarch'? What does the title mean?"

"The true Dharma, the sacred teachings of the Buddha, must be kept alive. When the monks talk of it, they say they are passing a lamp from teacher to student. If they fail to pass it along, the light is extinguished, the teachings die. Those who have performed this task over the ages are called the Patriarchs. In the land of the Brahmans there were twenty-eight or thirty-five Patriarchs, depending on which account one prefers. Since the Dharma arrived in the Middle Kingdom, brought by Bodhidharma—"

"One of my previous incarnations," the boxer said, proud of himself for recognizing the name.

The Empress ignored his comment. "Since Bodhidharma brought

the teachings to the Middle Kingdom, there have been six Patriarchs. Bodhidharma, Hui-k'o, Seng-t'san, Tao-hsin, Hung-jen, and the Sixth Patriarch, Hui-neng. The mad practice called Ch'an is the creation of Hui-neng. He is a very great master."

"Then why couldn't I get *him*? Why do I have to settle for one of his students?"

"We have invited the Sixth Patriarch to the palace on several occasions to bestow the purple upon him, and hear his teachings. He has always made some excuse, pleading sickness or inclement weather. If he will not come for the Chosen of Heaven, then he certainly would not come for you."

"Don't be so sure. After all, I am an abbot. And an important fellow in my former lives. I wonder, should I study with a mere monk, even if he does know this Ch'an? Perhaps he should study with me."

"The problem, precious one," she said, stroking the muscles that bound his chest like ropes, "is that you are too much an authority on the flesh, and not enough on the spirit."

"You'd be surprised. I'm not entirely the fool you think. Perhaps I never was Bodhikarma, or anybody else. Still, I've seen men die and I've wondered where they went, whether they changed form, as ice changes to water, or disappeared like the candle flame when the wick grows short."

The Empress smiled at him as she would at a child. "And which did you decide was the truth?"

"On sunny spring days, I knew it was the former. But when I was woken by the wolf's howl in the middle of the night, the latter seemed a certainty. So you see, I am priest and skeptic rolled into one, and thus more knowledgeable than either."

"Very good!" said the Empress, who always found a clever argument more entertaining than a simple truth. She clapped her hands with pleasure. "Oh, boxer, sometimes you amuse Us no end, and We are so glad to have found you."

"And other times?"

"Other times—other times, We are still glad. But then We wish that We were not Heaven's Chosen, and did not have to worry what these small-minded Confucian ministers thought about Our every word and gesture."

When he stepped out on the terrace of the water palace, he

saw that it had been snowing for some time. Big, soft flakes drifted to the water's surface. The simple monochromatic beauty of it made the Empress laugh like a little girl. She scraped the snow off a lacquer railing and brought it to the boxer's mouth, so that he might taste it.

As the eunuch poled the boxer back to shore, a cold wind blew along the waterway. The boxer wrapped his robe tight about him. The snow, catching and melting on his face, made his cheeks red. The park was white as a virgin scroll, the trees like the vertical slashes of the poet's brush, the horse's hoofprints a trickle of ink. Everything was, for an instant, hushed and pure, as though the world had just been born.

In front of the temple, a cone of snow remained where the little monk had been sitting that morning. At first the boxer thought it was a practical joke pulled by the Korean and the others, to make him think that the monk was still there. He was about to have the horse trample it, just for fun, the way children knock down towers of blocks, when he had second thoughts. He climbed down, walked to the pile of snow, brushed away a handful, and saw a blue nose, and eyelashes sparkling with ice crystals.

"Help me!" he screamed at the blind walls of the temple, and began to dig out the little monk.

The Korean knew all about a body losing heat, for Koguryu, his homeland in the north of Korea, had winters even colder and more bitter than those of the Middle Kingdom. He and the others carried the little monk into the cooking shed, undressed him, and sat him down beside the iron stove, which White Pheasant had been feeding with wood in preparation for cooking dinner. His wet robes were hung from a roofbeam to dry.

The little monk's skin was waxy and pale blue in color, his lips and eyelids purple. His breath came quick and uneven. He didn't seem to know where he was, and murmured about sunflowers, and about a cow that had wandered away and drowned in a stream.

The Korean warned against rubbing the little monk's skin, or pouring hot water on him, or moving him too close to the stove. Reheating, he insisted, had to be gradual. Instead he prepared a mat on the floor and ordered the two fattest monks, the eunuchs False Brush and White Pheasant, to undress and lie with the little monk between them like the filling of a dumpling, so he might absorb the heat of their bodies bit by bit.

Soon the trembling stopped. The little monk grew quiet and yawned, and his eyelids fluttered closed.

"Stay awake!" the Korean shouted at him. He wrapped the monk in dry robes and, holding him by the armpits, dragged him up and down the shed. His body was as limp and as heavy as a rice sack.

"You're wasting your time," Pinch Purse said. "He's dead."

The Korean kept on walking him.

"Why didn't anybody bring him in when it started to snow?" the boxer demanded.

"I would have," False Brush said, "but some prankster nailed my sandals to the floor, and painted a tree on my bald head."

"You said we should let him sit," Pinch Purse said.

"You don't have to do everything I say," the boxer said.

"You're the abbot."

"Somebody went out long enough," the boxer said, "to steal his begging bowl." He glared at Pinch Purse.

"I ain't stole nothing," Pinch Purse said. "I took it to the kitchen to fill it with grub so when he finished his meditating he'd have—"

"He's dead now," said the boxer, "and the Empress won't be pleased. She was looking forward to an audience with him."

"He's not dead," the Korean said, "but he will be if no one relieves me, and I'll be dead, too, from exhaustion."

"He's like a side of beef!" the boxer exclaimed, taking over the task, wrapping his arms around the little monk's chest and dragging him across the floor like some ungainly broom. "I don't feel any pulse in his chest."

"Sometimes when it's very cold the pulse goes and comes back," the Korean said.

"You're crazy," Pinch Purse said. "The pulse goes, it ain't never coming back."

"It will come back," False Brush said with certainty, "in the spring, with the geese."

A gurgling came from the little monk's open mouth.

"What was that?" the boxer asked, out of breath himself from his labors.

"His death rattle," Pinch Purse said. "He'll start to stink soon."

"Keep walking," ordered the Korean.

"I'm walking," the boxer said. "I'm walking."

A spasm passed through the little monk's body. He moaned and began to shake, very much alive.

"See?" the Korean said. "What did I tell you? Now let's put him to bed. Wrap him with blankets. Warm some wine."

They made a bed for him in the cooking shed—that being the warmest hall in the temple—and assigned White Pheasant to make sure that the oven was kept stoked and burning, day and night, until the monk was well enough to walk.

While the monk's overall health improved, the frostbite on the three small toes of his left foot and the little finger of his right hand grew more serious by the day. First the appendages turned shiny red, then purple, and finally black and blistery, like the peel of a rotting fruit. The nails curled away from the cuticles and dropped off. Everyone feared the worst.

The snow was too deep outside to go for help. White Pheasant studied some scrolls about medicine that he found among the dusty shelves of the temple's library, and reported back to the others.

"The yin, which is cold, has driven the warm yang out of the decaying digits. The five winds that maintain life in the body no longer circulate to these extremities. According to what I have read, they will shrivel and drop off of their own accord over a period of months. The process should be hastened by introducing a handful of maggots to cleanse the body of the bad flesh."

After dinner that night, the leftover food (they always had more than they could eat, thanks to the Empress's gifts) was heaped near the stove in order that it would rot more quickly. In a few days, scores of maggots had appeared on the stinking pile of fruit rinds and half-eaten bones. Pinch Purse, whose long, nimble fingers seemed particularly adept for the task, picked the tiny creatures out of the garbage and transferred them, one by one, to the patient's blackened extremities.

The boxer offered to cover these areas with a cloth, lest the sight of the waxy worms offend him, but the monk refused.

"What a privilege," he said, "to have this preview now of what will happen later, when *all* of me is maggot food."

The boxer wondered if, in the quiet of the night, the sound of their chewing disturbed the little monk's sleep.

* * *

A warm spell made it possible for the boxer to visit the Empress. The snow had a silvery crust from melting and refreezing, and his tarpan's hooves made a pleasing crunch as he gingerly tread the trails of the royal gardens.

The Empress was dismayed to hear about the little monk's predicament, for winter's long nights had filled her with questions about death. She arranged to send medicines concocted by her own herbalist, as well as imported fruits and other delicacies, to speed his recovery. She insisted that she be told daily of his progress, and that an audience be arranged the moment he was well enough to travel.

In the space of a week, the maggots had finished their meal. The shriveled digits were gone, and the stumps that remained were pink with blood and health. The little monk seemed pleased. He tried to stand up but, without the toes, could not keep his balance. A monk whom they called the Carpenter, because of his skill with a knife, whittled a crutch from a fig tree. Delighted, the little monk rose and, propping it under his right armpit, hobbled a few times around the kitchen, getting the feel of it. Then he hobbled outside, into the snow, despite the objections of the other monks, who pointed out that he had only his sandals and a tattered outer robe.

Fascinated, they followed him along the loggia, past the pagoda and the Buddha Hall. Dropping to his hands and knees, the little monk crawled under the fallen lintel of the front gate. When he reached the remains of the snow pile where the boxer had found him buried, he resumed his sitting, pulling left foot over right thigh, right foot over left thigh, folding his hands, half-closing his eyes, concentrating on the plume of breath that entered and escaped from his body.

The Korean groaned.

"He is as constant as the South Hill," White Pheasant said with admiration. "He teaches us a lesson without speaking a word."

The boxer knelt before the little monk and said to him, "If you are meditating to gain acceptance into my temple, I accept you. Now please come inside. *Please.*"

The monk opened his eyes and gazed directly at the boxer. Touching his palms together in front of his face, he bowed. Then he pulled himself up on his crutch and hobbled back to the temple.

The boxer and the other monks all exchanged looks of relief.

* * *

That night the boxer was lying on his mat, drinking rice wine and thinking about how an abbot of an important temple really deserved more than a little square chamber with one window and a smoky heating stove, when he became aware of the monk standing at the entrance. He bade him enter, and the monk hobbled in on his walking stick. When he reached the boxer's bed, he dropped the stick, knelt down, and bowed until his head touched the floor.

"That's all right," said the boxer. "You don't have to do all that. Want some wine?"

The little monk declined the wine pot.

"I have come to thank you for your hospitality," he said. This was the first time he had spoken more than a few words, and the boxer was surprised by the low, gravelly quality of his voice.

"Forget it."

"When a monk comes to live at a temple, he must greet the abbot and thank him for his hospitality. This is part of the order of our lives. Since I have come here as a Vinaya master, to teach you order, then I must be exemplary myself."

"You don't have to teach us anything. We're not a real monastery. You can take it easy and relax. We do some hunting, and we visit the wine shops. The Empress takes care of us because I'm her favorite. It used to be Princess T'ai-p'ing, but now it's me. She sent for you because we were getting a little too frisky. People were complaining. But now we're settling down. So you might as well enjoy it too. By the way, I'm sorry about what happened, the toes and the finger and all."

"As long as I still have *this* finger." The little monk held up the index finger of his right hand and grinned.

"Oh? And what's so important about that one?" the boxer asked.

Instead of replying, the monk picked up his crutch and hobbled away.

"Funny fellow," the boxer said to himself, leaning back and closing his eyes. Buoyed by rice wine, he drifted on the sea of sleep.

An instant later, or so it seemed, a loud, high-pitched bell woke him, its oscillating tone crisscrossing the space between his ears as if it had been emptied of matter. The boxer leaped to his feet and looked around, his heart pounding. He heard birds chirping, and saw the sky lightening in the east.

Who would dare wake him now, when it was barely the Hour

of the Rabbit? Whoever it was, he would have the man's head. He grabbed the mighty K'un-wu sword that the Empress had given him and ran out into the loggia that surrounded the main courtyard. Some of the other monks had already emerged from their chambers and stood in the loggia, swords raised, entertaining the same thought.

The bell sounded again and again. A moment later the little monk appeared, hobbling around the bend in the loggia, the crutch under his right armpit, the bell hanging from his right hand, the hammer in his left. He saw them all standing there, and smiled.

"Time to meditate," he said. He held out his hand. "When the lines of the palm can be seen, the hour is already late."

They pulled their robes tight for warmth, and stared at him dumbfounded. The air was bone-chilling at that hour.

"Hurry," he said. "Not a moment to spare." And, turning his back on them, he hobbled off in the direction of the meditation hall.

The other monks looked at one another. Then a few set off after him.

"Where are you going?" the boxer demanded of them.

"To meditate," they replied.

"*I'm* the abbot here," the boxer said, "and I'll say when it's time to meditate." He looked at their expectant faces. "I'm going back to bed. You can do what you want."

They turned their backs to him and started for the meditation hall.

"Oh, well, I'm up," he said to himself after a moment's indecision. "Might as well see what this is all about." And he fell into line with the rest.

For the boxer, meditation was excruciating. He could think of no worse punishment than being forced to sit so still for what seemed like half the day (but was really no more than the time he would spend on his toilet). His left ear itched, then his right knee, then the tip of his nose. A million errands came to mind that could not be put off another moment. The aches in his knees and hips seemed worse than any boxing injury. Yet to move would be to show himself inferior to all the others, who seemed to find sitting less of a chore.

Though the torture seemed endless, in time the little monk rang a bell, and they all bowed to the Buddha and their mats, and filed out of the meditation hall. The urgency of itches and errands forgotten, the boxer ambled back to his cell, took a drink, and lay down on his mat, hoping to catch up on the sleep he had missed. But a moment later Pinch Purse roused him to say that the little monk had let himself into the administration hall. Someone had better keep an eye on him, since the cash box was kept there. The boxer grumbled, rose, and went to investigate.

The cash box was safe; the little monk was on his knees, painting rows of characters upon a smooth plank he had found in one of the rubble heaps that were everywhere around the temple. Enviously the boxer watched his effortless brushstrokes. When the monk had finished, he borrowed an awl from the one they called the Carpenter, and bored holes in the corners of the plank, so that it could be hung by ropes from the eaves of the meditation hall.

"What does it say?" the boxer asked.

The little monk pointed to each character as he read it:

The matter of life and death is great.
Time flows quickly and nothing remains, it waits for no man.
Do not waste even an instant of it.

"But what do you consider wasting time?" the boxer asked, unconsciously aping the manner of a mandarin discussing an important philosophical issue. "I, for example, can think of no better way to pass an afternoon than sitting in a wine shop, holding a pretty, green-eyed Sogdian girl on my knee."

"In the south," the little monk said, "there are baboons who spend much of their lives pulling at their penises. They wile away the time, but they learn no Ch'an. Now you must excuse me, there is much to do."

The boxer glared at the others, who were hooting at him.

The boxer came across the little monk, Pinch Purse, the Korean, White Pheasant, and a few others gathered around the front gate of the monastery, raising a tall, triangular tower of lashed bamboo. Rather than using his cumbersome crutch, the monk moved about by clinging to parts of the tower, or dropped to his hands and knees when no supports were available. His robes were soaked from crawling in the snow, but he hardly noticed. The boxer, thinking how annoyed the Empress would be if, having only just recovered from his frostbite, the little man fell ill, pleaded with him to return to the kitchen and change into dry clothes, but the monk paid him no heed.

False Brush sat on a low wall a little distance away, observing the work and occasionally offering an opinion; but since he was under the misconception that they were constructing stocks in which the long-dead Taoist philosopher Lao-tzu would be displayed, his comments were of little use.

Once the tower was in place, and reinforced with stones and earth around the base of the poles, they threw some ropes over the top of it, and tied them to the fallen lintel.

"You're not going to try to lift that heavy timber?" the boxer said, laughing with disbelief.

"Pull!" the little monk shouted.

Some tugged on the rope while the rest leaned their weight against other bamboo poles they had slipped under the lintel's edge.

They strained and huffed until finally the reluctant lintel came free of the snow. Higher and higher it rose, the tower creaking under the weight, the lashings stretching to the breaking point. The boxer watched with amazement. When the lintel was high enough, some of the monks pulled on a second rope, and it swung forward and dropped into the indentations atop the vertical members of the gate as naturally as a displaced bone slips back in its socket.

All the monks cheered the little monk, bowed to him, and patted his back.

The imprint of the lintel in the snow, a rectangle of damp brown earth, teemed with insects, suddenly revealed, and rodent holes like miniature canals.

The boxer looked back and forth between the monk and the lintel. "You are a sorcerer!"

The monk shook his head. "I know how to raise gates and pavilions. Temples are always in need of repair and expansion. It's one of those skills a monk learns."

That evening, when the boxer visited the Empress in the gardens of Sui Yang-ti, at the lovely Lotus Palace, he had several amusing stories to tell of the little monk: about his waking them up so early, hanging his poem, and so forth. When she heard that he was well and moving about, she insisted on an audience with him the very next day.

"We shall see him at once! We dare not wait too long. When

We were young, We thought We would live forever. We believed We would have time for all things. Now We know better."

The boxer gazed contemplatively at the ceiling of the bed, with its intricate floral lacquerwork, and murmured, as though the thought had just struck him, "The matter of life and death is great. Time flows quickly and nothing remains, it waits for no man. Do not waste even an instant of it."

The Empress regarded her lover with surprise and admiration. "What wisdom you speak! We wonder if there was not more truth to the nun's prophecy than We gave her credit for."

The boxer smiled smugly.

10
AN AUDIENCE WITH THE EMPRESS

The Vinaya master, the tap of his crutch marking time, hobbled up the center aisle of the Great Audience Hall, which was also called the Dragon Hall because of its grandeur. Even the terra-cotta beasts tucked into the eaves appeared curious about the odd little visitor. In addition to the courtiers and officials, who numbered in the hundreds, the entire Yü-lin guard, the Empress's personal retainers, had been gotten out in show regalia, four troops in scarlet shirts and caps decorated with the tailfeathers of the Manchurian snow pheasant, the fifth troop in tabards of scarlet taffeta embroidered with the figures of wild horses. Even with all these occupants, the hall was not crowded. A sparrow that had somehow gotten trapped inside could fly about merrily, perching here and there, and never hit a wall or a supporting column.

Overlooking all this, the Empress and the puppet Emperor sat stiff and silent on their thrones, splendid in their silk robes and fancy headgear. The monk strode toward them, and behind him came the boxer, strutting like a rooster, his audience tablet gripped in his sweaty hands.

The officer of protocol presented the little monk with the Empress's gifts, a copy of the Lankāvatāra Scripture on a golden roller, a miniature tree of coral with green jade leaves, a sweet-voiced bird from the snowy Himalayas in a golden cage, ten bolts of the most beautiful silk, and the title of duke of the third rank, as well as the pale lavender robe and gold belt which accompanied it.

"Thank you," the little monk said, "but I have no use for such things." He ignored the usual obeisances and honorifics, for Buddhist monks, by custom, did not bow down to royalty. The boxer, who would have embraced any degradation to please her, cringed.

"Keep your Lankāvatāra Scripture for one who would study it," the little monk continued. "I know it by heart. Keep your coral tree and yellow songbird. The only tree I care for is the Bodhi tree where the Buddha had his enlightenment. The only tones I would listen to are the golden words of the Buddha. As for your title, give it to a man of virtue and please your ministers. As for your bolts of silk, give them to the poor and please Heaven."

"So much for our rice bowl," the boxer whispered without moving his lips, so that only the little monk could hear him.

"Our new monk is made of a very fine steel," the Empress said, impressed by his behavior. "We will honor his wishes and take back Our gifts without offense. If, at any time during his stay, he wishes a boon of Us, We will do Our best to comply."

The little monk made a small bow.

The boxer was amazed.

"Other Buddhist monks who have visited Us," the Empress went on, "have performed wondrous feats. One had a relic, a tooth of the Buddha, the sight of which would make a fierce lion roll on its back like a harmless housecat. Another could walk through fire, and hold it in his palm, and even swallow it. Still another tore out his tongue and stuck it back in his throat without shedding a drop of blood. What miracles can you do?"

"I wake in the morning and sleep at night. I eat when I am hungry and shit when my bowels are full. Sometimes a poem comes into my head, or I paint a pleasing vista with my brush. Surely I am the greatest magician of all."

Someone in the crowd snickered.

The Empress raised an eyebrow and glanced at the boxer.

"Magic is not his strength," the boxer said quickly. "He is better known for his profound knowledge regarding matters of life and death."

"Ahh." The Empress tilted her head a few degrees and smiled her cat's smile. "Then perhaps he would answer some simple questions for Us?"

"Careful," the boxer whispered, maintaining his smile. "When she gets that look it means trouble."

"I will be pleased to answer what questions I can," the monk replied.

"Very well," the Empress said.

The court grew still. Not even a sword clinked against a belt. The only sound was the sweet song of the caged bird, who neither knew nor cared that it had been rejected.

"Now that We are no longer young, We wonder more and more about the Pure Land. There were deeds in the past that We performed for the good of Our people, deeds that were not strictly in accordance with the precepts of Buddhism. Will they prevent Us from reaching the Pure Land?"

The little monk leaned against his crutch and shook his head. "No."

The Empress widened her smile.

"At last you've said something right," the boxer whispered with relief.

"And the good acts We do now, the building of Buddhist temples and carving of cave statues, they will improve Our chances?"

The little monk shook his head. "No."

The Empress's smile vanished. Her brow furrowed. "Then it is only the chanting of A-mi-t'o-fo that provides salvation?"

"Such chanting is of little use," the monk replied.

The Empress was clearly puzzled now. "Then how will We reach the Pure Land?"

"There is no Pure Land," the little monk said. "It is a fairy tale for simple people, to bring them peace."

"If there is no Pure Land, then where will We go after death?"

"Nowhere."

"Don't tell her that," the boxer whispered. "Please."

"You mean, then, that We will be reincarnated? That We will come back in another form?"

"A man has a lifetime as the grass has one summer. He must struggle for a thousand kalpas to attain it. Thus it is indescribably precious. Not even a moment must be wasted."

"And how shall We use this precious time?" The Empress was fascinated, outraged, sarcastic, sincere.

"To penetrate the Gateless Barrier. To learn the meaning of Nothing. To obtain the state where 'Kwatz!' is shouted and we stand as though on an endless sheet of ice and walk side by side with all the Patriarchs of the past."

"We have heard that these Ch'an monks are mad," the Empress said, "and now We see it is true."

The young Emperor nodded agreement.

"You are dismissed," the Empress said.

"Now wait a minute, Your Majesty . . ." the boxer interrupted, striding forward with a finger upraised.

"You are both dismissed."

"But he's the crazy one," the boxer hurried to explain. "I don't agree with anything he said. *I* believe in the Pure Land and—"

"Enough."

"And A-mi-t'o-fo, and life after death and—"

"*Enough!*"

She half rose from her seat, like a tigress about to spring.

Startled by the fury of the gesture, the boxer fell silent. He backed humbly out of the audience hall, under the eyes of several hundred courtiers who were delighted by what they imagined to be the beginning of the boxer's fall from favor.

"Why didn't you just tell her what the other monks tell her?" the boxer asked as he and the little monk rode back to the temple, side by side. Their horses stepped gingerly through the snow, plumes of steam rising from their nostrils. "Tell her she'll go to the Pure Land after she dies. That will make her happy."

"I could not lie regarding a matter of such importance," the little monk replied.

"I don't mind you turning the Empress against yourself. If you don't enjoy living and breathing, that's your business. It only troubles me because I told her what a wonderful, wise fellow you were. I aligned myself with you. Now we're both in trouble. I doubt that she'll have our heads. She's not as bad as that daughter of hers. Most likely she'll just have us degraded and banished to some cold, plague-ridden province in the north."

"Even the most skillfull seer," the little monk replied, "cannot tell what will happen one minute from now. Men's fortunes change as suddenly as the wind. You have seen it yourself. One day a commoner, the next a king. Don't fret over it."

The boxer was pleased to be comforted. Suddenly he felt a kinship with the monk. After all, they were in this together. "You're right. Let's go into town and forget our troubles with some good mare's-teat wine."

"I have taken the vows of the brotherhood," he said. "I cannot drink."

"Look," the boxer said, stopping his own horse and grabbing the reins of the other horse so that it sidestepped about and faced him. "We're dead men. Or, at very best, exiles to some horrible place where we'll spend our days wondering whether famine or the contagion will get us first. Let's suppose that what you said is true. No Pure Land. No A-mi-t'o-fo. Nowhere and nothing. Knowing this, are you going to die without visiting the wine shops of Lo-yang at least one time? Are you going to suffer the Common Change without tasting the best mare's-teat wine in the north? Are you going to walk the Dark Pathway without once laying eyes on a green-eyed Sogdian girl I know whose voice is as sweet as a nightingale's and who knows a hundred of the best Turkish songs by heart? Well? Are you?"

They took a private room on the second floor of the wine shop, and matched each other cup for cup. By the fifth round the little monk's face was purple. He rose and, propped on his crutch, sang a sentimental ballad with impressive feeling. The Sogdian girl said he was adorable, and the boxer grew jealous and sulked. To reassure him, she took him up to the old stepmother's room in the attic—she was out for the evening—and there, amid the musty piles of accounting scrolls, whispered a secret in his ear.

"I wasn't going to tell you," she said. "I was going to go away to the south and not return until it was all over."

"Until what was all over?" the puzzled boxer asked.

"And then, only if by accident you heard the baby crying and saw me go to it, and insisted on knowing who was the father . . ."

"What baby? What are you—?" But then his voice trailed off. "You don't mean—?" he began again. He noticed now that her breasts seemed unusually swollen beneath her green silk robe, her face pink with the flush of life. "You're not—?"

She nodded and looked down at the floor with a secret smile.

He howled with joy and, grasping her in his arms, swung her round and round. But then he stopped and, worried that he had overtired her, made her sit down and rest. She laughed at his concern.

The baby was his own, he knew, for he paid the old stepmother thirty thousand cash a month to guarantee that the Sogdian girl needed no other clients than himself.

"When is the baby due?" he asked.

"In half a year."

"And will it be a boy?"

"Silly thing! I cannot tell."

"I will buy a house for you, and servants to care for you. And I'll come and visit every day."

"You must not." Suddenly she was serious. "The Empress would find out. If she learned that you were its father, she would certainly have us killed. I care not for myself, but the baby must survive. Promise that you will not visit me, or even send me a message, until after the baby is born. Then you can visit me here, as in the past, and the old stepmother can see to our privacy."

"But you'll need money. At least let me give you some money."

"You have given me so much already that I am nearly a wealthy woman. The baby and I will be fine. Don't worry about us."

"A baby," the boxer said, grinning foolishly. "One to worship my ancestral plaque after I am gone." He was so happy that he began to cry. The Sogdian girl laughed and held his head tight against her breast.

"All the Empress's fine presents," he whispered, "seem like dross beside this."

Night had fallen by the time they left the wine shop. The little monk inquired as to the cause of the boxer's silly grin, and the reason why, and as they crossed the street and headed toward the stables where they had left their horses, the boxer kicked up his heels and whistled a gay tune. The boxer simply shook his head. The little monk didn't press him, but accepted this as he accepted everything else.

The stalls of the South Market were closed and shuttered, the street deserted and silent. All that remained of the day's hurly-burly, the shoving crowds and shrill-voiced merchants, were some rotten plums streaking the snow with purple, a few duck feathers, a piece of red silk ribbon, a broken saucer.

Hearing the soft crush of footsteps in the snow, the boxer glanced over his shoulder. Four figures in black robes and hoods were coming up behind him. They were carrying canes.

"We're being followed," he whispered. "You get out of the way. I'll handle this."

The footsteps were closer. The boxer could feel his heartbeat quicken, his body start to sweat. He wished he hadn't drunk quite so much wine, but there was nothing to do about it now.

The footsteps were almost upon them. He spun about in time to see a cane snap across his face. He fell to the snow and lay dazed by the sting of it. Meanwhile the assailants, their canes raised like battle staffs, turned toward the little monk. Not only did they outnumber him, but they were taller and heavier too. The odds were so unfair that the boxer, expecting nothing less than a massacre, couldn't bear to watch. Yet he did, and what he saw seemed like a dream. When they were almost upon him, the little monk balanced on his two feet, raised his crutch, and swung it as skillfully as any halberdier does his axe. They tried to block it with their own staffs, but he was too quick. The crutch moved so fast that it was almost invisible, yet struck with formidable precision. One assailant took a blow to the eye, another a poke in the groin. Each time the crutch made contact with a body, it touched a vital point that doubled a man over in pain, knocked the wind from him, or left him lying in the snow, momentarily unconscious. After a few moments of this, the four assailants turned and ran.

The boxer rose and gave the little monk his shoulder to lean upon. Together they stumbled toward the stable.

"Not bad," the boxer said, glancing back at the fleeing men. The bloodstains in the snow were scarcely distinguishable from the purple streaks of the plums. "I would have done it myself if the first one hadn't gotten in a lucky blow. Where did you learn to fight like that?"

"For a time I was a guest at Shao-lin Temple, renovating the old Buddha Hall. During my stay I practiced martial arts with the monks, who are adept at it. Legend has it that Bodhidharma, who became abbot there long ago, was unhappy with the physical condition of the students and taught them this style of boxing to invigorate their bodies after meditation."

"Well, you are a fair hand at it," the boxer said, "for an amateur. Sometime when I am not so busy, I will show you some powerful positions. I don't know if I told you this, but certain learned monks believe that I am the reincarnation of Bodhidharma. That may explain my skill as a boxer."

"You are who you are," the monk said. "The question remains: Who were they?"

The boxer shrugged. "I have many enemies. They may have been Confucians from the court who'd do away with me because I'm a farmer's son. Or Li family sympathizers who think that my assassination would unnerve the Empress and make her easy prey. Most likely they were Taoists. Some of my monks, when they've had too much to drink, run about town shaving those long-haired Taoist heads."

"Perhaps I am missing some obvious point, but what business is it of your monks, the length that the Taoists wear their hair?"

"Look. If these Taoists want to practice a different faith, they get what's coming to them. If they want to walk the streets in safety, they can be Buddhists. It's the way of the world."

"It is the way of a weasel," the monk replied.

"Careful what you say," the boxer said, "or I will punish you as I punished those muggers."

"You're not such a bad one," the boxer said, as they rode back to the temple at an easy trot. The full moon, reflected by the snow, suffused the world with a pale blue light. They could see deer nibbling the low branches of pine trees, and red squirrels rolling in the deep drifts.

"If I seem odd," the monk replied, "it's because the secular life is strange to me. I'm a traveler in a foreign land who doesn't know the customs. Fifty years old, and I've never lived outside the temple gates. That was why Venerable Uncle Hui-neng chose me to come here and teach you the Vinaya. He said that if I am to be a true master, I should learn the ways of the secular life as well as the monastic."

"So you will teach me about the monastery and I will teach you about the world." The boxer seemed pleased by the symmetry of it.

"In a manner of speaking."

"Did you learn anything tonight?"

The little monk laughed. "Do not go drinking at night with a man who shaves the heads of Taoists."

The boxer laughed too.

"Tell me more about yourself," the boxer said when they had ridden a ways farther.

"There is little to tell. In the book of Buddhist monks, my life will be a line or less. My parents died of the famine when I was seven. After much hardship I found my way to the Dharma Gate of the East Mountain, as my uncle's temple is called. Hui-neng took me in, raised me, and educated me."

"It's not so different from what happened to me," the boxer said. "But I found my way to the South Market at Lo-yang. I had no one. Who knows what I might have become, with a little help? I might have been the greatest boxer in the land! Which I am, nearly, anyway," he added quickly.

The little monk nodded. "I was fortunate. Hui-neng's Ch'an was as broad and deep as the East Sea. At first he frightened me, for he was dark-skinned and had the speech and the manners of the Lao."

"A barbarian? How could he be a master?"

"Just so did the Patriarch Hung-jen inquire of him. And he replied, 'Though our bodies differ, in the Buddha-nature we are all alike.' It is a very profound reply, I think."

"Tell me more about this barbarian master from the south."

"At first I thought he hated me, because he was so strict. He made me meditate day and night, until I had piles as big as goose eggs on my ass. I was so tired I would fall asleep in the midst of meditation, topple off the bench, and hit the floor with a thud. That woke me up! He never let me enter his chamber. I always had to remain kneeling at the entrance. Then, one afternoon when I was eighteen years old, he asked me in for a cup of tea. Just like that. I wept with joy."

"I would have kicked him in the butt."

The little monk shook his head. "You would have kowtowed to him, for his Buddha-nature shone so bright that even the blind could see it."

"Hold on! Are you saying that I'm—?"

"In later years I discovered that I had a talent for building. One of the other monks, an architect in lay life, taught me how to raise a wooden frame, hang screens, and mount the brackets that support a roof. Another monk taught me masonry. Soon I was in demand at those monasteries where monks were renovating old halls or adding new ones. My reputation spread. I even designed a summer palace for old Kao-tsung."

"The Empress's husband?"

"That's right. He liked it so much that he wished to bestow the purple on me."

"I'll bet that impressed your uncle."

"Worldly honors meant nothing to him. As long as I failed to answer the riddle, he thought me a fool. Each time I answered wrong, he hit me on the head with his wooden stick. In time my skull was as bumpy as a crocodile's back."

"What riddle?"

"The riddle of Hui-neng's flight."

"I like riddles," the boxer said.

"This is the hardest riddle of all. Men die trying to solve it. But those who succeed cross the Gateless Barrier. They are free from earthly woes. They neither cling to life nor fear death. Laughing with joy, they kneel in the palm of Buddha's right hand."

"Well, if solving it does all these fine things, then tell it to me at once! I'm quite good with riddles. I'm sure I can solve it."

"All right, then. This happened long ago, when Master Hui-neng first came to East Mountain Monastery. Being from the south, and illiterate, he could not even wear the monk's robe, and he was forced to tread the pestle in the threshing room. Meanwhile, Hung-jen, who was master of the monastery, held a contest to choose his successor. He was quite old and saw his death approaching like a visitor in the night. He announced that the monk who could write the most profound Ch'an verse would receive his begging bowl and Dharma robe, and become the new master, the Sixth Patriarch.

"The head monk, Shen-hsiu, wrote this verse on the wall:

> *The body is the Nirvana tree,*
> *The mind is like a clear mirror.*
> *At all times we must strive to polish it.*
> *Do not let the dust collect!*

"But Hui-neng sneaked out at night and wrote another verse beneath it:

> *In the beginning Nirvana has no tree,*
> *The mirror has no stand.*

If Buddha-nature is always clean and pure,
Where can the dust alight?

"Hung-jen instantly saw that Hui-neng's Ch'an was deeper. What a quandary! Would he pass the prized symbols of succession, the begging bowl and the Dharma robe, to a mere layman who worked in the threshing room? But he had no choice. He secretly declared him the winner, gave him the begging bowl and the Dharma robe, and told him to flee. You see, he knew there would be trouble.

"It happened just as he thought. No sooner had the other monks learned of the succession than they set off in pursuit of the upstart. One monk named Chen, a former general of coarse ways, caught up with him at Ta-yü-ling Mountain, and demanded that the robe and bowl be returned. Hui-neng laid them on a stone and said, 'This robe symbolizes faith; how can it be fought for with force? Take it.' But when Chen tried to take up the robe, it was as immovable as the mountain. Chen was terrified. Trembling with fear, he said, 'I have come for the Dharma, not for any robe. Teach me, please!'

"Now listen carefully, for here is the riddle that Hui-neng asked him that cold night on the mountainside, as the wind whistled about their heads, and the entire universe threatened to crack open like a crystal sphere:

" 'Think neither good nor evil. At such a moment, what is the True Self of Monk Chen?' "

"That is the riddle?" the boxer asked, his brows forming a mountain peak above his nose. "Hmmm. Let me see. Neither good nor evil . . . True Self of Monk Chen . . . Well, there's no way I can figure this out, for I've never met Monk Chen!"

"Then contemplate the True Self of Boxer Hsüeh. Work very hard. When you meditate, meditate on this riddle of 'neither good nor evil.' Think of it when you work and when you eat and when you shit. Immerse yourself in it day and night. Concentrate upon it with your three hundred sixty bones and eighty-four thousand pores, until your entire body is one great inquiry. And your reward will be the greatest treasure a man can possess."

"And what treasure is that?" the boxer asked, with interest and irritation in equal measure.

"This," the monk said, holding up his fist, slowly spreading his fingers.

The fist was empty.

"You're a madman all right," the boxer said, laughing, and spurred his tarpan to a gallop. The little monk galloped after him, his horse kicking up the snow like sprays of jewels in the moonlight.

"All right!" the boxer shouted as he strode into the residence hall. "Get up, all of you. I've got something to say."

The Korean, White Pheasant, and the others stuck their heads from the doors of their cells and regarded him blearily.

"This little fellow"—the boxer put his arm affectionately around the monk—"this little fellow has broken our rice bowl once and for all. He told the Empress that her beloved Pure Land was a fairy tale for simple folks. She'll probably exile and degrade every one of us, come morning. The way I see it, we can flee for our lives tonight. Or we can have one last maigre feast, eat everything in sight, drink what's left of the wine, send for the singing girls, and worry about tomorrow when tomorrow comes."

"Hear, hear!" shouted Pinch Purse.

The others shared his opinion.

"Already your understanding of Ch'an deepens," the little monk said approvingly.

THE EMPRESS HOLDS A DEBATE

The messenger from the palace found a great table laid in the Buddha Hall, covered with the remnants of a magnificent feast, and snoring monks sprawled everywhere, some of them even lying across the table, having keeled over into their wine cups and plates of dumplings and roast pig. Their red robes were smeared with grease, their white under-robes streaked with wine.

Sunlight and a flurry of new snow drifted through the gaping hole in the roof.

Having assured himself that no one was watching, the messenger grabbed an untouched pork rib from one monk's bowl, ripped off the meat with his teeth, and emptied a full wine cup to wash it down.

Then he located the boxer, lying stretched out on a pile of cushions, and shook him awake. The boxer stared at him a long moment, trying to decide whether he was friend or enemy, whether to bow or strike a fighting pose. Then he recognized the royal colors, the palace insignia, and a moment after that he recalled yesterday's audience, where the little monk had disappointed the Empress.

"I am ready to go," he said, struggling to stand up, brushing the crumbs off his face. He felt he should say something profound on the subject of exile, so that word of it would get back to the Empress and she would realize what a fine, sensitive soul he was, and feel remorse, but nothing came to mind. Finally he said, "Even though I am exiled to the farthest mountains of the north, my heart remains in the wine shops of Lo-yang."

"What?" said the messenger.

"You're here to exile us, aren't you?"

"No. I have an invitation from the Empress."

"An invitation? Well, read it. Be quick."

The messenger opened a scroll.

"Heaven's Chosen invites the Vinaya master and the Abbot of the White Horse Temple to defend the Buddhist faith at a debate with the Taoists at the Dragon Hall on this day at the Hour of the Goat. The faith judged to be the winner will become the faith of Heaven's Chosen."

The boxer scarcely heard the end of it, for by then he was dashing from one sleeping body to the next, roughly rolling them over, looking for the little monk. He found him asleep in the corner, curled up like a cat, a rib of pork in one hand, a wine cup in the other.

"Look at you!" the boxer said, shaking him awake. "A short time you've been with us and already I've corrupted you! Drinking and eating meat! Forgetting your meditation."

The little monk groaned and tried to roll away, but the boxer grabbed him by the ear and pulled him to his feet.

The little monk howled, opened his eyes, and vomited.

By now the Korean was awake. He joined the boxer, who explained the situation.

"We've got to get him cleaned up. We must prepare him for the debate. The future of Buddhism in the Middle Kingdom rests on his shoulders."

"Since when do you care a fig about the future of Buddhism?"

"Shut up, you foreign turtle spawn. As it happens, the little monk is teaching me all about Buddhism. You know, the riddle of Hui-neng's flight, the True Self of Boxer Hsüeh. The more I learn, the more it interests me."

The boxer lifted the little monk over his shoulder and carried him out into the snow.

"I know what's really worrying you," the Korean said, trudging after them, pulling his leopard skin tight around his shoulders for warmth. "If the Empress becomes a Taoist, you'll lose her favor. She'll stop protecting you. Then the Taoists, the Confucianists, the Princess T'ai-p'ing and her husband, and all your other enemies will see that you're skinned and sliced in five pieces."

The boxer ignored him. When he reached the bathhouse, he kicked open the door. Inside, the wooden floor creaked under his weight. The big wooden tub was still filled with water from a few days before, gray and swampy, with a skin of ice across the top.

The boxer dumped the little monk into the water.

His bald head emerged a second later, wide-eyed and sputtering. Quickly he pulled himself out of the tub and tumbled to the floor. Finding himself without his crutch, he started to crawl on all fours toward the door. His wet robe hung from his body like the loose skin of a starving dog. The boxer blocked his way.

"Listen—the Empress is giving us a second chance. She wants you to debate the Taoists today at the palace. The fate of Buddhism will be in your hands. Understand?"

The little monk crouched there, the water from his soaking robe making a little lake around him.

"My head," he murmured, "hurts."

"Of course it does," the boxer said. "It's what we call a hangover. Now wake up! Get in shape! You've still got a couple of hours to study. Lose today, and we're dead men tomorrow."

"You seemed much more philosophical about it last night," the Korean said. "Remember?" He imitated the boxer's bravado and swagger. " 'We can flee for our lives, or we can have one last maigre feast, eat everything in sight—' "

"I was drunk. The world seemed a jollier place."

He hoisted the wet bundle of the monk over his shoulder, and started for the residence hall, to dry him and dress him in clean robes. Meanwhile, Pinch Purse was dispatched to the South Market for a potion to clear the little monk's mind, and White Pheasant to the library to hunt for a document that might be of use in refuting the Taoists.

Some time later the eunuch, red-cheeked and breathing hard, burst into the residence hall with a scroll that he claimed would result in a decisive victory for Buddhism. He unrolled the Scripture to Propagate the Clear and Pure Law, opened it to a spot marked with a strip of silk, blew away the dust, and showed them the verse that would save their necks. Though he alone could read it, the very sight of the rows of complicated characters reassured the rest.

First of all, he explained, the scripture gave a very early date for the birth of the Buddha. This was important because recently the Taoists had been claiming that the Buddha was none other than their own founding sage, Lao-tzu, parading about in a second identity adopted during a trip to the Land of the Brahmans in ancient times. The dates in this scripture proved that the Buddha predated Lao-tzu by at least a century, indisputably refuting their claim.

White Pheasant looked for approval, but the little monk had just taken a gulp of Pinch Purse's herbal potion, a concoction of cardamom (to strengthen the mind), nutmeg (for the digestion), ginseng (to restore vitality), bezoar, python bile, and the ashes of human hair (simply so that the purchaser might feel that he was getting his money's worth), and all he could do was make a sickly smile.

Taking this as encouragement, White Pheasant went on to explain that, according to the scripture, the Buddha himself had sent three disciples to carry his teachings to the East. The men of the Middle Kingdom had called the first of the disciples Confucius and the last of them Lao-tzu.

In other words, not only was the Buddha not just another name for Lao-tzu, but Lao-tzu and Confucius were *both* merely students of the Buddha.

The boxer frowned and wrinkled his forehead. "I have never heard this teaching before. Could it be true?"

"Well, here it is on silk," White Pheasant said, "and painted in a most beautiful hand."

Again they looked to the little monk. He motioned for the scroll feebly, with the first finger of his right hand. Pinch Purse laid it respectfully in his lap, and bowed. They bowed often around him.

"Hmmm," the little monk said again and again, turning the rollers. He raised his eyebrows, he lowered them. The others hovered over him, breathing in unison with him, so hard were they wishing that the document would be useful.

"I know this Scripture to Propagate the Clear and Pure Law," he said after reading several verses. "It was written by those Buddhists who do not believe that the truth is weapon enough to slay their foes."

"You mean it's a forgery?" the boxer said.

"It is not part of the canon. It was composed only a hundred and fifty years ago, when Emperor Hsiao-ming of the Northern Wei dynasty held a debate like the one that Heaven's Chosen will hold tomorrow."

"Is it of any use?" Pinch Purse asked hopefully.

"Indeed it is," the little monk said, and before anyone could stop him, he tore a long section off the scroll and, lifting his robes, used it to wipe his ass.

The Taoist sorcerer wore a robe of blue kingfisher feathers adorned with the eight symbols of his faith—the fan, the sword, the pilgrim's staff and gourd, the clappers, the flower basket, the tube of rods, the flute, and the lotus flower—all depicted in peacock feathers of varying shades, and outlined in the blackest, shiniest raven feathers. When he moved, it shimmered like a many-colored flame. All these feathers reflected the Taoist admiration for the light, ethereal quality of the bird. The most powerful of the Taoist sorcerers, among which he was numbered, claimed to be capable of leaving their bodies and flying vast distances, over mountains and oceans. He carried a tall staff with a parchment at the top upon which was painted an image of the Sacred Mountain, the dwelling place of the Immortals.

His hair, which matched the raven feathers in the richness of its blackness, fell nearly to his waist. He was tall and gaunt, his skin vermilion from the cinnabar he ate to make himself immortal. Though his expression remained more or less dour, his coloring made him seem to be in a perpetual state of rage. His eyes were large, and hooded like the eyes of a hawk.

Only the brave approached a man of such frightening countenance, and only when very strong magic was required. To oppose him seemed the sheerest folly. Yet there was the little monk, standing opposite him in the middle of the Dragon Hall, still green-faced and red-eyed from his hangover, slumped over his crutch like some dying vine on a trellis.

The boxer, standing beside him to offer spiritual support, calculated his odds for success, and found them poor. Now the boxer considered the audience that had turned out in such numbers to witness his downfall, Confucians who resented his rise to power, Taoists whose heads he had forcefully shaved, even a few Buddhists who believed his behavior degraded their faith. Traitors, he thought. He glanced at the Empress on her Phoenix Throne, raised on the dais. Even his most captivating smile failed to melt her icy look. Beside her, the young Emperor was playing with his little wooden puzzle of a Buddha, trying to fit the pieces together. The boxer looked away in despair.

Now the audience grew hushed, and the officer of protocol read from a scroll that essentially repeated the message that had been brought to the temple the day before: that this was a debate between Buddhists and Taoists, the outcome of which would decide the faith to be embraced by Heaven's Chosen in years to come.

Owing to various astrological considerations, the Taoist sorcerer went first. His voice was deep and powerful, and his eyes blazed with an inner fervor.

"We of the Middle Kingdom have a most glorious and ancient history. Our achievements, such as the Long Wall of One Thousand Li that once kept our enemies at bay, and the marvelous canal that links the Yangtze and Yellow rivers, are looked on with awe by barbarian people. Our Empress"—and here he paused to bow to her—"has spread benevolence and virtue as far as Korea, Tibet, Japan, and the kingdom of Magadha. The words of our sages Lao-tzu, Confucius, and Mencius, to name a few, have inspired the men of Han to the greatest cultural and philosophical achievements. What need have we"—he turned to face the little monk—"for some foreign faith? Some import of a land where the men stretch their earlobes and cover themselves with trinkets, and the women walk about half-naked? Was it not Confucius who said, 'Barbarians with a ruler are not as good as our own people without one'? And Mencius who said, 'I have heard of using what is our own to change what is barbarian, but I have never heard of using what is barbarian to change what is our own'?"

The sorcerer raised his eyes to the Empress again, to indicate that he was finished.

The mandarins in the audience looked pleased.

"We are lost," the boxer murmured.

Now all eyes turned toward the little monk.

"These sayings are taken out of context," he began in a small voice. "The saying of Confucius was part of a larger argument meant to rectify the way of the world. Likewise, this saying of the sage Mencius is in truth an argument against one-sidedness. If my memory serves me, he is criticizing Ch'en Hsiang, not for studying foreign ways, but for abandoning his own education so completely."

The little monk cleared his throat and addressed the sorcerer directly.

"Good sir, you have studied the heavens, I assume?"

The sorcerer, puzzled, admitted he had.

"From observing the Pole Star, would you say that the Middle Kingdom is situated directly beneath the center of Heaven?"

"It is not directly beneath the Pole Star, no."

"And the borders that separate our country from its neighbors—these are certainly not the work of Heaven, for they change in times of conquest."

"That is so."

"According to the Buddhist scriptures, above, below, and all around, all creatures possess the Buddha-nature. Therefore I revere and study these scriptures. I do not distinguish between myself and barbarian people. Nor do I see a reason to reject the Way of Yao, Shun, Confucius, and the Duke of Chou. Gold and jade do not harm each other. Crystal does not cheapen amber, or vice-versa. Good sir, you say that another is in error, but it is you who err."

The boxer looked at the little monk in amazement.

The sorcerer made a face as if to show that what the little monk said was not even a rebuttal, but the prattle of an ineffectual child, and went on to his next argument.

"It is written in the Classic of Filial Piety that 'our torso, limbs, hair, and skin we receive from our fathers and mothers. We dare not do them injury.' Yet these Buddhists would have us all shave our heads! Furthermore, they regularly mutilate their bodies. They are fond of telling a story about their sage Bodhidharma, how he fell asleep while meditating and was so angered that he cut off his eyelids!"

"The Classic of Filial Piety," the little monk replied, "also says, 'The kings of yore possessed the ultimate virtue and the essential Way.' Was not T'ao-po one of these kings of yore?"

The little monk waited for a reply.

Finally the sorcerer said, "Yes."

"And did he not cut his hair short and tattoo his body?"

"He did," the sorcerer agreed, "but that was when he went to live in the barbarian land of Wu, where such grotesque customs were common."

"The fact is," the little monk said, "that Confucius cited him as a possessor of the ultimate virtue and the essential Way, and he did cut his hair short and tattoo his body. As for Bodhidharma, he cut off his eyelids so that he would not be lured away from his meditation by sleep. If a man does what is difficult, frightening, or painful in order to achieve an end, if he lets no barrier stand in the way, including the Six Emotions, the Five Desires, and the Ten Bonds, then we must praise his valor and not quibble over how he achieves his end. Your next argument?"

"But . . ." the sorcerer said.

"Your next argument," the Empress said.

"You Buddhists," the sorcerer began, "discourage seeking after wealth and pleasure. You wear red cloth, eat but one meal a day, bottle up the Six Emotions, and live out your lives in poverty. You even discourage marriage and children. Without children, who will worship the ancestors and make the sacrifices? Without ancestor worship and sacrifices, the Middle Kingdom will be doomed! Barbarians will conquer and enslave us. Future generations will perceive us with scorn."

The boxer looked around. The mandarins and the Taoists in the audience nodded and murmured approval, and even the Empress seemed at the point of being swayed.

"You have heard of the sages Hsü Yu and Chao-fu, who dwelt in a tree?" the little monk asked.

"Of course I have," the sorcerer responded.

"And Po-i and Shu-ch'i, who starved in Shou-yang?"

"Yes."

"Did they have wealth?"

"No."

"Or silk robes?"

"Not to my knowledge."

"Or children?"

"No, but . . ."

"And didn't Confucius say of them, "They sought to act in accordance with humanity and they succeeded in doing so?"

"Yes, he did, but—"

"I imagine the Empress and the court are busy, with many memorials to hear, and would appreciate your moving on to your next argument."

The sorcerer opened and closed his hands with frustration. His scarlet skin grew even brighter, making his hooded eyes even darker. He took on a sly look, and the boxer suddenly felt afraid.

"Those of my faith," he began, "have many techniques for obtaining immortality. Hence, Yao, Shun, the Duke of Chou, and Confucius and his seventy-two disciples became immortal using our techniques. Others may become immortal too, and never need to walk the Dark Pathway." He caught the Empress's eye. He was promising her what she desired most in the world, eternal life, and she was childlike in her eagerness to believe. He turned back to the little monk with a look of contempt. "What recipe for immortality does your Buddhism provide?"

"He's got you there," the boxer murmured.

"Is the sage Lao-tzu the authority by which you Taoists live?" the little monk asked.

"He and Chuang-tzu," the sorcerer agreed. "They are our authorities."

"And does not Lao-tzu say in his Tao Te Ching, 'Even heaven and earth cannot be eternal. How much the less can man?'"

"He does," the sorcerer conceded.

"And what of Confucius, who says, 'The wise man leaves the world, but humanity and filial piety endure forever'?"

"I suppose."

"You say that Yao, Shun, the Duke of Chao, and Confucius and his seventy-two disciples became immortal. Yet according to the records and commentaries that I have been fortunate enough to see, Yao died, and Shun had his death place at Mount Ts'ang-wu. We read of the Duke of Chou that he was reburied, and of Confucius that shortly before his death he dreamed of two pillars. As for his disciples, Po-yü, it is written, died before his father. Of Tzu-lu, it is said that his flesh was cut up and pickled. I can go on and on, but I believe that I have made my point." He pivoted around on his crutch to face the Empress, and smiled at her. "Perhaps now Heaven's Chosen would care to question me directly?"

"We wonder," she said after a few moments, "why you, a Buddhist, quote from the Confucian classics and the Taoist sages to prove your point?"

"To offer proof from the writings of one's opponent's faith is, to my mind, the most compelling rebuttal."

The Empress nodded her approval. "We agree that you have refuted the claims of your opponent," she went on. "Yet you have failed to put forth any reasons of your own why We should follow the Way of the Buddha. Can you do this?"

The monk thought for a moment.

"Are you familiar with a scripture called the Great Cloud?"

The Empress shook her head.

"It is a little-known scripture read mostly by those Buddhists who look forward to the coming of Maitreya, the future Buddha, the redeemer."

"And what of it?" the Empress asked.

"It differs from other such scriptures in that it predicts the coming of Maitreya as a woman. If I may quote?" He closed his eyes and rubbed his forehead. " 'You shall reign over the territory of a country with the body of a woman. . . . The people shall prosper; there will be no weaknesses, or sorrows from illnesses, or afflictions, or fears, or calamities; all propitious events will be completely realized. . . . All the countries of the Jambudvīpa will be obedient to you and none will oppose or resist you.

" 'You shall obtain great sovereignty. . . . You shall teach and convert the cities and villages that depend on you. . . . You shall destroy and subdue the external religions and the perverse and heretical visions. Then you shall in reality be a bodhisattva who will show and receive a female body in order to convert beings.' "

The little monk opened his eyes and stared at the Empress. He continued, "By Jambudvīpa, we mean, of course, that one of the four continents which is known as the Middle Kingdom. In other words, this excellent though little-known scripture predicts the reign of you yourself, the Chosen of Heaven. How could it, then, be false?"

The Empress's eyes gleamed. She looked at the little monk and the boxer. Then she looked toward the sorcerer.

"What have you to say about this?"

The sorcerer considered his words carefully. Were he to accuse the little monk of making up the quotation—which he suspected was the case, for he had never heard of this Great Cloud Scripture—it would be tantamount to accusing Heaven's Chosen of being an impostor. To refute it, assuming that he could think of some appropriate verse from the classics, would be to run the same risk. Nor could he present a Taoist scripture that made the same predictions, for no Taoist sect had an interest in future saviors. In immortality, alchemy, and birdlike flight, yes, but not in future saviors.

"There is nothing I can say," the sorcerer finally replied.

"Then you admit defeat?" the Empress said.

"I— Yes. I do." He glared at the boxer and the little monk.

"Then We declare the Buddhist monk the winner of this debate. From this day forward, Buddhism will be the faith of Heaven's Chosen. The sorcerer, because he sought to mislead us in our beliefs, will be degraded to the status of commoner and exiled to the province of Kuangsi for the rest of his days."

Though shocked by the harsh decree, the audience retained its composure.

The sorcerer, however, could restrain himself no longer, and cried out, like a spoiled child who has lost a game with his friends, "You care nothing for the truth!" He gestured vehemently as he spoke, making his feathered robe swirl and blaze like the blue flame that races across a film of oil. "You embrace his sophistries to gain your own ends. You discredit my sage, Lao-tzu, in order to discredit the dynasty that claims descent from him."

The T'ang princes claimed descent from Lao-tzu, since, like him, their clan bore the venerable surname of Li.

"Such outbursts will not be tolerated in the presence of Heaven's Chosen," the Empress said quietly. "Guards, remove him to the prison."

"Your Highness, if I may?" the boxer said, stepping forward.

"Speak," the Empress said, bestowing on him the smile of affection he had thought he would never see again. He breathed more easily than he had in days. He walked over to the sorcerer and put a hand on his back in a gesture of friendship. The sorcerer recoiled ever so slightly, as one might from the touch of a filthy dog. "This sorcerer is a good fellow. He simply had the bad luck to get mixed up with these Taoists in his youth. I suggest you let him stick around the court. He must know something useful. Maybe some of those recipes really do add a few years to your life. Who knows? I'd keep him around."

The Empress complimented the boxer on his compassion, and promised to give his suggestion due consideration.

The sorcerer, however, showed no gratitude.

A VICTORY AND A DEFEAT

When the boxer saw the monks waiting at the temple gates, he raised his arms in a gesture of victory and let out a mighty howl. The others cheered. White Pheasant appeared, rolling a wine cask along the path by the pagoda. The boxer knocked out the bung, hoisted it to his shoulders, and poured wine down the throats of the others, so it dribbled down their chins, and then he simply poured it over their heads. They picked up handfuls of wine-soaked snow and sucked on it, and mischievously stuffed more snow down the collars of each other's robes.

"We are back in the Empress's favor!" he shouted. "Our rice bowl overflows! Buddhism has triumphed, and that cur of a sorcerer has gotten what's coming to him! And the one we have to thank for it—aside from myself, of course—is our little Vinaya master."

They looked around for him so that they might shout his praises and hoist him to their shoulders, but he was nowhere to be seen.

They hunted through the temple, calling for him, dragging along the wine keg so they could douse him with it in playful appreciation.

They found him in the meditation hall, sitting on the bench, legs folded, eyes half-closed, breath slow. Those carrying the keg would have roused him by pouring wine over his head, but the boxer intervened. Out of gratitude and respect, he ordered them to join in the meditation, and they complied without complaint. They sat for as long as they could, a few minutes for some, as much as an hour for others. The boxer forced himself to sit longer than the rest. When he could bear the stillness no longer, he straightened his aching knees, stretched his back, opened his eyes. The little monk was still sitting.

That evening, when the boxer returned to the meditation hall, the monk's attitude was unchanged.

Likewise the next morning. Footprints and a ragged patch of yellow snow behind the hall showed where he had gone to urinate during the night. Puddles of water on the floorboards, tracked snow now melted, made him think of the broken vase, the scattered peonies. Suddenly the boxer grew terribly afraid. He knelt in front of the little monk, and gazed at him intently, as though to read his thoughts. Then he sat beside him and joined his meditation as an act of sympathy.

The Empress sent for the boxer. There, in the Lotus Palace, surrounded by a lake of ice that cracked and groaned and shifted as though trying to find comfortable repose, they made love. Afterwards, they curled together for warmth in a bed like a little house, painted with bright red lacquer and decorated with flowers and vines. The Empress praised the little monk, his knowledge of the classics, his quick mind and excellent memory. She spoke with particular interest of the Great Cloud Scripture he had quoted and its description of Maitreya, the Buddhist savior, returning as a great woman sovereign.

"This woman savior," the Empress asked in one of her fleeting moments of self-doubt, "are We truly she?"

"Without question," the boxer replied, tracing the line of her hip with his finger.

"There is," the Empress went on, "something We have long wanted to discuss with you. But We have waited because We wanted a further demonstration of your loyalty and wisdom."

The boxer pretended to be hurt. Outside, the ice on the lake shifted again, like the thunder of a coming storm.

"We, who occupy a position of great power, must also exercise great care. We must always place Our mind before Our heart. In the past We have trusted others and been disappointed."

"I understand," the boxer said.

"But now, after that splendid debate, We are convinced of your loyalty and wisdom. And so We shall share a plan with you. But let Us ask you a question first. Does it make sense to call this dynasty T'ang when the woman who rules is of a family named Chou?"

The boxer thought hard. What sort of answer was she looking for? Then it came to him: she planned to change the dynasty, as he had heard rumored. The question was meant to secure his support and assistance. He was overwhelmed with a feeling of his own importance at being cast for a lead in history's pageant, or at least a supporting role.

"It makes no sense at all. It is you who rule the Middle Kingdom, not the young Emperor."

"*My* military skill led to the conquest of Korea," she said. "*My* strategies kept back the Turks and the Tibetans. *My* acts of grace rewarded the aged, relieved the poor, pardoned those falsely imprisoned, and lifted the taxes that broke the farmers' backs. It was *I* who shortened the tour of duty and sent the border troops home so that they could practice their ancestral sacrifices, and *I* who began the recruiting of men of virtue to replace those treacherous and decadent aristocrats who would have betrayed me and everything I had worked for these many years."

"*I?*" the boxer said, smiling.

The Empress, her inner thoughts betrayed by her mistake, blushed. "Insolent thing," she said softly, licking him behind his ear.

"The fact is," she continued, "that *I* am responsible for the innovations that have brought untold prosperity and happiness to the people of the Middle Kingdom. Yet these woman-hating Confucian historians will paint me as the embodiment of evil, as they have the Empress dowagers before me. And when I die, that little fool Jui-tsung will destroy all the good I have done. What a tragedy, when there is one who could continue my rule and bring the seeds of my policies to flower."

"And who is that?" the boxer said, thrilling for an instant at the thought that it might be himself. After all, the power to rule had passed from Kao-tsung to the Empress through the simple expedient of marriage and the Jade Chamber. Might it pass as simply to him?

"Why, the Princess T'ai-p'ing, of course. Of all the royal heirs, male and female, she is the only one fit to rule."

The idea of female succession to the throne was so bizarre that for more than an instant the boxer was speechless. The thought of the Princess T'ai-p'ing sitting on the Dragon Throne iced his blood. Though his political concerns had never gone beyond wondering what effect a particular memorial might have on his own bumpy court career, he suddenly found himself worried about those whose world he shared, mandarin and peasant alike.

"Can the Dragon Throne pass to a woman?" he asked.

"All things are possible if Heaven mandates them. If the Chou dynasty receives the mandate of heaven, then it is meant to be.

"This is no whim," she went on, "but a plan We have played with since Our husband's death, just as Jui-tsung plays with his Buddha puzzle, trying to make the pieces come apart and fit back together in a different way. Until now We have hesitated, waiting for the proper omen. But when We heard the Great Cloud Scripture, We knew it was a sign of Heaven preparing to bestow its mandate, as a poet opens his scroll and makes his ink before the creation of a poem. Why else would the Vinaya master bring it to Our attention at just this time?"

She was We again, the boxer noted. The moment of intimacy had passed, leaving him lonely and distant from her.

"We are ashamed to admit it, but having never heard of this particular scripture, we doubted its validity. We wondered if the Vinaya master might have created it in order to win the debate. But Our Scholars of the North Gate have looked into the matter. They say it is a true scripture of the Mahāyāna canon, written in the Brahman land in ancient times. The problem is, it exists only in the Brahman script, that language called Sanskrit, which only a few of the most learned monks can read."

"I'm not sure I understand," the boxer said. "What exactly does this Great Cloud Scripture have to do with starting a dynasty?"

"It is the prophecy of my reign! It says that Maitreya will be reborn as a woman sovereign. Not an empress, nor an empress dowager, but a *woman sovereign*. Clearly, I am she. Does it make sense for such a sovereign to be called by the name of another emperor's dynasty, or to mark her calendar by another emperor's reign era?"

"I see," the boxer said. "Well, when are you going to announce it?" He licked his lips, anticipating the celebratory feasts to come.

"Oh, my Precious One." She smiled at him and touched his chin. "You cannot plant a tree in the morning and cut boards come noon. There are many, many preparations to make before my ministers and my subjects will accept such a revolutionary idea. But rest assured, Precious One, you will be part of it. You will supervise the translation of this Great Cloud Scripture into our own language, so that everyone can hear its wisdom. And you will see to it that the little monk writes a commentary along the lines of what he said at the debate, explaining how my reign fulfills each verse of the prophecy. When the translation is done, We shall establish Great Cloud temples in every city of the realm, and send out monks to read the scripture aloud and explain the commentary. We shall, in other words, create a special sect of Buddhism, the Great Cloud Sect, to support the glorious reign of the Chou."

"I cannot read my own language, much less the language of the Brahmans."

"You are good with people. They like you and are eager to work by your side. Others will read, translate, and check for meaning. You will be like the general who inspires his troops without ever lifting a sword."

"That is not a very good general, in my opinion."

"Our analogy is poor. A translation is not a war. There is no enemy but the obscure phrase, the sloppy brushstroke. Do as We say and have no doubts regarding your own ability."

The boxer was thoughtful as he rode his horse back to shore. The ice on the lake groaned and shifted like a beast caught in a snare.

When he returned to the temple, the Korean reported that the little monk still had not eaten. The boxer went to the meditation hall and, kneeling before the little monk, said, "Forgive me for disturbing your meditation, but I must ask if something is wrong. You haven't eaten in days."

The little monk opened his eyes and looked up at him.

"I have done something very, very evil," he said. "I have perverted the scriptures, the words of the Buddha himself, and made them seem other than what I know them to mean. To do this is like using golden chains to yoke a bullock."

"What are you talking about?" the boxer said. "You've been a hero. You saved Buddhism in the Middle Kingdom."

"I grew vain of my intellect, and proud. I wanted to show your Empress how clever I was. I trapped the sorcerer as a leopard might some poor rabbit, and showed him no mercy. I do not deserve to wear these robes, nor this scarf."

He pulled off the beautiful silk scarf he was wearing and hurled it away. It drifted, like some vast, sheer butterfly, past the statues of the Buddha.

"I think you're being too hard on yourself," the boxer said. "You made a very good impression on the Empress. For a while I thought she was through with me, but now, because of that Great Cloud Scripture, she likes me more than ever. But listen—here's exciting news. She wants us to render it into our own language. You'll be my chief translator and write the commentary. Your name will go down in history."

"The Great Cloud Scripture doesn't mean what I said it meant," the little monk went on angrily. "It is no prophecy of the coming of the Empress Wu. Its meaning is symbolic. It is the Buddha's way of saying that enlightenment is for all, peasant and mandarin, man and woman. The continent Jambudvīpa, which He prophesies that she will rule, is not the Middle Kingdom or any other continent of this earth, but a part of our cosmology. And even that is not actual, but a symbol of a certain level of enlightenment."

"Well, so what?" the boxer said gently. "You made the Empress happy and you saved our lives. Surely that's important too. I may not know a hundred scriptures, but I know that leftover millet is better than none."

The little monk shook his head. "I came to refine your Ch'an, but I have only succeeded in debasing my own. By perverting the Buddha's word, I have trapped myself in the web of karma. The more I struggle against it, the worse shall be its hold upon me. If I continue to live, I will simply propagate the lie. Death is my only escape. That is why I have chosen to starve myself."

The boxer lost his patience. "You'll do nothing of the sort! You're my new rice bowl. You're going to translate this Great Cloud and write a commentary, and when that's done you can hang yourself from the temple gate for all I care. But until then you can just forget about starving to death. Understand?" And he stamped out of the meditation hall.

Early next morning—the monk's third without food—a most subtle and exquisite aroma came drifting through the meditation hall: the smell of duck smoking in jasmine leaves, tangerine peel, and cassia, the pungent inner bark of the evergreen tree.

Saliva dripped from the corner of the little monk's half-open mouth. His Adam's apple rose and fell as he swallowed lest he drown in his own juices, but otherwise he maintained his stillness.

An hour later the aroma was replaced by a heartier smell. The duck was being steamed. The little monk worked his mouth. Determination replaced the peaceful look he had worn till then, and his muscles stiffened with resolve.

The next stage of this peculiar torture involved more a sound than a smell: the crackle of the same duck being deep-fried in peanut oil. Smoked, steamed, fried. It could only be that gourmet dish known as crispy perfumed tea duck! Soon other smells joined it, as harmoniously as the voices of the most cultivated singing girls join the strumming of the bent-necked lute: baking "flower rolls" seasoned with sesame oil and minced ham, cucumber steamed with cassia blossoms and wildflower honey, cabbage hearts with "glass noodles" stir-fried in chicken fat with roasted peppers from Szechuan.

The little monk screamed with frustration. He rose, grabbed his crutch, toppled to the floor from dizziness and the stiffness of his knees, rose a second time, and managed to reach the door of the meditation hall. What he saw then, no more than ten feet away, seemed like some ghastly apparition of the sort concocted by Maya to sabotage the meditation of the Buddha.

The snow had been cleared away, the iron stove dragged from the cooking shed, a banquet table set up alongside it. White Pheasant was busily putting the last touches on the magnificent feast the little monk had smelled being prepared. The boxer sat on a stool at the head of the table, waiting to be served, and the other monks were gathered on either side.

"You are the devil himself!" the little monk screamed at the boxer, and, weeping at his own weakness, took a flour roll from an enameled tray and ate greedily.

Something woke the boxer. He opened his eyes and lay very still, listening, for he knew that his enemies were not beyond sneaking into the temple and killing him in his sleep. No footsteps, no rustle of silk, no hiss of a dagger being unsheathed. What had awakened him was the feeling of wrongness, of things out of tune, misaligned.

He rose, pulled on his slippers and a fleece-lined robe over his sleeping robe, and walked through the residence hall on the balls of his feet, on guard for anything that might be amiss. He looked into the cell of the little monk and found it empty. Was he back in the meditation hall? How could anyone stay awake to meditate after such a huge feast and so many sleepless nights?

He stepped out into the cold air of the courtyard and stood very still, listening. A crackling sound seized his attention, and his eye was attracted by a flicker of light atop the knoll near the rolling mill. Someone had built a bonfire. Silhouetted by the flame, the pile of tangled brush resembled the intricate filigree around the pedestal of a piece of sacred art. A sweet smell in the air led him to believe that the brush had been soaked with hempseed oil, which the monastery kept in quantity for use in lamps and for other non-culinary purposes. Now that his eyes had adjusted, he saw, sitting in the middle of the circle of fire, the silhouette of a figure drawn into the pyramidal pose of meditation. Rising waves of heat rippled the image.

Self-cremation. He had heard stories of monks doing this kind of thing, but had never, until now, believed it.

The boxer began to run. He knew that he was too far away, and that the fire was spreading too fast, but he ran anyway. He tripped and slipped in the snow, fell and struggled to his feet again, kept at it till his robe was caked with snow and more had found its way into his slippers. He ran as in a dream, as though pushing his way through soft, suffocating obstructions, while nameless demons pursued him, snapping at his heels.

As the fire grew brighter, bathing the snow in an undulating red light, the image of the monk became wavering and insubstantial. Rather than burn like base, common matter, he was of such fine stuff that he would evaporate. The boxer saw his future evaporate with him: the regular meals, the cash he spent without thinking, the dignity of his office, the love of the Empress. He saw himself in the marketplace of a poor boarder town, splitting boards with the side of his hand, popping ropes tied about his chest, staging matches with the Korean for a few coins tossed at their feet.

He fell again and this time his foot twisted under him and sent a pain shooting through his leg. He tried to get up, but could not stand. "No!" he screamed with frustration. "No!" The air burned his throat. His lungs were a knot, his vision clouded with tears. Then he saw that his tears were mixed with rain. Not snow, as he would have expected, given the cold, but a cloudburst, a drenching, torrential rain. The cold had broken. It was spring's first thaw.

By the time he limped to the top of the knoll, the fire had been completely extinguished. The rain drove worm-holes into the snow, and tendrils of smoke rose from the circle of soaked, blackened brush. The little monk, sitting in the middle of it, was sopping wet but otherwise unharmed.

The boxer stood over him, hands on his hips, waiting.

Finally the little monk said, "It would seem that I am not meant to die at this time, after all."

He allowed the boxer to help him to his feet, and they limped back to the residence hall together.

RENOVATING THE TEMPLE

In the days that followed, the sun grew warm. Green buds appeared within the blackened brush where the monk had tried to immolate himself, and purple crocuses pushed through the crust of snow that remained in the temple courtyard.

As for accepting the job of translation supervisor, the little monk pondered it at some length. Though he did not believe in the supernatural, or in miracles, or in a personal God, he did see man and nature as two parts of the same cosmic device, intimately interacting toward some common though incomprehensible end. The drenching of his crematory fire seemed so deliberate that he could not ignore it. But if his life was being spared, for what purpose was it? To mislead a nation through a specious translation of a Buddhist scripture?

Another part of him argued that even if it was being put to a corrupt purpose, the Great Cloud Scripture was still part of the Mahāyāna canon, the Buddha's own words, and one always served the faith well who helped transmit its teachings. Although the Empress might insist on a twisting of the truth, time would always straighten it. Though the trees in the palace garden had been coaxed into the forms of dragons and deer, the cleverest gardener could not stop them from seeking the sun.

But perhaps the decisive issue was the effect that his choice would have on the boxer. Though the boxer often infuriated him, the little monk had also grown inordinately fond of him—he was so *human,* and so exciting to be around, compared with the virtuous monks he had known—and couldn't bear the thought of being the source of his ruin.

Once he had made up his mind, he went about the task of gathering a translation team with the same efficiency, ingenuity, and enthusiasm that he showed in every aspect of his life.

He called upon all the Buddhist temples in Lo-yang, regardless of whether they read the Three Treatises, or the Lotus of the True Law, whether they sought enlightenment through meditation or discourse, whether they repeated the name of A-mi-t'o-fo or awaited the coming of Maitreya, for all these sects, no matter how divergent, saw themselves as limbs of the same body.

The bodhisattvas must have been guiding his search, for him to have such good fortune. The first day, he located two visiting Brahmans of outstanding wisdom and scholarship, for the all-important task of enunciating and explaining the original Sanskrit text. Their skin was as dark as teak, their eyes round, their attitudes refined and pious, their incomprehensible speech as lovely as the babbling of a stream. Because they were of the same land and race as the Buddha, they were close to the river's source, and thus endowed with an aura of mystery and magic. No sooner had they moved into the White Horse Temple than stories began to circulate about their miraculous (though unwitnessed) talents: their ability to live for months on only a fig and a few drops of honey, to walk through fire and stand on water, to recollect a thousand previous incarnations.

Other Brahman monks, these bilingual, longtime residents of local temples, were assigned as Translators, Sanskrit Text Checkers, and Sanskrit Text Copiers.

The jobs of Scribes, Binders, Checkers of Meaning, Translation Checkers, and Chinese Text Copiers were given to distinguished Middle Kingdom monks.

Heaven's Chosen, exhibiting the love for endless bureaucracy that marked all Middle Kingdom endeavors, appointed four mandarins to oversee the project: the Specially Appointed Inspector and

Copier, whose regular title was Official First Class Scribe and Copier for the Regular Writing of the Emperor's Library Department; the Specially Appointed Commissioner, an official of the ninth grade, third class, provisionally holding the post of Administrator of the Service of the Troops of the Second Militia of the Wings of the Left Guard; the Commissioner and Inspector to Superintend the Translation, who was regularly Storeman and Scribe of the Court of Diplomatic Reception; and the Commissioner to Superintend the Translation, who was Registrar of the Court of Diplomatic Reception in Place of the Assistant.

The monks were pleased to be recruited, for the food at the White Horse Temple was rumored to be nearly as good as that at the palace, and after their work was finished, they were reasonably sure of receiving handsome cash rewards and perhaps income-producing titles.

The mandarins were also pleased, for their appointments provided prestige and a promise of promotion in rank and grade, while requiring little or no work on their part beyond the occasional progress report.

But most pleased of all was the boxer, for along with the title of Supervisor of Translation, and the honor of having all of the previously mentioned men beholden to him, the Empress had another treat in store, one he had dreamed of for some time.

"We are disturbed," she said to him one afternoon while they were walking in the palace garden, "at the thought of such distinguished scholar-monks being lodged in the decrepit White Horse. A historic enterprise such as this should only be attempted in the most beautiful and harmonious surroundings. The temple must be renovated. You will see that it becomes the most splendid temple in the city."

"I?"

"Yes. You will supervise the renovations. You will hire the architects and artisans. Whatever cash you require will be yours."

"But I thought I was unfit for the job."

"Much has changed since first we spoke of the topic. At that time you were naïve concerning politics and the court, and We were uncertain of your abilities. But in the past months you have proven yourself to Our satisfaction."

The boxer was thrilled. Finally he could turn the White Horse into a splendid palace of his own, where he could feel like an emperor. He deserved as much. The dangers and responsibilities of being the Empress's lover were great indeed, and it was only right that the rewards be commensurate.

The first thing he did was to order new costumes worthy of his exalted position. He had the Empress's own tailor make him a dozen robes of the best scarlet silk; six new scarves, each sewn from twenty-five strips of the most gorgeous floral brocade; and a dozen pairs of slippers embroidered with scenes from the Buddha's life on top, and Taoist images on the sole, so that every time he took a step, he raised the former toward heaven and ground the latter into the dirt.

Next he pulled the little monk away from the translation team and gave him the following instructions: he was to see exactly what the temple required in the way of restoration, then find the best workers and artisans for the job, negotiate contracts with them, and keep an eye on their work to make sure that they performed it honestly and in good time. Obviously the boxer could not do it himself, for he knew nothing of construction. He was, after all, an abbot, not some peasant who worked with his hands.

Soon the courtyard of the temple was as busy as the South Market. Potters built brick kilns to bake and glaze tiles to match the ancient tiles on the roof. Ivory carvers stacked their elephant tusks like firewood alongside heaps of white, green, and pink jade, and gorgeous pink coral. Carpenters brought in carts of hardwoods from the south: rosewood, sour jujube, camphorwood, paulownia, and sweet-smelling yellow sandalwood.

Bamboo scaffoldings were erected around each hall so that the artisans would have places to stand as they rebuilt the roofs and patched the walls. The eight Buddhist emblems of happy augury, the wheel of the Dharma, the conch shell, the parasol of state, the canopy, the lotus, the vase, the fishes, and the endless knot appeared everywhere, painted on the joists, sculpted in terra-cotta beneath the eaves, engraved on bronze brackets and hinges. Ox teams, dragging on block and tackle, lifted heavy beams into position. Sometimes the ropes broke or the oxen ran amuck, and the beams fell, but miraculously, no one, man or beast, was injured.

Dressed in his fine new robes, the boxer would strut along the temple walks, observing the artisans and laborers at their jobs, nodding with stern approval when he saw something he liked, boxing a worker's ears when he judged that his progress was too slow, or when some element displeased him.

When a real problem arose, the little monk was always available for advice. If the boxer was concerned about him holding two jobs, either one of which would have overwhelmed an ordinary man, it was for naught. He managed to be everywhere at once, one moment inside the administration hall, arguing with the Brahmans about the precise shade of meaning of a particular Sanskrit compound, the next moment out in the courtyard, arguing with a worker about the miter of a joint, then herding together the monks for meditation, then seeing that White Pheasant had the main meal under way. Yet he never seemed overwhelmed, or even busy.

Only in the renovation of his personal cell did the boxer rely entirely on his own whims, for in the course of innumerable daydreams he had worked out every inch of it. He ordered the workmen to remove the walls between several of the cells to create a suite of apartments like those of the Dragon Chambers at the palace, which the Empress had shown him one afternoon. The windows were enlarged to allow views of the pagoda and the courtyard. He had the cabinetmakers build him an enclosed, red lacquered bed like the one he shared with the Empress when he visited her, and he had the artists paint him a mural on the wall behind it of Maitreya standing in the clouds, the details highlighted with gold leaf, gems, and pearls.

One evening, while he was admiring his nearly completed apartments, one of those incidents occurred that a downtrodden man dreams of, particularly if he is of a petty and vindictive nature. He was gazing out a rear window at a small secondary courtyard, wondering if it might be a good place to have a pond so that the croaking of frogs could lull him to sleep, when he noticed a worker digging in a corner. This alone was odd at such a late hour, but the oddness was compounded by the man's familiarity, his wispy goatee and mustache, his watery eyes. One gesture—when the man pulled a handkerchief from his sleeve and wiped his nose—jarred the boxer's memory. Of course! Though dressed like a common worker in loincloth and coarse upper-robe, hair pulled back with a bandanna, he was undeniably the boxer's adoptive son, Prince Hsüeh Shao!

The boxer ran from his apartments, then slowed up lest he

appear overeager, and approached him from behind at a stroll, clearing his throat for attention. The prince looked up from the hole he was digging.

"Son," the boxer began in his most formal voice, "what a pleasant surprise, meeting you here."

"Son?" The watery eyes regarded him, puzzled. "I do not understand. Why do you call me that? I am simply a worker, a gardener."

"Come now! my son, don't you recognize me in my new robes? It's Huai-i, the boxer, whom you once berated for knocking over some foolish stone in your garden. Look at me now, the abbot of a great temple, the supervisor of an important translation!"

The prince hesitated a long time. Then he squinted at him and nodded. "Yes, of course. Forgive my lack of propriety, but you are so splendid in appearance only a sage would have known you for the same man."

To the boxer's delight, the prince fell to his knees and bowed and kowtowed. The single moment seemed to make up for every man who had ever slighted or mistreated him. It was the pinnacle of his life so far.

"Of course I forgive you," the boxer said magnanimously. "How could I expect you to recognize me? But you should learn a lesson from this. Do not judge men by their poor clothes or their lack of a title. The man you spit on one day may be a censor the next. It's the way of the world."

He gave that a moment to sink in before he went on; "But what of yourself, my beloved son? I see you no longer wear the purple robes of the highest ranks. Have you been degraded? What a good joke that would be, me nearly a mandarin, you almost a commoner."

Again the prince hesitated before he spoke. "I am still a prince, Father. It is my passion for gardening that has brought me here. Once I had overheard that you were remaking the temple and that you planned a new garden, I could not keep away. The thought that I might be the one to plan a new garden for the venerable White Horse Temple! I was worried you would hold a grudge and refuse me the honor, so I disguised myself as a common worker. Of course, I seek no wage, only the pleasure of exercising my artistry. But you were cleverer than I thought. You saw through my disguise in an instant. I can only throw myself on your mercy and plead that you allow me to stay and work. Do this for your poor son and I will always be grateful."

"I don't see why not. You are a fine gardener and a member of the family. But in the future, do not try to fool me. It is a useless task."

"I understand that now," the prince admitted.

"What are you digging?" the boxer asked, inspecting his son's work. What he had taken for a hole appeared to be a deep tunnel.

"A passageway to the temple's cellar," the prince explained.

"But I never knew my temple had a cellar!"

"It must have caved in some time ago. I only discovered it by accident, while shaping this flower bed. I thought I might please you by restoring it, so that you could make use of it someday. You must have many things you wish to store, temple treasures and the like."

"Yes. Yes, I do. How thoughtful of you, my son. But you must not work at this hour. Go home to the princess. Rest and write poetry as other learned men do in the evenings."

"Dear father, I'll confide in you." He pulled the kerchief from his sleeve and blew his nose. "My marriage is unsatisfactory at best. My wife, the princess—and this is just between the two of us—"

"Of course."

"My wife ignores me, or else she bosses me around as though I were a servant. My one great pleasure in life, my gardening, she mocks."

"Women are like this," the boxer said sympathetically, though in fact his own experiences had proven the contrary.

"Let me stay and work now, Father. With the other workers gone, it is so peaceful. I delight in the sound of the monks chanting their evening prayers. And as long as I work here, I need not go home."

"Of course, my son," the boxer said. "Work here all night, if you wish. And if you get thirsty from your work, stop by my suite of rooms—it's right over there—and share a pot of wine with me. I'll be up till a late hour."

"Father, judging from your sense of propriety, few deserve their good fortune as much as you."

The boxer saw the prince twice more during the temple renovation. The second occasion occurred thus:

One night the boxer was wandering through the temple garden when he heard a deep, creaking noise in an adjacent courtyard. Going to investigate, he discovered a number of monks in the moonlight, rolling big barrels along a path behind the kitchen.

"Why are you working at this late hour?" he asked.

"It is mysterious, nighttime work," False Brush replied. "You see, these barrels are filled with the wine of secret dissent. We will leave them in the temple cellar till they turn to the vinegar of rebellion."

"Shhh!" The boxer hushed him, and looked around to see whether any outsiders might be listening. "I know that your common sense took flight years ago, and that you confuse clouds and castles, but please don't say such things. The mere mention of rebellion will put us all back in prison."

Another monk came forward and the boxer saw that it was his adoptive son, the prince. It all seemed very odd.

"I hoped to surprise you," the prince said. "Knowing how you love mare's-teat wine, I purchased one hundred barrels. Alas, they are not yet aged to perfection. They must sit in some cool, dark place another two years before the flavor has reached its peak. So we are rolling them to the temple cellar."

"Aha," the boxer said. "So that explains it."

"At some future maigre feast, years hence, we had planned to break them out for your pleasure." His face fell. "But now the surprise is ruined."

The boxer smiled. "My memory is short. Already I have forgotten what these barrels contain. I'm sure that tomorrow morning I will remember nothing at all of what happened tonight. So you may continue your work. But be quick about it! I need my sleep if I'm not to have bags under my eyes and a sallow look."

As to the third meeting of the boxer and the prince:

A member of the Yü-lin Guard had just delivered several thousand strings of cash to the temple administration hall, to pay the artisans. The boxer, trusting no one else, was counting the money himself. Since he had never learned to use the abacus or write numbers, he kept a tally by scratching marks on a piece of slate. But sometimes he couldn't recall whether he had made a scratch or not, or else some stray thought crept into his head and he forgot what number he had reached, and then he had to start counting all over again.

After several frustrating hours of this, the boxer looked up and saw the prince, dressed as a common gardener again, kneeling on the floor a few feet away and observing him.

"What are you doing here?" the boxer asked with irritation. The little coins that slipped through his fingers like wet, squirming fish had put him in a bad mood.

"I announced myself, but you were so intent on your work that you seemed not to notice me."

"I'm trying to count this stupid cash so I'll know if they delivered the proper amount. But it's maddening! And I thought this job would be fun. I should never have agreed to it."

"If I might make a suggestion?" the prince said softly.

"Yes?"

He took a silk square out of his sleeve and blew his nose before he began. "You know how scarce metals are. They need the iron for swords to fight the Turks, and the copper to make coins."

"You don't have to tell me. One day the Empress says, 'Rebuild the temple, make it beautiful, I'll give you everything you need.' The next day there I am, begging for a few hundred catties of copper. Meanwhile the artisans are demanding their pay, and I can't even make these coins behave themselves and be counted."

"The point I'm making is this. You don't *have* to count the coins."

"I don't?"

"No. Why drive yourself mad? You're an important man—the abbot of a temple—with many more important things to do than this."

"That's true. So what do you suggest?"

"Melt them down instead. They're more valuable that way. Look—it takes six catties of copper to make one thousand cash, a string. The same six catties, fashioned into a pleasing incense burner or bell, could bring you thirty-six thousand cash."

"Why, I believe you're right," the boxer said, scratching his brow. "I never thought of that. But—wouldn't the Empress mind?"

"On the contrary, I think she'd be pleased. You'd be getting more value out of the cash. And by taking coins out of circulation, you'd inflate the currency. Everyone knows that the fewer the number of similar things that exist, the greater their value."

"It's rather clever, isn't it? Perhaps I should memorialize upon it to the court. I've been wanting to deliver a memorial on some important subject."

"I don't know if that would be wise. If too many people follow your example, no coins will be left for the rest of us. Why not keep the scheme to yourself? Someday you may need to regain the Empress's favor. You can reveal it to her then."

"I would give you credit, of course."

"The credit is yours. You would have thought of it yourself, given time."

And so the boxer discreetly hired a metalsmith to set up a little foundry in a shed at the rear of the temple, where he could melt down coins into copper and smelt it with tin to make bronze. Soon there was metal enough to repair the Buddhas in the Buddha hall, as well as to fabricate the ornate brackets and hinges to replace the worn and broken ones, and plenty left over to make into incense burners and bells of different sizes, and ritual cups and vases. In lieu of pay, the metalsmiths were permitted to keep some of the copper for their own use, while the other artisans were given little copper utensils and art objects. Everyone was satisfied by the arrangement and spoke of the boxer's wisdom.

Renovations continued throughout the spring, summer, and fall. The roof of the Buddha Hall was so perfectly patched that no one would have guessed there had ever been a hole in it. The rotten floorboards were replaced with new ones, the flaking paint of the murals scraped away, and new paint applied in brilliant, garish colors. The three bronze Buddhas at the head of the hall were cleaned and polished and decorated from head to toe with gold leaf and lacquers.

And so it continued with one hall after the next.

Even the vines were stripped off the wheel of the decrepit rolling mill so that it could turn upon its bearings, and the rotting teeth of the gears were extracted and replaced with new ones that meshed smoothly. When the sluice was opened, the machinery groaned like an old man rising from a long meditation, and within the mill, for the first time in years, the great stone wheels ground rice into flour.

Finally the golden finial was restored to its place atop the pagoda where Bodhidharma's begging bowl was enshrined.

And though it seemed that the dust and debris and the awful

smell of lacquer would never go away, that the workmen would be arguing forever and the dumb oxen wandering into the residence hall, one fall day they were all gone as suddenly as they had come, and the temple stood like a dazzling jewel in the sun, scrubbed and polished and as perfect as the Buddha-nature itself, or nearly.

The Empress came in her ivory carriage to gaze upon it, and was so pleased that she made the boxer an official of the ninth rank, and bestowed upon him the yellow robe and the brass belt, as well as an income of the taxes of three hundred families for as long as he should live.

Now he was a mandarin, an abbot, an architect. A rich man with a fabulous home. He had even enjoyed the rare satisfaction of seeing men grovel who had once sneered at him.

Yet his thoughts were not so much with the Empress, who had bestowed all this upon him, as with the flaxen-haired, green-eyed Sogdian girl who had, according to the best of his calculations, recently given birth to his first child.

14

THE TAOIST'S REVENGE

No sooner were the renovations completed than the boxer saddled his tarpan and rode to the market with the hope of visiting the new baby and its mother. Summer had come and gone, and fall was upon them. The branches of the trees that lined the way made an intricate tracery against the slate-gray sky. Leaves drifted beneath the tarpan's hooves.

When he reached the South Market, he left his horse at the stable and went to look for a present to commemorate the birth. He strolled through the bazaars, reveling in the chaotic displays of goods, the smells of foods and spices, the merchants bickering with customers over the worth of their goods. Here he was home. Every merchant knew him, and had heard the wondrous story of his success, for citizens of every age love to tell of a man passing from one of fate's extremes to the other. As he swaggered by their stalls, they winked at him or tossed him some fruit or trinket to cultivate his good grace. Those who knew him well enjoyed the honor of a few words of conversation and, when he was feeling particularly generous, some tidbit of palace gossip.

He stopped at the stall of a friend, a jeweler, to admire a jade stag small enough to fit in his palm. The deer was a symbol of long life. The Sogdian girl would like that.

"How much?"

"For you it's free. If you could just mention my work to the Empress."

"I'll do that," he lied, and, slipping the stag into his sleeve, moved along.

When he reached the wine shop, the Sogdian girl was nowhere in sight. He had a few glasses, thinking she would turn up sooner or later. He tried to enjoy the puppet show, but the antics of the puppets seemed foolish and irritating. Some mandarins of low rank who would curry favor with the Empress offered to buy his wine, but he would have nothing to do with them. He could simply have gone upstairs and asked the old stepmother where she was and when she was returning, but thoughts of death in childbirth had been plaguing him, thoughts he feared might be confirmed. The Hour of the Goat became the Hour of the Monkey, and still she did not show herself.

Finally he sought out the old stepmother. As he climbed the stairs to her third-floor office, a singing girl in a colorful robe brushed past him; recognizing him as a good customer, which is to say a wealthy one, she smiled boldly and let her hand brush against his, but his thoughts were only for the Sogdian girl.

The old stepmother was kneeling at a desk, calculating her worth. Her fingers, rattling the beads of the abacus, were as thin and knobby as a chicken's claw. Although she must have heard him, she didn't look up.

"Where's the Sogdian girl?" the boxer demanded, feeling the weight of the present in his sleeve.

Now she turned to him and fixed him with one eye that bulged from its socket.

"You don't know?"

Her voice creaked like the lid of a cash box.

"Of course not. How would I?"

"You sent her there."

"Where?"

"To the Land of Ghosts."

A knot formed in his stomach, and his throat began to constrict. "I don't like that kind of joke."

"It's no joke. One girl fewer in my stable, thanks to you." She held up the abacus and slid one bead along the wire, subtracting, to illustrate the point.

He felt a chill, even though, in a corner of the room, a fire crackled merrily within a heating stove. Outside in the street, two men were arguing over the price of a pig.

"If you're lying to me . . ." He turned his fists together, as if to wring her scrawny throat.

She reached behind the desk and brought out a big leather sack with a drawstring opening. From it she removed the four-stringed, bent-necked Kuchean lute, inlaid with mother-of-pearl unicorns and gazelles, on which the singing girl loved to play. He took it from her and held it in his arms as though it were the infant he had come to see.

"One of the Yü-lin Guard snuck into her home and strangled her in her bath. Didn't stop there, either. Slaughtered her three children and her brother so that no one would be left to avenge her."

"She had children?" he whispered.

The stepmother snorted contemptuously. "You're just like the rest. You love to believe you're the first and only, the start and the end."

"Tell me which member of the guard it was, and I'll bring you his head on a pike."

"It doesn't matter. He was a good soldier, carrying out his orders."

"And who gave these orders? Tell me quick!"

"A friend of yours. Heaven's Chosen. The wolf-woman Wu."

"You're lying, old whore . . ."

She laughed. "He calls the goat a goat and thinks to insult it."

He hurled the lute at the wall. The neck cracked and the strings sounded all at once in a terrible dissonant chord. Then he gave a savage kick to the table, sending the abacus, ink stick, and palette clattering to the floor. A scroll of cheap hemp paper on which she had been recording the accounts sailed across the room, unwinding like the dragon's tongue that seeks its prey.

Then he fled.

All was silent in the Dragon Hall, for the aged censor Hsü Yu-kung had just begun to speak. Suddenly the quiet was broken by the clatter of sandals, the swish of robes. A hundred mandarins turned their aloof, superior gazes in the direction of the sound. Recognizing the boxer, they smiled to themselves, for his appearance in court always boded an amusing incident of one sort or another.

He didn't bother to pick up his audience tablet, or join the queue waiting to deliver their memorials and petitions, or even perform the three kneelings and the nine kowtows, but simply strode before the throne, and made his demands of the Empress:

"I want to talk to you—now."

A dozen members of the Yü-lin Guard stepped forward, hands on their swords, and looked to the Empress for orders.

Censor Hsü opened his eyes wide with astonishment. He held up his ivory audience tablet for the boxer's inspection, and said in a quiet voice, "I am memorializing. You must wait your turn. This is not some tavern where all men shout at once, and comport themselves however the mood seizes them. This is the Palace of Heaven's Chosen. Please behave yourself accordingly."

The boxer glanced at the Empress. Her face had never been more masklike. The eyes glittered like jewels set in jade.

"Certainly," she began, "the honorable abbot of the White Horse Temple would not interrupt the proceedings of government except to report an emergency of the most dire sort, one that threatens the very existence of the Middle Kingdom. For this reason We shall ask the forgiveness of Censor Hsü, and request that the Officer of Protocol adjourn Our session until this afternoon."

With this, she rose and disappeared behind the curtain. Within minutes her favorite eunuch arrived to lead the boxer to her. The pretty fellow led him down long corridors and along loggias overlooking courtyards of naked plum and cherry trees, to the most distant part of the palace, a wise precaution lest voices be raised and harsh words overheard. The Empress was waiting in a tiny sitting room, bare but for a scroll of calligraphy on one wall. The screens were closed, the air stagnant.

"Is it true?" the boxer demanded. "Did you order her killed?"

"If you are referring to the Sogdian girl, yes." She was completely impassive, disinterested. She might have been discussing some drought in a southern province. "You cannot be permitted intimacy with such a woman, a woman of low birth who is lacking in propriety and virtue. It is too dangerous. You are privy to secrets of state."

"Miserable wolf of a woman! Who told you?"

"There was a scroll in the urn. Penetration of the Abstruse."

She was referring to a bronze urn that had recently been placed in the entrance of the Dragon Hall. It had four holes in its lid through which scrolls or slips of paper could be dropped, but removed only by a designated official, by opening the entire urn. "Delayed Favor," the opening to the east, was for receiving petitions from those who considered themselves worthy candidates for office; "Invite Rebuke," the south opening, was for criticism of government; "Redress of Grievances," the west opening, was for complaints of oppression and injustice; and the opening called "Penetration of the Abstruse" was intended for prophecies, predictions, and information about secret military schemes. Even in the few months since its installation, it had distinguished itself as an unusual instrument of vengeance. Among the first of its victims was its inventor, the son of a censor. A note in the north slot implicated him in supplying arms to the rebellion of the previous year.

"That stupid urn!" the boxer said. "How can you trust a scroll that has no signature? I used to know men who were such cowards they would not fight face to face. Instead, they snuck up on their enemy's house in the dead of night, threw a paving stone through a screen, and fled, weeping with fear. They are the ones who make reports to your urn."

"Nonetheless, it is true."

"I know! That cursed Taoist! That scum of a sorcerer! He did it. He would do anything to get back at me. Why did I ever ask you to spare his life? I will go find him now and cut off his balls as well as his hair!"

"You will not touch him."

"Don't order me! I'll listen to you no more. The stories about you are true. Your soul is blacker than the blackest weasel spirit. I would never see your dreadful face again."

He expected anything but what happened next. The Empress twisted away from him and held one hand like a fan over her face. A choking sound came from her, difficult to identify.

She was crying.

He was taken aback. He had never seen her cry before, never thought her capable of it. Her strength, discipline, and cunning were such that he tended to forget she was human. He grew concerned. He really did love her, he realized with surprise. Sometimes our own hearts are as mysterious as the earth's deepest caves. He approached her and pulled gently at the hand that covered her face.

"No!" she said, shaking her head.

He tried again and this time she allowed it. Her marvelous makeup had run like a scroll left in the rain, revealing all her flaws. Her face, he saw, was old, lined, dry, wrinkled. Kneeling beside her, he put his arms around her. A dusting of her face powder fell across his robe. He could feel her body heaving. He raised her face by the chin and kissed her.

They played at the Clouds and Rain and he pretended passion.

Afterwards he rose and began hunting through the pile of discarded clothing for his under-robe. The Empress gazed with fascination at the great, spent log of his penis, shifting from side to side as he moved, still turgid and red, shiny with a coating of fluid.

"Promise you will never take another lover?" she said.

"I promise," he said too easily.

She inclined her head a few degrees to the left and gave him that smile that made him so uncomfortable. Had her tears been real, or had she turned his rage to ardor with a few well-calculated gestures? The thought that he could be so easily manipulated terrified him.

"Then you have no objection to me applying a palace warder?"

"I don't know," he said. "What's that?"

"A gecko lizard is fed cinnabar until he turns as plump and red as the dragon that hangs between your legs." She tapped it with her finger and watched it swing like a pendulum. "Then he is killed and ground to a paste. A mark made with such a paste has magical properties. If the woman—or man—who wears it is unfaithful to the one who has applied it, the mark vanishes."

"Cinnabar, the favorite stuff of Taoist sorcerers. Could this, too, be the work of my rival?"

She didn't reply.

"And what if the mark comes off by itself?" the boxer pressed. "Must I never bathe again, or swim in the Lo, or press too hard against my bedding?"

"As long as you are faithful to Us, rest assured the mark will last."

"Don't you trust me?" he said feebly.

"Of course We trust you."

"Then what need have we of palace warders?"

"Then why resist Our suggestion?"

He sighed.

She brought out a jar of red paste and a brush of the sort that is used to apply makeup. No sooner had she removed the lid than the stench of it made him want to retch. Forcing him to lie still upon his back, she straddled him and painted a stylized blossom just over his solar plexus, his life-center. He laced his fingers behind his head, and watched her work with a strange detachment. He saw her, as if for the first time, a pampered old woman, narrow at the shoulders, the little globe of her stomach transversed by purple meridians where pregnancies had stretched the skin too far, her teats hanging flat against her chest, sucked dry by dozens of T'ang princes, most dead now by her own hand. Her body spoke more honestly of who she was than did her well-preserved face.

"Don't move," she said when she was finished, and, leaning very close, blew on the design she had painted. "There," she said, some time later. "Try to smear it or wipe it away."

The boxer picked at it with his fingernails, then scrubbed at it with a wet index finger. Rather than reassuring him, the permanancy of the foul-smelling glaze on his skin made him feel trapped, branded, bound. She might as well have planted one of her eyes there instead, so much did he feel that she now was witness to everything he said and did, and even thought.

Dressing, he lifted his robe and was surprised by a weight in the sleeve. He reached in and took out the jade stag. A symbol of long life. He wanted to laugh and cry at the same time.

"What's that?" the Empress asked.

"Nothing." He didn't know what to say. "Something I picked up in the marketplace." He hesitated for a moment and then handed it to her. "For you."

Not quite understanding what he was doing, or why, the boxer wandered the streets of Lo-yang past the time when the gates of the better neighborhoods were closed and barred for the night. He walked until he found himself in the worst part of the city, where the poor people lived crowded together in rickety bamboo tenements, where the streets were lined with taverns that stank of urine and old rice wine, and the kind of prostitutes known simply as "flowers" stood on the street because they had no one to pay for their rooms; where cutpurses, swindlers, and outlaw bands came to buy their liquor and spend their booty.

Once he had lived here too. Now it seemed as strange as a barbarian land.

He went from tavern to tavern, getting more drunk. At each tavern he would, as if by chance, take a seat beside the most sword-scarred, dangerous-looking patron, and after a few drinks he would begin to converse with him. The conversations began nicely enough. But little by little the boxer grew abusive, insulting him, provoking him, goading him on to a fight. He couldn't help it. He felt like one of the puppets at the wine shop, forced by some shadowy puppeteer to place itself in terrible jeopardy.

An ordinary man, under such circumstances, would not have lived long. But, just as Heaven had quenched the flames of the little monk's pyre, so She made the worst of men, for a few hours that night, even-tempered and prudent. Each time the boxer insulted a brigand, the brigand rose above it. Each time he spilled a drink on some lowlife, the lowlife, in a burst of good-heartedness, forgave him. Some even offered words of counsel, advising him to find strength at his ancestral shrine, or confess his woes to the abbot of his temple. In the last of the taverns he visited that night, two ruffians, acting with extraordinary compassion, raised him by the shoulders, carried him out to the river Lo, which ran nearby, and threw him in.

He emerged from it sputtering, cold, dead sober, and with a new resolve that was to prove even more dangerous than his activities to date.

THE BUDDHIST'S REVENGE

White Pheasant was waiting up at the temple, beside himself with worry. As soon as the boxer arrived, the eunuch sat him down near the stove in the cooking shed, pulled off his wet robes, dried him with silks, brought him fresh clothes, and fed him hot tea and a plate of his favorite dumplings, southern-style, stuffed with cabbage, ginger, scallions, and pork butt, seasoned with soy, sesame oil, and wine.

The boxer ate them all, then rose and walked out to the center courtyard. The eunuch ran after him, fearful of what madness he might try next. The boxer approached the great evening bell with its hundred and eight knobs, one for each of man's delusions, and pulled back the striker, which was suspended by two ropes from a wooden frame, so that it could swing horizontally.

"Sir," White Pheasant began, "it's the middle of the night, do you think it's appropriate to ring the—"

Before he could finish, the boxer hurled the striker toward the bell.

White Pheasant clapped his palms over his ears and grimaced.

The boxer rang the bell again and again. The deep, stomach-rumbling sound reverberated throughout the temple complex.

In moments the monks came straggling out of the residence hall, their under-robes glowing in the moonlight, and walked barefoot through the mud to where the boxer stood.

"Well?" said the Korean, who wore his leopard skin over his under-robe even when he slept. "You'd better have a good reason for waking me if you want to live to see the dawn."

"The Sogdian girl was executed," the boxer said, "and her family extinguished."

"I'm sorry to hear it," the Korean said. "She was clever, and a good lutist. Pretty, too, in a strange way." Then, in a soft voice, "And the baby?"

"There is no baby," the boxer said.

All the monks looked at the ground and were silent.

"Life is a dream," the Buddhist monk said. "I can perform a funeral service if you like."

The boxer didn't seem to hear him. "It's the fault of that black-souled Taoist sorcerer. He put a note in the urn saying that she and I had been sharing the pillow."

"But I'll bet the Empress gave the orders," Pinch Purse pointed out. "She kills her rivals the way you and me crack lice."

"Don't speak ill of your patron!" the boxer snapped. "She's only trying to do the virtuous thing."

"He's right," said False Brush. "Since the Empress kills, killing must be a virtue. Since she kills so many, it must be the greatest virtue. Since it is the greatest virtue, we should refrain from it, lest Heaven believe that we try to steal its glory, or—"

"Would someone shut him up," the boxer ordered, then went on, "It's the sorcerer who's behind it all, and don't anybody say otherwise. I'm going to his temple right now and shave his head bare. Then maybe I'll cut off his balls. Now what I want to know is who's coming with me? Four good men will do."

"Meeting him in the Dragon Hall is one thing," White Pheasant said nervously, "but at night in his chambers is another. He has powerful magic. What if he casts a spell and makes us think we are geese?"

"Then you'll hardly notice the difference," the Korean said.

The others laughed.

"We don't have to be scared of his magic," the boxer said, looking significantly at the little monk. "We've got magic of our own."

The little monk was so pious that everybody assumed he had supernatural powers, even though he denied it whenever he was asked.

"I'll come," said the Korean.

"Me too," said Pinch Purse.

White Pheasant and False Brush also volunteered, but the boxer judged the first too feminine, the second too mad.

"What we need," he went on, "is some good Buddhist magic to challenge their Taoist magic." And he stared at the little monk again.

"What you plan to do," the little monk said, "is violent and foolish. You tease the ripples of karma into waves. In time they will knock you off your feet and drown you."

"As the abbot of this temple, I order you to come."

The little monk gazed at him for a moment longer, then turned and hobbled back to his bed.

The boxer watched him go, opening his hands and making fists of them. Finally he shouted, "Go on! Go back to bed!" And added, in a lower voice, "Who needs him anyway."

The night, which had been clear, closed around them in a thickening mist as they urged their horses toward the Taoist temple. It was a cold, dank thing that seemed to track them like a predator. When viewed from the corner of the eye, it took the form of beasts and demons, but looked upon directly, it was as featureless as a vast expanse of snow. Finding their way became a game of chance. Even the Korean, who had an infallible sense of direction, grew uncertain about north and south. In time they arrived at a stony promontory overlooking a valley dotted with tall, slender pines. At the bottom it was a blackness, a void, a well dug down to the earth's core. An owl hooted. The horses whinnied and danced back and forth, and no amount of whispering would calm them.

"It should be down there," the Korean said.

As if in response to his words, a ray of moonlight pierced the mist, revealing, far below them, the tiled roofs of the Temple of the Prince of the Grand Tranquility. The procession of dark, gloomy meeting halls was surrounded by a high wall and gate. In the center courtyard, instead of the pagoda, which was a Buddhist symbol, stood the sorcerer's mysterious laboratory.

"It gives me the chills," Pinch Purse said.

"Let's go while the horses can see their way," the Korean said. The less time they had to reflect and feed their fear, the better. He pulled the leopard skin tight around his shoulders and, slapping the haunches of his mount, disappeared down the steep gravel path that led to the valley floor. The others paused only an instant before they followed.

As they neared the temple they could hear the monks chanting the Taoist prayers, prayers handed down from the nature cult of ancient times, one of several underground springs that fed the eclectic river of Taoism. The boxer held a finger to his lips. The tarpans, intuitively understanding, stepped lightly. Only the clatter of dislodged gravel betrayed their presence.

The temple gates were barred. By standing on the shoulders of the boxer, who in turn sat upon his mount, the Korean could reach the scalloped cornice that ran along the top of the wall. Grabbing it with both hands, he pulled himself up and over. They heard the grunt of him landing, the thud of punches being exchanged, gasps and groans, then silence. Moments later the gates swung open. The boxer and Pinch Purse ran inside and found the Korean tying and gagging the pair of long-haired Taoist monks who were supposed to be on guard.

The three of them sneaked along the loggia that surrounded the courtyard, keeping to the shadows. Seen up close, the sorcerer's laboratory was even more exotic. The materials and decoration of the four walls and the entryway had been inspired by the five elements—fire, water, earth, wood, and iron—and their associated symbols and compass orientations; thus the east wall, made of wood, displayed a green dragon with a curled tail; the south wall, made of gold to symbolize the element fire, displayed a scarlet bird; the iron west wall, a white tiger; and the north wall, cut of crystal to symbolize the element water, a black tortoise. The entryway, of earthen bricks baked in a magical fire, was painted with a great yellow dragon, the door disguised as his mouth.

"He's probably praying with the rest of them," the boxer said. "We'll break into his laboratory and wait for him. I've heard that he likes to work at night. The rays of the moon enhance his magic."

All three of them looked up at the moon. The mist raced across its yellow face like the veil of a harem dancer.

"The moon's nearly full," Pinch Purse observed in a trembling voice.

"You can still turn back," the boxer said.

"I ain't scared of these long-haired grandmothers," Pinch Purse assured him.

The door within the yellow dragon's mouth (the handle was an up-turned fang a foot long) opened easily. The chamber was dark, steeped in shifting shadows. A red glow came from coals smoldering in a brazier, and a cool blue moonbeam, magnified by a lens embedded in the roof, shone down on a cauldron of silvery liquid. Tendrils of lavender smoke rose from the surface, beckoning them like the fingers of a seductress.

The fire flared, and for an instant they could see the yin-yang symbol painted on the ceiling and, in concentric circles around it, the eight mystical trigrams, the sixty-four hexagrams. For a fleeting instant they were aware of tables and shelves crowded with pots of chemicals, with ingots of metals stacked in neat pyramids, with mortars and pestles, with scales and balances, with magical mixing spoons the size of the human heart, with scrolls of charms and recipes for making gold and prolonging human life for a thousand years. Then the fire burned low again, plunging them into darkness.

They moved forward on tiptoe, feeling their way. Something crashed. They stood dead still, scarcely daring to breathe. The distant chanting continued uninterrupted.

"Sorry," whispered Pinch Purse.

"Wait!" the boxer said. "I think I've found a candle."

"Light it from the coals," the Korean said.

"That's just what I'm doing, you rancid camel dung."

The next moment a firefly of light detached itself from the brazier and moved to illuminate the boxer's face. Thus armed, he began to investigate the laboratory more closely.

"Hadn't we better hide?" Pinch Purse asked nervously, while the boxer peered at a beaker of cinnabar.

"We've got plenty of time," the boxer said. "They're still praying. They'll be a while. Relax."

Curious, the Korean reached across the hearth and inserted his hand into the beam of moonlight. He gasped and pulled it back quickly, for the light was icy cold, and where it had struck him, the skin had turned transparent, permitting him to see the array of tiny bones in his hand, a sight that filled him with dismay.

"Hey, look at this," the boxer whispered.

The others crowded around him. He was holding the candle next to a melon-sized glass sphere. Within it, a tiny, scaly creature with webbed feet swam in a pale blue liquid.

"A dragon," Pinch Purse whispered. "A real one."

"Bah!" the Korean spat. "It's a lizard. We should eat him. They're good with lots of salt."

"You ignorant turtle spawn," the boxer said. "Break the glass and he'll grow to a hundred times this size and eat us instead. Now look at this."

He held the candle beside the next glass sphere. Inside it, suspended in a milky solution, was a human fetus, with a huge, translucent cranium and tiny, fragile limbs. Its umbilical chord penetrated the side of the sphere and connected with a pig's bladder filled with a mysterious fluid. Deep within the chest of the fetus, a heart throbbed and glowed like a jewel.

"Tell me *that's* not magic," Pinch Purse whispered.

"It's sorcery, all right," the boxer agreed. "We'd better be careful." He wrapped his fingers around the hilt of the K'un-wu sword he wore on his belt.

The Korean and Pinch Purse already had their daggers drawn.

The rest of the glass spheres contained equally remarkable specimens of botany and biology, miniature unicorns and mermaids, plants with sapphire blossoms, a stone that changed colors. But it was the figure imprisoned in the last of the spheres that gave them pause. He wore a tiny, tiaralike crown on his head, and his earlobes had been stretched until they nearly reached his shoulders, as was the practice of Brahmans in ancient times. Though he sat cross-legged in meditation, his eyes gazed up at them imploringly.

"Our Buddha," the boxer exclaimed with dismay. "The sorcerer has trapped him! We've got to set him loose."

"Wait," the Korean said, but he wasn't quick enough.

The boxer touched the glass sphere and it popped like a bubble. There was no Buddha within it, or any other material thing, but rather a sweet-smelling amber smoke.

"Where'd he go?" the boxer asked.

"It was only a dream," the Korean said. "What is this smoke? Some kind of incense. It makes my limbs cold and heavy."

"Mine too," Pinch Purse agreed. "Could this be some kind of enchantment? I can barely move. What about you?"

But the boxer, who had been standing directly over the sphere and had breathed most heavily of the smoke, could not even form a word, and simply stood there like some great dumb thing with his mouth hanging half-open.

The three of them retained barely enough mobility to turn their eyes toward the door, which was now opening. There was a flash of blue feathers, and the sorcerer appeared, staff in hand. He gazed at them from beneath his hooded eyes and smiled.

"Good evening, honorable visitors," he said with mock politeness. "How thoughtful of you to visit a poor, lonely priest like me—for lonely I am since my fall from the Empress's favor. How can I entertain you? Perhaps some wine, and delicacies, and singing girls might be in order. I know you love these things at your so-called Temple of the Wily Whore. Alas, I have naught but millet and turnips, for the Empress gives us no more cash, and the lay people are afraid to contribute now. Do millet and turnips suit you?"

He looked at them each, as though they might answer if he allowed enough time. Then he went on, "Why don't you speak? Have you nothing to say? You should have brought the Vinaya master. He had so much to say at the Empress's debate, so many confusing words that I forgot my own. But I will make my rebuttal tonight, of that you may be certain." Then he noticed the dagger in the Korean's hand. "But what's this? Have you come to trim my hair? Or make a worse cut, one that drains the life from my body? Cut yourself instead, Korean."

No sooner had he said this than the Korean was horrified to see his own hand, like the hand of an enemy, turn the dagger toward his own heart. Yet, being otherwise paralyzed, there was nothing he could do but try to will it away; he tried until he sweated and trembled from the effort, and all to no end. The tip of the blade pressed against his chest, harder and harder, until blood seeped into the weave of his robe.

"Enough," the sorcerer said.

The Korean's hand went limp, the dagger clattered to the floor. The bloody spot on the front of his robe slowly swelled.

"You must live," the sorcerer said, "to experience the humiliation to come. I plan to remove the mark of the palace warder from the boxer's broad chest. That should give you something to discuss the next time you see the Empress. I mixed the warder for her in the first place, and I alone know how to remove it. A bit of dragon spittle on a black silk towel. I'll attend to that later. First I must administer the potion, for it is nearly ready."

He tossed measured amounts of red clay, talc, sulfur, the ashes of a woman's hair, and the ground hoof of a pig into the cauldron. Finally he added a spoonful of cinnabar. The brew hissed, turned crimson, and tossed up billows of steam. Shadowy forms of strange creatures, part snake, part lizard, and part insect, seemed to scamper up and down the moonbeam as though it were a tunnel to another place. The sorcerer smiled. His face, illuminated from below by the hearth, took on a demonic aspect. Using an iron ladle, he scooped up some of the liquid and transferred it into a cup carved from a piece of stone and decorated all over with mystical designs.

"It is a very powerful potion," he said to the boxer. "You have only to touch your tongue to it and the yang will flow from your being and never return. Your breasts will swell, your skin grow soft, your beard vanish. And that Jade Stalk, the part of you that the Empress loves so well, will become a soft little thing, useless except for emptying the bladder. Let us see how such a change affects her passion for Buddhism."

The boxer's eyes darted back and forth nervously, and sweat beaded his brow.

"Here, boxer," the sorcerer said, approaching him. "Take the cup."

The boxer did as he was told, despite himself.

"Now raise the cup to your mouth," the sorcerer said. "Drink deeply of it."

The boxer felt his hand bring the cup close, his mouth open. He tried to close it again, but his muscles wouldn't cooperate. Concentrating with his entire being, he willed his arm to punch, his legs to run. It was like calling out to someone who wasn't there.

"Go on," the sorcerer said gently, enjoying every moment of it.

The boxer watched the cup approach, felt its rough surface against his lower lip.

The steam from it burned the delicate lining of his nose. Even the odor weakened him. He knew, for one horrible second, that what the sorcerer said was true, that once he had sipped from the stone cup he would be like a eunuch, stripped of the only thing he had ever possessed that was of any value. He saw himself living in the gutter, picking through garbage in search of a morsel of food, wrapping himself in rags come winter.

"Drink," the sorcerer said.

A rock knocked the cup from his hands. It hit the floor and split in two, the potion spreading along the cracks in the floor, hissing, leaving a trail of purple vapor.

The moment of unexpected violence broke the spell. The boxer and his compatriots found that they could move again. They turned toward the door of the laboratory to see who had saved them.

The little monk, leaning on his crutch near the doorway, bowed his head. "Karma or not, I couldn't leave you to be destroyed."

"Destroyed?" the boxer said, gathering his wits. He grabbed the sorcerer by the collar of his robe and lifted him to his toes. "No Taoist swine is going to destroy me. I'd just about figured out a way to break the spell, but I was waiting for the right moment to try it. Now who would like to deal this feathery rascal the first blow?"

The sorcerer's hooded eyes turned fearfully from one face to the next.

The little monk shook his head. "We must not touch him."

"If we don't kill him now," the boxer objected, "he'll get us next time."

"Perhaps he will show us the same mercy we have shown him," the little monk replied.

"Not likely," the Korean said. "I say we finish him off, once and for all."

"Let him be," the little monk said.

The boxer refused to let go of his collar. "But he was going to make an old lady out of me!"

"Let him be," the little monk said, "or I'll fight on his behalf."

The Korean raised his eyebrows. He had heard the story about the little monk beating away four assailants with his Shao-lin-style fighting.

"Then what are we supposed to do?" the boxer asked with indignation.

"Go home," the little monk said.

"Can't we even shave his—"

"Come," the little monk said, putting the crutch under his arm and hobbling toward the door.

The boxer looked back at the sorcerer, sighed, shook his head, and dropped him. The sorcerer fell to his hands and knees and remained in that position, eyes on the floor, motionless.

"You ain't seen the last of us," Pinch Purse said, shaking a fist at him. But then he turned and followed the others.

The Korean brought up the rear.

The Taoist monks were just finishing their prayers.

When the boxer and his friends were outside the temple, mounted and about to ride off, the Korean said, "I left my dagger on the floor. It was a gift from my father. I must go back for it. I'll just be a moment."

He jumped down from his horse and ran back inside the gate. A few moments later they heard shouts of anger and fear. A glow within the walls grew brighter as they watched. The Korean came running out of the gate, followed by the Taoist monks, who were screaming at him, shaking their fists, grabbing rocks off the ground and hurling them at him.

"Go!" the Korean screamed at his friends. He leaped onto his own horse, kicked it to a gallop, and sped away.

As they rode for their very lives up the gravel road out of the valley, they could hear the crackle of the fire spreading behind them, consuming the dry wooden walls of the sorcerer's laboratory and the halls beyond it.

THE BOXER IN MORE TROUBLE

Standing in the Dragon Hall before an audience of several hundred, clutching his ivory tablet in hands that shook with age though never with fear, Censor Hsü began to memorialize:

"The real menace to our empire is not the Turks who threaten our northern border, or the Tibetans who would attack us in the west, or the peasants who flee taxation, or the rampant inflation of our currency, or even the droughts and famines that beset the eastern provinces, but rather one lone man who wears the robe of an abbot and who is accompanied by a band of thugs who call themselves monks. Recently this 'abbot' supervised the renovations of the White Horse Temple, a task that should have cost, at the very most, three or four hundred thousand strings of cash. Instead he spent more than one million strings. On another occasion he and his monks visited the Monastery of the Prince of the Grand Tranquility in the middle of the night, and burned it to the ground. The last time I memorialized about this band of scoundrels, they intercepted me on the street and beat me until I was nearly unconscious. Learning that I was preparing another memorial about their exploits, these same 'monks' visited my home in the middle of the night, dragged me from my bed, tied me by the heels, and hung me upside down from a roofbeam. Once I was bound helpless in this manner, they searched my study until they found the scroll containing the memorial I had been composing, and defecated upon it. They told me that if I ever memorialized against them again, it would mean my death. For such scoundrels to be allowed to roam free, destroying property and attacking men of virtue at their whim, offends Heaven. Let them be executed this day, or banished to a frontier province where they may be of some use battling our enemies. Let us act with the wisdom of the sage kings of ancient times, and bring this matter to a quick resolution."

"We will consider your suggestion," the Empress replied with seeming indifference.

In fact, Censor Hsü's repeated memorializing against the boxer and his men upset her more than she dared show. She would have done away with the old man by fabricating his involvement in some treacherous scheme, were he not so singularly virtuous, unflaggingly loyal, forthright in his views, and above corruption and pettiness. To punish such a man unjustly, she had learned from experience, offended the court. While the mandate to rule was supposedly granted by Heaven, the court had been known, in the reigns of previous sovereigns, to revoke it with blinding speed.

She responded as she usually did to such dilemmas, by seeking the advice of her daughter. A messenger was dispatched to summon Princess T'ai P'ing to the Inner Palace with all possible haste. She arrived limping, her riding pants mottled with mud.

"What in the world happened to you?" the Empress asked, looking her up and down.

"I was in the middle of a polo match," the princess said. "And winning, too."

"Polo? You were playing polo?"

"Yes."

"With men?"

"No, Mother, with sheep. Of course I was playing with men! There are not enough women players in our kingdom to make a team, much less two. But it's all right. I hid my hair beneath my peaked cap so I looked like a man. Most of them thought I was Great-Aunt's Turkish groom. How I wish you had been there. Imagine me, galloping down the field with my mallet held high." Grabbing a fan from one of the servants, she straddled a stool and began to bounce as though on a mount. "The ball comes toward me and I lean so far over the side of my steed that I am nearly scraping the gravel. One of my opponents tries to block me. The whore's son strikes me in the calf with his mallet, as though by accident (that is why I limp). I knock him out of the way and hit the ball," she swung the fan furiously, "so it streaks through the air like an arrow, straight to the goal!"

"Will you never learn the proper behavior for a woman?"

The princess inclined her head a few degrees and regarded her mother with a catlike smile.

"Is being supreme sovereign of the Middle Kingdom proper behavior for a woman? If it is, than surely you can find no fault in my playing a little polo."

The Empress laughed. "Ah, daughter dear, you are my match and more. Of all the royal heirs, Lis and Chous, only you have the intelligence and strength to rule after me."

"Some say that in the ancient days of the Wu priests, women ruled over men, and passed the mandate to their daughters. Perhaps it will be that way again."

"Perhaps," the Empress agreed. "But the hour is still early for such discussions. We wish your counsel in another matter."

"It is the boxer again," the princess said with certainty.

"How do you know?"

"Everyone knows. Censor Hsü's latest memorial is the talk of the court."

"What can I do?"

"Send him to my house late tonight. Tell him that I have some new tricks of the Jade Chamber to teach him. When he arrives, I will have my servants beat him to death."

The Empress gasped and put a hand on her breast. "But We could not. He is too dear to Us. We have had so little happiness in Our life. Our years as consort to the Emperor and his father were as tedious as a prison sentence. When We became Empress, so many enemies arose that We could not relax Our vigilance for an instant. Only now, with the boxer, have We learned to laugh like a child. Oh, he is so amusing! We wish you could see him as We do. Sometimes, when he is feeling lighthearted, he teaches Us drinking songs and tells Us such comic stories, acting all the parts in different voices. And when he imitates the ministers, We laugh until Our sides ache and We lose control of Our water."

"I admit that is a side of him I have not seen," the princess said dryly.

Reaching out, she took her mother's hand and stroked it gently, as if to soften the effect of what she was about to say.

"You will have to get rid of him sooner or later. Every day he becomes more of a threat to you. He is like an animal, with no sense of propriety, blundering here and there, creating havoc at every turn."

Her mother looked away. "Do not talk about him so. Every day he becomes more refined. Some days he is even sagelike. Here is a poem he wrote, as best I can remember it.

The matter of life and death is great.
Time runs quickly and nothing remains; it waits for no man.
Thus it must not be wasted.

"Is it not a profound sentiment? And you liken him to an animal."

"Mother, you know as well as I that it is a very popular poem among these death-loving Buddhists, and probably dates back to the coming of Bodhidharma. You will find it scribbled on every monastery wall."

"It did seem familiar," the Empress admitted.

"Take my advice and put an end to him now. You've worked too hard and too long to sacrifice everything for a few pleasant afternoons with this rascal."

The Empress smiled and shook her head. "When you grow old, Death becomes as familiar as the servant who pours your bath. He sits opposite you at dinner, and strolls beside you in the garden. Sometimes he comes so close that you can feel his breath on your neck. Then all the Taoist spells and Buddhist discourse are to no avail, and the only reassurance is of a strong young man's arms."

"There are other young men with strong arms," the princess pointed out.

"I must have him," the Empress said, starting to weep.

The princess rose and put her arms around her mother. "I'm sorry, Mother. I will make no more objections." And then: "I have a thought. What if we could move him inside the palace? Then you could keep an eye on him."

"Yes, that's a good idea," the Empress agreed. "Let us think of a pretext."

"We shall, I know it."

"Ah, you are a wonderful daughter indeed," the Empress said, and held the princess tight, not minding in the least the mud that soiled her pink robes.

The boxer had heard about Censor Hsü's latest memorial against him and, knowing that love was like a sapling that could only bear to be bent so far, he wondered if this, following so closely upon the revelation of his affair with the Sogdian girl, was the end. Holding his ivory audience tablet, he crept toward the Empress's platform and kowtowed, then looked up with dread. (The young Emperor was nowhere in sight.)

She was smiling.

He exhaled. Somehow he had gotten off again. He must have stored up some very good karma in those other lives.

"We are of Chou, a venerable family of the northwest," she began. "As you know, there was another Chou dynasty in ancient times who were virtuous emperors, honored by Heaven. The Duke of Chou was a great sage who invented writing. One reason, as We see it, for their long reign was the building of a Ming-t'ang, a hall to honor Heaven. The emperors who preceded Us wished to build such a hall, but their small-hearted and literal-minded officials could not reach an agreement about its size or shape, its style of construction or placement. My own Scholars of the North Gate have fared better. By poring over the histories and the classics, by consulting with astrologers and seers, and by exercising their own resourcefulness and ingenuity, they have discovered the true nature of such a hall. Now it waits only for a man of virtue to superintend the job. After your splendid work at the White Horse, you were the obvious choice."

"Thank you," the boxer said. "I promise I will do my best to make this Ming-t'ang pleasing to Heaven." He thought of the cash he had diverted to his own pocket during the temple renovations. How much more might he make off with on a project such as this? His senses reeled at the prospect, as his heart soared from the honor. "Where will it be built?"

"Here, on the site of the Phoenix Hall where we now meet."

She regarded the roof beams and walls with a frown. "This hall, with its faded colors and dour statues, has never pleased Us."

The boxer looked around too. "Yes," he agreed, "we'll build something much fancier, as big as a mountain, with dragons and phoenixes all over it. We'll build a Ming-t'ang that people will talk about for centuries to come."

"Of course, you will have to live at the palace during its construction." She performed a lascivious gesture, opening her lips slightly and revealing the point of her tongue.

The boxer grinned, trying to look as though more time for intimacy was what he dreamed of, when the contrary was the case. In fact, he was no longer the young man who could make the Vigorous Peak three times a night. She was draining him. Yin and yang were in imbalance. He worried that soon nothing would remain of him but a brittle shell like that of an insect who dies beneath a hot sun.

"I will send a dozen servants to pack your things, and carts to carry them here. Meanwhile, you must appoint someone to supervise the translation in your absence. The Vinaya master would be a wise choice."

"I'll talk to him about it as soon as I get back."

"So. Very good. That takes care of it all, except for the clipping."

"The clipping?" the boxer said, his flesh beginning to crawl.

"When Censor Hsü learned that you would be coming to live in the palace, he insisted on it. It is only proper that a man who lives in the palace endure the 'palace punishment.'"

The boxer opened his mouth but could not speak. He had broken out in a cold sweat. He looked down and saw that without his even knowing it, his fingers had spread protectively across his groin.

"We recall," she went on, "when We were young and Emperor T'ai-tsung engaged a music master to teach Us to sing and accompany Ourselves on the lute. He did not seem to mind being clipped, for such was the honor of being Our mentor."

"A musician is one thing," the boxer said, trying to think. "They are not much better than dogs."

"Others have endured it too," the Empress said thoughtfully. "Poets and painters. Even architects like you."

"But—" he said, searching, "but what of the Clouds and Rain?"

"Only the jewels will be taken away. It is a simple operation, and nothing to fear. I have watched it done. The doctor slits the skin of the sack, then pops out the jewels. They hang from their stems like twin cherries. He clips the stems and sews the sack closed again with silk thread. Perhaps, if we asked him, he would put in balls of jade to replace those he has removed. Then no one would know the difference. The Jade Stalk would remain, and form the Vigorous Peak as always. If it is pain you worry about, he will use the silver needles so that you feel nothing. Be thankful, and do not sweat and grimace so! Were you a little boy, they would simply crush them with pliers."

"But—" he began again. "But I would like children someday, to worship at my shrine when I am gone."

"Make your choice," the Empress said, as though indifferent to the whole affair. "Lose your jewels and enjoy the life of the court, or have your children and go begging for their food."

"I had a fine life before I met you," the boxer protested. "I lived as I liked and saw whom I chose to see. I did not have pork and duck at every meal, but I did not go hungry. I can survive without you." But even as he said it, the words were hollow.

The two of them gazed at each other as boys do when they exchange dares and then wait to see who will first cross that line drawn by a toe in the dust.

Suddenly the Empress burst out laughing and covered her face with her hands.

"Oh, I am sorry," she said, "but I could not resist my little joke."

"Joke?"

"Precious One, I swear, you will live in the palace unclipped and as a man. You know I would not touch your body but to caress it, nor would I permit your skin to be cut unless it were to excise some unsightly mole. But I could not resist teasing you this little bit. Do you forgive Us?"

The boxer breathed deeply. "Yes, of course. I knew it was a joke all along. And a good one too!"

He complimented the Empress on her sense of humor, and thanked her again for his important assignment. When he left her, he went straight to the wine shops, and drank cup after cup until he stopped shaking.

17

THE BOXER LEARNS TO PAINT

Despite his new palace chambers, which surpassed even those of the temple in luxury, the boxer was not happy. He missed the company of his men: the talk, the pranks, the forays, the brawls. What surprised him was how much he missed the little monk, with his quiet dignity and puzzling, tantalizing stories of the Sixth Patriarch. Once he thought he heard the tap of the crutch moving along the loggia outside his chambers, but when he rose from his bed to look, it was only the branch of a tree tapping against an oiled screen.

He was not entirely alone, for White Pheasant had been permitted to come along as his butler. Yet he would have been happier without his endless mothering, his fussing and fretting over the boxer's health.

He could no longer come and go as he liked. If he tried to sneak off to the wine shops or the South Market, two members of the Yü-lin Guard, stationed outside his chambers, would demand his destination. If the guards judged the errand worthwhile, the boxer was permitted to go—but with the two guards tagging behind, observing his every move. They did not relax their vigilance until he was safely returned to the palace. Later he heard that the Empress, determined to avoid further confrontations with the immaculate Censor Hsü, had ordered execution for any guard on duty during the boxer's next bit of mischief.

Most wearisome of all was his doting Empress. His new apartments were in a far corner of the inner palace, surrounding a courtyard where few ventured. In former times they must have housed her handservants, for they were situated directly behind her "phoenix" apartments, and connected with them by a short corridor. This proximity allowed the Empress to visit him on even her busiest days, and on those days when work was light, she might come to him two or three times. He felt as helpless as the swatch of silk that a woman hangs by the toilet and uses to wipe herself. Yet he always forced himself to smile when he saw her, and to please her when they performed the Clouds and the Rain. He did this not entirely out of fear—though that was a part of it, to be sure—but also from reluctance to hurt her feelings or disappoint her. Pleasing women was terribly important to him.

The courtyard outside his chambers featured a pond with a rocky bank and a willow growing beside it. In the warm months, pink lotuses bloomed on the water's surface, and carp with scales of mottled gold and silver, and fins like billowing veils, gulped for air at the surface. Now the lotuses had withered and the carp had swum deep, where nothing could be seen of them but the occasional glint and glimmer of gold through the mire, like so many lost coins. The few leaves that remained on the willow were crisp and curled. When the boxer could bear his confinement no longer, he would come here and practice shadow-boxing, or merely sit by the willow and remember other days. Despite the differences, it began to remind him of the courtyard in the prison where he had once been interned.

One afternoon when he stepped out on the loggia, he saw a young woman standing beside the willow. Her mouth was small, her eyes as large and lovely as a doe's. Those high, arching eyebrows known as "moth antennae," which were all the fashion, had been drawn in indigo kohl on her domed forehead, and a tiny lotus painted in the center of her brow. Her hair, piled high, was held in place with jeweled combs and silk ribbons, and the smoothness of her skin would have shamed those South Market potters who took pride in their porcelain.

She wore a lower robe of pink decorated with large flowers of a darker pink, and tied across the bosom with a pale blue sash. Her upper robe was red, diamond-patterned, full-sleeved. A gossamer shawl was draped across her shoulders. Her fingers seemed as long and fragile as icicles. The very thought of her ankles made his heart race. He wasted no time in approaching her and wishing her a good day.

She looked at him, but did not smile. "You are the abbot of the White Horse Temple. I had heard that Heaven's Chosen brought you here."

"I have come to build a Ming-t'ang at the palace, to please Heaven," he said, trying to impress her. "And you?"

"I am the Virtuous Consort of Jui-tsung," she said.

The consort of Jui-tsung? He tried to imagine the docile, pimply, adolescent Emperor acting the Clouds and Rain with the sylph who stood before him. He himself was a much more appropriate mate for her. Though such observations were purely speculative, (only a fool would betray the Empress in her own home) a shred of his consciousness began to catalogue the corners of the palace where people rarely tread, the alcoves where the gasps and groans of passion would go unnoticed.

"What are you doing here, in this back courtyard?" he asked.

"All of us who are associated with the young Emperor try to keep out of the Empress's sight. The sparrow does not fly when the falcon is hunting."

"Now wait a moment. The Empress's justice is famous from the South Hill to the East Sea. She only punishes those who betray her."

"She has already executed a dozen Li princes. Did they betray her?"

"I don't know. Maybe some of them were planning to usurp the throne. I try not to get involved in politics."

"Did you betray her?" the Virtuous Consort asked.

"Certainly not!"

"Then why are you a prisoner?"

"I am no prisoner. I come and go as I like."

"Yet you pace like a caged jackal."

"I do not pace like a jackal. If anything, I prowl like a lion!"

The Virtuous Consort hid her face behind her hand.

"Do you laugh at me?" the boxer asked. "Yes, you do!" Yet she was so charming that he could not be angry.

"Forgive me. Living in fear makes me laugh at the most inappropriate moments."

"You worry with no cause. I will talk to the Empress about it. She'll reassure you."

"Please. You mustn't. Promise you will make no mention of me, or of our meeting. As long as the Empress does not think about the young Emperor and his family and consorts, the better our odds of survival."

"Well, all right. But I think you've got the wrong idea about her."

"We've talked too long already," she said, looking at the loggias around the courtyard. "If anyone sees us . . . I'd better go."

"No, wait. Stay a moment longer."

She smiled at the boxer. "Why?"

"I'm so bored and lonely. I like having someone to talk to."

"But if, as you said, you are free to come and go as you like . . ."

"Perhaps," the boxer admitted, "I am not quite so free as I had imagined."

"Still, I do not understand. How can you be idle when you have the Ming-t'ang to build?"

"The Scholars of the North Gate are still conferring. I must wait for their report before I can begin."

"And didn't I hear that you were preparing a translation of some important scripture?"

"That work, too, is in its early stages. First the great Brahman scholars must enunciate the text. So I find myself idle. Tell me, please, how you pass the time here," he asked, and it was no casual question, but as urgent as a dying man's final request.

"I play on my lute and sing."

"I do not know music."

"Or I write letters to my family. I tell them the smallest details of my life, the intrigues of my servants, my dreams, scraps of conversation I have overheard. Living thus, ordinary things take on extraordinary importance."

"I have no family," the boxer said. He was embarrassed to admit that he could neither read nor write. Most monks were intellectuals.

"Then write about your faith. Study your scriptures. Make copies of them so that others may benefit. Isn't that what other monks do?" She was genuinely puzzled. Monks were busy people and even a monk in isolation should not have suffered from this problem of boredom.

"I . . ." He hesitated. "I cannot write. I hurt my finger." He held up his hand, bending his index finger in an awkward way to make it appear broken. It was a trick he had learned while showboxing, to win the audience's sympathy.

She guessed the truth and her eyes softened. He was no more a real abbot than she was an Emperor's wife. In truth, they were nothing but fellow prisoners awaiting sentence.

"Have you ever tried painting?" the Virtuous Consort asked.

The boxer shook his head.

"It is a good distraction, and one that a man can teach himself." Then abruptly she added, "I must go," and turned and walked away. Her step was so smooth and even that she seemed to glide rather than walk like common people.

He thought no more about her until the next day, when White Pheasant brought him a writing kit and a scroll of virgin paper. It could have only been a gift from the Virtuous Consort. The boxer asked White Pheasant to recommend a gift for him to send in return.

White Pheasant suggested sending nothing; moreover, he recommended that the boxer pretend the meeting had never taken place. The Empress, once a consort herself, mistrusted other consorts most of all. Among the changes she had wrought during her husband's reign was a reduction in the number of his concubines from one hundred twenty-two to six, renaming them "Assistants to Virtue" and "Monitors of Propriety" to emphasize the behavior expected of them. She would not risk another woman doing to her what she had done to the previous Empress.

The writing kit was contained in a beautiful rosewood case, the cover inlaid with a snow scene of mother-of-pearl, with ebony line and shadow. Inside it, in little compartments, he found several sizes of deer-hair brushes with bamboo handles, an ink palette carved from stone, deep at one end to hold the water and shallow at the other to provide a surface for scraping the ink stick, several ink sticks in a small leopard-skin bag, and a dish and a double-welled bowl of white porcelain.

The boxer permitted White Pheasant, who was nearly as accomplished in the other arts as he was in cooking, to instruct him. The eunuch spread out the writing implements on a low wooden desk below a screen that let in the somber autumn light. Kneeling before the desk, he poured water from a little pitcher, filling the well of the stone palette. Then he dipped the ink stick into the water and, drawing it up onto the dry part of the palette, gently rubbed it against the stone until the water turned a rich blue-black. He showed him how to use the double-welled bowl to moisten and wash the brush, and the dish to mix lighter shades of ink. Finally he demonstrated three ways of holding the brush, and the various strokes required to depict the four subjects that men most loved to paint: the bamboo, the chrysanthemum, the plum blossom, and the orchid. He would have shown him more, but the boxer, impatient to try what he had already witnessed, grabbed the brush from his hand and shooed him away.

He was dismayed at the difficulty of imitating even the preparatory steps. First his ink was too thin, then too thick and lumpy with bits of carbon. His brush was dry, then so charged with ink that it ran down the paper. He tried painting bamboo, as White Pheasant had shown him, and then put his hand to a complicated cluster of chrysanthemum petals. His strokes were as primitive as a child's, cramped and nervous, lacking the prized quality of spontaneity.

Still, it felt wonderful. All his life he had dreamed of sitting at such a desk, drawing a fine deer's-hair brush across smooth, excellent paper, just like the most learned scholar-official. Why, he might have been preparing a memorial, or a bit of the dynastic history, or even writing a poem! Although painting and writing were not identical, they were certainly close kin.

He tried capturing the essence of various items in the room, the bed with its fretwork screens, the lacquered armchair, the writing box itself. Had he any critical sense at all, he might have hurled his work across the room in frustration, but his pleasure was like that of a child's. He painted the view from his window, the lake with the rocky bank, the willow tree. When he tired of that, he painted the flaxen-haired, green-eyed Sogdian girl as he remembered her, lying naked in bed. One thought led to another, and he found himself painting the Empress, but the picture turned into a kind of caricature, with crossed eyes and a mustache. He painted Censor Hsü skewered with a sword, in one side and out the other, and the Taoist sorcerer with a great, heavy boulder falling on his head.

He completely lost track of time, as one does when engrossed in such a pleasant diversion, and was only brought back to the present by the sound of the Empress's voice inquiring of White Pheasant as to whether the boxer was in. Quickly he rolled up the scroll and hid it under the cushion he was sitting on, and stuffed the writing things back in the box and hid the box under the cushion too. Then he sat there, his heart pounding, listening to their conversation in the anteroom.

"The boxer is in his bedchamber," he heard White Pheasant say, "wielding his brush."

"Come now," the Empress said. "We have known this man for two years and have never seen him raise a brush or read a character."

"Nevertheless, that is how he occupies himself this afternoon."

"I will see this with my own eyes before I believe it."

"Then take a look," the eunuch said.

Hearing this, and wishing not to make a liar out of the man who fed him so well, the boxer grabbed the scroll and the writing box from beneath the cushion and frantically spread them out on the desk. Water spilled, ink smeared, but a few seconds later he was holding the brush over the paper, painting a stalk of bamboo, his hand shaking so much that the bamboo looked more like a lightning bolt. Hearing the screen being pushed aside, he hunched over his work, pretending to be blind to any reality beyond the paper's border.

"He does indeed wield the brush," the Empress remarked, back in the anteroom, talking to the eunuch. "But to what purpose?"

The eunuch had a shrug in his voice. "Perhaps he draws sparrows, or clouds, or whirlpools, or pomegranates. Who knows? Perhaps he draws the Ming-t'ang as he sees it in his mind's eye. There is much about our abbot that we do not know. He is a constant source of surprise to us all. Shall I announce you?"

"That is not necessary," she replied. "We would not disturb him during the time he spends improving himself. We shall return later."

The boxer was doubly pleased. First he had impressed her as being more than a Jade Stalk for her to ride upon during her every moment of leisure; and at the same time he had found a means of keeping her at bay, at least temporarily. He smiled at his own cleverness and returned to his work, a childlike drawing of himself and the Empress fornicating like dogs.

* * *

While occasionally, during the course of the following days, the boxer tried his hand at a plum blossom or orchid, mostly he painted erotic cartoons, caricatures of the courtiers, or fantasies of a violent or perverse nature. What a good time he had! At the end of each session, he would put away his drawing materials and hide the scroll beneath his cushion for the next day, lest anyone else see it. He looked forward to covering the entirety of its long, white emptiness with his brushstrokes, as he would yearn to trample a field of virgin snow.

One morning the scroll was gone. Panicking, he ran to White Pheasant's chambers and, grabbing the eunuch by the lapels of his robe, demanded to know what had become of his drawings.

"The Empress took them," White Pheasant replied.

"The Empress?" He banged his own bald head with his fists. "No. No! Why did you give them to her? Why didn't you ask me first?"

"You were in the bath. But don't be upset. She doesn't care if your bamboo lacks resiliency, or your plum blossoms lie heavy on the paper. She only wished to see what progress you were making."

"Listen, camel dung," the boxer screamed at him, "they weren't pictures of bamboo plants and plum trees, they were drawings—" He hesitated and said more softly, "Drawings of another sort." Flopping down on the floor, he went on, "Oh, I'm finished, now I'm really finished."

"I'm sorry," White Pheasant said, "I didn't realize—"

The boxer had no further desire to discuss it. He simply sat there on the floor, looking morose, waiting for the ax to fall.

After imagining the alternatives open to him, he decided that his best course was to blame another. When the Empress arrived at his chambers, the scroll tucked beneath her arm, he said, "I am so sorry that White Pheasant gave you his own scroll instead of mine. I have heard that sometimes he indulges in crude caricatures of members of the court. I certainly hope you did not have to endure looking at any such thing, for I know how they would offend you. My opinion is that you should not punish him too harshly. He is a good-hearted fellow and an excellent cook."

"We are disappointed to learn this," the Empress said. "We were hoping the scroll was yours, for we have rarely seen brushwork of such sensitivity, pictures so filled with life."

"Really? Let me look. Perhaps it was my scroll after all."

He rolled it from one end to the other, searching nervously for a caricature or a dirty cartoon, but finding only masterful studies of waves crashing against rocks, of prancing horses and long-legged cranes, of mysterious mountains and tranquil bamboo groves. Though the scented kudzu paper, sandalwood rollers, and crystal knobs were all identical to those of the scroll he had decorated, it was obviously a different scroll.

"Mine, after all," the boxer announced.

"We are so impressed by your skill with the brush," she said. "Where could a man of low origins have learned such subtlety of expression? It is miraculous."

"I am a complicated person," the boxer admitted. "That is why I do not scoff when fortune-tellers say I was once Bodhidharma. With all there is inside me, I wonder that I have not been a dozen people in former lives."

She inclined her head a few degrees to the left and said, with her catlike smile, "I would love to see you paint. Would you paint something for me now?"

"If only I could. But just this morning I hurt my hand in the lid of the clothes box. See?" He held up his right hand, performing his trick of bending the index finger so that it appeared broken.

"You must paint for me when it heals."

"You can be certain I will."

As soon as the Empress had left, the boxer told White Pheasant to arrange for him to meet with the Virtuous Consort in the courtyard. White Pheasant reiterated the dangers involved in such a meeting but, seeing that the boxer was adamant, did as he was told.

The following evening he saw her standing by the willow beside the pond, a creature of such supernatural beauty and repose that it occurred to him she might be a fox fairy.

"It's a lovely evening," he said, approaching her from the loggia where he had been waiting. "A little chilly, perhaps. Winter will be here soon enough."

"Why did you want to see me?"

"You switched the scrolls. Who else had one like it? Admit it was you. Admit it."

"It is so," she said, looking boldly back at him. "I was on my way to the gardens, scroll and paintbox in my sleeve, hoping to capture the essence of the autumn trees as the last leaves fell. On my way I met the Empress, who asked for my opinion of a scroll she carried beneath her arm. Though she bears no love for me, she knows that I am skilled with the brush. I unrolled it, hiding my disgust at what I saw. I think she had not looked at it herself, for she certainly would have burned it in an instant."

The boxer nodded gravely. "The work of the eunuch White Pheasant. He delights in drawing these lurid pictures. I plan to talk to him about it this very afternoon."

"I surmised that she had taken the scroll from you in secret. While her head was turned, I exchanged your scroll for my own."

"Thank you," he whispered.

He was standing very close to her now. He looked into her eyes with an expression midway between passion and indigestion. After a good bit of this, he seized her and pressed her body against his. She slid her knee up and into his groin with surprising force for one so slight. The world went white with pain. The blow left him breathless, red-faced, and goggle-eyed. He wrapped his hands around his testicles and doubled over.

"I am the Virtuous Consort of Jui-tsung," she said in a placid voice. "I did not save your life out of any sense of sympathy. When first we met, I felt pity, but now I feel only contempt. You are no more than a crude, illiterate peasant, full of bluster, bravado, and self-delusion. I did what I did not for you, but to spite the wolf of a woman who keeps my husband prisoner here, in what is rightly his own palace. Tell whom you like what I have said today, for I have been too long silent, and no longer fear the consequences of the truth."

She turned from him and glided across the courtyard, back to her chambers.

The boxer found himself in a stone palace on a mountain peak, with all the world below obscured in mist. The rooms themselves were bare and deserted, the ramparts crumbling. Though he walked from chamber to chamber, through the courtyards and along loggias, he saw no other soul. He grew more and more anxious. A boy of fifteen appeared as if from nowhere. The hour was late, he said, and he would show the boxer to his bedchamber. The boy had green eyes, flaxen hair, and a smile of extraordinary sweetness. The boxer found his presence immensely comforting. He undressed, but then grew nervous as he saw that the boy was about to take away his monk's robe and scarf.

"Don't worry," the boy reassured him. "You'll have no need for these. I'll see that they are cared for."

The boxer entered his bedchamber and found the servant girl and the Sogdian girl awaiting him. The servant girl, he noticed, still had the dagger wound on her chest. Yet she was of excellent color, and radiant, even lovelier than he remembered her.

"You must be careful," he warned them. "The Empress will find out."

"Don't worry about her," they said.

"That boy," the boxer said. "Who was he?"

"Didn't you recognize him?" The Sogdian girl laughed. "That is our son. He is growing up to be a fine young man, isn't he?"

"But I thought—"

"Hush," the Sogdian girl whispered, and stopped his words with an embrace. Then all three acted the Clouds and Rain together.

He woke to the first light filtering through the latticework screens of his enclosed bed, and experienced an indescribable sense of sadness to realize it had been a dream. As he lay there mourning it, he grew aware of a strange sensation, a small circle of heat on his chest. He threw back the blankets, pulled open his sleeping robe, and saw to his dismay that the vermilion mark of the palace warder was gone.

Hearing his name, he opened the little doors to the bed, swung out his feet, and sat up on the edge. He looked across the room and saw White Pheasant at the entrance, bowing.

"Heaven's Chosen comes to call," he said.

"What?" the boxer said. He grabbed the lapels of his sleeping robe and pulled them tight across his chest and held them there, over the vanished warder, with clenched fists. "But it's barely the Hour of the Rabbit."

White Pheasant raised his palms in a gesture of helplessness. "She must not be kept waiting."

"Of course not," the boxer agreed, heart pounding. "Send her in." He sank back into the recesses of the bed and pulled the covers over him as extra protection.

She was carrying a scroll under her arm—not his own collection of lurid cartoons, he saw with relief, but a thick scroll of silk, with a rash of official stamps upon it.

He forced himself to smile, and said in a sincere voice, "Good morning, my beloved. The sight of you gladdens my heart."

"Forgive Us for waking you," she said. "We know how you love your sleep. But We were so excited We could not restrain Ourself." She sat down on the edge of the bed and offered the scroll to him. "It is the report from Our Scholars of the North Gate. They have reached an accord regarding the details of the Ming-t'ang. This means We can begin the building at once. Here, have a look at it. You must be as eager as We were to learn what they have discovered in their research."

"I certainly am," the boxer said. He took the scroll from her and unrolled it in his lap, while trying to remember if he had ever admitted to her that he could not read. To stay on the safe side, he pretended he could, and studied the columns of characters with interest. "Hmm," he said, and "Yes," and "Well," all the time nodding his head. Then he quickly rolled it up, lest she ask him about any specific detail, and said, "Of course, I'll have to study it at my leisure, but it certainly looks thorough. I see no reason why we should not begin construction immediately."

"How deeply you concentrate."

Actually, he was thinking about the palace warder. The little monk would know a way to bring it back. He had to have him brought to the palace.

"We should have the Vinaya master take a look at this report and make sure that nothing in it violates Buddhist law."

"You are so wise. Additional opinions are always useful in a project such as this, in order to avert controversy and criticism from different quarters. We will send it to him at once."

"Better yet, have him come here. Then we can review the report together."

"An excellent suggestion," the Empress agreed.

The boxer silently applauded his own cleverness.

"Why do you pull the covers over your chest in that way?" she asked.

"I do not."

"You do."

"It is the cold."

"Come here in the light and take off your robe."

"Why should I?"

"So that We may caress your body."

"If that is the only reason, caress it here, in the dark of my bed, as we usually do."

"And also We wish to gaze upon your form. Sometimes the very sight of you makes Our Golden Cleft flood like the Yangtze."

"Then seeing me in your mind's eye must stimulate you even more, for there I am perfect while in life I am flawed."

"Obstinate thing! Usually you love nothing more than to parade around naked, as though you were a sledge dragged by that fierce dragon that lives between your legs."

"Usually you do not test me. Usually you trust me."

"We trust you."

"Then why this insistence on seeing me naked in the light? Admit the real reason."

The Empress looked away, and said in a soft voice, "I have heard stories."

"What sort of stories?"

"About you and the Virtuous Consort."

The boxer laughed. "I would have nothing to do with that stuck-up orchid."

"If you have nothing to do with her, then how do you know she is stuck-up?"

"One can tell simply by looking at her."

"You have seen her, then?"

"Well, everybody has seen her. Haven't they? I think I noticed her walking through the courtyard one day."

"And how did you know it was she?"

"I asked White Pheasant."

"Why did you ask White Pheasant? Do you ask him every time you see a person walking through the courtyard?"

"I—I don't know. I was bored, so I asked him." The boxer was getting angry. "If I had more to do, I wouldn't be so bored. You can't expect a vigorous man such as I to spend his life locked up in his apartments."

He climbed out of the bed, pulled on an outer-robe, and began to pace the bedroom.

"You are free to come and go as you like," the Empress said, rising to sit on the edge of the bed and watch him.

"With a dozen soldiers following me."

"They are there to protect you."

"I can protect myself."

"By burning down Taoist temples?"

"That wasn't my fault."

"Well." The Empress cleared her throat. "The Ming-t'ang will keep you busy enough. Meanwhile," she added curtly, "We shall await your apology," and she turned and left his apartments.

The boxer could not face the Empress until he had done something about his palace warder, for an apology would entail its display. Ponder the problem as he would, he could think of no technique to bring the mark back, or a lie to explain its disappearance. His only hope lay in the little monk, who, he believed, could deal with any crisis, no matter how dire. He only hoped that she would not, in her anger, forget her promise to send for him.

He was relieved when, later that afternoon, White Pheasant announced the Vinaya master's arrival. The little monk seemed nearly as pleased to see the boxer as the boxer was to see him. They bowed and knelt on the floor, facing one another. While White Pheasant prepared tea, the little monk spoke of the other monks, of the translation effort, and of the condition of the White Horse, whose operation, the boxer noted forlornly, seemed only to have improved since his departure.

The boxer would have brought up the subject of the palace warder immediately, but they were being observed by two of the Yü-lin Guard, and by a secretary whom the Empress had sent to take notes of their discussion, lest any valuable idea be forgotten. The boxer would have to wait for the moment when they were alone. In the meantime, he showed him the report on the Ming-t'ang.

The little monk pored over the scroll for nearly a half hour. When he looked up, he was not pleased.

"These Scholars of the North Gate say they have designed the Ming-t'ang," the monk said, "but in truth they have given us nothing but a bunch of quotes from the dynastic histories and the treatises on architecture. They say that it might have been this or it might have been that, but as for concrete examples or recommendations, they offer us nothing."

He rolled up the scroll, placed it on the floor in front of him, and continued, "All work done by committee is of this useless nature, for a committee is like a dragon with a hundred heads, each wishing to set out in its own direction and promote its own welfare.

As a result, it goes nowhere and accomplishes nothing. And if, by chance, the committee should contain a man of unique vision, whose opinion would be worth hearing, the others will grind down his ideas until they are smooth and featureless, as inoffensive and conventional as their own drivel. Fortunately, reports such as this can be ignored."

The little monk turned to the secretary and ordered him, as though he were a servant, to hand over his scroll and writing kit at once. The boxer, having tried the brush himself, was awed by the speed and sureness with which his companion ground the ink stick into the stone palette.

"Are you going to write a letter demanding a new report?" the boxer asked

The little monk shook his head. "Why waste more time? We will draw our own plans."

"Here? Now? But we know nothing about a Ming-t'ang!"

"True. But it is like making up a story about some mysterious, ancient place. If no man knows the truth, then who can throw stones at the storyteller?"

"I suppose," the boxer said, uncertain

"We do have some idea about what the Empress wants. First of all, she wants a very big and splendid hall that will win the hearts of all the people of Lo-yang. She wants a hall that is different from the other halls, as she is different from past sovereigns, but will blend harmoniously with them. And I imagine that she would like a hall . . ." He went on and on, piecing it together from what he knew of the Empress, pausing every now and then to ask the boxer's opinion.

The boxer listened, nodding thoughtfully, filled with the most wonderful feeling of confidence now that the little monk had taken charge. Anyone who could design a Ming-t'ang could find a way around this business of the palace warder.

"Let us make it as big as we can," the boxer said. "A giant pagoda with ninety-nine floors!"

"Yes, I think that's an excellent idea. A Buddhist structure for a Buddhist Empress. A giant pagoda, three hundred feet high at least." As he spoke, his brush danced across the paper, sketching big, simple shapes. "But only three floors. Then we can make the ceilings so high that they seem like the very dome of Heaven. The first floor must be the most splendid of all, since that will be the great audience hall. People will gather there for ages to come and recall the grandeur of the Empress Wu."

"Remember the laboratory of the Taoist sorcerer? How the walls represented the five elements? Might we employ such a scheme of symbols here?"

"Yes, yes. But instead of the five elements, we shall make the first floor square, to symbolize August Earth, and the second, twelve-sided, one for each period of the day, Hour of the Rabbit, Hour of the Snake, Hour of the Horse, and so forth. As for the third floor, let it be circular, for it is closest to Heaven, and Heaven loves the circle above all other shapes." His brush moved faster and faster. "And atop it all, a great bronze dragon."

"No, no, no." The boxer held up his hand. "A phoenix. Let it be supported by dragons. Dragons of a base metal. Phoenix above dragons—that will please her."

The little monk ground more ink and set about making a clean sketch of the building they had conceived together. It took him only minutes. Then he passed the scroll to the boxer, who felt a kind of satisfaction he had never known to see his own ideas so beautifully realized in ink. The Ming-t'ang the monk had rendered was of awesome proportions, as reflected by a few human figures sketched at the base, yet possessed of grace and lightness, thanks to vast, overhanging, turned-up roofs that seemed to float in space. The phoenix at the very top was so appropriate as to leave no doubt that the Middle Kingdom was meant to be ruled by a woman.

"How will we support such a vast structure?" he asked the monk.

"Just as we would a small pagoda—with a central beam. But one of magnificent proportions."

The conventional pagoda, the wooden kind as opposed to those of stone, had for structural support a central timber, one-quarter of which was buried in the earth. The joists and rafters that supported its small, parasol-like roofs were anchored into this timber and what walls existed were nonsupporting, hung like screens from the roofs. But pagodas were tall, narrow structures. The Ming-t'ang they had designed was bigger than any pagoda in existence, and as broad as it was tall.

"Do such timbers exist?" the boxer asked.

"I have seen them in the distant south, in the steaming forests of Kwangtung province. To drag one to the Yangtze and then float it to the capital will require many men. But if we send for it at once, then perhaps we can begin construction by spring. And if we begin by spring, and have a great many workers, then perhaps we may finish by New Year's. It is not impossible. You must have the Empress approve our plans immediately."

The boxer replied that he would love to do just that, but—and here he grew slightly guileful—he was prevented by a pain in his chest. He glanced at the secretary and saw, to his satisfaction, that the man had lost interest in the proceedings and was organizing his ink sticks. Turning back to the little monk, the boxer urged him to look at his chest and see if he could divine the source of the problem. The little monk, not perceiving the secret meaning of his words, was puzzled, but agreed nonetheless.

The boxer pulled open his robe. The little monk noticed at once that the palace warder was gone. He lowered his brow and frowned with concern. Then he reached forward and touched the area with his finger.

"I was unfaithful in a dream," the boxer whispered.

"One reality is as transient as another."

"Can you save me?"

"Perhaps," the little monk whispered. "Close your eyes and make your mind still, as when you are meditating."

"Well, you know, I don't get much time to meditate, with all my responsibilities toward the—"

"Hush, and do as I say."

The boxer closed his eyes and tried to meditate. The presence of the little monk made it easier, for his concentration was such a powerful force that it seemed to spill over the boundaries of his body, enhancing the abilities of those around him.

"Recall your dream," the monk went on. "Remember the setting of it, the smells, the colors. Now think about the woman."

"There were two of them."

Though his eyes were closed, he heard the little monk chuckle. "Imagine both of them, as they appeared in your dream. But now, instead of sharing your pillow with them, repel them. Though they may be young and pretty, you have sworn your fidelity to the Empress."

The boxer's face grew sadder and sadder.

"Tell them," the monk went on, "that you can have no more to do with them now, but that someday you will all be together again, in a place without fear or suffering. Tell them that."

Tears welled in the corners of the boxer's eyes. Finally he opened them and looked at the little monk. "I told them."

The little monk reached forward and opened the collar of the boxer's robe. The mark of the palace warder was precisely where the Empress had painted it, the vermilion more brilliant than ever.

The boxer looked at the little monk with wonder. "How did you . . . ?"

"I did nothing. You did it yourself."

"But I dreamed it."

"This life is a dream. Is a dream within a dream any less real?" Before the boxer could reply, the little monk went on, "It is all to no point unless you wake up from all dreams. Only then will you see the darkness and confusion of your old life."

"But how can I do that?" the boxer asked, having for an instant a vision of how marvelous such an existence might be.

"Slap yourself! Tear off your eyelids! Knowing neither good nor evil, stare at the face you had before you were born!"

"I don't understand," said the boxer.

"In time you will," the little monk said.

BUILDING THE MING-T'ANG

The Empress was cool when the boxer presented himself at her Phoenix Chambers. Though his apology, along with the sight of the palace warder, even darker than when she had first applied it, warmed her, what won her over were the drawings of the Ming-t'ang. The boxer himself took credit, believing that since he had contributed so much to it, he was perpetrating only a slight untruth. Having made a few more changes so that she might take credit as the real architect of the hall, she approved the drawings, and that very day sent a messenger to Kwangtung to arrange for the cutting of a great tree, and the floating of it back to Lo-yang.

The winter passed peacefully, the Empress and the boxer happy in their way. Convinced of his fidelity, she even began to let him roam, unchaperoned, through the wine shops and the South Market (though she contrived to act the Clouds and Rain with him in daylight at least once a week, so that she could inconspicuously check the warder). He, feeling less resentful, was more loving. When she was not too busy, they would walk in the gardens, or go together to worship the memory of the Empress's mother at the great Fu-hsien temple founded in her honor, or attend a polo match where they could watch the Princess T'ai P'ing, disguised as a man, galloping to and fro like a wild Turk, swinging her mallet, terrifying the other contestants.

While Censor Hsü had been quiet on the subject of the boxer, he had not retired from the court's eye. One of the most impassioned memorials of the winter was his criticism of the building of a Ming-t'ang. In his opinion, metal shortages were so severe that the casting of the nine enormous iron dragons that were to serve as supports for the third story, and the giant bronze phoenix that was to ornament the roof, would cause grave hardship to the economy. To get enough laborers, tens of thousands of men would have to be taken from their farms. This in turn would lead to famine, and famine to rebellion.

He evoked the name of Sui Yang-ti, the emperor whose extravagant building projects (among them the Lotus Palace where the Empress and the boxer whiled away their afternoons) had contributed to the fall of his dynasty. He quoted the words of Emperor Kao-tsu, who had said, after establishing his new dynasty of the T'ang and returning the Middle Kingdom to a degree of peace and prosperity, "I do not want you to dig ponds! Nor to make gardens! Nor to build pleasure parks at the expense of our farmers! I forbid you to indulge yourselves!"

The Empress, acknowledging the merit of his memorial, agreed, with an air of sacrifice, to cast the phoenix in iron rather than bronze, and plate it. Censor Hsü was not impressed by the concession.

All winter they followed the reports of the great timber and its progress from the forests of Kwangtung, near the south sea. Now, they heard, it was being felled; now dragged by a thousand men through the hot, mosquito-ridden rain forests (a tackle broke, it rolled and crushed a dozen men); now floated up the Yangtze, five hundred oxen towing the load (it collided with a barge and a hundred more men were drowned, a hundred oxen dragged into the river); now floated up the great Canal (they felt more comfortable, for this was the familiar route the tax grain took from southern farms to northern granaries); now along the canal, from one teeming entrepôt to the next, places with names like Hang-chou, Ch'ang-chou, Sung-chou, and Pien-chou; and finally, like a herald of spring, down the serene Lo, into the middle of town, where it was fished from the water with elaborate block and tackle, while festive crowds cheered as though for a great philosopher or an outstanding poet.

The stately visitor from the south was carried down Heaven's Way to the site where the Ming-t'ang would stand, just within the South Gate of the palace. The old Phoenix Hall had already been razed to make room, and a giant post hole dug to accommodate it. Before the timber could be raised, it had to be finished. Hundreds of carpenters set about scraping off the bark and smoothing it with adzes and chisels. In three days it was as round and even as if it had been turned on a monumental lathe. Then a thousand lines were looped around the top of it, and ten thousand men bent their backs and pulled. Bit by bit, the great timber swung up from the ground until it stood erect. Even the Empress, watching from a balcony, was awed by the size of it, and assigned one of the court poets to write an ode celebrating this "auspicious shaft."

Construction began immediately. The boxer sat, like a general, in a pavilion specially erected to shade him from the sun, sipping mare's-teat wine and observing his army of artisans and laborers dragging and measuring, cutting and hammering. When one of the foremen came to him with a question regarding the length of a timber, or the manner in which two beams should be joined, he grew indignant at being bothered with such trivia, and hit the man with a bamboo cane. The foremen attributed the eccentric behavior to Ch'an, bowed respectfully to him, and solved the problems on their own.

Once or twice a week the little monk would arrive and take the boxer on a tour of the construction, quietly pointing out which parts, cunningly dadoed and dovetailed, would bear the weight of the structure to come, and which, shoddily joined, would give way within a few years. After he had left, the boxer would seek out the guilty workers and threaten them with death and the extinction of their families if the faults were not corrected.

Thanks to the army of workers, the quality and detail of the little monk's preparations, and the endless wealth at their disposal, construction progressed quickly. By midsummer the stone terraces were cut and in place, the first floor completed, the second story framed, the roof brackets awaiting their rafters and joists. Potters were mixing a rare golden glaze for the roof tiles, while in a foundry on the west side of the city, molds were being made for the iron dragons and the great phoenix.

At this time the boxer received a message from the little monk, summoning him to the White Horse Temple for an important meeting. Although irritated by the disruption, he was also pleased by the opportunity to carry more cash to the temple, to be melted down in the foundry there. He loaded up his tarpan with four saddlebags of coins and set off for the temple, the poor pony weaving like a drunkard under its load.

As he trotted through the city, he marveled at his good fortune. Censor Hsü was leaving him alone; the Taoist sorcerer, busy rebuilding his own temple with a handsome subsidy from the Empress, also seemed willing to forget their differences. The boxer was more than ever in the Empress's good graces, as evidenced by the liberty he enjoyed, nearly as much as he had before the unfortunate incident with the Sogdian girl.

He had learned a lesson. You could not have everything, even in your dreams. Maturity was disillusionment. Now that he had accepted it, his life was secure. He was staying out of trouble. He had wealth, power, and prestige. Wasn't love a simple thing to give up in return? It was the way of the world.

He found the little monk in his cell, sitting cross-legged on the floor, making notes on hemp paper while referring to a dozen other scrolls arranged on the floor around him, each opened to a different verse. The boxer began to rail about the imposition, an important man such as he being called away from his work, but the little monk, who was in the midst of a thought, shushed him until he had finished writing. He motioned for the boxer to sit beside him, and brought him up to date on the progress of the translation.

The Sanskrit had been enunciated and explained, the scripture translated. Most of the team, their work done, had returned to their home temples. Those who remained were occupied with the mundane tasks of checking and copying, gluing one long sheet of paper to the next and winding them onto scrolls. As for the commentary—the collection of arguments that would prove that the Empress Wu was the reincarnation of Maitreya and destined to rule as supreme sovereign—the little monk was in the midst of composing it.

"But why did you bother calling me here?" the boxer demanded irritably. "I trust you with your work. Read it to me when you are done, if you like, and I will give you my opinion."

"I am not interested in your opinion," the little monk replied, irritated by the boxer's vanity. "I called you here because it happens that I must modify the plans of the Ming-t'ang to comply with certain details in the commentary. When the Empress sees the modifications, she will ask questions, and if you are to appear other than a fool, you must be able to supply answers. This, in turn, requires having at least a rudimentry understanding of the commentary. Do you understand?"

"Of course I understand. What do I look like? Some stupid camel?"

The little monk ignored him.

"The creation of this commentary is a large and complex task. The Empress wants a text that can be preached all over the land, to the simple and the learned alike, and that will identify her indisputably as the incarnation of Maitreya. To establish this, in certain cases we must twist the meaning of the text by interpreting the characters in an unlikely way, or obscure the text by introducing other texts. Now here is an example of a verse that lends itself to the Empress's scheme: 'The Buddha then praised the goodness of the Queen Ching-kuang . . . and said that she would rule over the land in the body of a woman.'

"This Ching-kuang is one of the audience to whom the Buddha is preaching the scripture. In another verse, the Buddha says to her: 'You shall obtain a quarter of the places governed by a chakravartin king. The people shall prosper, there will be no weaknesses or sorrow from illness, nor afflictions, nor fears, nor calamities; all propitious events will be completely realized. All the countries of Jambudvīpa will be obedient to her, and none will resist or oppose her.'

"Since the earth is divided into four continents, and the Middle Kingdom is the southern continent, it is obviously the 'quarter' referred to. By the way, *chakravartin* is Sanskrit for 'he who sets the Wheel in motion,' referring to the Great Wheel of the Law, or Dharma. In other words, a very great ruler. And of course I'll say that all these optimistic prophecies have become fact under the Empress's rule."

"But didn't you once tell me that Jambudvīpa wasn't a real place?"

The little monk shrugged. "This sort of commentary is more an exercise in ingenuity than in finding the truth."

"But when you first debated the sorcerer, you cursed yourself for abandoning the truth. You were so upset you tried to kill yourself."

"What a piece of vanity," he said, shaking his head, "setting myself up as arbiter of the truth. How do I know what the Buddha really meant? At the temple we interpret it one way—but who's to say which way is right?"

The boxer stared at him in wonder. "You used to be unshakable in your faith. Now you pretend you don't know truth from lie, and spend your time making this confusing document even more confusing. It's one thing for *me* to go along with the Empress's lies. I never understood the truth to begin with. But you, you were incorruptible. What brought about this change?"

"What change?" the little monk said briskly, and with a trace of anger. "I'm the same monk I always was. Why are you stirring up the tea leaves?"

"You know what I think?" the boxer said. "I think you've lost your integrity. The awarding of titles has swelled your head. Being chief-of-this and head-of-that has made you as big a fool as any mandarin. I've taught you about the secular world, all right. But I've done my job a little too well."

"If the worthy Scholar of the Kick to the Groin is through memorializing, I would proceed to discuss the translation with him."

The boxer had never heard sarcasm from the lips of the little monk, and it saddened him no end. He felt as though he were responsible for breaking some exquisite porcelain vase. Was it his fate to destroy all that was good and beautiful as he went along his way?

"I have no more to say," he said.

"Good." The little monk turned back to his scrolls. "What do you know of the Kuang-wu Ming prophecy?"

The boxer shook his head. "Nothing."

He felt the urge to cry, something he had not felt since he was a child.

"It's another scripture," the monk droned on, "like the Great Cloud, that prophesies the coming of the Empress—according to the Empress. It's so obscure that most of it could mean anything, which makes it useful for constructing rebuses and anagrams. Supposedly it was found within a round white stone that was split open by a bolt of lightning one stormy night. My guess is that her Scholars of the North Gate composed it as part of her legitimation campaign. Whatever the case, I have been instructed by the Empress to drop in a verse from the Kuang-wu Ming when I cannot make the Great Cloud say precisely what I want it to say. Please pay attention, for all this, as you will see, harks back to the building of the Ming-t'ang. Now here's a very odd passage from the Kuang-wu: 'Three times six youths will sing a ballad. Later they will change the ballad to that of Wu Mei-niang. The ballad says that she is neither too young nor too old.'

"Three times six is eighteen, and eighteen sons means Li, the surname of the T'ang dynasty."

"Your thoughts rush by like the west wind," the boxer complained.

"Forgive me," the little monk said with some sympathy. "I forget that you cannot write. Come look over my shoulder." He wet his brush on the stone palette, shaped it to a point, and drew on the paper as he spoke.

"You see, the character li 李 can be broken down into the three characters shih-pa tzu 十八子, which mean 'eighteen boys.' "

"That is fascinating," the boxer said enviously. How he wished he could write, so that he could play such wonderful games with the characters! He longed to grab the brush out of the monk's hand and try it then and there, but was too embarrassed, afraid he might make a fool of himself. Perhaps later, when he was alone in his apartments.

"As for the line about their changing the ballad to that of Wu Mei-niang, it means that after the three sages of the T'ang—that is to say the three T'ang emperors—the dynasty will 'change' to Wu. In fact, Wu Mei, Wu the Beautiful, was the Empress's consort name when she first came to the palace."

"I didn't know that," the boxer said.

"I've been reading the reign records, the ones assembled in preparation for the dynastic histories. They're filled with puzzles like that. If you like rebuses, I'll show you a really complex one that took me hours to work out. Again, it uses a quote from the Kuang-wu Ming: 'Under the recumbent mountain, invert the exit and you will find a saint.'

" 'Recumbent' means that if we put the upper part of the 帚 of the character for 'woman' 婦 on its side, it becomes the character for 'mountain' 山. "Invert the exit" means that if we invert the lower part of 帚 we have the character for 'exit' 出 . Thus we get the character for 'woman' 婦 proving that the Empress Wu has the virtue of a saint."

"How wonderful," the boxer said, enchanted.

"One more," the little monk said, enjoying this showing off, "also from the Kuang-wu inscription. You see, the beauty of the Kuang-wu is that it is so obscure that it resembles the clouds that drift by on a spring day, taking the form of whatever thought is on your mind. Here it is: 'A splendid cat will protect the four regions for you.'

"The animal symbol for Wu is the cat."

"Sometimes she looks just like one," the boxer said, smiling to think of it.

"She is without question a 'splendid cat' who protects the four regions for us, these being the four borders of our kingdom. But 'splendid,' when represented by the character *li*, has another meaning too. In the Classic of Changes, it is the trigram of two solid lines above and below, with a broken line in the middle ☲ . Because the broken line is in the middle, it is also called the 'middle daughter,' and its 'position' is south. Now, the Empress Wu is the middle of three daughters, and as you will recall from my previous commentary, she governs the south continent."

"It is clever indeed!" the boxer said with enthusiasm, all bad feelings forgotten. "But what has this to do with the Ming-t'ang?"

The little monk laughed. "I was so taken with my work that I nearly forgot. There is one more passage—this one from the Great Cloud Scripture." He turned the scroll until he found it. " 'The Respectable One prays to Maitreya, "Construct a magic city for me. Above, there will be a silver pillar, and below there will be an inscription for the ten thousand generations. Goddesses wearing celestial garments and golden bells hanging on the pillar will at the same time summon my disciples to enter the magic city." ' "

The monk looked up at the boxer. "Does it suggest anything to you?"

The boxer thought, then shook his head.

"The Ming-t'ang," the little monk said impatiently. "The 'silver pillar above' is the giant timber we floated from Kuangtung. The 'prophecy below' is the Kuang-wu Ming prophecy. 'Goddesses wearing celestial garments'—well, that could be read in the singular and taken to mean the Empress herself in her inaugural robes. And the golden bells summoning the disciples are her teachings summoning representatives of the provinces to pay homage."

"In other words, we plate the pillar in silver, place a copy of this Kuang-wu Ming manuscript at the base of it, and start referring to the hall as the Heavenly City."

"At last you understand," the monk said with a sigh.

19

THE GIANT BUDDHA

When next the Empress visited the Ming-t'ang, the boxer pointed out the silver plate on the pillar and the addition of the carved box at the base of it that would hold the strange Kuang-wu Ming prophecy. He even quoted for her from memory (he had spent hours learning it) the relevant passage from the Great Cloud Scripture.

The Empress, tilting back her head to take in the immensity of it, grew dizzy, and had to grab the boxer's arm for support.

"Heaven's Chosen is pleased," she said, smiling, recovering herself.

Her words echoed throughout the cavernous room. Soon there would be platforms for sacrifices, and fabulous murals, but now the floor was empty, the walls blank but for the endlessly repeating patterns of brick and mortar. Overhead they could see the second- and third-floor balconies with their ornate railings, the complicated, cantilevered roof brackets known as *tou-kung*, the lattice-work ceiling that allowed in light from the eaves of the highest roof.

"Is it not everything it could have been?" the boxer asked,

basking in the glory of what he thought of as his own work, however slight his contribution may have been.

"Only one thing is lacking."

"What?" He looked around, irritated that any fault should be found in the vast perfection of it.

"We see no place for a Buddha."

"You knew how it would look," he said, trying not to sound too defensive. "You saw the plans." He surveyed the hall with a critical eye. "I suppose we could still put in an alcove or something. It's never too late."

The Empress shook her head. "My Scholars of the North Gate have deemed it improper. They point out that the Ming-t'ang is the embodiment of an ancient ideal, a monument to Heaven, the Supreme Deity. They suggest, instead, a second structure behind it, a pavilion to house the grandest Buddha of all, one so vast that he will make the great Vairocana Buddha at the Lung Men cave shrines seem like a toy. What do you say to the building of such a Buddha?"

"I think it's a fine idea. A beautiful hall like this should have a Buddha nearby, if not within. I'll confer with the Vinaya master and draw you some pictures."

"Excellent. And," she added, almost as an afterthought, "We should like it completed by New Year's."

The boxer squinted at her. "New Year's of what year?"

"Of this year. In time for the great celebration. The astrological signs are auspicious. We dare not lose this opportunity."

"But that's only three months from now."

"Do whatever you need to do. Men, money, materials—take what you require. But please see that it is done on time."

She was not gone a minute when he ordered his tarpan saddled and set off for the White Horse.

"Now she wants a Buddha," he said, striding into the monk's cell, rousing him from his meditation.

"The Empress, you mean?"

"And we're the ones who will be building it."

"Such work is usually enjoyable."

"Yes, but this Buddha is supposed to be bigger than the Vairocana Buddha at the cave shrines outside of town."

"That's not impossible," the little monk said thoughtfully.

"And it's supposed to be finished by New Year's. *This* New Year's."

The little monk grew silent. After a minute he said, "Certainly in nine months. Perhaps in seven, with enough men and good luck. But never in three."

"Well, that's what I told her, but she wouldn't listen. She said, 'Do what you have to do, but get it done.'" He shook his head in disgust and dropped down on the floor beside him. "Women. You do everything you can for them and it's not enough."

The little monk gazed out the window, appraising the position of the sun, which was just tangent to the horizon. The days were shorter now, and the air took on a chill at dusk. "If we ride straight to the palace, we should catch the Empress between her bath and her supper. She is always in a good mood at that time and open to suggestions."

"Then you've got a plan?" the boxer said.

"No. Nothing comes to mind. But I'm sure I'll think of something by the time we arrive."

"Yes?" The boxer's pleasure turned to anger. "And if you don't?"

"Then we'll have a nice evening's ride and be no worse off than when we started."

The Empress received them in her sitting room. Though her tolerance, if not her affection, for the boxer varied from hour to hour, she was always pleased to see the little monk. The servants brought hot tea for them, with fire-dried walnuts from Nan-chao and soy-dipped radish fans to snack on.

"We are delighted by the visit of these two who spread the words of the golden mouth. What brings you here this evening?"

"It's about the giant Buddha," the boxer said.

"Oh," said the Empress, her voice growing cold. "We have no desire to hear excuses as to why Our will cannot be obeyed."

"No excuses," the boxer said quickly. "But an idea. Something the Vinaya master came up with. Tell her."

"Yes," the little monk said. "An idea. Let me see."

The Empress stared at him, waiting.

"The idea is simply that if we are to make a Buddha of such vast proportions, for all the world to see, then we should employ the finest artist in the kingdom. I speak of the poet-painter Wei, whose Buddhist images are without equal."

The corners of the Empress's lips rose in a smile. "He is excellent indeed. A specimen of his calligraphy hangs in Our bedchamber, and though We have looked at it a thousand times, each time Our gaze falls upon it We marvel anew at the grace, the spontaneity, and the life within every line. Once he was an official of Our court, vice-president of the Board of Rites. Alas, he found the life of the bureaucrat a betrayal of his personal principles. He wished to spend his remaining days in a quiet retreat, tending his chrysanthemums and writing his poems. So he resigned and traveled to a distant province. We do not know where to find him."

"But I do," the little monk said. "On several occasions he visited our monastery at Shao-chou, and we, in turn, visited his thatched lodge on the High Eyebrow Mountain, in the west of Szechuan province. Let the boxer and me go to him. I know we can convince him to design our Buddha."

"We've got plenty of good artists here," the boxer said, dreading the thought of a long trip. Why was the little monk filling her head with such troublesome ideas? What possible point could there be in traveling all that distance for some poet-painter, even if he was the best in the world? A Buddha was a Buddha.

"But would the painter sculpt?" the Empress asked, ignoring the boxer. "As far as I know, he loves only the brush."

The monk looked thoughtful. "Perhaps we could persuade him to."

"He does only as he wishes," the Empress pointed out. "Even the orders of Heaven's Chosen leave him unimpressed. In that sense, artists are like monks, outside the rules and manners of our society."

"I suppose you're right," the little monk said. "We'd best forget the whole idea. I'm sure we can find a good enough artist here in Lo-yang. The only other possibility . . ." he seemed on the verge of saying something of the greatest ingenuity, but at the last instant changed his mind, shook his head, fell silent.

"Yes?" the Empress urged.

"Nothing."

"Please tell Us."

He leaned close to her and said with excitement, "I was thinking that if, instead of a statue, we were to make this a massive silk banner, four hundred feet high at least, he could draw the Buddha on a scroll and then other artisans could scale it up to massive proportions."

"But We wanted a *sculpted* Buddha."

"That is why I refrained from voicing my thought."

She was silent for a few moments, sipping her tea. Then: "How would such a banner be held aloft?"

"By a wooden frame within a pavilion," the monk replied.

"You would need more great timbers from the south."

"Now that we know how to move them, we can deliver them without difficulty."

"So the banner would hang like a screen?"

"Yes. That is correct."

"It would not last long."

"As a Buddhist, the Empress knows that nothing but the void is eternal. Its transience would be a lesson in itself. It might even be an advantage, for duplicate banners could be made to replace the first if it were torn or consumed by flame. How much simpler and more economical than rebuilding a tremendous statue. And if you ever decided that you wanted another image to hang in place of the Buddha, the change would be child's play."

The Empress's eyes gleamed. An image of herself as Maitreya!—that was what the monk was hinting at. The boxer was awed by his friend's cunning.

"While this idea is very different from what We had envisioned," she said, "you have impressed Us with its advantages. Might it also be completed more quickly?"

"That is a consideration," the little monk agreed, but in such a way as though to imply that it was of little importance.

"We don't know if Huai-i told you," the Empress said, "but We should like the project done in time for New Year's, that all the people of Lo-yang might venerate it."

"He mentioned something about that."

"Let me consider it more carefully. We will give you Our decision in the morning."

When they had left the Empress, the boxer laughed and slapped the little monk on the back.

A TRIP TO THE SOUTH

In the company of a squad of the Yü-lin Guard, the monk and the boxer set off on horseback for the province of Szechuan. The soldiers wore shingled armor and cowlings that rattled as they rode, and carried banners of the royal purple trimmed with gold. Their sergeant, a fat man with a face like a bull, wore boots with upturned toes, a shingled skirt, an ornate breastplate of layered buffalo hide, and a helmet that curled up at the ears.

They rode for ten days along river valleys and through mountain passes, spending the nights at temples and monasteries along the way, or buying their lodgings from townfolk. When nothing better could be found, they pitched tents. As they traveled, the weather grew warm and humid, the vegetation dense and green. Rain forests replaced the barren, rolling hills of yellow loess soil. A permanent mist covered the land, and the fields of wheat and barley and sugarcane glistened in the morning light. The sweating soldiers stripped off bits of their armor and bound them to the backs of their saddles with leather thongs, until they were down to their underclothes. Far from civilization, they recognized signs of wild animals, bear droppings, the remains of a stag torn apart by lions. When they pitched camp for the night, they piled their campfire with green sugarcane so that the noise of it crackling and exploding would frighten away predators.

The boxer should have enjoyed the freedom and adventure of it, particularly after months of semi-confinement in the palace, but time had changed him. Though he always complained about the Empress's demands, he felt useless and inconsequential without them. Having grown accustomed to the comforts of the palace, he found it difficult to sleep on the straw mats that the monasteries kept for guests, and even harder outside in tents, like a nomad, with rocks and twigs digging into his back and a stick of sugarcane exploding every time he was about to drift off. The soldiers mocked his softness behind his back.

One evening, when he and the little monk had gotten undressed and were lying on their mats in the tent they shared, talking softly about men they had known and places they had seen, they heard the murmur of women's voices. The boxer rose, pulled on his robe, and went to investigate. In the light of the bonfire he saw fifteen of the loveliest girls he had ever seen, waiting at the edge of camp. They stood together, their eyes lowered shyly, while their chaperon, a small, plump, gray-haired woman of fifty or so, talked seriously with the sergeant.

"What's this about?" the boxer demanded, striding to their side.

The sergeant looked at the boxer and blushed. He seemed to be retaining his dignity only with effort.

"They want us to choose the prettiest of them to spend the night with us," he said, unable to look the boxer in the eye.

"You mean they're concubines?" The boxer examined them with interest.

"No, no," the sergeant replied quickly. "It's a queer custom of these parts. Whenever travelers pitch camp near their hamlet, they send all their young women to visit. Those whom the strangers choose to share their pillow think it a great honor. In the morning they ask for some trinket to remember the man by. They wear the trinkets on strings around their necks, and those women with the most trinkets are considered the most attractive and are sought out by the young men of the area as wives."

"You're joking," the boxer said, a smile spreading across his lips. He looked at the plump old lady, who confirmed the story with a nod of her gray head.

"What shall I do, sir?" the sergeant asked. "Send them away?"

The boxer walked among the girls, grinning at one, winking at another, lifting the chin of a third so he might gaze upon her comely young face.

"After all," he said to the sergeant, "it is a local custom. We should not be insensitive to the needs of the people of this fine province. You come with me," he said to a round-faced girl whose skin was fresh as a peach. "And you too," he added, indicating another girl with enormous black eyes. And to the sergeant, "Let your men have their pick of the rest of them. But be sure to remind them to be gentle and sensitive lovers, lest these young ladies speak ill of us in days to come."

And with that he removed the girls from their disappointed companions as a well-trained dog cuts sheep from a herd, and, with an arm around each of them, began to lead them back to his tent. They giggled and nestled against his side. Then suddenly he let go of them and doubled over with pain.

"Are you all right, sir?" the sergeant shouted from behind him, while the girls looked on with concern.

"The cursed warder," he gasped. "It burns like a hot coal in my breast."

He pulled back the collar of his robe in time to see the mark of the palace warder nearly fade from sight. "I don't want them," he whispered to himself. "I don't want them. I don't, I don't, I don't." The pain eased, the mark darkened. He stood up, straightened out his robes, made his breathing normal.

"Sergeant," he said, "you and your men make these girls happy. As the abbot of a great temple, I have forsworn the companionship of women."

He returned to the tent and lay on his mat, trying to fall back asleep. But now, in addition to the exploding bamboo, he had a second distraction, the grunting and moaning of the soldiers as they enjoyed themselves with the village girls. It was a sound that made him grind his teeth and rue the day he had met the Empress Wu.

Now, as they neared the Yangtze, the great river of the south, many of the farms and hamlets they passed were abandoned. Later their horses would overtake bands of refugees in coarse robes, loincloths, and woven bamboo hats, carrying all their earthly possessions in wicker baskets balanced on poles across their backs, or in carts that they pulled by hand. These peasants, hearing the hoofbeats, would drop their belongings, run off the road, and crouch in the ditches, trembling with fear. Soldiers, they knew, were only a cut above brigands. There was a saying, "Good iron is not beaten into nails."

Each time this happened, the little monk would make the entire party stop and wait while he comforted the cowering peasants and gave them gifts from his own stock of food, cash, and clothing. The soldiers thought him mad. When he had exhausted his supplies, he gave away the clothing off his back, since it was warm now, and he had no use for it. Noticing a peasant with a broken basket pole, the little monk offered his own crutch to replace it.

He seemed indifferent to the comic spectacle he made, riding his tarpan in his underclothes and bright silk Buddhist scarf.

"You'll starve," the boxer said. "And when we go back north you'll freeze."

"Heaven will provide for me," the little monk replied with assurance.

Shamed, the boxer joined in the charity and gave away his own provisions, though he would not go so far as to part with his robes. For the Vinaya master, who lived and breathed monkhood, the robes were merely cloth, a device to satisfy modesty and provide warmth. For the boxer, they were the embodiment of his achievement (as well as a device to conceal the K'un-wu sword, which he carried at his side). Without them he would have felt like a peasant.

The parade of refugees filled him with sadness. They reminded him of his childhood, of the last, desperate trek he had made with his father and mother, fleeing the tax collector, looking for a place to start again. He remembered the famine, and trying to fill his belly with pebbles and bark. He remembered his mother's raging fever, his father's slow starvation, how each had gone to walk the Dark Pathway within a few weeks of the other, leaving him alone and friendless in a strange province. No wonder he could not sleep.

While riding through a bamboo forest, laughing at the antics of the monkeys who swung from bough to bough overhead, they encountered another one of these refugee families, slightly bolder than the rest in that they did not flee when they heard the horses approaching. They were twelve in number: the head of the clan, a wizened old man with a beard like silk floss; three younger men and their wives; and some half-dozen sons and daughters ranging from infancy to a marriageable age. Coming alongside them, the little monk and the boxer offered food and cash, which they shyly accepted. The boxer, making small talk to put them at ease, asked their destination.

"The city of Tung-chou," the old man replied, "to look for work."

"But why would you abandon the honorable life of the farmer?"

"How can we farm without a plow?"

"What became of your plow, old man?" the boxer asked with concern.

The old man hesitated.

A parrot, his red feathers only just visible through the rich green foliage overhead, squawked and took flight.

One of the young men spoke up, his voice as bitter as spoiled wine: "The wolf-woman Wu seized our plow to make iron dragons for her Ming-t'ang. She has taken the plows of all the farmers. What are we to do? Turn up the soil with our chopsticks?"

The sergeant swung his weight down from the pony and strode over, his face flushed, his eyes large and protruding, making his resemblance to a bull all the more striking. He had shed all his armor in deference to the heat, and his white under-robe, soaked with sweat, adhered to the bulge of his stomach.

"You would call Heaven's Chosen a wolf-woman?"

"I would call Confucius a fox-fairy if I thought he was one," the young man said.

"Then kneel so I may chop off your head," the sergeant said, drawing his sword, "and make a neat job of it."

"I will not," he said, and, grabbing the pole he had used to balance his baskets, held it in both hands like a staff. The other two young men copied his example, as did the older man with the white beard. They faced the soldiers, a brave little army.

The forest was silent. No creature stirred. The canopy of foliage overhead was impossibly still.

"You are no farmers," the sergeant said, "but common outlaws. You shall die for this—every man, woman, and child among you."

Hearing this, the younger children wept, and hid behind their mother's robes.

"In the reign of the wolf-woman," the young man replied in

a voice rapturous with excitement, "the outlaw is the virtuous man, and the mandarin is the outlaw."

"Kill them," the sergeant ordered, and his men rushed forward, intending to make quick work of them with their blades. Suddenly all was turmoil. The older children grabbed the younger ones in their arms and ran. The jungle animals fled too, driven from their hiding places by the scuffle. Screaming monkeys leaped through the branches, and the birds took to the sky with a great show of color and flapping of wings.

Observing the fighting, the boxer felt the same kind of envy he had felt when listening to the soldiers share their pillows with the village girls a few nights before. How he loved a good fight, and longed to join in! The refugees were surprisingly skilled with their poles—obviously this sort of fighting was an art they had trained in, for defense or pleasure—and they managed to block nearly every sword thrust. When their staffs got split, they used the short pieces in a different style, raining blows or stabbing with them. There came a point when the boxer could resist the temptation no longer, and he drew the K'un-wu sword hidden under his robes and charged, howling like a beast.

Which side did he fight on? If one had asked him while he was standing on the sidelines, he would have answered: the Yü-lin Guard, of course. But no sooner had he closed his fingers around the sharkskin hilt than he felt an electric bond between his heart and his hand, and turned the blade against the very same men whose authority, by all rights, he should have defended. Never had he fought so gracefully, never had his strokes been so sure and powerful. He acted without a moment's premeditation, observing neither himself nor his audience in order to calculate the theatrical effect of his moves, one of his worst failings in combat. He was all of one piece, a single entity with his weapon, a devastating fighting force.

The soldiers, despite their efforts, fell like quail. The K'un-wu sword dispatched five of them with clean, quick strokes while the refugees hacked away at the rest. When all the soldiers were dead, the refugees turned toward the sergeant, slapping their broken staffs against their palms. He held up his hands and backed away, whispering, "Do not hurt me, please. I will give you cash, my fine horse, a hundred bolts of silk . . ." His bowels let loose, and fecal matter stained his white under-robes.

"If we let him live," the old man said, "he will come back for us. If he cannot find us, he will kill others. Who knows how many refugees will lose their lives in retribution for those whom we killed today?"

For this reason they decided to execute him, but while they were arguing over who would do the deed and how (execution being a dreadful task for any man of character), one of the wives suddenly whispered, "He is mine," and, grabbing a sword from a dead soldier by her feet, sprang forward and buried its blade in the sergeant's gut. She moved so quickly that no one had time to object. His eyes opened very wide, and he toppled over backwards, taking the sword with him.

The refugees bowed solemnly to the monks. The boxer, carried away with sympathy, urged them to take all the soldiers' possessions. Instead they satisfied themselves with the ponies, which were rare in the south and of great value. Tying one to the next, they led them on their way.

The boxer stood for some time, trying to understand the implications of what had occurred. The bodies lay about him in crazy positions, some shorn of arms and legs and heads, some hacked to pieces or sliced in the gut so that viscera spilled out and turned the earth black with blood. The killing did not bother him so much as the fact that he had defied agents of the Empress, which act was not so different from defying the Empress herself.

"You are a rebel," the little monk said, as if reading his thoughts.

"I am not! And if you ever say that again, you'll die for it."

"Like it or not, you are," the little monk whispered. "You are a good man at heart, but you haven't the courage to break the royal rice bowl. You love your luxury too much, and your power even more."

"Listen, turtle spawn, I have the courage of a dozen men. See how I killed those soldiers? But I am not a rebel! I did what I did—" He stopped to think, and to clean his sword in the dirt. "I did what I did because I felt sorry for the children. I did not wish to see them harmed. But this was an exception, a freak occurrence. It will never happen again. I am a mandarin, a baron, abbot of the White Horse, humble servant of the Empress Wu. Do you understand?"

As they hacked down dead trees with the dead soldiers' swords (one could not insult the great K'un-wu sword with such work) for wood to feed a funeral pyre, the little monk said, "Do you recall how you felt, fighting?"

The boxer threw a log on the pyre they were preparing, and grinned. "As though I did not care whether I lived or died."

"That was Ch'an fighting. You knew neither good nor evil. And perhaps you almost glimpsed your original face."

The boxer regarded him with absolute amazement. "For the first time," he whispered, "it does not seem like nonsense. I think I understand."

"You understand nothing," the little monk said, and laughed at the boxer's angry look.

Suffice it to say that the sergeant and his soldiers were neither mourned nor missed. The boxer and the little monk could protect themselves, and as for finding their way, the monk had traveled through this part of Szechuan and knew the roads and rivers.

Cantering up a ridge the next morning, they found themselves overlooking the sweeping Yangtze River valley, a quilt of bright green rice paddies, amber wheat, gray barley, and red cane. The river itself was dark and turbulent, as broad as a sea, and crowded with every sort of barge, dinghy, raft, and junk. Men and oxen in vast numbers trudged along the banks, hauling the barges behind them with ropes of hemp and bamboo. To the east the boxer could see the walled city of Tung-chou, and to the west, craggy, mysterious foothills swathed in mist. The little monk pointed out four distant peaks, the Four Great Peaks of the Buddha, the tallest of which, the High Eyebrow Mountain, was their destination. There, midway between base and summit, the poet-painter had escaped the petty world of the court for something pure and rare.

As they rode their ponies along the river valley, the little monk said, "If we are asked, we might be wise to identify ourselves as members of my temple, the Dharma Gate of the East Mountain, rather than of your White Horse. You and your temple are known as favorites of the Empress, and the Empress does not seem to be well liked in these parts."

Had anyone else had the effrontery to make such a suggestion, the boxer would have cursed him and drawn his sword. But, the little monk's words having been amply supported by yesterday morning's skirmish, he quietly agreed.

That afternoon they reached the foothills, and that night, the base of the High Eyebrow. Though the area seemed desolate, the only inn was so crowded with pilgrims, lay brothers, and monks that they were forced to sleep in the courtyard on coarse gravel, the texture of which was only slightly disguised by their mats. A phenomenon called the Precious Light of the Buddha, which often took place near the summit at dusk, an exquisite rainbow seen through the mist, had made the High Eyebrow a holy place where pilgrims might acquire merit simply by visiting. More than seventy temples and monasteries were scattered around the mountaintop to receive visitors and house the several thousand monks who lived there permanently.

In the morning they left their ponies with a groom and started along the tortuous footpath that led up the mountain. The little monk set off with a new cane and new robes, the former cut from a bamboo tree, the latter presented to him by a fellow monk he had befriended that morning. In places the path skirted rock face and grew so narrow that the climber had to hug the wall, and in other places it was so steep that steps had been chiseled in the stone. Despite the little monk's handicap, he nearly kept pace with the boxer. Where the path was wide and flat, they would rest on some comfortable bit of moss, catch their breath, and enjoy the wondrous view of the Yangtze winding through the mist. The boxer was fascinated by the rapport between his friend and the other monks they met at such times. Regardless of what sect they represented, whether they longed for the Pure Land and chanted the name of A-mi-t'o-fo, or read the Three Treatises of Nagarjuna, or pondered the queer riddles of Ch'an, they were all brothers in the Buddha. They would always ask where the other was from, if he had visited such and such a temple in that vicinity, and if so, what news he had of the monks who resided there; was this one still abbot, and had that one gained the state of joy where "Kwatz!" is shouted? The boxer envied them their closeness and wondered why, though he wore the robes, he did not share it.

That afternoon, still well below the timberline, yet high enough that the Yangtze resembled a serpent and Tung-chou a gem lost in a sea of mist, they reached a place where the way forked, and the little monk guided them on the less-trodden path, insisting, even though he had not visited the place in five years, that it led to the lodge of the great poet-painter.

Indeed, his memory was not faulty. Another hour of walking at a quick pace found them at the gate of a rustic garden of small, twisted pines and poplars. Wild grasses grew among smooth white stones. A babbling creek emptied into a pool where golden carp swam. All this was combined so subtly and artfully that it might have been some happy accident of nature rather than the conscious work of man. (In this respect it was the opposite of the formal garden of Prince Hsüeh, with its pitted stone and rare plantings.) A path that wound through the garden, affording many beautiful vistas, led to a hut with daub-and-wattle walls, a thatched roof, and unfinished fretwork screens on either side of the entrance. Bamboo shades, gathered at the top of the doorway, let in the sun and smells.

A middle-aged man, clearly visible through the entryway, sat cross-legged on the floor, wearing a mandarin's robes and a humped black cap and reading a scroll. A few other scrolls were stacked in a drum beside him.

The little monk cleared his throat.

21

THE GREAT POET-PAINTER

"My dear friend," the mandarin said, rising and bowing. "Too many months have passed since last we spoke. My heart overflows with joy to see you once again. Here in my thatched hut I have few guests beyond the birds that sing for me in the morning, and the deer who pose for me in the evening."

He had a long, drawn face, a scraggly beard, and drooping mustaches. His complexion was sallow, and his almond eyes glittered with sensitivity.

"Have you come to admire this splendid mountain," he continued, "and witness the Precious Light of the Buddha, which alleviates all sorrows?"

"In fact," the little monk said, "we've come to see you." He introduced the boxer, and explained, without actually mentioning the Empress's name or the fact that any official patronage was involved, that thay had decided to construct an enormous banner of the Buddha, and that they wanted the greatest artist in the kingdom to make the sketch for it.

"I am hardly a great artist," the poet replied. "My brushwork is a poor and awkward thing. Still, I am flattered that you came all this distance, and I will do my best. Certainly, in such a noble undertaking, the bodhisattvas will take pity and guide my hand. But what a poor host I am! You must be exhausted from your long climb. Come sit in my lodge and share some wine with me. I rarely have the pleasure of guests."

The hut contained only two rooms and four windows. As for furnishings, there were four wooden beds (for the rare occasions when he did receive friends, the poet explained), a bent-necked lute, a painting kit, paper, and the drum of scrolls that included poetry, anthologies, a few of the Confucian classics, and the popular Buddhist scripture called the Lotus of the True Law. One chest held lacquerware, another his clothes. Thus his possessions were few and simple, and served him rather than made him their slave.

They seated themselves on the floor, in such a way that they could admire the garden and the view of the valley, and drank delicately scented ginger wine from cups of green lacquerware.

At first the little monk and the great poet exchanged gossip about this monk and that, much like the conversations that had taken place during their climb. The boxer listened but dared not speak, awed as he was by the refined surroundings and the fame of his host. Presently, when his host seemed to have run out of questions, he felt a little more at ease and ventured a comment:

"Don't you get lonely up here, all by yourself? What I mean is, don't you miss city life? The crowds and excitement of the wine shops and the market?"

The great poet laughed, perhaps a trifle condescendingly, the boxer thought. "There are many distractions and joys in nature, too. I once wrote a poem on this subject. Would you care to hear it?"

The little monk and the boxer urged him on, the latter admittedly more out of politeness than enthusiasm.

The great poet gazed into the distance and began:

I lean on the south window and let my pride expand.
I consider how easy it is to be content with a little space.
Every day I stroll in the garden for pleasure.
There is a gate there, but it is always shut.
Cane in hand, I walk and rest,
Occasionally raising my head to gaze into the distance.
The clouds aimlessly rise from the peaks.
The weary-winged birds know it's time to come home.

*As the sun's rays grow dim and disappear from view,
I walk around my lonely pine tree, stroking it....*

He would have gone on, but at that moment three peasants appeared, running up the garden path carrying wicker baskets balanced on poles across their backs. The boxer expected the great poet to become furious at such an interruption, and was surprised to see that he was pleased. The peasants hurried up to the front steps of the hut and lay down their baskets in a row.

"I'll finish the poem in a moment," the great poet told his guests. Rubbing his hands together in anticipation, he said to the peasants, "Well, what have we got today, boys?"

In response to which they opened the baskets and revealed the most marvelous assortment of foodstuffs that the boxer had seen outside the palace kitchen. There were plucked ducks, chickens, and quail, baby pig, crisp bean sprouts, snow peas, yellow squash, winter melon, lotus root, celery heart, bamboo shoots, cassia bark, straw mushrooms and oyster mushrooms, lily buds, scallions, and tree ears, as well as a variety of fruits and nuts.

The great poet looked through the food, sniffing, fingering, and otherwise ascertaining the quality of each item, and then directed the boys to prepare certain elaborate dishes using the foods he had chosen. They bowed several times, put the foods back in the baskets, shouldered the poles on which the baskets hung, and ran off.

"Of course you'll join me for dinner?" the great poet said.

"I thought you lived all alone up here," the boxer said.

"So I do."

"Then who were they?"

"My servants. They live at the bottom of the mountain." Noticing the look on the boxer's face, he went on, "Do you live without servants?"

"No."

"Then why would you expect me to?"

"I—I don't know. I thought you came here to enjoy a simpler life."

"Would it be simpler without servants to do my bidding?"

"I see your point," the boxer said, though in truth something still confused him.

"What I fled was the artificiality of government life, the pretension, the competition, the endless chitchat, the false smiles one wore while socializing with men of culture. It happens I have another verse on the subject. That is, if you are not bored with my work."

"Far from it," the boxer said, wondering if they would have to spend the entire day listening to the great poet recite.

He began:

> When I was young I was out of tune with the herd;
> My only love was for the hills and mountains.
> Unwittingly I fell into the web of the world's dust
> And was not free until my thirtieth year.
> The migrant bird yearns for the old wood;
> The fish in the tank thinks of its native pool.
> I had rescued from wilderness a patch of mountainside
> And still rustic, I returned to garden and field.
> Long I lived checked by the bars of a cage;
> Now I have turned again to Nature and Freedom.

He dropped his head forward as though the work of reciting it had exhausted him utterly.

"I like that line, 'web of the world's dust,'" the boxer said.

The great poet nodded. "Thank you."

Then, hearing the gravel of the garden path crunch beneath visitors' slippers, he looked up eagerly.

Three mandarins were approaching. Two of them wore purple robes, belts of gold, and jade plaques indicating that they were dukes at the very least, or perhaps even princes, while the third wore a dark green robe with a silver belt, indicating that he was a marquis. They all wore humped black caps with ties that hung down like drooping rabbits' ears, and black slippers.

Judging from the great poet's effusive welcome, he was not unduly angered by this invasion from the web of the world's dust. He introduced them to the boxer and the little monk. The first, a man in his sixties, tall, with a drawn face and a sad, weary look to his eye, was no less a personage than Li Chuan, T'ang prince, granduncle of the emperor Jui-tsung, and prefect of Tung-chou. The young man who accompanied him was his son, Li Chan, tall like his father but not yet so debilitated by life. He had kind black eyes, fine white teeth, and smiled often. The third man, a local magistrate, was short and plump, with small eyes girdled in fat, and a mole growing on the side of his nose.

"We must speak with you," the elder prince said.

"Then join us," the great poet said generously, "for nothing encourages speech like a good wine, a pleasant view, and the company of virtuous friends."

"We do not wish to trade verse," the elder prince said, irritated by the poet's cavalier attitude. "This is a matter that may decide our futures."

"The past and future are but a dream," the poet said. "All that truly matters are the knotted pines of my garden."

"We acknowledge your sensitivity and appreciation of nature. However, what we need now is your counsel. Please tell us when we can speak to you regarding this pressing matter."

The great poet gazed up at the sun. "Come back at the Hour of the Monkey. We will dine together and you can tell me your problem then. These two fine monks will join us."

"We must speak with you *alone*," the elder prince said.

"They can be trusted," the poet said. "They are visitors from the Dharma Gate of the East Mountain, where the virtue of the monks is beyond calculation."

The elder prince leaned forward and whispered into the great poet's ear.

The great poet responded, "They are enemies of the Empress Wu, just as we are. Yesterday this big monk"—he indicated the boxer—"slaughtered a dozen of the Empress's personal guard who had threatened a poor band of refugees. What greater show of loyalty could you require?"

"How do you know about that?" the boxer asked.

"In these parts, news of rebellion spreads like wildfire."

The boxer looked uncomfortable, but said nothing.

The elder prince examined the face of the boxer carefully, as though the truth might be written there in the fold of his eye or the cave of his nostril. Finally he nodded and agreed. "We will dine and tell you of our problem then."

The more the boxer saw of it, the more complex the simple life of the poet appeared. When the boxer and the Vinaya master returned from their afternoon trek to the summit of the mountain, where they had gone in hopes of seeing the Precious Light of the Buddha (they had seen nothing but a hundred other sightseeing monks and an endless vista of mist), they found a low table erected in a clearing in the garden, and the three servant boys setting it with lacquerware cups and bowls and ivory chopsticks. Meanwhile, a cleaver-wielding chef was preparing dozens of dishes on a stove behind the hut. Smells of earth and pine had given way to the most delicious fragrances of frying pork, soy sauce, and peppers.

When all the guests had arrived, they were seated on low stools around the table. Torches were lighted and the courses presented, as many as there were guests, each artfully arranged on a platter of contrasting color. Among the dishes were regional specialties the boxer had never seen before, such as soft-fried lotus blossoms, and shredded chicken with orchid petals. Although the food of these parts was famous for its spiciness, the true gourmet dishes were distinguished more by their use of fragrant and colorful flowers.

The evening was perfect, less damp than it had been, with a warm breeze rustling the pines. The conversation, revolving as it did around poetry, Ch'an, gardens, and tales of the antics of eccentric monks, was lively, and the food was fresh and faultlessly prepared. By the time dessert came—pears steamed in cassia, honey, and wine—the elder prince, though far from gay, was in a better temper than he had been in that afternoon.

The great poet leaned across the table and said, "Unburden yourself. Allow us, your friends, to share the dreadful weight you carry."

The elder prince regarded them one at a time. "The wolf-woman Wu has summoned us to the capital to celebrate the discovery of the white stone. We fear it is a trap."

"First things first," the poet said. "What sort of stone is this that warrants a celebration? Be patient with me, for here on my mountain I am out of touch with the world."

"It is a white stone dredged by a fisherman from the River Lo. Eight characters appear upon it in smooth lines and curves, as though engraved by the elements. These characters say: A Sage Mother shall come to rule mankind, and her reign shall be eternally prosperous." The Empress insists it is the work of Heaven, another augury of her reign."

The poet laughed. "Whenever has Heaven spoken so specifically? I have seen a stone with a pit in it that looked like the Buddha, and another stone that the river had shaped to resemble a stooped old man. But never have I seen a stone with a whole sentence carved in it. Particularly one of such political utility."

"It is another stunt," the young prince said, "to legitimize her rule. She means to evoke the memory of the great Emperor Yü of antiquity, and the tortoise he found in the River Lo, upon whose shell were written the characters of our language."

"The Empress is in love with this white stone," the elder prince said. "She memorializes about it before the court, claiming it to be 'pure of heart.' She has made the fisherman who found it a 'roving general,' and she has forbidden fishing in the River Lo."

"First she takes the plows from the farmers," the magistrate murmured. "Now she forbids fishing in the Lo. How are men to eat?"

"No sooner do we hear of this white stone," the elder prince said, "than a messenger arrives with her invitation."

"Ah yes," the poet said. "The invitation."

"She wishes us to attend the festival celebrating the discovery of this white stone, as well as the opening of the Ming-t'ang she has constructed."

"This Ming-t'ang is yet another manifestation of her endless corruption," the poet said. "The rumor is that she gave her male concubine a million cash to build it, though he is a peasant who cannot even read or write."

"Concubine?" the boxer said.

"You know," the poet said. "This so-called abbot whom her daughter picked up in the marketplace."

"There must be *something* special about him," the magistrate said, winking lewdly and rubbing the place between his legs.

The poet and the younger prince laughed, and even the elder prince, with all his misery, smiled. Only the boxer and the Vinaya master failed to see any humor in it.

"So what if he is a peasant?" the boxer demanded, unable to tolerate another moment of this. "We all share the Buddha-nature. Perhaps he was a Patriarch in a former life. Perhaps he was Bodhidharma himself. I understand he is quite wise and gentle."

"I hear he is a conceited lout," the poet said, "who takes advantage of his status to bully and humiliate others."

"Lies and slander!" the boxer objected, half rising from his seat.

"Then you know him?" the young prince inquired. "You must tell us all about it. Where did you meet? What was he like?"

"My brother monk," the Vinaya master interrupted, "has such compassion that he cannot bear to hear ill spoken of anyone, and comes to their defense even if they be the blackest criminal. But I fear we have wandered from the subject at hand." He turned to the elder prince. "You were saying that you were summoned by the Empress."

"Yes. To attend the opening of the Ming-t'ang, and celebrate the augury stone. I have been in touch with my cousin Li Ch'ung, governor of Pao-chou in Shantung, and he has received a similar invitation. Apparently all the Li princes have been invited."

"It is not enough that she degrades them," the magistrate said, "and sends them to govern frontier provinces. Now she calls them back to humiliate them—"

"Or annihilate them," the poet said grimly.

"So I thought, too," said the elder prince. "No sooner have the Li princes arrived at the Ming-t'ang than the building catches fire. The doors are barred. There is no escape."

"Or else," his son said, "we sit down to a banquet of poisoned food that we cannot refuse."

"Then don't go," the boxer said. "It seems simple enough." He was losing patience with them. All this derogatory talk about the Empress made him edgy. Even though she was hundreds of miles away, he imagined that she could somehow overhear them.

The elder prince shook his head. "For us Li princes to refuse as a group would be to admit conspiracy and to condemn ourselves. She has set a cunning trap. Either way we lose."

"Then you have only one choice," the poet said.

"Rebellion," the young prince whispered.

The boxer and the little monk exchanged glances.

"Can you find sufficient support?" the little monk asked.

"Not in Szechuan," the young prince said. "Here life is too sweet. Even those farmers who have lost their plows to the iron collectors are unwilling to lose their lives. But in Shantung there are many valiant fighting men and there is much talk of separatism. That is where we will find the spine of our army. Cousin Li Ch'ung will lead their march on Lo-yang."

"It is a dangerous undertaking," the poet said. "If you fail, it will mean your own lives and the probable extinction of the Li clan.

But if you succeed, then the T'ang will be restored to power and the Middle Kingdom will cast aside the yoke of the wolf-woman's rule."

"We must act quickly and boldly," the elder prince said, "yet with caution, for the slightest mistake will mean our undoing. Tomorrow, at the Hour of the Rabbit, couriers on fleet ponies will leave for every corner of the kingdom where Li princes have been exiled. They will take with them an edict composed in the name of Cousin Jui-tsung, imploring them to march on the capital and rescue him."

"Then Jui-tsung is a part of your rebellion?" the boxer asked, remembering the docile, slouch-shouldered adolescent who seemed interested in nothing beyond his wooden puzzles.

"We will use his name," the young prince replied, as if explaining it to a child, "to legitimize the rebellion. It is something he would want us to do. Once we have captured Lo-yang and disposed of the Empress, we will restore Jui-tsung as true sovereign of the land."

"And let us not forget," the elder prince went on, "to send an edict to the loyal servant of Li-hung, who still waits for rebellion under his guise of madness. After all these years of pretending, he will be gratified by the opportunity for action."

But the boxer wasn't listening, for a certain question had occurred to him: "What will become of the Empress's favorites when this rebellion finally takes place? For example, oh, I don't know. That fellow you were talking about before. The abbot of the White Horse Temple."

"He will be sliced, or strangled," the young prince said, "for decapitation would be too kind."

"Much too kind," the boxer agreed uncomfortably.

The dinner guests spent the night at their host's hut. In the morning, when they were about to depart, the poet asked the monks if they had forgotten something. He watched with amusement as they tried and finally succeeded in remembering the sketch of the Buddha that had been their reason for coming. Revelations of the previous evening had shunted the matter to the rear of their minds.

The great poet took out his writing set, ground some ink on his stone palette, dipped his brush, and, with a few quick strokes created a Buddha that conveyed the stillness of a stone, yet at the same time nearly pulsated with life. Even the boxer, whose aesthetic sense was raw, to say the least, realized the genius of it. If this were not enough, the poet dashed off a second, that they might make a choice, and three more, so that the two princes and the magistrate might each have a reminder of their visit. Each was perfect and spontaneous, and completely different from the previous painting.

"Ch'an brush," the little monk murmured.

On the elder prince's drawing he included the following verse, in a wonderfully powerful hand:

> *When the hills are flat*
> *And the rivers dry,*
> *When it lightens and thunders in winter*
> *When it rains and snows in summer,*
> *When Heaven and Earth mingle—*
> *Only then will our friendships cease.*

Together the five guests bid their host farewell and descended the steep footpath to the mountain base, where they parted ways. Sedan chairs were waiting to take the princes and the magistrate back to Tung-chou. The boxer and the Vinaya master returned to the inn to pick up their horses. Neither said a word to the other. Rebellion hung like a black shroud over their thoughts. The groom delivered their horses, and the boxer paid him from his leather pouch of cash. They rode a little way along the river valley before the monk stopped his horse and climbed down. Dark, rolling clouds had massed over the Yangtze. The distant rain appeared as a crosshatching of diagonal lines so fine as to be nearly invisible. Now a few drops began to fall from overhead. Peasants standing knee-deep in rice paddies peered up at the sky in appreciation, as if it had told a good joke. Others ran for the shelter of little huts, holding their broad-brimmed bamboo hats to their heads.

"What are you doing?" the boxer demanded.

"I cannot come with you," the little monk apologized. "I will stay here."

"What are you talking about?"

"I have learned too much about the Empress. I can no longer serve her with a clear conscience. I never should have, but I deceived myself because I enjoyed the attention and acclaim."

"Don't be silly! Where will you go?"

"There are many monasteries and temples where I can be of service."

"You won't join the rebellion, will you? It cannot succeed. Everyone involved will die a terrible death."

"Alas, I like the rebels no better than I like the Empress. I will take no side in this dispute. Time will settle it justly, as it does all matters. And now we will say farewell. Unless you care to come with me."

The boxer sat on his mount, gazing at the monk and contemplating the offer. The rain became a downpour, putting a gleam to his bald dome, soaking his robes. The ground was quickly turning to mud, and the river roared down from the mountains like a quiet man goaded to violence.

"How could I?" the boxer asked.

"Simply do it. You may never have another chance. Come with me and learn what it is to be a real monk. I promise you, no joy can equal it! We could travel together to the Dharma Gate of the East Mountain and listen to the teachings of the Sixth Patriarch. He has brought men like you to enlightenment in a matter of years."

The boxer thought about it. A light came to his eyes, and for an instant he might actually have contemplated doing it. But then he smiled and shook his head.

"No."

"If you go back"—the little monk hesitated—"you will not live long. So many enemies. And it is only a question of time before the Empress turns on you, too."

"I can take care of myself," the boxer said, the old swagger coming back to him. "And don't worry about the Empress. I'm the only man who can please her."

The monk turned and began to trudge off into the rain.

"Wait!" the boxer shouted. "What about the pavilion for the great Buddha?"

The monk turned. He had to shout to be heard over the downpour. "The plans have been drawn. The workmen know what to do. You need only give them the sketch."

"And the commentary on the Great Cloud Scripture?"

"Alas, it is done. Would that I could undo it, for that document will prove my most dangerous lie."

"What about—" he began, desperate to make the little monk stay. "What about our friendship?"

Here the little monk's voice grew very sad. "That is the thing I will miss most of all."

All the way home he considered telling her about the rebellion. In the last year he had caused her mostly embarrassment, and this might be an opportunity to remind her of how clever and useful he could be. He hesitated only out of fear that, by dining with the rebels, he had hopelessly implicated himself. It was a difficult decision, and the boxer was not good with problems that required intellection.

Even after he had returned to the palace, the problem plagued him. One morning he would rise resolved to tell her, change his mind halfway to her chamber, change his mind again that afternoon, and wake up in the middle of the night with still another opinion.

In order to postpone the decision, he did not go to her, but waited for her to summon him. When the summons never came, he grew irritated and sent a note demanding that she visit his apartments immediately to learn some very important news. She didn't respond to that, either, but sent a eunuch in her stead, who explained that she was occupied with a crisis and would have no time for him until it had been resolved.

At such a time, the boxer decided, it was only proper that he be counted among the Empress's valued advisers. He insisted that he be taken to her. He bullied his way into the temporary Phoenix Hall, where he found Heaven's Chosen surrounded by her most important ministers and generals. Everywhere he looked, he saw purple robes and belts with gold plaques. When the Empress noticed the boxer, her eyes burned like coals and she thrust a finger at him.

"You were there! You were in Szechuan at the very instant this rebellion was being hatched, yet you caught no clue of it! Were you so busy ogling the girls that you could not see the traitors behind every tree? Did you spend so much time in the taverns that you missed the rebels marching through the fields? How could you have been so stupid and blind? How could you?"

"Rebellion?" he said, as though it were news to him. "What rebellion?" He shouldn't have been in such a rush to see her, he decided. He should have waited a couple of weeks.

"The rebellion of the Li princes," she said furiously.

"No one in Szechuan would tell me of such things. They know

I am your most vehement supporter. Why, had I even heard mention of the word rebellion, I would have drawn my sword and—"

He pulled his K'un-wu sword from beneath his robe and made as if to stab one of the ministers for whom he bore a particular dislike. The mandarin froze with terror, eyes riveted on the blade poised inches from his breastbone.

"This is no time for play," the Empress said. "The rebel forces are gathering at Wu Shui in preparation for crossing the Yellow River."

"I do not play! I am only saying that I would lay down my life for you in an instant. Send me to battle those rebel forces. I will bring them to their knees, I swear it."

The Empress stared at him, and shook her head in wonder. "Do you really think that you could lead an army? You could not even lead your little band of monks without the help of the Vinaya master."

"May I remind you that I am a fighter by profession? I know what it means to face a dangerous opponent in battle. I know how it feels to defend one's benefactor."

"We have no patience for him today," the Empress said to her eunuchs.

"Well, if you have no use for me, then I will leave. I am a busy fellow with many matters to attend to." Pouting, he waited for the Empress to stop his departure, but she merely turned away from him and conferred with her ministers.

"I," he said loudly, "am leaving."

Nobody even turned in his direction.

"Hah!" he said, and stomped out of the audience chamber. Striding along the loggia, face twisted in its worst scowl, he nearly ran down a handservant who happened to get in his way.

He retired to his apartments and spent the next two days drawing vicious caricatures of the Empress (though now he took the precaution of burning them afterwards, lest they fall into the wrong hands). He vowed never to speak to her again. He would simply remain in his rooms and not come out, no matter how hard she pleaded.

So he had resolved.

But when, four nights later, he heard a knocking at his door and opened it and saw the Empress standing on his doorstep, as sad and vulnerable as a waif, his heart opened to her.

"I am weary and frightened," she said, "and need these strong arms of yours to hold me."

She felt like a trembling sparrow against his chest. For a long time he simply held her without speaking a word. Then he picked her up in his arms and carried her into the bedchamber. They acted the Clouds and Rain, but with so little artifice on her part that it seemed like some newly discovered rite, filled with unexpected tenderness and melancholy. Afterwards, they lay together and he stroked her thigh and whispered about how much he loved her. Still later, they sat up in bed and drank mare's-teat wine that the servants brought, and ate the golden peaches of long life.

"The rebellion has been crushed," she said to him. "The treacherous Li Ch'ung led five thousand men on the city of Chi Nan. We sent the imperial army under the command of Ch'iu Shen-chi, my finest general, to fight them. If We could have sent you, Precious One, We would have, but We dared not alienate Our court at such a perilous time by indulging in an act that Our critics would certainly cite as favoritism. Some other time you will be Our general, We swear it before the eyes of Heaven. Perhaps you will lead an army against the Turks—would you like that?"

"Whatever enemies I challenge, I will vanquish in your name. I will force their kings and ministers to kowtow before your throne, and I will make them send gold and dwarves and horses in tribute."

"I know you will, my Precious, my wonderful Precious One."

"Now tell me about the battle for Chi Nan."

"There was none, for first they had to cross the Yellow River, and that entailed seizing the little town of Wu Shui for a base from which to depart. Li Ch'ung tried to storm the town by rolling carts filled with burning grass against the gates. But the wind changed, blowing the fire back over his own troops so that some were killed by the flames or by the hot smoke in their lungs, and the rest were forced to retreat."

"Well, losing one battle early on should not have discouraged them."

"Indeed not. But Li Ch'ung was a poor leader of men. When one of his officers expressed doubts about the rebellion, he had him beheaded as an example. The other rebels were so dismayed by his cruelty that they disbanded, and he was left with only his household guard. He tried to return to his home in Liao Ch'eng, but the guards at the city gate, having heard of his failure, slew him and chopped off his head in hopes of regaining Our favor. When the imperial army arrived, the city's officials came forward in mourning clothes, that they too might be forgiven. Alas, the general did not accept this gesture, and put them and their families to death."

"How many?"

"One thousand and a few more. Now Li Ch'ung's father, Li Chen, who was prefect of Yu Chou in northern Anhui, had raised troops too. Yet they were so lacking in enthusiasm that when they saw Our imperial army approaching, they disbanded and fled like rabbits. Li Chen retreated to his city and closed the gates. As he stood on the parapet watching Our troops surround him, one of Our captains called to him and said, "Prince, why are you sitting up there, waiting for death?" Since he had no answer to the question, he took his own life, as did his son and daughter, and her husband, too."

"And that was the end of it?"

"Nearly. There were, as always, a few loose threads to be bound. My watchdogs made a list of all the Li princes involved in the rebellion, so that they and their families could be executed. These include Li Yüan-k'uei, Li Yüan-chia, and the Princess Ch'ang Lo, to name a few. And there was another member of the conspiracy whose identity may shock you."

The boxer's heart stopped. Had the little monk changed his mind and joined the rebellion after all? Or, worse, had the Empress learned of his presence at the dinner with the rebel leaders? It was not unlike her to prolong such an embarrassing revelation in order to deepen her victim's discomfort and thus milk the most satisfaction from it. He'd seen it before. If she had learned about it, no amount of tender feelings would save his life; he knew this for a certainty. Yet, study her as he would, he saw no hint of the cat's smile that usually boded her more disastrous revelations.

"Your son, Hsüeh Shao." She had a twinkle in her eye, knowing how the boxer disliked that particular prince whose home he had once shared.

"My son?" The boxer noticed that his own laughter had an hysterical edge to it. "How did he get caught up in it?"

"He supplied crossbows and blades to Li Ch'ung. He vowed vengeance against Us, and do you know why? Because We had given you his name. At least that is the theory of Princess T'ai-p'ing."

The boxer laughed some more. "Is the princess sad to lose him?"

"She had tired of him. All he ever spoke of was his gardening. In truth, she has little affection for men. Still, he was her husband. In deference to this, I have permitted him to starve to death in prison, rather than endure the humiliation of public execution."

"An act of charity," the boxer agreed.

22

THE BOXER IS BETRAYED

The months preceding the opening of the Ming-t'ang passed quickly, for the boxer had much to attend to. Artists had to be engaged to enlarge the great poet's sketch of the Buddha and transfer it to a vast scroll of silk, as wide and long as a river, and carpenters had to be hired to finish and miter the timbers from the south, so that they could be assembled into a towering, open pavilion in which the banner could be hung.

In the past, the little monk had taken care of all such important decisions, making them appear effortless. But now that he was gone, all responsibility rested on the boxer's shoulders. Losing him was like losing a limb, a part of himself that he took for granted. Every time he gave an order he wondered, Is this right? Is this what the little monk would have said? Yet he dared not hesitate or reverse himself, for fear of appearing weak or unsure. Better to make mistakes with conviction, that much he knew.

Inspired by the sketch, the artists worked quickly and well. Soon it was nearly done; all that remained was the ceremony called "Opening the Eyes of the Buddha," in which the chief artist, stocking-footed so as not to tear the silk, knelt beside the Buddha's huge head and, wielding a long-handled brush, painted in his eyes, half-closed, secretly smiling. Meanwhile, a monk chanted a verse from one of the scriptures about men opening their eyes to the true reality. Then, like the sail of some magnificent junk bound for the high seas, the banner was raised on its wooden frame until it seemed to overlook the entire kingdom.

As for the Ming-t'ang itself, the boxer walked around and around it, examining it with meticulous care. Wherever he discovered an empty space beneath an eave, or a bare patch of plaster wall, he ordered an artisan to fill it with dragons and phoenixes, lions, tortoises, stags, bats, the four symbols of literature and science, the eight symbols of precious things, the symbols of happiness and long life, and, most important, the scepter of Heaven, for the hall had been built in Heaven's name.

Under the direction of the Scholars of the North Gate, who had been consulting the ancient texts to learn how best to please Heaven, he had had his men construct a vast altar, five tiers high, with sweeping stairways to the topmost platform, where libations could be offered to Heaven and August Earth, to ancestors and emperors past. The penultimate tier had sixteen alcoves to offer sacrifices to the five emperors of ancient times, the planets, and the three hundred and sixty stars.

Yet even when it was done, it was not done, for the scholars could not come to an agreement. No sooner had a tier been completed than they informed him that it was too high or too low, or wrong in shape. They were no more in accord about the placement of the alcoves, or whether the stairways should be oriented north and south or east and west. They changed their minds as the talentless poet changes a word back and forth a dozen times, hoping to turn doggerel into a masterpiece. Finally the boxer lost patience and told them there would be no more alterations; the sacrificial platforms would stand as they were, whether Heaven liked them or not.

Yet he felt that all his hard work went unappreciated, for every day when the Empress and her ministers came to rehearse the elaborate choreography of the sacrifice, the most splendid and complex of all the Confucian rites, he would be banished from the hall as though he were just another worker. Nor did she visit him in the evenings, for celibacy was a part of the preparations, too.

His anxiety about having everything "just so" increased with every passing day. Setbacks brought him to the verge of nervous collapse. A windstorm tore a gash in the great silk Buddha banner, while in the hall a patch of wall plaster somehow got moisture behind it, making one of the murals bubble and crack and peel. (Another sovereign, less sure of himself, might have taken these as omens.) But with an endless supply of artisans on hand, as well as rewards of wealth and honor and punishments of torture and death, repairs got done on schedule.

The Veneration of the Augury Stone, as the Empress's beloved white stone was called, preceded the Sacrifice to Heaven by fifteen days, as "little dishes" did a banquet, to stimulate the appetite. At dawn on the twelfth day of the twelfth month, the Empress led a procession down to the banks of the Lo, where a ceremonial platform had been erected. The young Emperor, Jui-tsung, followed close behind her, admirably concealing whatever emotions he felt at the recent loss of nearly his entire clan to his mother's executioners. His son, the Crown Prince, and all the officials of the court, both civil and military, and even the chiefs of certain border tribes and tributary states, all decked out in their barbarian regalia, followed them. The boxer had been instructed to walk about four-fifths of the way toward the end of the procession, just behind the ambassador of the Uighurs, an unbearably haughty fellow in jewels and brocaded robes, who was suffering from flatulence.

When they reached the river, the waters were as thick as mercury, the sky overcast and iron-colored. There was a heaviness in the air, as when a storm approaches, yet no sign that the clouds would break to relieve the tension.

The procession silently re-formed around the base of the altar to admire the treasures that had been arrayed there: the imperial seal, a rock crystal throne, a fire-bead the size of a hen's egg from the Chams, a pearl the size of a goose egg from Kuangtung, a savage two-horned rhinoceros in a bronze cage, an albino lion with blazing red eyes from Magadha, a goat with two heads, a black-skinned dwarf, and many other tribute objects. Taking its place before them all was the "pure-hearted" white augury stone with its wondrous inscription.

When everyone had found their places, Heaven's Chosen bowed three times to the white stone and recited an ode to it composed by one of the court poets. Excellent makeup had revived the beauty of her youth, and her voice rang out as pure and firm in its conviction as the notes of a martial trumpet. She announced a new title for herself, Sage Mother, Sovereign Divine, borrowing the phraseology from the white stone. Her Confucian critics noted that the word *sovereign* was without gender, free of the connotations of the traditional titles. She would be a second-class empress no longer. She proclaimed a new reign era, also borrowing it from the stone, called Eternal Prosperity. Feeling the first drops of rain on the back of her hands, she hurried through the rest of it, thanking the different factions gathered there, the court for supporting her decisions, the army for crushing the rebellion of the Li princes, the prefects for keeping peace within their provinces. The Middle Kingdom, she promised the representatives of tribes and tributary empires, would always be a friend and a protector to them. Then she climbed down the stairway, entered the one of her five carriages that was known as the "gold carriage" just as the clouds opened and the downpour began. Servants rushed to the riverbank to collect the tribute objects before they were soaked. Soldiers ran about chasing the two-headed goat, who had escaped his pen in the confusion.

Twelve days later she began the ritual fast that preceded the Sacrifice to Heaven. She put on the Hat of Communication with Heaven and isolated herself for three days in order to create sanctity within herself.

The bad weather continued, raining on and off, and only cleared on the morning of the Sacrifice. A clamor of drums and trumpets ascertained that no man or beast would oversleep this day. The Empress appeared, riding along the Way of Heaven in her most splendid vehicle, the "jade carriage," decorated with a painting of a blue dragon on the right side, a white tiger on the left. Soldiers stood in an endless procession on either side of the road, illuminating the darkness with smoking torches. She rode all the way across the city and back again, so that any peasant who wished could seize his shred of glory by gazing at her profile, however briefly.

The Ming-t'ang had been cleaned and polished until it shone like a fantastic bauble. The boxer, consumed with anxiety that some oversight of his own might spoil the display, ran here and there, renailing a loose step at the altar, blowing upon the still-wet spot where the mural had been repainted, running outside to assess the wind and pray it would not rip another hole in the Buddha.

The same crowd of mandarins and emissaries who had attended the ceremony on the banks of the Lo found their way to the

Ming-t'ang. Overhearing one of the most sophisticated of the tributary kings marveling at the craftsmanship, the murals, and the metalwork, the boxer felt a flush of pride. The Empress appeared in her most elaborate imperial garb and a headdress topped by a horizontal board with rounded ends, strings of beads hanging like curtains before and behind her face. Cradled in her right arm she carried the jade scepter known as the *kuei*, the most ancient symbol of imperial authority. She seemed to drift up the altar stairs like a spirit. Reaching the platform, she faultlessly recited the prayers and performed the ancient rituals, offering the libations to Heaven and August Earth.

Watching her, the boxer experienced an instant of timelessness. It seemed as though the Empress, or her spirit, in one guise or another, had performed this rite a thousand times in ages past, and would perform it a thousand times again in ages to come. For once he almost believed that a supreme deity called Heaven was more than a convention to justify the madness of monarchs; for one moment he believed that it truly did exist, and that it cared deeply about the affairs of men; that life was more than some slow-paced and random tavern brawl where those with the best punches survived and those with crystal jaws did not.

The Empress offered libations to her ancestors, and read the inscriptions on jade tablets dedicated to them, which she then placed in the interior of the altar. While offering libations to the four T'ang emperors, she promoted her father posthumously to Emperor, thus laying the cornerstone for a new dynasty, the Chou. The offhand manner in which she did this fooled no one. A few members of the audience, awed by her ingenuity, her disregard for tradition, and her brazen nerve, began to whisper, despite the sanctity of the occasion. That the Empress's father had been a vendor of lumber, a member of the despicable merchant class, whose status of duke had been awarded for a political favor, bothered her not one whit. All that remained was for the silent Jui-tsung to abdicate in her favor, and she would have achieved her dream, the end of the T'ang, the start of the Chou.

There, before an audience still dazed by her father's sudden divinity, she drank the "wine of happiness" and brought the ceremony to a close. She descended the stairway, climbed into her jade carriage, and, to the beat of the drum and the blast of the trumpet, led the loyal Yü-lin Guard back to the palace. There she changed into robes more appropriate for the New Year's Eve service and maigre feast that were to follow at the White Horse Temple.

The boxer rode directly to the temple, to make sure that everything was in order. He had not been there in many months, and was delighted to see the Korean, Pinch Purse, and his other old friends. He inquired about False Brush, who was not among them, and learned that the mad monk had vanished during a lightning storm a few weeks ago and had not been seen since. Some thought the Taoist sorcerer had stolen him and shrunk him to fit in one of his glass spheres, while others of a less fanciful turn of mind believed he had fallen in the Lo while drunk and drowned.

The boxer was upset by the state into which the monastery had fallen since the little monk's departure. The film of dust on the benches was so thick that a man could write in it with his finger. Piles of ash from old incense lay on the altar, and no one had bothered to remove the withered flowers from the vases. The glow of the great bronze Buddhas had dimmed with tarnish, and the iron bell had a patina of rust. Though White Pheasant had done his best to maintain it, the temple was only barely presentable.

Although the guests would be arriving within a few hours, the boxer vowed to do what he could to get the temple in shape. He assigned each monk a housekeeping chore, and promised a thousand cash to the one who did his best. He personally lighted all the lanterns and saw to it that the stoves in the monks' cells were filled with bamboo leaves and grass, in order to produce voluminous smoke in the sky above the monastery, as was appropriate to this particular holiday.

The Empress and fifty or so of her favorites began to arrive near midnight. Among them were the Princess T'ai-p'ing, the Princess Ch'ien Chin, the Taoist sorcerer, and other monks, ministers, and members of her family. At midnight the great bell sounded, and monks and lay people alike gathered in the dining hall to pay reverence to the Buddha. When they were all seated, the Empress looked to the boxer for his command. Seeing this, everyone else did the same. The boxer, elated by the attention, led them as they climbed down from the benches, spread their mats on the floor, and paid reverence to the Buddha. Those few moments made up for months of being slighted and ignored. The Empress bowed lowest of all and remained down the longest. When she rose, her face was radiant with pleasure.

After chanting some scriptures to the beat of the wooden fish, and ringing the bell again, monks and lay people mingled and exchanged congratulations. According to custom, a meal of gruel and fruit should have followed, but because the guest of honor was the Empress, and this was a special occasion, a superb maigre feast was served instead. First came a platter of thinly sliced meats and vegetables arranged, in honor of Heaven's Chosen, as a multihued phoenix; then a rare bird's-nest soup made from mucus extracted from the salivary glands of the small salangane and collected by boiling their nests; sea slugs with abalone; snakeskin stew from the south; bears' paws; hundred-year-old eggs, which were really quail eggs that had been cooked in a lime bath; and many other wonderful and exotic dishes from all over the Middle Kingdom.

Before they began, the empress held up a chopstick.

"The chopstick," she began, "is round at one end, to symbolize Heaven, and square at the other, to symbolize Earth. In the center of the chopstick, round becomes square, Heaven becomes Earth. So do We, Sovereign Divine, intercede between you, Our subjects, and the powers of the universe. By Our perfect sacrifice this night, We assure the Middle Kingdom of happiness, peace, and plenty in years to come."

Everyone applauded her.

She went on to announce that in gratitude for building the Ming-t'ang, the boxer would from this day on be a duke of the third class, with an income equal to the taxes of one thousand families.

The boxer bowed deeply before her. His joy was such that he nearly wept.

While they ate, White Pheasant, who was temple administrator, and Pinch Purse, who was controller (the boxer had appointed him out of the belief that the only way to prevent him from stealing the temple's money was by putting him in charge of it), read aloud from the temple's books an accounting of the year's profits from the rolling mill, the hemp presses, the land leased to local farmers, and the donations made by pious citizens, rich and poor. This too was a custom, an opportunity for the temple to be evaluated as a business.

The boxer stood with his arms folded across his chest, smiling and nodding as though he were listening to a sprightly tune. A rich man, he thought. A duke! At one point he managed to catch the sorcerer's eye and made a face as if to say, "There! See what real faith can do!"

In counterpoint to the singsong recitation came the far-off sounds of peasants celebrating the new year, the explosions of sticks of bamboo stuffed with gunpowder, the joyful shouts of "Bonzai!"

One by one the courtiers rose and toasted the Empress with the finest grape wine. They toasted the augury stone, the new reign era, and the Empress's father. Then suddenly a eunuch was apologizing that they had run out of wine.

"How is this possible?" the Empress demanded, half rising from her stool, eyes blazing with anger. "I ordered ten casks brought here for the night."

"My apologies," the eunuch said, "but some vandal has crept out to the carts and split the kegs open with an ax."

The Empress's eyes blazed for a moment more; then she smiled and said, "No matter, send our fastest rider to the palace for ten casks more."

"If I may make a suggestion?" It was the Taoist sorcerer, and he had the slightest smile on his thin lips. "I understand that the temple has a wine cellar and that it is well stocked."

"Is this true?" the Empress inquired of the boxer.

"Why, yes," he said. "I had forgotten all about it. False Brush had it dug during the renovations. I recall him rolling the casks along the monastery path late one night."

"You are fond of doing things late at night," the sorcerer said, "that you would not do in the daylight."

"Is there any reason why we should not drink it?" the Empress asked the boxer, irritated that he had not offered it immediately.

"I cannot vouch for its quality, or its ripeness. But bad wine, I suppose, is better than none at all." He directed four of the monks to go down to the wine cellar and bring up as many barrels.

"Have the barrels opened here, before us," the Taoist sorcerer said.

The Empress looked at him with curiosity.

"My reasons will become clear," the sorcerer said. He glanced at Princess T'ai P'ing and Censor Hsü, who were sitting near the head of the table.

Four wine barrels were rolled one by one into the dining hall and turned to stand upright. The monks knocked out the bungs with a mallet, but when they tipped the barrels forward, nothing poured out.

"And yet they are full of *something*," one of the monks commented, puzzled by the tremendous weight of them.

"Break them open," the Empress ordered.

The monks brought in axes and began to chop at the metal hoops. After the hoops had popped, one more chop split open the staves like the petals of a flower, and the contents of each barrel clattered out onto the floor for all to see.

There, lying amid the balls of silk floss in which they had been packed, were suits of armor, crossbows and arrows, swords and battle-axes.

The Taoist sorcerer rose to his feet and, pointing at the boxer, shouted in a triumphant voice, "There is your rebel leader! I will tell you why he found it necessary to travel to Szechuan just when the rebellion of the princes was being planned. He went there for no other reason than to dine with Li Chan and his son, and plan his treachery!"

"The rebel Hsüeh Shao is his son!" Princess T'ai P'ing cried, joining in. "Night after night he went to the White Horse Temple to store these very weapons and armor in the cellar."

"It is not true," exclaimed the boxer. "He came to garden!"

"In the middle of the night?" the sorcerer asked skeptically.

"His accomplice," she went on, "the monk named False Brush, was the loyal servant of Prince Li Hung. He pretended to be mad while all the time he and this false Buddhist plotted your destruction."

"No!" the boxer shouted. "I mean, you may be right about False Brush, but—"

"You know it as well as we do," the princess said with disgust at his pretense. "That is why he fled the moment he heard the rebellion was crushed."

"If you need more evidence of the man's treachery," Censor Hsü said to the Empress, his voice an eye of calm in the midst of the storm of accusations, "I have learned of a metalsmith employed by the abbot to debase the currency, to melt down cash coins and turn them into incense burners and the like. By his estimate, more than a million cash has been diverted by this means."

"But I thought I was doing you a favor," the boxer protested. "I thought if I made the coins scarcer, they would increase in value, and I would get more value from them by turning them to copper."

"No man could be so stupid," Princess T'ai P'ing said, "as not to realize that the destruction of coins is the destruction of trade. The truth is, you knew all the time precisely what you were doing."

"I did not," the boxer objected. "It was all Hsüeh Shao's idea. Ask him yourself."

"He died this morning," she said, as though discussing the weather. "He starved to death in prison."

"Vulture of a woman! Your husband dead not a day, and you without a tear in your eye! You are even worse than your mother!"

The Empress made a sound midway between a gasp and a hiss to hear this sentiment expressed in public. She gestured to the head of the Yü-lin Guard, who in turn ordered his men to seize the boxer and take him away.

The boxer kicked over the table so that it became a wall to block his pursuers; food and bowls flew everywhere, and the spilled wine made the floor as slippery as ice. One of the soldiers fell, impaling himself on his own drawn blade. The boxer ran for the exit, the Yü-lin Guard at his heels. His tarpan was tied near the door; if only he could reach it, he could easily outdistance them. He would ride and ride until he reached the south, not Szechuan or Kuangtung, but the far south, the land of Nam-viet, where the dark-skinned Man and Lao lived in ignorance of empresses and the changing winds of royal fancy. He even had some cash in his saddlebags as well as an extra robe and a jug of wine.

Then he was through the door, out into the cool night. With a pull he untied the reins, and with a leap he lifted himself into the saddle. Then he was slapping the tarpan's flank, clicking his tongue, goading it to a gallop. The road from the temple was narrow and treacherous in the dark, lined with trees whose low limbs could yank a man from his mount if he veered too far. The boxer rode bent low so the wind swept over his shaven head, and ripped at his scarlet robes. A maniacal smile spread across his face. He had outwitted them, he had escaped. For all their pretensions of aristocracy and refinement, they were no match for a quick-witted farmer's son.

He looked back to gauge the progress of his pursuers, and when he turned forward again he saw a bunch of drunken revelers standing in his path. They were young men, students, dressed in the robes and caps of the aristocracy. "Bonzai!" they shouted, waving cheerfully at him, hardly seeming to realize that if they did not move aside in a few seconds they would be trampled. "Bonzai! Bonzai!" One of them lit a fuse sticking out of a length of bamboo and tossed it in the air; then all of them ran. The boxer knew what was going to happen, but what could he do? The bamboo stick exploded nearly on top of him. The tarpan reared and rolled its great white eyes with terror. The boxer managed to hold on, but then the horse twisted again, unexpectedly, and flung him sideways onto the road, his head into a tree trunk. After that he remembered no more.

He thought that he had been unconscious only a moment, but when he reached up to rub his aching head, he felt a stiff bristle of hair where, since becoming a monk, he had never permitted more than the merest stubble to grow. All his muscles ached. When he moved, he felt painful sores on his buttocks, his shoulder blades, everywhere his body touched the bed. Still denying his senses, he looked around for the members of the maigre feast, which he believed was still in progress.

Gradually he understood that much time had passed, that he was in his bed, in his fine apartments at the White Horse Temple. He couldn't understand why his chest felt so heavy until he pulled down the sheets and saw, padlocked around his neck, an iron collar of the sort he had seen men wearing in prison. Again and again he tried to rise from the bed, but he was weak with hunger and the weight of it held him down. When he finally did manage to stand up, he became nauseated and his head spun, and he lost his balance and hit the floor with a thud. He cried out for help, but no one came. He crawled out into the courtyard. The air was frigid, the sun blinding. The gravel cut into his knees and the palms of his hands. The pagoda seemed like a dagger in the underbelly of the sky. A light snow had begun to fall. Seeing smoke streaming from the cooking shed, he started in that direction. There he found White Pheasant cooking soup.

"Thank Heaven you are all right!" the eunuch said, rushing to his side, "but you shouldn't be up like this. Let me carry you back to your bed."

"How did I get this way?" the boxer asked.

"Don't you remember fleeing the maigre feast? A firecracker scared your horse and you fell and hit your head."

"But what of this?" he said, tugging at the iron collar.

"Some people believed that you were involved in the rebellion. The Empress decided—simply to please them, I believe—that something had to be done to," he hesitated, searching for the right word, "*restrain* you."

"Now I remember," the boxer said, "though it's all a little fuzzy. Where are the others?"

"Around and about. Now, sir, I must insist that you go back to bed this instant. You're weak. You need rest and food."

"What do you mean, 'around and about'?"

White Pheasant looked more and more uncomfortable. "I believe they went to visit the wine shops. They should be back sometime tonight. Now why don't we go and—"

"You're lying. Tell me where they are."

White Pheasant looked down at the floor. He was crying.

"Did something happen to them?"

White Pheasant nodded.

"They're not dead, are they?"

"Some of them were implicated in the rebellion. The others she considered guilty by association."

"Executed?"

White Pheasant nodded.

"All of them? Even the Korean?"

White Pheasant nodded.

"No!" the boxer shouted. He raised his fists in agony and shook them at the ceiling. "A curse on her, the vulture! They were good, loyal men, each one worth a dozen mandarins."

"Please, sir, you mustn't get too excited."

The boxer took a few deep breaths. "The Korean was the finest. He had the dignity and courage of a general. Do you know, he was only fifteen when he became a soldier? Our imperial army was marching against Koguryu, his homeland. He was one of fourteen thousand who dared to resist. They were taken prisoner, every one of them, and marched through the streets of the old capital, Ch'ang-an, while the crowds jeered and threw stones. He used to tell me about it. The general gave them to the Emperor—it was T'ai-tsung then—for slaves, but he was impressed by their courage and set them free. So there he was, barely a man, in a strange country where he knew no one, without a coin, ignorant of the language and customs. Yet he did well for himself."

"I'd say he did very well," White Pheasant agreed.

"If only I had something to remember him by. They didn't leave behind his leopard skin, by any chance?"

White Pheasant shook his head.

"I'll miss him," the boxer said, staring at the floor. "I will."

"Let me walk you back to your apartments," White Pheasant said, offering his arm. "You must be very tired."

"Tired," said the boxer. "Yes, I am." And he allowed the eunuch to take his arm.

When he woke again, he was starving. He found a beautifully prepared meal of mild dumplings, along with a vegetable broth and some shredded chicken, waiting on a tray near his bed. As he was wolfing it down, White Pheasant appeared and sat down at the edge of the bed.

"Eat slowly, sir. You don't want to overdo it and get sick."

When he had finished everything on the tray, he said to White Pheasant, "You've got to help me get to the palace. If only I can speak to the Empress, I can explain everything. I'm innocent, you know. I had no part in this rebellion. It's all just a lot of coincidence and misunderstandings. You believe me, don't you?"

He looked hopefully into the eunuch's face.

"Of course."

"Now be a friend," the boxer said, "and saddle my tarpan. I'll be out in a moment. I just need to gather my strength."

"I'm sorry, but the tarpan isn't here. They're keeping him at the palace stables, at least till you're better."

"Then we'll walk to the palace," the boxer said, "or find a sedan chair somewhere along the way. Let's get going."

"Wait till you're feeling better, sir, I beg of you."

"I'm feeling just fine," the boxer said.

White Pheasant helped him as far as the temple gate. The boxer staggered outside, where a half-dozen guards with halberds and crossbows blocked his way.

"Let me by!" the boxer demanded. Though he tried to make use of his big, commanding voice, the sounds that came out were feeble, choked, and constricted.

"Sorry, sir," one of them said, "but we have orders that you're to stay here for the time being."

"Whose orders?"

"Heaven's Chosen."

The boxer looked back and saw White Pheasant standing at the gate, watching sadly, as though he had known this all along.

The boxer had barely enough strength to return to his bed. When he was under the covers, he said to the eunuch, "I'll have to fight my way out. Where is the K'un-wu sword?"

"It was gone when they brought you here."

"He who dares touch my K'un-wu sword will feel its blade!" the boxer exclaimed. "Bring me another sword."

"There are none."

"What of all the caches where the men hid their weapons in the old days?"

"Empty now."

The boxer thought about it. "Then there's only one thing to do. You must go to the Empress and have her come here."

"I don't want to leave you alone in your present state, sir."

"What state? You talk about me as though I were a sick man. But I'm as healthy as an ox. Now go, you fat grandmother, and do not return without the Empress in tow, or I'll twist your nose."

Despite this threat, White Pheasant returned with no more than a message. The Empress, he said, sent her regrets regarding the present situation and hoped that it might be improved in the future. Meanwhile, she promised to visit as soon as her schedule permitted. Unfortunately, a new border crisis had arisen. Mo-ch'o, the ambitious new Khan of the eastern Turks, was harassing the tribes that had settled along the Long Wall of a Thousand Li in the north.

"She's waiting for some time to pass, so the others will forget," the boxer said. "Then she'll come for me. Things will be just like before. All I have to do is wait and be patient." But as the weeks crept by, there were moments when he saw the truth. Her promises resembled those she made to placate bothersome envoys from countries too little to warrant her attention.

More snow came, and freezing cold. In time the air turned warm, buds appeared on the trees, and squirrels leaped from the roofs of the pagoda.

Summer, fall, winter. Another year passed.

Every week he sent White Pheasant to talk to the Empress, and every week the eunuch returned with the same message, that she sent her regrets and would see him when time permitted. Some days he would believe it, and the hope would sustain him. On other days his anger and frustration were such that he would attack White

Pheasant, whom he blamed for all his travails, as we tend to do when the real source of our grief is beyond our reach, and beat him with his fists until the eunuch wept and cried for mercy.

Having nothing better to do, the boxer ate and drank to excess. With his movements restrained by the neck weight, his body grew soft and fat, his skin pale from the time he spent indoors, his eyes ringed and sunken from lack of sleep.

White Pheasant was always trying to cheer him up. One day he arrived with two packages from the South Market, wrapped in mulberry paper and silk ribbon. The boxer tore the paper off the big one. It was the first time in many months that the eunuch had seen him smile. Puzzled, he lifted from the nest of open paper a robe of gorgeous light lavender silk.

"What is this pretty thing?"

"The Empress made you a duke for your excellent work on the Ming-t'ang. Don't you recall? These are the robes of your office."

The smaller package contained a belt with gold plaques, also appropriate to a duke of the third rank.

"Are these from the Empress?" the boxer asked in a feeble voice.

The Empress knew nothing about them. White Pheasant had ordered them at the South Market, with his own cash. But he could not bear to tell the boxer that, so instead he said, "Yes, from the Empress," and looked away.

"Then she hasn't forgotten me, after all. She is simply waiting for the time when my supposed crimes are forgotten. Quick, help me try them on. When she sees me dressed as a duke, she will certainly invite me back to the palace."

The boxer rose shakily from the bed, and White Pheasant helped him slip his arms into the sleeves. But his stomach had grown so large that the robe would not cover it, nor would the splendid belt close. Dismayed, the boxer sat back down on his bed and contented himself with holding the excellent robe in his lap and stroking it as though it were a kitten, while he looked off into the distance, imagining himself as he might have appeared in it.

The following fall, White Pheasant, returning from a trip to the palace, brought important news. Three times petitions had been submitted to Heaven's Chosen, one with sixty thousand names, pleading with her to take the dragon throne, and three times, as was the polite custom, she refused. But then a phoenix had been sighted resting on the palace roof, and a flock of vermilion birds, symbols of prosperity, had been observed fluttering through the Great Audience Hall; both of these were portents whose meaning could not be denied.

Standing atop the palace gate, with a vast crowd gathered below, she announced the change of dynasty. The T'ang was over, the Chou had begun. Long life to the Chou. Three days later she proclaimed herself Holy and Divine Emperor. Jui-tsung, wisely abdicating, was made imperial heir. Visiting the Temple of the Imperial Ancestors, she replaced the ancestral tablets of the T'ang with those of her own family.

"I made it possible," the boxer said bitterly, "and yet I could not be there to share in her glory."

"But there's something else," White Pheasant added quickly. "Along with the change of dynasty, she announced an amnesty for all prisoners. Perhaps she will let you go free now."

"I am no prisoner!" the boxer objected. Yet hope bloomed again, like some bulb deceived by a warm day in winter.

With nothing to distract him, he began to live more and more in his memories. He lay on the broad bed in his luxurious apartments, the mural of Maitreya gazing down at him with his beatific smile, and dreamed of the days when he was a show-boxer, when he strutted through the South Market, his robe open to show his muscles, the envy of all who saw him. He remembered lying on the banks of the Lo with the servant girl on a spring afternoon, watching the limbs of the willows move like curtains in the breeze. And touring the taverns with his good friend the Korean, indulging in friendly tests of strength, drinking cheap rice wine, and talking about women and battle until late into the night.

One day, noticing an iron door hinge worn through with rust, he wondered if he could not rid himself of his heavy collar in the same way, and to this end he began to pour water on it night and day. It did rust, as he had hoped, but rather than weaken the iron, this simply worsened the pain by abrading his neck whenever he moved. The skin of his throat began to bleed and swell until it puffed out on either side of the collar, like a pillow cinched with a cord.

White Pheasant tried to comfort the boxer by slipping a swath of silk beneath the collar, but even so slight an object restricted his breathing. The situation grew ever worse, the rust opening the sores, the sores swelling on account of it, the rust then biting even deeper.

The skin took on a greenish cast and hot pockets of pus rose beneath the surface. The boxer grew feverish and sweaty. He mistook the lacquer fretwork of his bed for the walls of a prison and screamed for help lest the lice crawl into his wounds and kill him. White Pheasant moved his own mat into the boxer's suite and slept on the floor beside his bed, the better to wait upon him. He spoke gently to him, fed him hot broth, and put cold cloths on his forehead and wrists. Seeing that the boxer's skin was growing hotter and hotter, with no break to the fever in sight, the eunuch announced that he was going to the palace for help.

"Don't bother," the boxer murmured. "She's forgotten me. She'll be happy to get rid of me. I should have watched my step while I had her. I could have been her husband. I could have been emperor. Instead I will die here in this awful way."

White Pheasant returned some time later with the new palace doctor and two assistants. The doctor was a tall, good-looking man with long-lashed eyes, who bore some resemblance to the boxer as he had appeared in better days. But the resemblance vanished as soon as he moved or spoke (so much does a man's nature influence his appearance), for the doctor was a mandarin, an heir to wealth and influence. He wrote poetry and was well schooled in the Confucian classics. His surname was listed among the venerable clans of the northeast.

One of his assistants immediately set to work sawing off the iron collar.

Meanwhile, the palace doctor held the boxer's head in his hands and closely examined his complexion, his eyes, the color of his lips, the texture of his hair. He felt the pulse in his finger for strength and speed and vitality.

Then he turned to White Pheasant, who was observing all of this with concern, and said, "He has experienced an upheaval in his life, has he not? A disorder of the Seven Sentiments? Of joy, anger, sadness, fear, love, hate, desire?"

"Of all of those, I fear," White Pheasant replied.

"The body," the doctor said, "is a microcosm of the cosmos. The five organs have their parallels in the five elements and the five winds. If there is to be health, there must be harmony."

He broke off there, for his assistants had managed to remove the heavy collar from the boxer's throat. The festering of the wounds was far worse than it had appeared. They gave off a smell like rotting fruit. The palace doctor suggested that the boxer be made drunk with rice wine so as to be less bothered by the pain to come, and White Pheasant set about the simple task. Then the doctor ordered a fire started in the stove.

When the boxer seemed sufficiently drunk, and the fire was blazing, the doctor took a coal from the stove and held it to a heap of moxa, a kind of down prepared from dried mugwort leaves, that he had poured onto a ceramic plate, until it began to smolder and smoke. Then he poured some of it into the wound on the boxer's neck and placed a cup over it, so that the vacuum would draw out the poisons. At the height of his health and self-esteem, the boxer might have borne the pain silently, but now, weakened by fever, despair, and neglect, having lost even the desire to appear brave, he screamed and squirmed and tried to escape, and had to be held down by the doctor's assistants until each of his wounds had been cauterized in the same manner.

Once this was done, the doctor set to work mixing ingredients from his bag—herbs, bits of toad skin and insect, ground rhinoceros horn and crushed pearl—into a base of beeswax and rice flour, then formed the paste into little balls that the boxer was to ingest several times a day with a cup of rice wine. *Not* grape wine, the doctor repeated, for grape wine was a creation of barbarians, and only native food and drink could restore harmony to the body. As he said this, he frowned at the painting of the Buddha Maitreya on the wall, as though to make it clear that he included not only barbarian victuals in his prescription, but barbarian faiths too. These opinions were less those of the medical profession than an expression of the doctor's own deep-seated Confucian beliefs.

Despite these ministrations, the boxer's condition continued to worsen. Now that he no longer troubled to shave his head, his hair grew in gray, making him appear far older than he was. Labored breathing and stomach pains woke him in the middle of the night. Food lost its savor for him and, where before he had been fat, he now grew frighteningly thin. Though he was barely thirty, he looked like an old man.

Each week, when the doctor came to visit, he was more concerned. After several months of this, he took White Pheasant aside and asked him if there was anything they could do to improve the boxer's mood.

"A visit from the Empress," the eunuch replied, "would mean everything to him."

"It is precisely what she wishes to avoid," the doctor murmured. "Yet she still cares for him. Why else would she send me back here, week after week, to see that he survives? I will ask her."

"Thank you," White Pheasant said, overwhelmed with emotion.

23

THE BOXER BECOMES A GENERAL

When the boxer learned that the Empress was coming to see him, he performed a meticulous toilet. For the first time since the maigre feast, White Pheasant shaved the boxer's head and used his own rouge to heighten the color of the boxer's cheeks so that he might have a semblance of health. He dressed him in his new pale lavender robes and gold belt, which were voluminous on his sticklike frame. The desperation with which the boxer fussed over his appearance brought to mind those poor courtesans who primped for hours in the hope of attracting the notice of the Emperor. When he asked White Pheasant how he looked, the eunuch responded, "Handsome and filled with vitality," though he thought the opposite.

The boxer asked White Pheasant if he thought the Empress would want to meet in his bedchamber, so they could act the Clouds and Rain, a practice they had neglected for more than two and a half years. When he suggested the Buddha Hall instead, the boxer seemed relieved. A sick man, White Pheasant pointed out, was expected to hoard his vital fluid if his health was to improve. Furthermore, Buddhist monks always looked best meditating, since that was the practice around which their lives, costumes, and ritual had been designed.

This having been decided, the boxer leaned on White Pheasant's shoulder and they walked together to the Buddha Hall, where he took a place on the bench, arranging his lavender robes around his knees, and waited as though meditating.

Although the doctor must have prepared the Empress, she still betrayed her dismay upon seeing her lover in this decrepit state. Although in the past she had always ordered them left alone together, this time she permitted White Pheasant, the doctor, and his two assistants to remain, or, rather, she insisted that they do so, fearing what embarrassing situations might occur otherwise.

"How handsome you look in your new robes," she said. She knew him well enough to know what words would please him most.

"It's been a long time," he said casually, as if seeing her was no special event in his life. "What brings you to my temple?" His voice, despite his efforts, was a hollow croak.

"We desired to see you. We had heard you were sick, and wished to offer Our hope that your health improves soon."

"That's very thoughtful of you."

He made small talk, congratulating her on the change of dynasty. She told him that many copies had been made of the Great Cloud Scripture, and Great Cloud temples had been established all over the empire so that the scripture could be read and explained to the populace.

And so the interview continued, with a formality that filled everyone with discomfort. Even the boxer was relieved when the Empress finally rose to mark the end of it.

"Is there anything We can do to speed your recovery?" she asked solicitously as she was leaving.

"My freedom," he whispered.

"You have been relieved of your collar, I notice. Isn't that enough?"

"If only I could go outside and ride my tarpan and visit the wine shops."

"When in the past We gave you such freedom, you abused it. You created situations that were an embarrassment to Heaven and difficult to rectify."

"It will not happen again, I swear it!"

"We will take it under consideration."

She turned her back on him and walked toward the door.

"Wait!" he shouted.

She faced him, controlling her irritation.

"Once you said you would make me a general. You promised. I have heard that the Eastern Turks cause trouble at the Long Wall of a Thousand Li. Why not send me to fight them? I could not embarrass Heaven if I were so far away. And perhaps I could subdue them. I have been a fighter all my life. I know how to fight. It is the one thing I do know."

"We will take it under—"

"Please, let me go. I can't bear another day in this prison."

The Empress was no longer smiling. "Be glad that I did not put you in a real prison," she snapped.

"Forgive me," the boxer said softly, kneeling and lowering his face to the floor.

"He wishes to be a general," the Empress said to the doctor, as they rode back to the palace in the ivory carrage. "He wants to fight the eastern Turks. Never has a man had so little sense of his own limitations. He is the kitten, always finding its way into mischief, and We are the mother who cannot find it in Our heart to drown it. What will We do with him?"

She sat in the Emperor's seat, facing forward, and he in the seat usually reserved for the Empress, his back to the horses, his knees only inches from hers. Chessboard patterns of sun, coming through the fretwork of the carriage windows, slid across their fine silk robes.

"A long trip like that would surely be the end of him," the doctor said. "Even healthy men perish on such journeys."

"And yet it would be a good way to die, wouldn't it? Fighting for one's Empress in a distant land?"

"Better than to end it lying in bed, drinking rice wine and dreaming of the past. After all, the quality of a man's life is no greater than the honor that surrounds his death."

The wheels groaned on their axles as the carriage jogged along the paving stones. The doctor's knee touched the Empress's, but she made no effort to move away.

"Of course, he could not lead a regiment," she mused. "What

is it you Confucians say? 'How do you expect to lead others when you cannot even lead yourself?' "

"So the Sage says in his Analects."

"But would he truly have to lead a regiment? Wouldn't it be enough if he believed he was leading it? Let Us explain Our thoughts. By coincidence, Our excellent general Li To-tso has brought his army home to Lo-yang so they can worship their ancestors. He plans to return with them to the Long Wall of a Thousand Li in a few months. We see no reason why Huai-i should not march alongside them. We could tell a few of the soldiers to pretend that he is a general, to bow and kowtow to him, and address him with many honorifics. It could do no harm."

"And if they meet the enemy?"

"There is no enemy."

"But what of Mo-ch'o?" the doctor asked.

"The Khan has ceased his hostilities. An envoy arrived only yesterday with a fine tribute and a note expressing interest in a marriage between him and my own family."

"And what will the boxer do when he reaches the Long Wall and finds no Turkish army awaiting him?"

"Knowing him," the Empress said, smiling, "he will probably be greatly relieved. On his return he will make up many amusing stories of how he chopped off the head of this Turk, and stabbed that one in the chest, and finally brought his troops to victory."

"There will be no return."

She seemed not to hear him. "We shall send him a suit of lacquered armor. Such things make him so happy, for he is like a little boy. And we will give him back his precious K'un-wu sword. Up north he can carry on as he likes."

"You care for him still. I'm surprised."

"Does it make you jealous?"

He smiled but did not reply.

"He made Us feel young," the Empress went on. "Without him, We might have never dared to overthrow the T'ang and establish the Great Chou."

"Then he has done something vital indeed."

"So it is settled. Ah, it tires Us so, worrying over him." She sighed and worked her shoulders back and forth.

"Are you stiff?" the doctor inquired solicitously.

She nodded. "You must return to Our apartments, and ease Our tensions with your skillful fingers."

The doctor gladly obliged.

The boxer loved the armor as much as the Empress had anticipated, and though he was so weak he could barely stand, he insisted on trying it on as soon as it arrived. The bronze helmet had a veil of floral brocade that covered his neck. Shoulder pads were designed to resemble dragons' heads, from which his arms emerged like tongues. An ornate breastplate hung from the shoulder pads by belts, and a sectional iron girdle protected his abdomen. Over a floral lower robe he wore a skirt of iron shingles. His K'un-wu sword hung at his side, the blade crying for Turkish blood. The armor seemed a more potent medicine than all the pills, massage, and moxa combined; no sooner had White Pheasant fastened the last piece in place than the boxer was transformed. His sagging posture grew erect, his sunken chest swelled, his chin jutted forward, and the fire returned to his eyes. He wanted to go straight outside and practice dueling with his shadow, but White Pheasant wouldn't allow it. He argued that if the boxer was to be of service to his Empress, he must rest and regain his strength. Reluctantly, the boxer undressed and returned to bed.

By spring he was able to walk about for several hours without growing fatigued. After a dozen requests, his tarpan was returned to him from the palace stables. The horse, delighted to be back on familiar ground, nuzzled him with his cold, moist nose. He swung into the familiar saddle and rode around the temple courtyard. But when he tried to leave the temple, the guards still refused to let him pass.

"When I am your general," the boxer said to them, "I will make you pay for your insolence."

"When you are our general," the guards replied, "tortoises will fly and sparrows crawl in the mud."

As the days grew longer and the weather warmer, the boxer began to wonder if the Empress had again forgotten him. But then a palace messenger arrived with a scroll, which the boxer, furrowing his brow, spent some time pretending to read. As soon as the messenger left, he brought it to White Pheasant, who was in the cooking shed, preparing lunch. The eunuch read it and wept with joy. It was an official document, he explained, appointing the boxer Commander-in-Chief of the Northern Frontier, and ordering him to meet his army in two days' time at a certain specified place outside the city, and march them to the desert outpost of Shan-yu, beyond the Long Wall of a Thousand Li, to repulse Mo-ch'u, the Khan of the eastern Turks.

The boxer was breathless with excitement. He ran around his apartments collecting his blankets, under-robes, socks, slippers, handkerchiefs to wipe his teeth, the razor he used to shave his head, his chopsticks and lacquerware bowl, his teapot, and all the other things he might need for his travels. On the morning of the appointed day, he dressed in his boots and armor, which he was determined to wear until the heat made him swoon, mounted his taipan, and waited. Soon a squadron of soldiers arrived to accompany him to the plain north of the city, where the army was gathering.

He had prepared, after hours of reflection, a phrase to shout to the guards outside the temple when they saw him in his armor with his squadron, a phrase to bring them to enlightenment regarding what fools they had been for mocking him, but when he rode out the gate, they were gone. Apparently they had received orders, too.

The pleasure of being outside those walls after the years of sickness and internment! His eyes, deprived of the sight of anyone except White Pheasant, feasted on the faces of the peasants leading their water buffalo along the river. The rows of houses fronting on the banks seemed feats of marvelous ingenuity, and the rolling yellow hills beyond the city walls were a wonder beyond compare.

But was his freedom real, he wondered, or illusory? Was the squadron truly under his command, or was he under theirs? He could have found out by ordering them to disperse or to ride to the wine shops with him, and seeing if they obeyed. He could have done that easily enough—but fearing the results, he did not.

His heart soared when he rode over a rise and saw his army gathered in the valley below: infantry, with spears and shields; artillery, with lethal crossbows and quivers of quarrels; the cavalry, their restless ponies kicking up the yellow dust called loess; the charioteers, their brightly lacquered vehicles flying the red banners of the Chou. The soldiers wore tunics of jade green with loose white cuffs, blue pants with tan leggings, breastplates of iron shingles held together with gold rivets and purple cords, red ribbons around their topknots. Trains of oxcarts, camels, and asses carried more weapons, armor, and chariot parts; felt tents and tent poles; rations of soy sauce, millet, pickled vegetables, and rice for the officers. The camels in particular were so burdened that they wove when they walked. For the boxer, who had spent so much time in isolation, they seemed a great many men and beasts.

As he rode among them, basking in their salutes and endearing addresses, he decided that this sensation was the headiest a man could experience, beyond love or the consummation of the Clouds and Rain, or even the knowledge of painting and reading characters. If their voices were ironic, their smiles mocking, he did not notice, so intoxicated was he with his power.

Obviously he had been wrong about his fortunes. Though perhaps he had fallen temporarily from the Empress's favor, his karma was providing him with an opportunity to win her back and silence his critics once and for all. He had only to find the troublesome Turk Mo-ch'o and put an end to him, and he could return to Lo-yang a hero whom no man could fault. Then he could retire from such strenuous adventures and return to the quiet of the monastery. He could no longer deny the truth about himself: he was not the man he had once been. The march was yet to start, and already he was weary. Since his confinement, even the simplest tasks exhausted him.

The boxer had no more idea how to lead an army than how to run a temple, translate a scripture, or build an audience hall, but that had never stopped him in the past. He did as he always did in such situations, and sought out the man below him in command, whom he hoped would have the expertise he himself lacked. Such a man, he learned after inquiring of a knowledgeable-looking cavalry sergeant, was the famous Li To-tso, a general whose exploits on the northern frontier were legend. He was said to know the ways of the khans as other men know their own wives and children.

He found the general meeting with his men in a felt pavilion painted with snarling tigers and noble stags. He was a barrel-chested, energetic old man whose skin was leathery from the outdoor life. He had bushy white brows, scars and wounds in profusion, and buckteeth that made his lips protrude like a tortoise beak. He wore simpler, lighter armor than the boxer's, an old breastplate battered by sword and arrow, and a shingled skirt over his robe. The sword that hung by his side carried a wonderful patina of age.

The boxer had been concerned that the general might resent

his interference, and was pleased when the old man greeted him in a fatherly way. No sooner had he finished his briefing than he sent the other officers away so that the two of them could speak in private.

"Of course, I've had experience in battle," the boxer began when they were alone, "but it was in the rain forests of the south. The terrain was quite different, as was the temperament of our foes. What I'm trying to say is, I wonder if you would advise me on the best way to move the army up to meet the Turks. In turn, I'll teach you some of the tactics that won me the name 'The Empress's Invincible Leopard.' "

"So that is what they call you, eh?" the old general said, looking at him with one eye. "You must have struck fear into the hearts of the Lao. Or was it the Man?"

"Both," the boxer said soberly. "And others. I was also called 'The Scourge of the South.' "

"I have my marching orders planned out," he said. "Why don't I repeat them to you, and you can give them to the men."

"I wouldn't mind assisting you in that way," the boxer said. "After all, you are a venerable old man who has served the Empress nobly over the years."

"Thank you for your kindness," the general said without a trace of sarcasm. He was a remarkable man indeed.

Although the trek was not much farther than that which he had made to Szechuan some years before, it seemed, because of his weakened health, ten times the distance. At times, overwhelmed with fatigue, he would swoon and tumble from his mount and land, with a clatter of armor, in the loess. Then the general would order his men to make a stretcher for him, and carry him along like an old woman in a sedan chair. No sooner had he recovered than he would stagger up from the stretcher, screaming insults at the soldiers who had been good enough to carry him, slap the dust from his armor, and climb back onto his mount.

The boxer gave only one order on his own initiative, and he gave it again and again. Though it puzzled and angered the other officers, costing them days of the march and making no sense, they hesitated to interfere, for they had been ordered by the Empress herself to let him have his head. Every time the army passed a Buddhist monastery or temple, he insisted on stopping to inspect the place, supposedly to see if it was being run up to standard. As abbot of the kingdom's greatest temple, it was his duty. The officers would watch, baffled, as the boxer ordered that all resident monks be gathered in the courtyard for his inspection. Then, when they were assembled, would ask, "Are there no more?" as if there were some monk in particular he was searching for. And when they said no, his face would fall, and his step leaving the temple would be heavy as that of a man in mourning.

In a few weeks they caught sight of an extraordinary structure following the horizon like the tail of a sleeping dragon. It was all of stone, with a broad highway along the top, upon which cavalry could be seen riding to and fro. Sturdy battlements bordered the highway, and square watchtowers rose every thousand yards, bristling with soldiers. This was the first time the boxer had seen the Long Wall of Ten Thousand Li, and it was a revelation to him, an inkling of the Middle Kingdom's true grandeur.

The old general, seeing the boxer's expression of awe, matched the step of their horses and, riding alongside him, expounded on the wall's construction and history. It was an earthwork faced with uniform pieces of stone, wide enough for horses to ride along the top of it five abreast, so long that even the fleetest horse could not cover its distance in a week. Sections of it had been built by the ancient kings of Chao and Yen to protect the mountain passes from invasion. These sections had been linked and further fortified by the infamous Ch'in emperor Shih Huang Ti, the burner of books and reviser of history. Tens of thousands of exiled convicts had been employed to perform the labor. Those who died of fatigue or injury were buried where they fell, there at the base of the wall, earning it the title of the Long Grave. Once it had repelled barbarians; now the empire had grown so vast that certain barbarian tribes, the Khitans for example, lived within the boundary of the wall, while certain citizens of the Middle Kingdom inhabited cities beyond it.

The army pitched camp at the base of the nearest tower. When the soldiers who were patrolling the wall heard the clang of the great gong that ended their duty, they ran down the narrow stone stairways within the tower to greet the new arrivals. Old friends embraced. Letters were exchanged, as well as news from the capital. The more enterprising soldiers sold food and trinkets they had bought in the markets of Lo-yang. When night came, torches were lit and casks of rice wine rolled out to celebrate the arrival of the army. Several of the soldiers, dressed like girls, strummed their lutes, sang, and danced to favorite Turkish songs, such as "Tune for Releasing a Goshawk" and "Crushing the Southern Barbarians."

The men were a mixed lot, conscriptees, convicts, barbarians who had been taken prisoner in other battles, and even a few volunteers, though this last group was the smallest, for in the Middle Kingdom a soldier's life was without honor. They were all of low birth, coarse and brutal, and for these reasons the boxer felt more comfortable among them than in the company of the officers, who were mostly mandarins of venerable lineage.

After spending what he judged sufficient time with the officers in their felt pavilion, he gave the excuse of needing fresh air (he did indeed appear ill, pale, with sweat beading on his brow) and snuck away to join the common soldiers in their celebration. After a dozen cups of wine, the blood pulsed fast in his veins. Drawing his sword, he boasted about how he would cut a swath through the Turkish troops, battle them one by one, up through the ranks, until he came face to face with the Khan himself, and then he would make old Mo-ch'o taste the tempered bronze of the K'un-wu sword. The Turks would be cowed, the western border safe forever. When the Empress saw the Khan's ugly head on a pike, she would certainly reconsider and take him for a husband, and he would be Emperor of all the Middle Kingdom.

The other soldiers, seeing from his behavior that despite his fancy armor and sword he was a simple man like themselves, abandoned pretense and laughed at him. Those who had been posted at the Long Wall for many months did not know of the lies they were supposed to tell the "general," while those of his own regiment, who had been ordered to lie, had grown tired of the charade, and longed to expose the buffoon of an officer.

"How will you fight Mo-ch'o when he is our ally?" they asked.

At first he thought they were joking, that it was part of the drunken camaraderie they were enjoying that evening. But they would not permit him to escape from the truth; they held him there and ground his face in it. They told him of the Khan's change of heart, of how a rebellion within his own tribe, as well as difficulties with the Uighurs and Khitans, had weakened his position dangerously, leading him to seek alliance with the Middle Kingdom through marriage and tribute.

The boxer finally understood that Heaven's Chosen had deceived him at every turn. She had made him believe that he was being entrusted with troops when he was merely traveling alongside them. She had sent him to do battle for her when she knew there was no battle to be done. She had outwitted him, arranging all this simply to lure him to this distant outpost where he could do all the bumbling he liked without causing her embarrassment or invoking the wrath of her critics. His fury blinded him to the compassion of the arrangement; how much simpler it would have been for her to arrange a midnight assassination.

He would not be stopped, he told them. He had come to kill Turks, and kill Turks he would. With that he climbed on his tarpan and galloped across the scrub, in the direction of some distant lights, which he took to be a town.

The lights were guard fires burning atop the earthwork walls of a frontier village. The guards at the gate, impressed by the boxer's armor, assumed he was a soldier of high rank and opened the huge timber doors for him, even though it was late at night. They told him where he would find the taverns and the whorehouses, for soldiers of all times are the same in their needs. He rode down the main street, past a sprawling stone caravanserai, a splendid home that must have belonged to the local magistrate or warlord, and a temple for Persian fire-worshipers, or so he judged from the exotic paintings on the walls of it. There was a Buddhist temple, too, but for lack of patronage it had been converted to an inn. He turned down another street where the buildings were smaller, of fire-baked brick, with colorful vertical banners and signs. A stable, a noodle factory, a tailor. The tavern. The boxer tied the reins of his tarpan to a bit of broken fence in front, and swaggered through the entrance.

He had been in bad taverns before, but he could not recall ever seeing a place such as this. The air was foul with sweat and urine, the oil lamps barely bright enough to let a man see where he was walking. The floor was covered with sand, and rats scurried beneath the long wooden tables, scavenging for scraps.

As for the patrons, they reminded him of paintings he had seen of crimson-faced, bulging-eyed Buddhist demons. One man had no nose, while another's lip had been sliced away so that his gums and black teeth could be seen. Wine poured down his chin when he drank. He saw Uighurs, Turks, Khitans, a party of short, barrel-chested Tibetans with flat, round faces. All of them carried swords and daggers in their sashes and across their chests.

He ordered a pot of rice wine from a humpbacked old lady

with milky eyes. It tasted like piss, but he didn't care. He sat down on a three-legged stool and watched a game the patrons were playing, a game unlike any he had seen before, in Lo-yang or anywhere else he had traveled. It didn't take long to understand the rules.

The player whose turn it was would hold one hand behind his back and, grasping a dagger by its tip with the other, toss it in the air so that it spun like a water mill. While it was airborne, he had to raise his glass and empty it using the same hand. Then he had to put down the glass and catch the dagger before it hit the table. It was not only a question of catching the dagger, but of catching it by the handle, for the blade was so sharp that to do otherwise would mean losing a piece of a finger at the least, as happened several times while the boxer was watching. (There seemed to be a trick to it that the Tibetans knew and the rest did not.) The other patrons of the bar found these accidental amputations riotously funny. If the player succeeded, the others paid for his drink. If he failed, he bought theirs.

One of the Tibetans had his eye on the boxer and, after a few more rounds of the dagger game, invited him to try it.

"I'm looking for Turks," the boxer said, ignoring the question. "Any Turks here?"

"No more fight Turks," the Tibetan said in his oddly accented voice. "Khan make peace with Empress. Fight Khitans now."

"I didn't say anything about fighting, did I? I just want to know if there are any Turks here." His fingers, closing around the sharkskin hilt of his sword, belied his words.

Several men who, judging from their round eyes, hooked noses, and thick beards, might have been Turks, began to talk among themselves in a corner, occasionally glancing at him.

"No need fight. Play game," the Tibetan said, offering him the knife. "You get hurt bad enough." And he laughed.

One of the men who had been talking in the corner now approached him.

"You say you are looking for Turks," he said. "I am a Turk. I was once a general of the great Khan. How can I be of service to you?"

"You can draw your sword," the boxer replied. "When I'm through with you, I'll take on your tribesmen. And when your heads are laid out in a row like the beads of an abacus, then I'll be on my way."

"If we were to fight, it might be an excuse for other soldiers to do the same. One thing leads to the next. Soon the peace treaty between our rulers would mean as little as the stick you use to wipe your ass."

"Is there a man speaking somewhere?" The boxer cupped a hand behind his ear, as though to improve his hearing. "All I hear is the slobbering of some cowardly turtle spawn."

"Perhaps we can play the dagger game instead," the Turk said, not in the least provoked.

"I haven't come all this way to play games."

"Hear me out," said the Turk. His thick mustache curled up at the ends and his smile was filled with big, square teeth. "Instead of tossing the dagger into the air, we will toss it at each other."

"It hardly seems a fair contest. Whoever goes first will win, since no man can catch a dagger thrown full force."

"We will throw it underhand. Does that satisfy you? And you can go first."

"What if we both catch it?" the boxer asked. "What then?"

"We will keep tossing it until one of us moves from his spot, or calls off the game. If I call it off, you may have my necklace." He fingered a golden necklace he wore around his neck, all inlaid with rubies and emeralds. "It's quite valuable, I assure you."

"And if I call off the game?" the boxer asked.

"That fine sword you carry at your side will be mine."

"This is the K'un-wu sword," the boxer protested, "a gift of the Empress herself." Then he said, "Why these games? Why not duel to the death and be done with it, like real men?"

"Because when war is over, men become civilized. And civilized men need more refined ways to kill each other."

The boxer was trapped. To decline now would be to admit he was less refined than a barbarian. He could not suffer the loss of face in front of so many. After all, he was a duke of the third degree, an abbot, a man of many distinctions.

"All right," he said, and took the dagger.

"We'll stand ten paces apart," the Turk said, measuring off the distance, "to add to the sport of it."

The owner of the tavern, a little mole of a man with jaundiced skin and a black cap, grabbed the humpbacked woman and dragged her into the storeroom so that they might avoid witnessing whatever mayhem was to come. The rest of the patrons, although pretending to be indifferent to the event, rearranged their stools for a better view.

Now the Turk and the boxer faced each other. The murmuring stopped, the room grew silent. Even the rats ceased scavenging beneath the tables. The boxer held the dagger by the tip of the blade and aimed. Everyone was watching him. The heat was oppressive, and his head began to spin. He clutched the edge of the table and waited for it to pass. Then he aimed again and tossed the dagger underhand.

It clattered against the wall, having missed his opponent entirely.

"My turn now," the Turk said, retrieving the dagger from the floor. Holding it by the tip, he swung his arm back by his side, an awkward gesture, and squinted at his opponent in concentration.

The boxer felt himself break out in sweat. Facing an enemy with a weapon, while he himself was unarmed and forbidden to move, was a terror quite unlike any other he had known. He put his hands up in front of his chest, palms out, fingers spread, a fragile shield, and, using what few techniques of meditation he had learned from the little monk, concentrated his entire being on the dagger.

He didn't know exactly what happened next, but he felt something hit his palm, like a hard slap, and heard the dagger drop to the sandy floor.

"Not even a cut," he thought to himself. He looked at his palm and saw that it was split open, so the skin curled up, like a dumpling sliced half through. He felt nothing, for the skin was dead. When he tried to press the cut closed with the fingers of his other hand, blood coursed over his hands. The Tibetan came forward with a strip of silk and wrapped it expertly so that the game could continue.

"No winner on the first round," the Turk said. "Your turn."

The boxer took the dagger and aimed. He was feeling feverish now, and his eyes wouldn't focus. If the game went on too long, he knew, he would be hacked like pork beneath the cook's cleaver. He had to wound the Turk with this throw. He had to. He pulled back his arm and, swinging it forward, let loose the dagger.

The Turk nearly caught it by the hilt, but it bounced out of his hand, and buried its blade in his boot. He shouted with pain. Squatting, he pulled it out and remained in that position, massaging the skin and grimacing. Some of his colleagues pulled the boot and the sock off his foot and dressed the wound, which was small but deep.

When the Turk stood up again, he looked less pleased with himself. His skin was clammy and the boxer was gratified to note a tremor in his throwing hand.

"My turn," the Turk said, no longer smiling.

He grasped the blade by the tip, pulled his arm back by his side, and flung it very fast, though somewhat wildly.

Without moving his feet, the boxer leaned his whole body to the left. He laughed with relief to realize that the dagger had missed him altogether.

"No winner on the second round," the Tibetan said.

The Turk was frowning now and breathing hard.

"My turn," said the boxer. He pulled back the dagger and let it fly. The Turk raised his hand to catch it but miscalculated and the blade went into his forearm, severing an artery. He pulled it out at once, but the damage had been done. The blood came out in spurts, blackening the sand on the floor. Quickly the Tibetan tied a silk tourniquet around the Turk's elbow and tightened it until the bleeding stopped.

"I'll take that necklace now," the boxer said, holding out his hand.

"Not so fast," said the Turk. "I haven't given up yet." He limped back to his friends and whispered with them for a few moments. Then he returned to his position and said, "My turn."

He raised the dagger beside his ear. The boxer began to protest that they had agreed to throw it underhand, but he only got out a word before the weapon flew, straight and fast as only an overhand throw can propel it, into his breast. He bent over from the pain, fell to the floor, and rolled around on the dirty, bloody sand, trying to pull it out. He had the impression of commotion, of men running every which way. As he lost consciousness he felt someone rip the K'un-wu sword from his belt.

The cool night air revived him. He was lying in somebody's arms, on the floor of a battle chariot, jogging along a rough path. Overhead, the stars jiggled sickeningly. His first thought, logic being as weak as flesh at such moments, was that the Turk had repented for his unfair behavior and was taking him to a doctor. He tried to turn and felt a pain like a hot coal in his chest.

"Keep still," said the man who was holding him. "You're badly hurt."

He recognized the voice of the old general.

"Am I going to die?" he said. "Don't let me die, please."

"There's a monastery near here. The Buddhist monks know their herbs and medicines. They'll do what can be done."

He knew he should pretend indifference to his death, but he could not. The sight of the blood flowing down his chest, soaking his robes, scared him enough, and when he realized that the hot liquid he was lying in was more of the same, he was seized with panic. How much blood did a man's body hold? How much could he lose and still survive?

As weak as a newborn, he dozed and woke, and dozed again. Drifting in and out of consciousness, life was no longer a continuity, but a succession of dim, disparate images: him being lifted out of the chariot, into a sedan chair; the chair being hurried up a hillside of steep stone steps; the reassuring sight of monks' robes and a monastery gate; a clean, dry cell with a heating stove and a mat on the floor; the excruciating pain of moxa being burned in his wound. He struck out at the darkness and felt hands around his arms, restraining him, while gentle voices reassured him. His lips were forced open and liquid was trickled down his throat, pungent with medicinal herbs, gritty with ground rhinoceros horn and powdered gold. Only then did real sleep come.

That night he dreamed he saw the traitorous Turk wearing his K'un-wu sword, swaggering through the loggias of the palace, while mandarins turned and bowed to him. A woman, sometimes the Empress and at other times Princess T'ai P'ing, came out of her chambers and kissed him on the lips, then drew him to her bed.

Another time he woke to find the little monk sitting beside him, putting cold silks on his forehead.

"If only you were really here," the boxer said, "you could solve everything. You always did."

The little monk laughed and shook his head. "I am as real as everything else in this dream life. Your karma brought you to the same monastery where I chose to settle after my wandering."

"No, no, I am not so easily fooled. With all the thousands of temples in the land, the odds against you and me being thrown together like this are impossible."

"What an obstinate fellow!"

"You are just another phantom of my troubled sleep," the boxer said in his world-weary way.

"What about this?" the little monk said, grasping the boxer's nose and giving it a twist. "Is this a dream?"

"You yourself once told me how the philosopher Chuang-tzu, stung by a mosquito in his sleep, believed himself skewered with a sword. What I took for a tweak of the nose was probably no more than the settling of a dust mote."

"It's my fault," the little monk muttered to himself, "for teaching him half the truth."

When the boxer woke the next morning, the little monk was still sitting cross-legged beside his mat, sunk in meditation.

"It really is you," he said, "you miserable turtle spawn!" And he began to cry with happiness.

"I told you so last night," the little monk said, "but you argued me away with Chuang-tzu."

"Like a mandarin," the boxer said proudly.

"Like a fool."

"How did you get here?"

"I might ask the same of you."

"I was on my way to vanquish the Turks and win back the Empress, but she'd already made a treaty with them. I decided to fight them anyway, and found a few in a local tavern. No, a dozen of them. They were ferocious in battle! My mighty K'un-wu sword cut a swath through them, like a sickle through a field of hemp. Finally only one remained. He pleaded for mercy. I took pity on him and let him go. No sooner had I turned my back than the treacherous fellow stabbed me."

"In the chest?"

"I meant to say 'turned my head.'"

"I see."

"Then the camel dung stole my sword. I must get it back. It was a present from the Empress. If she sees me without it . . ." Another thought occurred to him. "What of my tarpan? Is he in the stables?"

"We have no stables," the little monk replied.

"Then I've lost him, too. The finest horse I've ever ridden."

"There are many horses and swords."

"But not like these! Don't you understand anything? They were presents from the Empress. One of a kind. Irreplaceable."

"If you must worry, worry about yourself, boxer."

"Is it that bad?" the boxer asked, gazing down at his chest wound.

The little monk nodded solemnly.

"Will I . . ." The boxer hesitated. "Will I die?"

"Perhaps."

"But it doesn't hurt so much now."

"Be thankful for that."

"What should I do?"

"Ponder the question I've asked you so many times before: Thinking neither good nor evil, what was your true face before you had a face?"

"Don't talk your silly riddles to me!" the boxer said, half rising from the mat with anger. "I'm dying!"

"So the question becomes more important than ever."

"But what of the Empress? I will certainly lose her if I cannot turn this campaign into a victory for myself."

"Win her, lose her. The matter is of no importance."

"Don't tell me what's important. It's the only thing that's of any importance at all. If you want to help me, figure out a plan."

The little monk shrugged. "Tell her you fought the Turks. After all, you did. Have you cash?"

The boxer nodded.

"Hire some artisans to erect a stela to commemorate your victory. Everyone believes what they read on a monument. Then go back to the Empress and show her your wound. Tell her you are dying for her. Any woman would like that."

"You're the cleverest man I've ever met. If only you could come with me."

The monk sighed. "I suppose someone has to look after your wound."

"Then you will?"

"The truth is, you've spoiled me for monastic life. I've grown too used to the excitement and danger of your company. And . . ."

"And what?"

"And I sense we have only a short time left."

"You're not sick, are you?" the boxer asked with concern.

The little monk laughed again and told him to rest.

24

THE BOXER RETURNS

The boxer nearly did not survive the return to Lo-yang. He had to ride in the back of an oxcart, all wrapped in blankets, and every bump made him moan with pain. He began to bleed intermittently from the mouth, the rectum, and the nose. Sometimes he slept, and sometimes, half-conscious, he muttered and gestured as though believing himself to be in some other place, conversing with people long dead. At other times he woke to a kind of heightened awareness, where, to the wonder of the little monk, he spoke of the predicament of his life with a deeper understanding than he had shown before.

When finally they arrived at the White Horse, White Pheasant ran out to great them. He gasped when he saw the boxer's condition. Together the eunuch and the little monk carried him to his chambers and put him to bed beneath the watchful eye of Maitreya, the future Buddha, the savior, the redeemer of mankind. Together they cared for him as best they could.

Day and night the boxer's ramblings had a common refrain, that he must see the Empress. White Pheasant reported that he had approached her personally and that she was simply trying to find time in her schedule for a good, long visit. In fact, he had sent messages to her twice and, receiving no reply, had ceased for fear of irritating her.

Some say that before a man's death he experiences a surge of strength, just as a lamp flares brightly before the oil is exhausted.

One night the boxer woke, feeling as he had felt ten years before, when he'd first met Heaven's Chosen. He sat up in bed and thought: She does not visit me because she thinks that I am too feeble to make the Vigorous Peak. But tonight I am better. I have recovered from my long illness and I am filled with the yang essence. I will go to the Inner Palace, to her bedchamber, and act the Clouds and Rain with her until the monk sounds his morning bell.

Quietly, so as not to disturb his two attendants who were sleeping in the next room, the boxer crawled out of bed, dressed in his scarlet monk's robes, which was his lightest and most comfortable costume, and, stealing White Pheasant's horse from the stables, rode through the sleeping city to the palace. As he came to the gate of each neighborhood, he ordered the guards to let him pass. Cowed by the vague memory that he was someone important, they swung back the gates.

The guards at the palace, seeing the boxer so sickly and pale, were solicitous. Knowing they would never allow him to visit the Empress—especially at this late hour—he improvised a story about urgent business regarding the Buddha banner, ominous astrological indications requiring that a scripture be chanted immediately by a monk standing beside it in order that the Kingdom be spared from disaster. As he passed through the first gate, he saw, on the nearest terrace, the Ming-t'ang silhouetted against the moon, and beyond it the silk Buddha in its towering pavilion. Torches had been left burning so that it could be admired at any moment of the night or day. His chest swelled with pride at the grandeur of it, the gloss of its finish, the intricacy of its detail. Reminded of his mortality by an ache in the spot where he had suffered the Turk's dagger, he thought, Whatever happens to me, the Ming-t'ang will survive as my monument. Though I have no children, the Ming-t'ang is my child. The Ming-t'ang is my immortality.

Deeper and deeper he penetrated into the palace, into the maze of walls and gates and guards that surrounded the Phoenix Chambers, until he reached a place where even the most cunning lie would carry him no further. After ten years of visiting and living in the palace, he was intimate with the layout of every courtyard and hall. While the guards were out of sight, he climbed onto a railing and, grabbing hold of a dragon's head beneath the eaves, pulled himself onto the roof. One of the monster's fangs broke off and struck the gravel. He lay motionless on the roof, on the cool corrugation of the tiles, listening to the guards running every which way, investigating the sound. How fatigued he suddenly was! He felt as though he could not take another step even if his life depended on it. His breath sawed at his lungs like a blade. A lump formed in his throat. When the guards were gone, he coughed it up and spat. The discharge was black against the golden yellow of the tile.

When the pain eased, he rose to his feet and, keeping low, crept across one roof after another until he was looking down on the courtyard of the Phoenix Chambers. More guards patrolled here, their footsteps softly crunching on the gravel, their helmets shining like pearls in the moonlight. Five marched back and forth along the loggia while five more patrolled the paths of the courtyard. They moved like the planets, coming in and out of conjunction with one another. A time came when all ten guards were facing away from him; then he hung from the eaves by his fingertips and dropped to the ground. They heard him and turned, but by then he was in the anteroom of the Empress's apartments. He grabbed an oil lamp and pushed ahead, through the sitting room, into the bedchamber.

"Who's that?" the Empress cried, seeing the lamplight shining through the fretwork screens of her bed.

The sound of her voice filled him with a tingling, nostalgic pleasure. In the fear of losing her, he had discounted her importance to him. She was everything: wife, mother, vocation, faith. She was his world.

"It's me," he whispered, crossing to the bed, "returned from vanquishing the Turks. Forgive me for this late visit, but I couldn't wait another minute."

He pulled open the doors of her bed.

"Stop," she cried. "Go away!" But she was too late. He saw them lying twined together naked within the bed, the Empress and the palace doctor. The corona of the lamplight illuminated the Empress's face, and he read many things in her eyes: anger, compassion, regret—but not love.

"Excuse me," he said softly, backing away. "I only meant to—"

Then he turned and ran for the door.

He ran through courtyards and loggias, not knowing where he was running, seeking escape not so much from the palace but from existence itself. Hot tears streaked his cheeks. How could he have allowed himself to care so much for a woman? How could he have made himself victim to such pain?

Now there were shouts, sounds of pursuit, boots running on gravel, arrows whistling past him so close that he felt a breeze from their feathers. They would have caught him in a moment were it not for the mazelike quality of the loggias, the confusion created by courtyards populated by tall rocks and stunted trees specially chosen for their resemblance to human figures.

He ducked around a corner and found himself standing directly behind the towering silk Buddha banner, and the Ming-t'ang. Without a thought he grabbed a flaming torch from its sconce—the heat of it, and the smell of the burning hempseed oil, nearly made him sick—ran to the pavilion where the Buddha was displayed, and lit the bottom of the banner. The flame leaped up the silk, fed by the oil-based paints, blossoming like a fabulous flower that illuminated the entire palace grounds. The guards who had been pursuing him stopped short, frozen as if by enchantment, their faces suddenly crimson in the reflected light, their mouths open in astonishment. There was something stupefyingly wonderful about the speed of the destruction, the monumental proportions of it. The flame, at the zenith of its climb, seemed to lick the moon. No one moved, for the calamity was so sudden and of such a scale that no one could think precisely how to react.

Then came the cracking of timber. The pavilion that held the banner aloft had been eaten through by flames. The banner teetered and toppled forward onto the Ming-t'ang, a tinderbox of dry wood, flammable lacquer, silks, gauzes, and taffetas, all of which obediently burst into flame. The enchantment was ended; everyone came alive again, running every which way, their forms blurred and distorted by the rising waves of heat. Their mouths were open as though they were screaming, but their voices were outdone by the roar of the fire.

The boxer had an easy time losing himself in the subsequent chaos.

* * *

The fire took all night to subdue. When the first light of morning shone over the palace roofs, all that remained of the Ming-t'ang was a forest of short, jagged, blackened timbers, releasing curling tendrils of smoke into the crystalline air.

The Empress, having sent away everyone but her eunuch, walked alone through the wreckage, not so much assessing the damage, as she had told the guards, but rather mourning the memories of herself and the boxer. For surely the Ming-t'ang best represented, in its gaudiness, grandeur, and unorthodoxy, as well as in its initial impossibility and final ruin, their wonderful love.

Hearing a sniffling sound, she grabbed a daggerlike shard of burnt wood and raised it with the intention of spearing or scaring away whatever rat or rodent was lying in wait for her. But then she saw that it was the boxer, fetally curled in an unburned corner of the ruins.

"Precious," she whispered, coming closer, "are you hurt?"

The boxer stared straight at her, yet seemed not to recognize her. His face and his bald head were smeared with ashes, and he had cut himself badly on the cheek.

She knelt beside him and put her arms around him, made him rest his head against her shoulder.

"I lost the sword," he whispered, as a child confesses losing his cap. "The K'un-wu sword."

"It doesn't matter," she said, caressing his back.

Then she said, "Precious One, you have suffered so much pain and indignity on my account. I should have left you where I found you, on the street. Though of all women who ever lived, or ever will, I am most powerful, I cannot turn common bone into jade, or low blood into carnelian. In future lives, precious, our fates will be better balanced. Whether we are both peasants or members of a venerable lineage, we shall be together, I feel it in my heart."

She held him a moment longer and then she said, "Good-bye, my precious, my stallion, my Jade Stalk. Good-bye."

She turned her back and ordered the eunuch who accompanied her to return him to the White Horse Temple.

Princess T'ai P'ing came at the Empress's summons.

"How can I please you, Mother?" she asked.

"It is the boxer," the Empress said. "Despite mortal wounds

and illness, he has found his way back from the Long Wall of a Thousand Li. He has the spirit of a dragon."

"And, if I may say so, the evil of a weasel."

"You speak of the burning of the Ming-t'ang?"

"Everyone says it was his work. Censor Hsü, I am told, prepares to memorialize about it tomorrow."

"Oh, spare me his honesty, piety, and long-suffering tones."

"Would that I could, Mother."

"We have a question. Suppose your favorite polo horse broke a leg and had to be destroyed. Does propriety demand that you wield the blade yourself? Must you comfort the dumb beast with your presence during his last moment of life? Or can you assign the bloody work to some groom and spare yourself the pain?"

"It depends," the princess replied gently. "A horse is not a man."

"We are a foolish old thing. You know of whom We speak."

"Once, long ago, I made you an offer, and I will make it again. I brought the boxer into your life, and so it is my duty to dispose of him."

"Be quick," the Empress said, pain in her eyes, "and merciful."

"We will see that the job is done," the princess replied.

The boxer was so exhausted that he slept for two days.

What finally woke him was the sound of a messenger in the next room, conversing with White Pheasant. The boxer lifted himself on one elbow and listened. The messenger was inviting the boxer to the home of the Princess T'ai P'ing for tea, and the eunuch was responding that the boxer was too feeble to go anywhere right now.

"Wait!" the boxer shouted. He rose from the bed, found his footing, and stumbled into the anteroom.

"Tell the princess I happily accept," he told the messenger.

"You'd better not," White Pheasant whispered behind his hand. "I really do advise against it."

"Quiet, you old grandmother," the boxer said. "I'll do as I please. If you're worried about my health, well, I'm like a buffalo. Look!" He went over to the heating stove and actually managed to raise it a few inches, before letting it crash to the floor.

"It is not your health I worry about," White Pheasant admitted, as soon as the messenger had left. "This invitation gives me a queer feeling. The princess does not normally extend social invitations. I have heard rumors around the palace that you are being blamed for the destruction of the Ming-t'ang. I wonder if she plots against you."

"That is my fear too," added the little monk, who had been observing all this from an armchair.

"The princess invites me," he said, grinning at them, "to act the Clouds and Rain. She felt my yang essence long ago, when she first tested me, to see if I was suitable for the Empress. Of course, while I was the Empress's lover, I could not be her lover too, for such things are forbidden to mandarins like ourselves. But now that the mother has taken a new lover—I speak of the palace doctor—I am again free to please and delight the daughter."

His voice was full of self-assurance, but they could not help but notice how his hands trembled.

"I don't know," White Pheasant said, stroking his chin. He looked very worried.

"You must remember," the boxer went on, "that the princess lost her husband during the rebellion. She needs a man to care for her. Someone who's her equal, if you know what I mean. When the Empress dies, the Dragon Throne will pass to the princess. And whoever happens to be her husband"—he winked at them—"will become emperor."

White Pheasant and the little monk waited at the temple gate.

Late that afternoon, an old man appeared in the distance, leading an oxcart. He trudged along, back bent, eyes on the dusty road, leaning on a walking stick.

In time he reached the gate and they saw that the cart contained the boxer's body. Judging from the marks on him, he had been beaten to death with canes.

The little monk sighed.

White Pheasant began to weep, and held his sleeve over his eyes.

The old man helped them unload the body—the boxer was a big man—and then led his cart away as quietly as he had arrived.

Later that day they built a pyre to burn him, as was the custom with Buddhists.

The little monk watched the flame and considered the strange ways of karma, its punishments and rewards. Afterwards he buried the bones and the ashes. He had to do it himself, for White Pheasant was so grief-stricken as to be useless. Nearby he found a large white rock, nicely rounded, and rolled it onto the grave. Then he got out his writing kit, ground some ink, made a point on the brush, and wrote:

>THIS IS THE GRAVE OF HUAI-I, BOXER, ABBOT,
>DUKE, TRANSLATOR, ARCHITECT, GENERAL,
>DHARMA BROTHER AND BELOVED FRIEND.
>THOUGH HE DID NOT LIVE LONG,
>HE DRANK DEEP AND OFTEN FROM LIFE'S GOBLET.
>MAY HE PASS ETERNITY IN THE PURE LAND.

And, having finished his business there, he packed up his few things in a bundle, flung the bundle over his shoulder, and, leaning on his crutch, began the long journey home.